DAVID COPPERFIELD

CHARLES DICKENS

David Copperfield

abridged

A Purnell Classic

OTHER TITLES IN SERIES

SBN 361 03523 3
First published in this edition 1976
by Purnell Books, Berkshire House, Queen Street, Maidenhead,
Berkshire
Made and printed in Germany

CONTENTS

CHAPTER 1

I Am Born

WHETHER I shall turn out to be the hero of my own life, or whether that station will be held by anybody else, these pages must show. To begin my life with the beginning of my life, I record that I was born (as I have been informed and believe) on a Friday, at twelve o'clock at night. It was remarked that the clock began to strike, and I began to cry, simultaneously.

I was born at Blunderstone, in Suffolk, or "thereby," as they say in Scotland. I was a posthumous child. My father's eyes had closed upon the light of this world six months, when mine opened on it.

An aunt of my father's, and consequently a great-aunt of mine, of whom I shall have more to relate by and by, was the principal magnate of our family. Miss Trotwood, or Miss Betsey, as my poor mother always called her, when she sufficiently overcame her dread of this formidable personage to mention her at all (which was seldom), had been married to a husband younger than herself. He was strongly suspected of having beaten Miss Betsey, and even of having once, on a disputed question of supplies, made some hasty but determined arrangements to throw her out of a two pair of stairs' window. These evidences of an incompatibility of temper induced Miss Betsey to pay him off, and effect a separation by mutual consent. He went to India with his capital, and from India tidings of his death reached home, within ten years. How they affected my aunt, nobody knew; for immediately upon the separation she took her maiden name again, bought a cottage in a hamlet on the sea-coast a long way off, established herself there as a single woman with one servant, and was understood to live secluded, ever afterwards, in an inflexible retirement.

My father had once been a favourite of hers, I believe; but she was mortally affronted by his marriage, on the ground that my mother was "a wax doll." She had never seen my mother, but she knew her to be not yet twenty. My father and Miss Betsey never met again. He was double my mother's age when he married, and of but a delicate constitution. He died a year afterwards.

This was the state of matters on the afternoon of, what I may be excused for calling, that eventful and important Friday.

My mother was sitting by the fire, that bright, windy March afternoon, very timid and sad, and very doubtful of ever coming alive out of the trial that was before her, when, lifting her eyes as she dried them, to the window opposite, she saw a strange lady coming up the garden.

My mother had a sure foreboding at the second glance, that it was Miss Betsey. She came walking up to the door with a fell rigidity of figure and composure of countenance that could have belonged to nobody else.

When she reached the house, instead of ringing the bell, she came and looked in at that identical window, pressing the end of her nose against the glass to that extent that my poor dear mother used to say it became perfectly flat and white in a moment.

She gave my mother such a turn, that I have always been convinced I am indebted to Miss Betsey for having been born on a Friday.

My mother had left her chair in her agitation, and gone behind it in the corner. Miss Betsey, made a frown and a gesture to my mother, like one who was accustomed to be obeyed, to come and open the door. My mother went.

"Mrs. David Copperfield, I *think*," said Miss Betsey; the emphasis referring, perhaps, to my mother's mourning weeds, and her condition.

"Yes," said my mother, faintly.

"Miss Trotwood," said the visitor. "You have heard of her, I dare say?" My mother answered she had had that pleasure.

"Now you see her," said Miss Betsey. My mother bent her head, and begged her to walk in.

They went into the parlour and when they were both seated, and Miss Betsey said nothing, my mother, after vainly trying to restrain herself, began to cry.

"Oh tut, tut, tut!" said Miss Betsey, in a hurry. "Take off your cap, child," said Miss Betsey, "and let me see you."

My mother was too much afraid of her to refuse. Therefore she did as she was told, and did it with such nervous hands that her hair (which was luxuriant and beautiful) fell all about her face.

"Why, bless my heart!" exclaimed Miss Betsey. "You are a very Baby!"

My mother was, no doubt, unusually youthful in appearance even for her years; she hung her head, as if it were her fault, poor thing, and said, sobbing, that indeed she was afraid she was but a childish widow, and would be but a childish mother if she lived.

"In the name of Heaven," said Miss Betsey, suddenly, "why Rookery?"

"Do you mean the house, ma'am?" asked my mother.

"Why Rookery?" said Miss Betsey. "Cookery would have been more to the purpose, if you had had any practical ideas of life, either of you."

"The name was Mr. Copperfield's choice," returned my mother. "When he bought the house, he liked to think that there were rooks about it."

"David Copperfield all over!" cried Miss Betsey. "David Copperfield from head to foot! Calls a house a rookery when there's not a rook near it, and takes the birds on trust, because he sees the nests!"

"Mr. Copperfield," returned my mother, "is dead, and if you dare to speak unkindly of him to me——"

My poor dear mother, I suppose, had some momentary intention of committing an assault and battery upon my aunt. But it passed with the action of rising from her chair; and she sat down again very meekly, and fainted.

When she came to herself, the twilight was shading down into darkness; and dimly as they saw each other, they could not have done that without the aid of the fire.

"Well?" said Miss Betsey, "and when do you expect——"

8

"I am all in a tremble," faltered my mother. "I don't know what's the matter. I shall die, I am sure!"

"No, no, no," said Miss Betsey. "Have some tea."

"Oh dear me, dear me, do you think it will do me any good?" cried my mother in a helpless manner.

"Of course it will," said Miss Betsey. "It's nothing but fancy. What do you call your girl?"

"I don't know that it will be a girl, yet, ma'am," said my mother innocently.

"Bless the Baby!" exclaimed Miss Betsey, unconsciously quoting the second sentiment of the pincushion in the drawer up-stairs, but applying it to my mother instead of me, "I don't mean that. I mean your servant."

"Peggotty," said my mother.

"Peggotty!" repeated Miss Betsey, with some indignation. "Do you mean to say, child, that any human being has gone into a Christian church, and got herself named Peggotty?"

"It's her surname," said my mother, faintly. "Mr. Copperfield called her by it, because her Christian name was the same as mine."

"Here, Peggotty!" cried Miss Betsey, opening the parlour-door. "Tea. Your mistress is a little unwell. Don't dawdle."

Having issued this mandate:

"You were speaking about its being a girl," said Miss Betsey. "I have no doubt it will be a girl. I have a presentiment that it must be a girl. Now child, from the moment of the birth of this girl——"

"Perhaps boy," my mother took the liberty of putting in.

"I tell you I have a presentiment that it must be a girl," returned Miss Betsey. "Don't contradict. From the moment of this girl's birth, child, I intend to be her friend. I intend to be her godmother, and I beg you'll call her Betsey Trotwood Copperfield."

"And was David good to you, child?" asked Miss Betsey, when she had been silent for a little while. "Were you comfortable together?"

"We were very happy," said my mother. "Mr. Copperfield was only too good to me."

"What, he spoilt you, I suppose?" returned Miss Betsey.

"For being quite alone and dependent on myself in this rough world again, yes, I fear he did indeed," sobbed my mother.

"Well! Don't cry!" said Miss Betsey. "You were not equally matched, child—if any two people *can* be equally matched—and so I asked the question. You were an orphan, weren't you?"

"Yes."

There was an interval of silence, only broken by Miss Betsey's occasionally ejaculating, "Ha!", as she sat with her feet upon the fender.

"David had bought an annuity for himself with his money, I know," said she, by and by. "What did he do for you?"

"Mr. Copperfield," said my mother, answering with some difficulty, "was so considerate and good as to secure the reversion of a part of it to me."

"How much?" asked Miss Betsey.

"A hundred and five pounds a year," said my mother.

"He might have done worse," said my aunt.

The word was appropriate to the moment. My mother was so much worse that Peggotty, coming in with the teaboard and candles, and seeing at a glance how ill she was—as Miss Betsey might have done sooner if there had been light enough—conveyed her up-stairs to her own room with all speed; and immediately despatched Ham Peggotty, her nephew, who had been for some days past secreted in the house, unknown to my mother, as a special messenger in case of emergency, to fetch the nurse and doctor.

The doctor having been up-stairs and come down again, and having satisfied himself, I suppose, that there was a probability of this unknown lady and himself having to sit there, face to face, for some hours, laid himself out to be polite and social.

"Well?" said my aunt.

"Well, ma'am," returned Mr. Chillip, "we are—we are progressing slowly, ma'am."

"Ba—a—ah!" said my aunt, with a perfect shake on the contemptuous interjection.

Mr. Chillip sat and looked at her, notwithstanding, for nearly two hours, as she sat looking at the fire, until he was again called out. After another absence, he again returned.

He sidled into the parlour as soon as he was at liberty, and said to my aunt in his meekest manner:

"Well, ma'am, I am happy to congratulate you."

"What upon?" said my aunt, sharply.

"Well, ma'am," resumed Mr. Chillip, as soon as he had courage, "I am happy to congratulate you. All is over now, ma'am, and well over."

During the five minutes or so that Mr. Chillip devoted to the delivery of this oration, my aunt eyed him narrowly.

"How is she?" said my aunt, folding her arms with her bonnet still tied on one of them.

"Well, ma'am, she will soon be quite comfortable, I hope," returned Mr. Chillip. "Quite as comfortable as we can expect a young mother to be, under these melancholy domestic circumstances. There cannot be any objection to your seeing her presently, ma'am. It may do her good."

"The baby," said my aunt. "How is she?"

"Ma'am," returned Mr. Chillip, "I apprehended you had known. It's a boy."

My aunt said never a word, but took her bonnet by the strings, in the manner of a sling, aimed a blow at Mr. Chillips' with it, put it on bent, walked out, and never came back. She vanished like a discontented fairy.

CHAPTER 2

I Observe

LOOKING back, into the blank of my infancy, the first objects I can remember as standing out by themselves from a confusion of things, are my mother and Peggotty.

There comes out of the cloud, our house—not new to me, but quite familiar, in its earliest remembrance. On the ground-floor is Peggotty's kitchen, opening into a back yard.

Here is a long passage—what an enormous perspective I make of it!—leading from Peggotty's kitchen to the front-door. Then there are the two parlours; the parlour in which we sit of an evening, my mother and I and Peggotty—for Peggotty is quite our companion, when her work is done and we are alone—and the best parlour where we sit on a Sunday; grandly, but not so comfortably.

And now I see the outside of our house, with the latticed bedroom windows standing open to let in the sweet-smelling air, and the ragged old rooks'-nests still dangling in the elm-trees at the bottom of the front garden. Now I am in the garden at the back, and where my mother gathers some in a basket, I stand by, bolting furtive gooseberries, and trying to look unmoved. A great wind rises, and the summer is gone in a moment. We are playing in the winter twilight, dancing about the parlour. When my mother is out of breath and rests herself in an elbowchair, I watch her winding her bright curls round her fingers, and straightening her waist, and nobody knows better than I do that she likes to look so well, and is proud of being so pretty.

That is among my very earliest impressions. That, and a sense that we were both a little afraid of Peggotty, and submitted ourselves in most things to her direction, were among the first opinions—if they may be so called—that I ever derived from what I saw.

Peggotty and I were sitting one night by the parlour fire, alone. I had been reading to Peggotty about crocodiles. I was tired of reading, and dead sleepy; but having leave, as a high treat, to sit up until my mother came home from spending the evening at a neighbour's, I would rather have died upon my post (of course) than have gone to bed.

"Peggotty," says I, suddenly, "were you ever married?"

"Lord, Master Davy," replied Peggotty. "What's put marriage in your head?"

She answered with such a start, that it quite awoke me. And then she stopped in her work, and looked at me, with her needle drawn out to its thread's length.

"I don't know!—You mustn't marry more than one person at a time, may you, Peggotty?"

"Certainly not," says Peggotty, with the promptest decision.

"But if you marry a person, and the person dies, why then you may marry another person, mayn't you, Peggotty?"

"You MAY," says Peggotty, "if you choose, my dear. That's a matter of opinion."

"But what is your opinion, Peggotty?" said I.

I asked her, and looked curiously at her, because she looked so curiously at me.

"My opinion is," said Peggotty, taking her eyes from me, after a little indecision and going on with her work, "that I never was married myself, Master Davy, and that I don't expect to be. That's all I know about the subject."

"You an't cross, I suppose, Peggotty, are you?" said I, after sitting quiet for a minute.

I really thought she was, she had been so short with me; but I was quite mistaken: for she laid aside her work (which was a stocking of her own), and opening her arms wide, took my curly head within them, and gave it a good squeeze.

"Now let me hear some more about the Crorkindills," said Peggotty, who was not quite right in the name yet, "for I an't heard half enough."

I couldn't quite understand why Peggotty looked so queer, or why she was so ready to go back to the crocodiles.

We had exhausted the crocodiles, and begun with the alligators, when the garden-bell rang. We went out to the door; and there was my mother, looking unusually pretty, I thought, and with her a gentleman with beautiful black hair and whiskers, who had walked home with us from church last Sunday.

He patted me on the head; but somehow, I didn't like him or his deep voice, and I was jealous that his hand should touch my mother's in touching me—which it did. I put it away as well as I could.

"Oh, Davy!" remonstrated my mother.

"Dear boy!" said the gentleman. "I cannot wonder at his devotion!"

I never saw such a beautiful colour on my mother's face before. She gently chid me for being rude; and, keeping me close to her shawl, turned to thank the gentleman for taking so much trouble as to bring her home. She put out her hand to him as she spoke, and, as he met it with his own, she glanced, I thought, at me.

"Let us say 'good night,' my fine boy," said the gentleman, when he had bent his head—I saw him!—over my mother's little glove.

"Good night!" said I.

"Come! Let us be the best friends in the world!" said the gentleman, laughing. "Shake hands!"

My right hand was in my mother's left, so I gave him the other.

"Why, that's the wrong hand, Davy!" laughed the gentleman.

My mother drew my right hand forward, but I was resolved, for my former reason, not to give it him, and I did not. I gave him the other, and he shook it heartily, and said I was a brave fellow, and went away.

At this minute I see him turn round in the garden, and give us a last look with his ill-omened black eyes, before the door was shut.

Peggotty, who had not said a word or moved a finger, secured the fastenings instantly, and we all went into the parlour. My mother, contrary to her usual habit, instead of coming to the elbow-chair by the fire, remained at the other end of the room, and sat singing to herself.

—"Hope you have had a pleasant evening, ma'am," said Peggotty, standing as stiff as a barrel in the centre of the room, with a candlestick in her hand.

"Much obliged to you, Peggotty," returned my mother in a cheerful voice, "I have had a *very* pleasant evening."

"A stranger or so makes an agreeable change," suggested Peggotty.

"A very agreeable change, indeed," returned my mother.

Peggotty continuing to stand motionless in the middle of the room, and my mother resuming her singing, I fell asleep, though I was not so sound asleep but that I could hear voices, without hearing what they said. When I half awoke from this uncomfortable doze, I found Peggotty and my mother both in tears, and both talking.

"Not such a one as this, Mr. Copperfield wouldn't have liked," said Peggotty. "That I say, and that I swear!"

"Good Heavens!" cried my mother, "you'll drive me mad! Was ever any poor girl so ill-used by her servants as I am! Why do I do myself the injustice of calling myself a girl? Have I never been married, Peggotty?"

"God knows you have, ma'am," returned Peggotty.

"Then, how can you dare," said my mother—"how can you have the heart—to make me so uncomfortable and say such bitter things to me, when you are well aware that I haven't, out of this place, a single friend to turn to?"

"The more's the reason," returned Peggotty, "for saying that it won't do. No! That it won't do. No! No price could make it do. No!"—I thought Peggotty would have thrown the candlestick away, she was so emphatic with it.

"How can you be so aggravating," said my mother, shedding more tears than before, "as to talk in such an unjust manner! How can you go on as if it was all settled and arranged, Peggotty, when I tell you over and over again, you cruel thing, that beyond the commonest civilities nothing has passed!"

Peggotty seemed to take this aspersion very much to heart, I thought.

"And my dear boy," cried my mother, coming to the elbow-chair in which I was, and caressing me, "my own little Davy. Am I a naughty mama to you, Davy? Am I a nasty, cruel, selfish, bad mama? Say I am, my child; say 'yes,' dear boy, and Peggotty will love you; and Peggotty's love is a great deal better than mine, Davy. *I* don't love you at all, do I?"

We went to bed greatly dejected. My sobs kept waking me, for a long time; and when one very strong sob quite hoisted me up in bed, I found my mother sitting on the coverlet, and leaning over me. I fell asleep in her arms, after that, and slept soundly.

Whether it was the following Sunday when I saw the gentleman again, or whether there was any greater lapse of time before he reappeared, I cannot recall. I don't profess to be clear about dates. But there he was, in church, and he walked home with us afterwards.

Peggotty began to be less with us, of an evening, than she had always been. My mother deferred to her very much—more than usual, it occurred to me—and we were all three excellent friends; still we were different from what we used to be, and were not so comfortable among ourselves. Sometimes I fancied that Peggotty perhaps objected to my mother's wearing all the pretty dresses she had in her drawers, or to her going so often to visit at that neighbour's; but I couldn't, to my satisfaction, make out how it was.

Gradually, I became used to seeing the gentleman with the black whiskers. I liked him no better than at first, and had the same uneasy jealousy of him.

One autumn morning I was with my mother in the front garden, when Mr. Murdstone—I knew him by that name now—came by, on horseback. He reined up his horse to salute my mother, and said he was going to Lowestoft to see some friends who were there with a yacht, and merrily proposed to take me on the saddle before him if I would like the ride.

The air was so clear and pleasant, and the horse seemed to like the idea of the ride so much himself, as he stood snorting and pawing at the garden gate, that I had a great desire to go. So I was sent up-stairs to Peggotty to be made spruce; and, in the meantime, Mr. Murdstone dismounted, and, with his horse's bridle drawn over his arm, walked slowly up and down on the outer side of the sweetbriar fence, while my mother walked slowly up and down on the inner, to keep him company.

Mr. Murdstone and I were soon off, and trotting along on the green turf by the side of the road. He held me quite easily with one arm, and I don't think I was restless usually; but I could not make up my mind to sit in front of him without turning my head sometimes, and looking up in his face. He had that kind of shallow black eye—I want a better word to express an eye that has no depth in it to be looked into—which, when it is abstracted, seems, from some peculiarity of light, to be disfigured, for a moment at a time, by a cast.

We went to an hotel by the sea, we walked about on the cliff after that, and sat on the grass, and looked at things through a telescope—I could make out nothing myself when it was put to my eye, but I pretended I could—and then we came back to the hotel to an early dinner.

We went home early in the evening. It was a very fine evening, and my mother and he had another stroll by the sweetbriar, while I was sent in to get my tea. When he was gone, my mother asked me all about the day I had had, and what he had said and done.

I write of her just as she was when I had gone to bed after this talk, and she came to bid me good night. She kneeled down playfully by the side of the bed, and laying her chin upon her hands, and laughing, said:

"Don't tell Peggotty; she might be angry." And we kissed one another over and over again, and I soon fell fast asleep.

It seems to me, at this distance of time, as if it were the next day when Peggotty broached the striking and adventurous proposition I am about to mention; but it was probably about two months afterwards.

We were sitting as before, one evening (when my mother was out as before), in company with the stocking and the yard measure, and the bit of wax, and the box with Saint Paul's on the lid, and the crocodile book, when Peggotty, after looking at me several times, and opening her mouth as if she were going to speak, without doing it—which I thought was merely gaping, or I should have been rather alarmed—said coaxingly:

"Master Davy, how should you like to go along with me and spend a fortnight at my brother's at Yarmouth? Wouldn't *that* be a treat?"

"Is your brother an agreeable man, Peggotty?" I inquired, provisionally.

"Oh, what an agreeable man he is!" cried Peggotty, holding up her hands. "Then there's the sea; and the boats and ships; and the fishermen; and the beach; and Am to play with——"

Peggotty meant her nephew Ham; but she spoke of him as a morsel of English Grammar.

I was flushed by her summary of delights, and replied that it would indeed be a treat, but what would my mother say?

"Why then I'll as good as bet a guinea," said Peggotty, intent upon my face, "that she'll let us go. I'll ask her, if you like, as soon as ever she comes home. There now!"

"But what's she to do while we are away?" said I, putting my small elbows on the table to argue the point. "She can't live by herself."

If Peggotty were looking for a hole, all of a sudden, in the heel of that stocking, it must have been a very little one indeed, and not worth darning.

"I say! Peggotty! She can't live by herself, you know."

"Oh bless you!" said Peggotty, looking at me again at last. "Don't you know? She's going to stay for a fortnight with Mrs. Grayper. Mrs. Grayper's going to have a lot of company."

Oh! If that was it, I was quite ready to go. The day soon came for our going. We were to go in a carrier's cart, which departed in the morning after breakfast. I would have given any money to have been allowed to wrap myself up over-night, and sleep in my hat and boots.

It touches me nearly now, although I tell it lightly, to recollect how eager I was to leave my happy home; to think how little I suspected what I did leave for ever.

I am glad to recollect that when the carrier began to move, my mother ran out at the gate, and called to him to stop, that she might kiss me once more. I am glad to dwell upon the earnestness and love with which she lifted up her face to mine, and did so.

As we left her standing in the road, Mr. Murdstone came up to where she was, and seemed to expostulate with her for being so moved. I was looking back round the awning of the cart, and wondered what business it was of his. Peggotty, who was also looking back on the other side, seemed anything but satisfied; as the face she brought back in the cart denoted.

CHAPTER 3

I Have a Chance

THE carrier's horse was the laziest horse in the world, I should hope, and shuffled along, with his head down, as if he liked to keep people waiting.

We made so many deviations up and down lanes, and were such a long time delivering a bedstead at a public-house, and calling at other places, that I was quite tired, and very glad, when we saw Yarmouth.

As we drew a little nearer, and saw the whole adjacent prospect lying a straight low line under the sky, I hinted to Peggotty that a mound or so might have improved it; and also that if the land had been a little more separated from the sea, and the town and the tide had not been quite so much mixed up, like toast and water, it would have been nicer.

When we got into the street (which was strange enough to me), and smelt the fish, and pitch, and oakum, and tar, and saw the sailors walking about, and the carts jingling up and down over the stones, I felt that I had done so busy a place an injustice; and said as much to Peggotty.

"Here's my Am!" screamed Peggotty, "growed out of knowledge!"

He was waiting for us, in fact, at the public-house. Our intimacy was much advanced by his taking me on his back to carry me home. He was, now, a huge, strong fellow of six feet high, broad in proportion, and round-shouldered; but with a simpering boy's face and curly light hair that gave him quite a sheepish look. He was dressed in a canvas jacket, and a pair of such very stiff trousers that they would have stood quite as well alone, without any legs in them. And you couldn't so properly have said he wore a hat, as that he was covered in a-top, like an old building, with something pitchy.

We turned down lanes bestrewn with bits of chips and little hillocks of sand, and went past gas-works, rope-walks, boat-builders' yards, shipwrights' yards, ship-breakers' yards, caulkers' yards, riggers' lofts, smiths' forges, and a great litter of such places, until we came out upon the dull waste I had already seen at a distance; when Ham said,

"Yon's our house, Mas'r Davy!"

I looked in all directions, as far as I could stare over the wilderness, and away at the sea, and away at the river, but no house could *I* make out. There was a black barge, or some other kind of superannuated boat, not far off from where we stood, high and dry on the ground, with an iron funnel sticking out of it for a chimney and smoking very cosily; but nothing else in the way of a habitation that was visible to *me*.

"That's not it?" said I. "That ship-looking thing?"

"That's it, Mas'r Davy," returned Ham.

If it had been Aladdin's palace, roc's egg and all, I suppose I could not have been more charmed with the romantic idea of living in it. There was a delightful door cut in the side, and it was roofed in, and there were little windows in it; but the wonderful charm of it was, that it was a real boat which had no doubt been upon the water hundreds of times, and which had never been intended to be lived in, on dry land.

It was beautifully clean inside, and as tidy as possible. There was a table, and a Dutch clock, and a chest of drawers, and on the chest of drawers there was a tea-tray with a painting on it of a lady with a parasol, taking a walk with a military-looking child who was trundling a hoop. The tray was kept from tumbling down, by a bible; and the tray, if it had tumbled down, would have smashed a quantity of cups and saucers and a teapot that were grouped around the book.

All this, I saw in the first glance after I crossed the threshold—child-like, according to my theory—and then Peggotty opened a little door and showed me my bedroom. It was the completest and most desirable bedroom ever seen—in the stern of the vessel; with a little window, where the rudder used to go through; a little looking-glass, just the right height for me, nailed against the wall, and framed with oyster-shells; a little bed, which there was just room enough to get into; and a nosegay of seaweed in a blue mug on the table.

We were welcomed by a very civil woman in a white apron, whom I had seen curtseying at the door when I was on Ham's back, about a quarter of a mile off. Likewise by a most beautiful little girl (or I thought her so), with a necklace of blue beads on, who wouldn't let me kiss her when I offered to, but ran away and hid herself. By and by, when we had dined in a sumptuous manner off boiled dabs, melted butter, and potatoes, with a chop for me, a hairy man with a very goodnatured face came home. As he called Peggotty "Laas," and gave her a hearty smack on the cheek, I had no doubt, from the general propriety of her conduct, that he was her brother; and so he turned out—being presently introduced to me as Mr. Peggotty, the master of the house.

"Glad to see you, sir," said Mr. Peggotty. "You'll find us rough, sir, but you'll find us ready."

I thanked him, and replied that I was sure I should be happy in such a delightful place.

"How's your Ma, sir?" said Mr. Peggotty. "Did you leave her pretty jolly?"

I gave Mr. Peggotty to understand that she was as jolly as I could wish, and that she desired her compliments—which was a polite fiction on my part.

"I'm much obleeged to her, I'm sure," said Mr. Peggotty. "Well, sir, if you can make out here, for a fortnut, 'long wi' her," nodding at his sister, "and Ham, and little Em'ly, we shall be proud of your company."

Having done the honours of his house in this hospitable manner, Mr. Peggotty went out to wash himself in a kettleful of hot water, remarking that "cold would never get *his* muck off." He soon returned, greatly improved in appearance; but so rubicund, that I couldn't help thinking his face had this in common with the lobsters, crabs, and crawfish—that it went into the hot water very black and came out very red.

After tea, when the door was shut and all was made snug (the nights being cold and misty now), it seemed to me the most delicious retreat that the imagination of man could conceive. Mr. Peggotty was smoking his pipe. I felt it was a time for conversation and confidence.

"Mr. Peggotty!" says I. "Did you give your son the name of Ham, because you lived in a sort of ark?"

Mr. Peggotty seemed to think it a deep idea, but answered:

"No, sir. I never giv him no name."

"Who gave him that name, then?" said I, putting question number two of the catechism to Mr. Peggotty.

"Why, sir, his father giv it him," said Mr. Peggotty.

"I thought you were his father!"

"My brother Joe was *his* father," said Mr. Peggotty.

"Dead, Mr. Peggotty?" I hinted, after a respectful pause.

"Drowndead," said Mr. Peggotty.

I was very much surprised that Mr. Peggotty was not Ham's father, and began to wonder whether I was mistaken about his relationship to anybody else there. I was so curious to know, that I made up my mind to have it out with Mr. Peggotty.

"Little Em'ly," I said, glancing at her. "She is your daughter, isn't she, Mr. Peggotty?"

"No, sir. My brother in law, Tom, was *her* father."

I couldn't help it. "—Dead, Mr. Peggotty?" I hinted, after another respectful silence.

"Drowndead," said Mr. Peggotty.

I felt the difficulty of resuming the subject, but had not got to the bottom of it yet, and must get to the bottom somehow. So I said:

"Haven't you *any* children, Mr. Peggotty?"

"No, master," he answered, with a short laugh. "I'm a bacheldore."

"A bachelor!" I said, astonished. "Why, who's that, Mr. Peggotty?" Pointing to the person in the apron who was knitting.

"That's Missis Gummidge," said Mr. Peggotty.

"Gummidge, Mr. Peggotty?"

But at this point Peggotty—I mean my own peculiar Peggotty—made such impressive motions to me not to ask any more questions, that I could only sit and look at all the silent company, until it was time to go to bed. Then, in the privacy of my own little cabin, she informed me that Ham and Em'ly were an orphan nephew and niece, whom my host had at different times adopted in their childhood, when they were left destitute;

and that Mrs. Gummidge was the widow of his partner in a boat, who had died very poor. He was but a poor man himself, said Peggotty, but as good as gold and as true as steel—those were her similes.

Almost as soon as the sun shone upon the oyster-shell frame of my mirror I was out of bed, and out with little Em'ly, picking up stones upon the beach.

"You're quite a sailor, I suppose?" I said to Em'ly.

"No," replied Em'ly, shaking her head, "I'm afraid of the sea. I have seen it very cruel to some of our men. I have seen it tear a boat as big as our house all to pieces."

"I hope it wasn't the boat that——"

"That father was drownded in?" said Em'ly. "No. Not that one, I never see that boat."

"Nor him?" I asked her.

Little Em'ly shook her head. "Not to remember!"

Here was a coincidence! I immediately went into an explanation how I had never seen my own father; and how my mother and I had always lived by ourselves in the happiest state imaginable, and lived so then, and always meant to live so.

"Your father was a gentleman and your mother is a lady; and my father was a fisherman and my mother was a fisherman's daughter, and my uncle Dan is a fisherman," said Em'ly, as she looked about for shells and pebbles.

"Dan is Mr. Peggotty, is he?" said I.

"Uncle Dan—yonder," answered Em'ly, nodding at the boat-house.

"Yes. I mean him. He must be very good, I should think?"

"Good?" said Em'ly. "If I was ever to be a lady, I'd give him a sky-blue coat, with diamond buttons, nankeen trousers, a red velvet waistcoat, a cocked hat, a large gold watch, a silver pipe, and a box of money."

"You would like to be a lady?" I said.

Emily looked at me, and laughed and nodded "yes."

"I should like it very much. We would all be gentlefolks together, then. Me, and uncle, and Ham, and Mrs. Gummidge. We wouldn't mind that, when there come stormy weather.—Not for our own sakes, I mean. We would for the poor fishermen's, to be sure, and we'd help 'em with money when they come to any hurt."

We strolled a long way, and loaded ourselves with things that we thought curious, and put some stranded starfish carefully back into the water—I hardly know enough of the race at this moment to be quite certain whether they had reason to feel obliged to us for doing so, or the reverse—and then made our way home to Mr. Peggotty's dwelling. We stopped under the lee of the lobster-outhouse to exchange an innocent kiss, and went in to breakfast glowing with health and pleasure.

"Like two young mavishes," Mr. Peggotty said. I knew this meant, in our local dialect, like two young thrushes, and received it as a compliment.

Of course I was in love with little Em'ly. I am sure I loved that baby quite as truly, quite as tenderly, with greater purity and more disinterestedness, than can enter into the best love of a later time of life, high and ennobling as it is.

We used to walk about that dim old flat at Yarmouth in a loving manner, hours and hours. The days sported by us, as if Time had not grown up himself yet, but were a child too, and always at play. I told Em'ly I adored her, and that unless she confessed she adored me I should be reduced to the necessity of killing myself with a sword. She said she did, and I have no doubt she did.

I soon found out that Mrs. Gummidge did not always make herself so agreeable as she might have been expected to do, under the circumstances of her residence with Mr. Peggotty. Mrs. Gummidge's was rather a fretful disposition, and she whimpered more sometimes than was comfortable for other parties in so small an establishment. I was very sorry for her; but there were moments when it would have been more agreeable, I thought, if Mrs. Gummidge had had a convenient apartment of her own to retire to, and had stopped there until her spirits revived.

Mr. Peggotty went occasionally to a public house called The Willing Mind. I discovered this, by his being out on the second or third evening of our visit, and by Mrs. Gummidge's looking up at the Dutch clock, between eight and nine, and saying he was there, and that, what was more, she had known in the morning he would go there.

It was a very cold day, with cutting blasts of wind. Mrs. Gummidge's peculiar corner of the fireside seemed to me to be the warmest and snuggest in the place, as her chair was certainly the easiest, but it didn't suit her that day at all. She was constantly complaining of the cold, and of its occasioning a visitation in her back which she called "the creeps." At last she shed tears on that subject, and said again that she was "a lone lorn creetur' and everythink went contrairy with her."

"It is certainly very cold," said Peggotty. "Everybody must feel it so."

"I feel it more than other people," said Mrs. Gummidge.

Accordingly, when Mr. Peggotty came home about nine o'clock, this unfortunate Mrs. Gummidge was knitting in her corner, in a very wretched and miserable condition.

"Well, Mates," said Mr. Peggotty, taking his seat, "how are you?"

We all said something, or looked something, to welcome him, except Mrs. Gummidge, who only shook her head over her knitting.

"What's amiss?" said Mr. Peggotty, with a clap of his hands. "Cheer up, old Mawther!" (Mr. Peggotty meant old girl.)

Mrs. Gummidge did not appear to be able to cheer up. She took out an old black silk handkerchief and wiped her eyes; but instead of putting it in her pocket, kept it out, and wiped them again, and still kept it out, ready for use.

"What's amiss, dame!" said Mr. Peggotty.

"Nothing," returned Mrs. Gummidge. "You've come from The Willing Mind, Dan'l?"

"Why yes, I've took a short spell at The Willing Mind tonight," said Mr. Peggotty.

"I'm sorry I should drive you there," said Mrs. Gummidge.

"Drive! I don't want no driving," returned Mr. Peggotty with an honest laugh. "I only go too ready."

"Very ready," said Mrs. Gummidge, shaking her head, and wiping her eyes. "Yes, yes, very ready. I am sorry it should be along of me that you're so ready."

"Along o' you! It an't along o' you!" said Mr. Peggotty. "Don't ye believe a bit on it."

"I an't what I could wish myself to be," said Mrs. Gummidge. "I am far from it. I know what I am. My troubles has made me contrairy. I feel my troubles, and they make me contrairy. I wish I didn't feel 'em, but I do. I wish I could be hardened to 'em, but I an't. I make the house uncomfortable. I don't wonder at it. I've made your sister so all day, and Master Davy."

Here I roared out, "No, you haven't, Mrs. Gummidge," in great mental distress.

"It's far from right that I should do it," said Mrs. Gummidge. "It an't a fit return. I had better go into the house and die. I am a lone lorn creetur', and had much better not make myself contrairy here."

Mrs. Gummidge retired with these words, and betook herself to bed.

At last the day came for going home. I bore up against the separation from Mr. Peggotty and Mrs. Gummidge, but my agony of mind at leaving little Em'ly was piercing. We went arm-in-arm to the public-house where the carrier put up, and I promised, on the road, to write to her. We were greatly overcome at parting; and if ever, in my life, I have had a void made in my heart, I had one made that day.

Now, all the time I had been on my visit, I had been ungrateful to my home again, and had thought little or nothing about it. But I was no sooner turned towards it, than my reproachful young conscience seemed to point that way with a steady finger; and I felt, all the more for the sinking of my spirits, that it was my nest, and that my mother was my comforter and friend.

This gained upon me as we went along; so that the nearer we drew, and the more familiar the objects became that we passed, the more excited I was to get there, and to run into her arms.

Blunderstone Rookery! How well I recollect it, on a cold grey afternoon, with a dull sky, threatening rain!

The door opened, and I looked, half laughing and half crying in my pleasant agitation, for my mother. It was not she, but a strange servant.

"Why, Peggotty!" I said, ruefully, "isn't she come home?"

"Yes, yes, Master Davy," said Peggotty. "She's come home. Wait a bit, Master Davy, and I'll—I'll tell you something."

Between her agitation, and her natural awkwardness in getting out of the cart, Peggotty was making a most extraordinary festoon of herself, but

I felt too blank and strange to tell her so. When she had got down, she took me by the hand; led me, wondering, into the kitchen; and shut the door.

"Peggotty!" said I, quite frightened. "What's the matter?"

"Nothing's the matter, bless you, Master Davy dear!" she answered, assuming an air of sprightliness.

"Something's the matter, I'm sure. Where's mama?"

"Where's mama, Master Davy?" repeated Peggotty.

"Yes. Why hasn't she come out to the gate, and what have we come in here for? Oh, Peggotty!" My eyes were full, and I felt as if I were going to tumble down.

"Bless the precious boy!" cried Peggotty, taking hold of me. "What is it? Speak, my pet!"

"Not dead, too! Oh, she's not dead, Peggotty?"

Peggotty cried out, "No!" with an astonishing volume of voice; and then sat down and began to pant, and said I had given her a turn.

I gave her a hug to take away the turn, or to give her another turn in the right direction, and then stood before her, looking at her in anxious inquiry.

"You see, dear, I should have told you before now," said Peggotty, untying her bonnet with a shaking hand, and speaking in a breathless sort of way. "What do you think? You have got a Pa. A new one," said Peggotty.

"A new one?" I repeated.

Peggotty gave a gasp, as if she were swallowing something that was very hard, and, putting out her hand, said:

"Come and see him."

"I don't want to see him."

—"And your mama," said Peggotty.

I ceased to draw back, and we went straight to the best parlour, where she left me. On one side of the fire, sat my mother; on the other, Mr. Murdstone. My mother dropped her work, and arose hurriedly, but timidly I thought.

"Now, Clara my dear," said Mr. Murdstone. "Recollect! control yourself, always control yourself! Davy boy, how do you do?"

I gave him my hand. After a moment of suspense, I went and kissed my mother: she kissed me, patted me gently on the shoulder, and sat down again to her work. I could not look at her, I could not look at him, I knew quite well that he was looking at us both; and I turned to the window and looked out there at some shrubs that were dropping their heads in the cold.

As soon as I could creep away, I crept up-stairs. My old dear bedroom was changed, and I was to lie a long way off. I rambled downstairs to find anything that was like itself, so altered it all seemed; and roamed into the yard. I very soon started back from there, for the empty dog-kennel was filled up with a great dog—deep-mouthed and blackhaired like Him— and he was very angry at the sight of me, and sprang out to get at me.

CHAPTER 4
I Fall Into Disgrace

I WENT up to my room, hearing the dog in the yard bark after me all the way while I climbed the stairs; and, looking as blank and strange upon the room as the room looked upon me, sat down with my small hands crossed, and thought.

I was crying all the time, but, except that I was conscious of being cold and dejected, I am sure I never thought why I cried. At last in my desolation I began to consider that I was dreadfully in love with little Em'ly, and had been torn away from her to come here where no one seemed to want me, or to care about me, half as much as she did. This made such a very miserable piece of business of it, that I rolled myself up in a corner of the counter-pane, and cried myself to sleep.

I was awakened by somebody saying, "Here he is!" and uncovering my hot head. My mother and Peggotty had come to look for me, and it was one of them who had done it.

"Davy," said my mother. "What's the matter?"

"Nothing." I turned over on my face, I recollect, to hide my trembling lip, which answered her with greater truth.

"Davy," said my mother. "Davy, my child!"

"This is your doing, Peggotty, you cruel thing!" said my mother. "I have no doubt at all about it. How can you reconcile it to your conscience, I wonder, to prejudice my own boy against me, or against anybody who is dear to me? What do you mean by it, Peggotty?"

Poor Peggotty lifted up her hands and eyes, and only answered, in a sort of paraphrase of the grace I usually repeated after dinner, "Lord forgive you, Mrs. Copperfield, and for what you have said this minute, may you be truly sorry!"

"Oh, dear me!" cried my mother, turning from one of us to the other, in her pettish, wilful manner. "What a troublesome world this is, when one has the most right to expect it to be as agreeable as possible!"

I felt the touch of a hand that I knew was neither hers nor Peggotty's, and slipped to my feet at the bed-side. It was Mr. Murdstone's hand, and he kept it on my arm as he said:

"What's this? Clara, my love, have you forgotten?—Firmness, my dear!"

"I am very sorry, Edward," said my mother. "I meant to be very good, but I am so uncomfortable."

"Indeed!" he answered. "That's a bad hearing, so soon, Clara."

"I say it's very hard I should be made so now," returned my mother, pouting; "and it is—very hard—isn't it?"

He drew her to him, whispered in her ear, and kissed her. I knew as well, when I saw my mother's head lean down upon his shoulder, and her arm touch his neck—I knew as well that he could mould her pliant nature into any form he chose, as I know, now, that he did it.

"Go you below, my love," said Mr. Murdstone. "David and I will come down, together. My friend," turning a darkening face on Peggotty, when he had watched my mother out, and dismissed her with a nod and a smile: "do you know your mistress's name?"

"She has been my mistress a long time, sir," answered Peggotty. "I ought to know it."

"That's true," he answered. "But I thought I heard you, as I came up-stairs, address her by a name that is not hers. She has taken mine, you know. Will you remember that?"

Peggotty, with some uneasy glances at me, curtseyed herself out of the room without replying. When we two were left alone, he shut the door, and sitting on a chair, and holding me standing before him, looked steadily into my eyes.

"David," he said, making his lips thin, by pressing them together, "if I have an obstinate horse or dog to deal with, what do you think I do?"

"I don't know."

"I beat him."

I had answered in a kind of breathless whisper, but I felt, in my silence, that my breath was shorter now.

"I make him wince, and smart. I say to myself, 'I'll conquer that fellow', and if it were to cost him all the blood he had, I should do it. What is that upon your face?"

"Dirt," I said.

He knew it was the mark of tears as well as I. But if he had asked the question twenty times, each time with twenty blows, I believe my baby heart would have burst before I would have told him so.

"You have a good deal of intelligence for a little fellow," he said, with a grave smile that belonged to him, "and you understood me very well, I see. Wash that face, sir, and come down with me."

He pointed to the washing-stand, which I had made out to be like Mrs. Gummidge, and motioned me with his head to obey him directly. I had little doubt then, and I have less doubt now, that he would have knocked me down without the least compunction, if I had hesitated.

"Clara, my dear," he said, when I had done his bidding, and he walked me into the parlour, with his hand still on my arm; "you will not be made uncomfortable any more, I hope. We shall soon improve our youthful humours."

God help me, I might have been improved for my whole life, I might have been made another creature perhaps, for life, by a kind word at that season. A word of encouragement and explanation, of pity for my childish ignorance, of welcome home, of reassurance to me that it *was* home, might have made me dutiful to him in my heart henceforth, instead of in my hypocritical outside, and might have made me respect instead of hate him.

We dined alone, we three together. He seemed to be very fond of my mother—I am afraid I liked him none the better for that—and she was very fond of him. I gathered from what they said, that an elder sister of his was coming to stay with them, and that she was expected that evening.

After dinner, when we were sitting by the fire, and I was meditating an escape to Peggotty without having the hardihood to slip away, lest it should offend the master of the house, a coach drove up to the garden gate, and he went out to receive the visitor. My mother followed him. I was timidly following her, when she turned round at the parlour-door, in the dusk, and taking me in her embrace as she had been used to do, whispered me to love my new father and be obedient to him.

It was Miss Murdstone who was arrived, and a gloomy-looking lady she was; dark, like her brother, whom she greatly resembled in face and voice, and with very heavy eyebrows, nearly meeting over her large nose.

She was brought into the parlour with many tokens of welcome, and there formally recognized my mother as a new and near relation. Then she looked at me, and said:

"Is that your boy, sister-in-law?"

My mother acknowledged me.

"Generally speaking," said Miss Murdstone, "I don't like boys. How d'ye do, boy?"

Under these encouraging circumstances, I replied that I was very well, and that I hoped she was the same; with such an indifferent grace, that Miss Murdstone disposed of me in two words:

"Wants manner!"

Having uttered which with great distinctness, she begged the favour of being shown to her room.

As well as I could make out, she had come for good, and had no intention of ever going again. She began to "help" my mother next morning, and was in and out of the store-closet all day, putting things to rights, and making havoc in the old arrangements.

On the very first morning after her arrival she was up and ringing her bell at cock-crow. When my mother came down to breakfast, and was going to make the tea, Miss Murdstone gave her a kind of peck on the cheek, which was her nearest approach to a kiss, and said:

"Now, Clara, my dear, I am come here, you know, to relieve you of all the trouble I can. You're much too pretty and thoughtless"—my mother blushed but laughed, and seemed not to dislike this character—"to have any duties imposed upon you that can be undertaken by me. If you'll be so good as give me your keys, my dear, I'll attend to all this sort of thing in future."

From that time, Miss Murdstone kept the keys in her own little jail all day, and under her pillow all night, and my mother had no more to do with them than I had.

My mother did not suffer her authority to pass from her without a shadow of protest. One night when Miss Murdstone had been developing certain household plans to her brother, my mother suddenly began to cry, and said she thought she might have been consulted.

"Clara!" said Mr. Murdstone sternly. "Clara! I wonder at you."

"Oh, it's very well to say you wonder, Edward!" cried my mother, "and it's very well for you to talk about firmness, but you wouldn't like it yourself."

"It's very hard," said my mother, "that in my own house——"

"*My* own house?" repeated Mr. Murdstone. "Clara!"

"*Our* own house, I mean," faltered my mother, evidently frightened—"I hope you must know what I mean, Edward—it's very hard that in *your* own house I may not have a word to say about domestic matters."

"Edward," said Miss Murdstone, "let there be an end of this. I go to-morrow."

"Jane Murdstone," said her brother, "be silent! How dare you to insinuate that you don't know my character better than your words imply?"

"I am sure", my poor mother went on at a grievous disadvantage, and with many tears, "I don't want anybody to go. I should be very miserable and unhappy if anybody was to go. I don't ask much. I am not unreasonable. I only want to be consulted sometimes."

"Clara," he continued, looking at my mother, "you surprise me! You astound me! Yes, I had a satisfaction in the thought of marrying an inexperienced and artless person, and forming her character, and infusing into it some amount of that firmness and decision of which it stood in need. But when Jane Murdstone is kind enough to come to my assistance in this endeavour, and to assume, for my sake, a condition something like a housekeeper's, and when she meets with a base return——that feeling of mine is chilled and altered."

"Don't, my love, say that!" implored my mother very piteously. "Pray let us be friends," said my mother. "I couldn't live under coldness or unkindness. I am so sorry. I have a great many defects, I know, and it's very good of you, Edward, with your strength of mind, to endeavour to correct them for me. Jane, I don't object to anything. I should be quite broken-hearted if you thought of leaving——" My mother was too much overcome to go on.

"Jane Murdstone," said Mr. Murdstone to his sister, "it is not my fault that so unusual an occurrence has taken place to-night. Let us both try to forget it. And as this," he added, after these magnanimous words, "is not a fit scene for the boy—David, go to bed!"

I could hardly find the door, through the tears that stood in my eyes. I was so sorry for my mother's distress; but I groped my way out, and groped my way up to my room in the dark, without even having the heart to say good night to Peggotty, or to get a candle from her.

Going down next morning rather earlier than usual, I paused outside the parlour-door, on hearing my mother's voice. She was very earnestly and humbly entreating Miss Murdstone's pardon, which that lady granted, and a perfect reconciliation took place. I never knew my mother afterwards to give an opinion on any matter, without first appealing to Miss Murdstone, or without having first ascertained by some sure means, what Miss Murdstone's opinion was; and I never saw Miss Murdstone, when out of temper (she was infirm that way), move her hand towards her bag as if she were going to take out the keys and offer to resign them to my mother, without seeing that my mother was in a terrible fright.

There had been some talk on occasions of my going to boarding school. Mr. and Miss Murdstone had originated it, and my mother had of course agreed with them. Nothing, however, was concluded on the subject yet. In the meantime I learnt lessons at home.

As to any recreation with other children of my age, I had very little of that; for the gloomy theology of the Murdstones made all children out to be a swarm of little vipers (though there *was* a child once set in the midst of the Disciples), and held that they contaminated one another.

The natural result of this treatment, continued, I suppose, for some six months or more, was to make me sullen, dull, and dogged. I believe I should have been almost stupified but for one circumstance.

It was this. My father had left a small collection of books in a little room upstairs, to which I had access (for it adjoined my own) and which nobody else in our house ever troubled. From that blessed little room, Roderick Random, Peregrine Pickle, Humphrey Clinker, Tom Jones, the Vicar of Wakefield, Don Quixote, Gil Blas, and Robinson Crusoe, came out, a glorious host, to keep me company. They kept alive my fancy, and my hope of something beyond that place and time—they, and the Arabian Nights, and the Tales of the Genii—and did me no harm; for whatever harm was in some of them was not there for me; *I* knew nothing of it.

This was my only and my constant comfort.

One morning when I went into the parlour with my books, I found my mother looking anxious, Miss Murdstone looking firm, and Mr. Murdstone binding something round the bottom of a cane—a lithe and limber cane, which he left off binding when I came in, and poised and switched in the air.

"I tell you, Clara," said Mr. Murdstone, "I have been often flogged myself."

"To be sure; of course," said Miss Murdstone.

"Certainly, my dear Jane," faltered my mother, meekly. "But—but do you think it did Edward good?"

"Do you think it did Edward harm, Clara?" asked Mr. Murdstone, gravely.

"That's the point," said his sister.

To this my mother returned, "Certainly, my dear Jane," and said no more.

I felt apprehensive that I was personally interested in this dialogue, and sought Mr. Murdstone's eye as it lighted on mine.

"Now, David," he said—and I saw that cast again as he said it—"you must be far more careful to-day than usual." He gave the cane another poise, and another switch; and having finished his preparation of it, laid it down beside him, with an impressive look, and took up his book.

This was a good freshener to my presence of mind, as a beginning. I felt the words of my lessons slipping off, not one by one, or line by line, but by the entire page; I tried to lay hold of them; but they seemed, if I may so express it, to have put skates on, and to skim away from me with a smoothness there was no checking.

We began badly, and went on worse. I had come in, with an idea of distinguishing myself rather, conceiving that I was very well prepared; but it turned out to be quite a mistake. Book after book was added to the heap of failures; my mother burst out crying.

"Clara!" said Miss Murdstone, in her warning voice.

"Why, Jane, we can hardly expect Clara to bear, with perfect firmness, the worry and torment that David has occasioned her to-day. David, you and I will go up-stairs, boy."

As he took me out at the door, my mother ran towards us. Miss Murdstone said, "Clara! are you a perfect fool?" and interfered. I saw my mother stop her ears then, and I heard her crying.

He walked me up to my room slowly and gravely—I am certain he had a delight in that formal parade of executing justice—and when we got there, suddenly twisted my head under his arm.

"Mr. Murdstone! Sir!" I cried to him. "Don't! Pray don't beat me! I have tried to learn, sir, but I can't learn while you and Miss Murdstone are by. I can't indeed!"

"Can't you, indeed, David?" he said. "We'll try that."

He had my head as in a vice, but I twined round him somehow, and stopped him for a moment, entreating him not to beat me. It was only for a moment that I stopped him, for he cut me heavily an instant afterwards, and in the same instant I caught the hand with which he held me in my mouth, between my teeth, and bit it through. It sets my teeth on edge to think of it.

He beat me then, as if he would have beaten me to death. Above all the noise we made, I heard them running up the stairs, and crying out— I heard my mother crying out—and Peggotty. Then he was gone; and the door was locked outside; and I was lying, fevered and hot, and torn, and sore, and raging in my puny way, upon the floor.

It had begun to grow dark, and I had shut the window (I had been lying, for the most part, with my head upon the sill, by turns crying, dozing, and looking listlessly out), when the key was turned, and Miss Murdstone came in with some bread and meat, and milk. These she put down upon the table without a word, glaring at me the while with exemplary firmness, and then retired, locking the door after her.

I never shall forget the waking next morning; the being cheerful and fresh for the first moment, and then the being weighed down by the stale and dismal oppression of remembrance. Miss Murdstone reappeared before I was out of bed; told me, in so many words, that I was free to walk in the garden for half an hour and no longer; and retired, leaving the door open, that I might avail myself of that permission.

I did so, and did so every morning of my imprisonment, which lasted five days. I saw no one, Miss Murdstone excepted, during the whole time—except at evening prayers in the parlour; where I was stationed, a young outlaw, all alone by myself near the door. I only observed that my mother was as far off from me as she could be, and kept her face another way, so that I never saw it; and that Mr. Murdstone's hand was bound up in a large linen wrapper.

The length of those five days I can convey no idea of to any one. They occupy the place of years in my remembrance.

On the last night of my restraint, I was awakened by hearing my own name spoken in a whisper. I started up in bed, and putting out my arms in the dark, said:

"Is that you, Peggotty?"

There was no immediate answer, so I groped my way to the door, and putting my own lips to the keyhole, whispered:

"Is that you, Peggotty, dear?"

"Yes, my own precious Davy," she replied. "Be as soft as a mouse, or the Cat'll hear us."

I understood this to mean Miss Murdstone, and was sensible of the urgency of the case; her room being close by.

"How's mama, dear Peggotty? Is she very angry with me?"

I could hear Peggotty crying softly on her side of the keyhole, as I was doing on mine, before she answered. "No. Not very."

"What is going to be done with me, Peggotty dear? Do you know?"

"School. Near London," was Peggotty's answer.

"When, Peggotty?"

"To-morrow."

"Shan't I see mama?"

"Yes," said Peggotty. "Morning."

Then Peggotty fitted her mouth close to the keyhole.

"My own!" said Peggotty, with infinite compassion. "What I want to say, is, that you must never forget me. For I'll never forget you. And I'll take as much care of your mama, Davy, as ever I took of you. And I won't leave her."

"Thank you, dear Peggotty!" said I. "Oh, thank you! Thank you!"

From that night there grew up in my breast a feeling for Peggotty which I cannot very well define. She did not replace my mother; no one could do that; but she came into a vacancy in my heart, which closed upon her, and I felt towards her something I have never felt for any other human being.

In the morning Miss Murdstone appeared as usual, and told me I was going to school; which was not altogether such news to me as she supposed. She also informed me that when I was dressed, I was to come down-stairs into the parlour, and have my breakfast. There I found my mother, very pale and with red eyes: into whose arms I ran, and begged her pardon from my suffering soul.

"Oh, Davy!" she said. "That you could hurt any one I love! Try to be better, pray to be better! I forgive you; but I am so grieved, Davy, that you should have such bad passions in your heart."

"Master Copperfield's box there!" said Miss Murdstone, when wheels were heard at the gate.

I looked for Peggotty, but it was not she; neither she nor Mr. Murdstone appeared. My former acquaintance, the carrier, was at the door; the box was taken out to his cart, and lifted in.

"Clara!" said Miss Murdstone, in her warning note.

"Ready, my dear Jane," returned my mother. "Good bye, Davy. You are going for your own good. Good bye, my child. You will come home in the holidays, and be a better boy."

Miss Murdstone was good enough to take me out to the cart, and to say on the way that she hoped I would repent, before I came to a bad end; and then I got into the cart, and the lazy horse walked off with it.

CHAPTER 5

I Am Sent Away From Home

WE might have gone about half a mile, and my pocket-handkerchief was quite wet through, when the carrier stopped short.

Looking out to ascertain for what, I saw, to my amazement, Peggotty burst from a hedge and climb into the cart. She took me in both her arms, and squeezed me to her stays until the pressure on my nose was extremely painful. Not a single word did Peggotty speak. Releasing one of her arms, she put it down in her pocket to the elbow, and brought out some paper bags of cakes which she crammed into my pockets, and a purse which she put into my hand, but not one word did she say. After another and a final squeeze with both arms, she got down from the cart and ran away.

The carrier looked at me, as if to inquire if she were coming back. I shook my head, and said I thought not. "Then, come up," said the carrier to the lazy horse; who came up accordingly.

I had now leisure to examine the purse. It was a stiff leather purse, with a snap, and had three bright shillings in it, which Peggotty had evidently polished up with whitening, for my greater delight. But its most precious contents were two half-crowns folded together in a bit of paper, on which was written, in my mother's hand, "For Davy. With my love."

"Are you only going to Yarmouth?" I asked.

"That's about it," said the carrier. "And there I shall take you to the stage-cutch, and the stage-cutch'll take you to—wherever it is."

As this was a great deal for the carrier (whose name was Mr. Barkis) to say—I offered him a cake as a mark of attention, which he ate at one gulp, exactly like an elephant, and which made no more impression on his big face than it would have done on an elephant's.

"Did *she* make 'em, now?" said Mr. Barkis, always leaning forward, in his slouching way, on the footboard of the cart with an arm on each knee.

"Yes. She makes all our pastry and does all our cooking."

"Do she though?" said Mr. Barkis.

By-and-by, he said:

"No sweethearts, I b'lieve?"

"Sweetmeats did you say, Mr. Barkis?" I thought he wanted something else to eat.

"Hearts," said Mr. Barkis. "Sweethearts; no person walks with her?"

"With Peggotty?"

"Ah!" he said. "Her."

"Oh, no. She never had a sweetheart."

"Didn't she, though?" said Mr. Barkis.

He sat looking at the horse's ears.

"So she makes," said Mr. Barkis, after a long interval of reflection, "all the apple parsties, and doos all the cooking, do she?"

I replied that such was the fact.

"Well. I'll tell you what," said Mr. Barkis. "P'raps you might be writin' to her?"

"I shall certainly write to her," I rejoined.

"Ah!" he said, slowly turning his eyes towards me. "Well! If you was writin' to her, p'raps you'd recollect to say that Barkis was willin'; would you?"

"That Barkis was willing," I repeated, innocently. "Is that all the message?"

"Ye—es," he said, considering. "Ye—es. Barkis is willin'."

"But you will be at Blunderstone again to-morrow, Mr. Barkis," I said, faltering a little at the idea of my being far away from it then, "and could give your own message so much better."

But he repudiated this suggestion with a jerk of his head, so while I was waiting for the coach in the hotel at Yarmouth that very afternoon, I procured a sheet of paper and an inkstand and wrote a note to Peggotty, which ran thus:

"My dear Peggotty. I have come here safe. Barkis is willing. My love to mama. Yours affectionately. P.S. He says he particularly wants you to know—*Barkis is willing*."

I slept soundly until we got to Yarmouth.

The coach was in the yard, shining very much all over, but without any horses to it as yet; and it looked in that state as if nothing was more unlikely than its ever going to London. I was thinking what would ultimately become of me, when a lady looked out of a bow-window where some fowls and joints of meat were hanging up, and said:

"Is that the little gentleman from Blunderstone?"

"Yes, ma'am," I said.

The lady then rang a bell, and called out, "William! show the coffeeroom!" upon which a waiter came running out of a kitchen, and seemed a good deal surprised when he was only to show it to me.

He brought me some chops, and vegetables, and took the covers off in such a bouncing manner that I was afraid I must have given him some offence. But he greatly relieved my mind by putting a chair for me at the table, and saying very affably, "Now, six-foot! come on!"

I thanked him, and took my seat at the board. "What have we got here?" he said, putting a fork into my dish. "Not chops?"

"Chops," I said.

"Lord bless my soul!" he exclaimed, "I didn't know they were chops. Why a chop's the very thing to take off the bad effects of that beer! Ain't it lucky?"

So he took a chop by the bone in one hand, and a potato in the other, and ate away with a very good appetite, to my extreme satisfaction. He afterwards took another chop, and another potato; and after that another chop and another potato. When he had done, he brought me a pudding, and having set it before me, seemed to ruminate, and to become absent in his mind for some moments.

"How's the pie?" he said, rousing himself.

"It's a pudding," I made answer.

"Pudding!" he exclaimed. "Why, bless me, so it is! What!" looking at it nearer. "You don't mean to say it's a batter-pudding?"

"Yes, it is indeed."

"Why, a batter-pudding," he said, taking up a table-spoon, "is my favourite pudding! Ain't that lucky? Come on, little 'un, and let's see who'll get most."

The waiter certainly got most. He entreated me more than once to come in and win, but what with his table-spoon to my tea-spoon, his dispatch to my dispatch, and his appetite to my appetite, I was left far behind at the first mouthful, and had no chance with him. I never saw anyone enjoy a pudding so much, I think; and he laughed, when it was all gone, as if his enjoyment of it lasted still.

Finding him so very friendly and companionable, it was then that I asked for the pen and ink and paper, to write to Peggotty. He not only brought it immediately but was good enough to look over me while I wrote the letter.

The blowing of the coach-horn in the yard was a seasonable diversion, which made me get up and hesitatingly inquire, in the mingled pride and diffidence of having a purse (which I took out of my pocket), if there were anything to pay.

"If I hadn't a family, and that family hadn't the cowpock," said the waiter, "I wouldn't take a sixpence. If I didn't support a aged pairint, and a lovely sister,"—here the waiter was greatly agitated—"I wouldn't take a farthing. If I had a good place, and was treated well here, I should beg acceptance of a trifle, instead of taking of it. But I live on broken wittles—and I sleep on the coals"—here the waiter burst into tears.

I was very much concerned for his misfortunes, and felt that any recognition short of ninepence would be mere brutality and hardness of heart. Therefore I gave him one of my three bright shillings, which he received with much humility and veneration, and spun up with his thumb, directly afterwards, to try the goodness of.

It was a little disconcerting to me, to find, when I was being helped up behind the coach, that I was supposed to have eaten all the dinner without any assistance. I discovered this, from overhearing the lady in the bow-window say to the guard, "Take care of that child, George, or he'll burst!" and from observing that the women-servants who were about the place came out to look and giggle at me as a young phenomenon.

We had started from Yarmouth at three o'clock in the afternoon, and we were due in London about eight next morning. It was Midsummer weather, and the evening was very pleasant.

What an amazing place London was to me when I saw it in the distance. We approached it by degrees, and got, in due time, to the inn in the White-chapel district, for which we were bound.

The guard's eye lighted on me as he was getting down, and he said at the booking-office door:

"Is there anybody here for a yoongster booked in the name of Murd-stone, from Bloonderstone, Sooffolk, to be left till called for?"

Nobody answered.

"Try Copperfield, if you please, sir," said I, looking helplessly down.

"Is there anybody here for a yoongster, booked in the name of Murd-stone, from Bloonderstone, Sooffolk, but owning to the name of Copper-field, to be left till called for?" said the guard. "Come! *Is* there anybody?"

No. There was nobody.

A ladder was brought, and I got down. The coach was clear of passengers and backed off by some hostlers, out of the way. Still, nobody appeared, to claim the dusty youngster from Blunderstone, Suffolk.

More solitary than Robinson Crusoe, who had nobody to look at him, and see that he was solitary, I went into the booking office, and, by in-vitation of the clerk on duty, passed behind the counter, and sat down on the scale at which they weighed the luggage. Supposing nobody should ever fetch me, how long would they consent to keep me there? Would they keep me long enough to spend seven shillings? Should I sleep at night in one of those wooden bins, with the other luggage, and wash myself at the pump in the yard in the morning; or should I be turned out every night, and expected to come again to be left till called for, when the office opened next day? Supposing there was no mistake in the case, and Mr. Murdstone had devised this plan to get rid of me, what should I do? If they allowed me to remain there until my seven shillings were spent, I couldn't hope to remain there when I began to starve. These thoughts, and a hundred other such thoughts, turned me burning hot, and made me giddy with ap-prehension and dismay. I was in the height of my fever when a man entered and whispered to the clerk, who presently slanted me off the scale, and pushed me over to him, as if I were weighed, bought, delivered, and paid for.

As I went out of the office, hand in hand with this new acquaintance, I stole a look at him. He was a gaunt, sallow young man, with hollow cheeks. He was dressed in a suit of black clothes rather short in the sleeves and legs; and he had a white neck-kerchief on, that was not over clean.

"You're the new boy?" he said.

"Yes, sir," I said.

I supposed I was. I didn't know.

"I'm one of the masters at Salem House," *he* said.

"If you please, sir," I said, when we had accomplished about the same distance as before, "is it far?"

"It's a good step," he said. "We shall go by the stage-coach. It's about six miles."

I was so faint and tired, that the idea of holding out for six miles more was too much for me. I took heart to tell him that I had had nothing all night, and that if he would allow me to buy something to eat, I should be very much obliged to him. He appeared surprised at this—I see him stop and look at me now—and after considering for a few moments, said he wanted to call on an old person who lived not far off, and that the best way would be for me to buy some bread, or whatever I liked best that was wholesome, and make my breakfast at her house, where we could get some milk.

Accordingly we looked in at a baker's window, and we decided in favour of a nice little loaf of brown bread, which cost me threepence. Then, at a grocer's shop, we bought an egg and a slice of streaky bacon; which still left what I thought a good deal of change, out of the second of the bright shillings, and made me consider London a very cheap place. These provisions laid in, we went to the poor person's house, which was a part of some alms-houses, as I knew by their look, and by an inscription on a stone over the gate, which said they were established for twentyfive poor women.

The Master at Salem House lifted the latch of one of a number of little black doors, and we went into the little house of one of these poor old women, who was blowing a fire to make a little saucepan boil. On seeing the master enter, the old woman stopped with the bellows on her knee, and said something that I thought sounded like "My Charley!" but on seeing me come in too, she got up, and rubbing her hands made a confused sort of half curtsey.

"Can you cook this young gentleman's breakfast for him, if you please?" said the Master at Salem House.

"Can I?" said the old woman. "Yes can I, sure!"

I sat down to my brown loaf, my egg, and my rasher of bacon, with a basin of milk besides, and made a most delicious meal. While I was yet in the full enjoyment of it, the old woman of the house said to the Master:

"Have you got your flute with you?"

"Yes," he returned.

"Have a blow at it," said the old woman, coaxingly. "Do!"

The Master, upon this, put his hand underneath the skirts of his coat, and brought out his flute in three pieces, which he screwed together, and began immediately to play. My impression is, after many years of consideration, that there never can have been anybody in the world who played worse. He made the most dismal sounds I have ever heard produced by any means, natural or artificial. I don't know what the tunes were—if there were such things in the performance at all, which I doubt—but the influence of the strain upon me was, first, to make me think of all my sorrows until I could hardly keep my tears back; then to take away my appetite; and lastly, to make me so sleepy that I couldn't keep my eyes open.

When I seemed to have been dozing a long while, the Master at Salem House unscrewed his flute into the three pieces, put them up as before, and took me away. We found the coach very near at hand, and got upon the roof; but I was so dead sleepy, that when we stopped on the road to take up somebody else, they put me inside where there were no passengers, and where I slept profoundly, until I found the coach going at a footpace up a steep hill among green leaves. Presently, it stopped, and had come to its destination.

A short walk brought us—to Salem House, which was enclosed with a high brick wall, and looked very dull. Over a door in this wall was a board with SALEM HOUSE upon it; and through a grating in this door we were surveyed, by a surly face, which belonged to a stout man with a bull-neck, a wooden leg, overhanging temples, and his hair cut close all round his head.

"The new boy," said the Master.

The man with the wooden leg eyed me all over and locked the gate behind us, and took out the key. We were going up to the house, among some dark heavy trees, when he called after my conductor.

"Hallo!"

We looked back, and he was standing at the door of a little lodge, where he lived, with a pair of boots in his hand.

"Here! The cobbler's been," he said, "since you've been out, Mr. Mell, and he says he can't mend 'em any more. He says there ain't a bit of the original boot left, and he wonders you expect it."

With these words he threw the boots towards Mr. Mell, who went back a few paces to pick them up, and looked at them (very disconsolately, I was afraid) as we went on together. I observed then, for the first time, that the boots he had on were a good deal the worse for wear, and that his stocking was just breaking out in one place, like a bud.

Salem House was a square brick building with wings, of a bare and unfurnished appearance. All about it was so very quiet, that I said to Mr. Mell I supposed the boys were out; but he seemed surprised at my not knowing that it was holiday-time. That all the boys were at their several homes. That Mr. Creakle, the proprietor, was down by the seaside with Mrs. and Miss Creakle. And that I was sent in holiday-time as a punishment for my misdoing. All of which he explained to me as we went along.

Mr. Mell having left me while he took his irreparable boots up-stairs, I went softly to the upper end of the room, observing all this as I crept along. Suddenly I came upon a paste-board placard, beautifully written, which was lying on the desk, and bore these words: *"Take care of him. He bites."*

I got upon the desk immediately, apprehensive of at least a great dog underneath. But, though I looked all round with anxious eyes, I could see nothing of him. I was still engaged in peering about, when Mr. Mell came back, and asked me what I did up there?

"I beg your pardon, sir," says I, "if you please, I'm looking for the dog."

"Dog?" says he. "What dog?"

"That's to be taken care of, sir; that bites."

"No, Copperfield," says he, gravely, "that's not a dog. That's a boy. My instructions are, Copperfield, to put this placard on your back. I am sorry to make such a beginning with you, but I must do it."

With that he took me down, and tied the placard, which was neatly constructed for the purpose, on my shoulders like a knap-sack; and wherever I went, afterwards, I had the consolation of carrying it.

What I suffered from that placard nobody can imagine. I recollect that I positively began to have a dread of myself, as a kind of wild boy who did bite.

There was an old door in this playground, on which the boys had a custom of carving their names. It was completely covered with such inscription. In my dread of the end of the vacation and their coming back, I could not read a boy's name, without inquiring in what tone and with what emphasis *he* would read, "Take care of him. He bites." There was one boy —a certain J. Steerforth—who cut his name very deep and very often, who, I conceived, would read it in a rather strong voice, and afterwards pull my hair. There was another boy, one Tommy Traddles, who I dreaded would make game of it, and pretend to be dreadfully frightened of me.

In the monotony of my life, and in my constant apprehension of the reopening of the school, it was such an insupportable affliction! I had long tasks every day to do with Mr. Mell; but I did them, there being no Mr. and Miss Murdstone here, and got through them without disgrace. Before, and after them, I walked about—supervised, as I have mentioned, by the man with the wooden leg. At one we dined, Mr. Mell and I, at the upper end of a long bare dining-room, full of deal tables, and smelling of fat. Then, we had more tasks until tea, which Mr. Mell drank out of a blue teacup, and I out of a tin pot.

I picture myself going up to bed, among the unused rooms, and sitting on my bedside crying for a comfortable word from Peggotty. I picture myself coming down-stairs in the morning, and looking through a long ghastly gash of a stair-case window at the school-bell hanging on the top of an outhouse with a weathercock above it; and dreading the time when it shall ring J. Steerforth and the rest to work.

Mr. Mell never said much to me, but he was never harsh to me. I suppose we were company to each other, without talking. I forgot to mention that he would talk to himself sometimes, and grin, and clench his fist, and grind his teeth, and pull his hair in an unaccountable manner. But he had these peculiarities. At first they frightened me, though I soon got used to them.

CHAPTER 6

I Enlarge My Circle of Acquaintance

ONE day I was informed by Mr. Mell, that Mr. Creakle would be home that evening. In the evening, after tea, I heard that he was come. Before bed-time, I was fetched by the man with the wooden leg to appear before him.

"So!" said Mr. Creakle. "This is the young gentleman whose teeth are to be filed! Turn him round."

Mr. Creakle's face was fiercy, and his eyes were small, and deep in his head; he had thick veins in his forehead, a little nose, and a large chin. He was bald on the top of his head; and had some thin wet-looking hair that was just turning grey, brushed across each temple, so that the two sides interlaced on his forehead.

But the circumstance about him which impressed me most, was, that he had no voice, but spoke in a whisper. The exertion this cost him, or the consciousness of talking in that feeble way, made his angry face so much more angry, and his thick veins so much thicker, when he spoke, that I am not surprised, on looking back, at this peculiarity striking me as his chief one.

"Now," said Mr. Creakle. "What's the report of this boy?"

"There's nothing against him yet," returned the man with the wooden leg. "There has been no opportunity."

"Come here, sir!" said Mr. Creakle, beckoning to me.

"I have the happiness of knowing your father-in-law," whispered Mr. Creakle, taking me by the ear; "and a worthy man he is, and a man of a strong character. He knows me, and I know him. Do *you* know me? Hey?" said M. Creakle, pinching my ear with ferocious play-fulness.

"Not yet, sir," I said, flinching with the pain.

"Not yet? Hey?" repeated Mr. Creakle. "But you will soon. Hey?"

I was very much frightened, and said I hoped so, if he pleased. I felt, all this while, as if my ear were blazing; he pinched it so hard.

"I'll tell you what I am," whispered Mr. Creakle, letting it go at last, with a screw at parting that brought the water into my eyes. "I'm a Tartar. When I say I'll do a thing, I do it," said Mr. Creakle; "and when I say I will have a thing done, I will have it done."

"I am a determined character," said Mr. Creakle. "That's what I am.

I do my duty. That's what *I* do. My flesh and blood," he looked at Mrs. Creakle as he said this, "when it rises against me, is not my flesh and blood. I discard it. Has that fellow," to the man with the wooden leg, "been here again?"

"No," was the answer.

"No," said Mr. Creakle. "He knows better. He knows me. Let him keep away. I say let him keep away," said Mr. Creakle, striking his hand upon the table, and looking at Mrs. Creakle, "for he knows me. Now you have begun to know me too, my young friend, and you may go. Take him away."

I was very glad to be ordered away, for Mrs. and Miss Creakle were both wiping their eyes, and I felt as uncomfortable for them as I did for myself. But I had a petition on my mind which concerned me so nearly, that I couldn't help saying, though I wondered at my own courage:

"If you please, sir——"

Mr. Creakle whispered, "Hah! What's this?" and bent his eyes upon me, as if he would have burnt me up with them.

"If you please, sir," I faltered, "if I might be allowed (I am very sorry indeed, sir, for what I did) to take this writing off, before the boys come back——"

Whether Mr. Creakle was in earnest, or whether he only did it to frighten me, I don't know, but he made a burst out of his chair, before which I precipitately retreated, without waiting for the escort of the man with the wooden leg, and never once stopped until I reached my own bedroom, where, finding I was not pursued, I went to bed, as it was time, and lay quaking, for a couple of hours.

Next morning Mr. Sharp came back. Mr. Sharp was the first master, and superior to Mr. Mell. Mr. Mell took his meals with the boys, but Mr. Sharp dined and supped at Mr. Creakle's table.

Tommy Traddles was the first boy who returned. He introduced himself by informing me that I should find his name on the right-hand corner of the gate, over the top-bolt; upon that I said, "Traddles?" to which he replied, "The same," and then he asked me for a full account of myself and family.

It was a happy circumstance for me that Traddles came back first. He enjoyed my placard so much, that he saved me from the embarrassment of either disclosure or concealment, by presenting me to every other boy who came back, great or small, immediately on his arrival, in this form of introduction, "Look here! Here's a game!" Happily, too, the greater part of the boys were not so boisterous at my expense as I had expected.

I was not considered as being formally received into the school, however, until J. Steerforth arrived. Before this boy, who was reputed to be a great scholar, and was very good-looking, and at least half-a-dozen years my senior, I was carried as before a magistrate. He inquired into the particulars of my punishment, and was pleased to express his opinion that it was "a jolly shame;" for which I became bound to him ever afterwards.

"What money have you got, Copperfield?" he said, walking aside with me when he had disposed of my affair in these terms.

I told him seven shillings.

"You had better give it to me to take care of," he said. "At least, you can if you like. You needn't if you don't like."

I hastened to comply with his friendly suggestion, and opening Peggotty's purse, turned it upside down into his hand.

"Do you want to spend anything now?" he asked me. "You can, if you like, you know," said Steerforth. "Say the word."

"No, thank you, sir," I repeated.

"Perhaps you'd like to spend a couple of shillings or so, in a bottle of currant wine by-and-by, up in the bedroom?" said Steerforth. "You belong to my bedroom, I find."

It certainly had not occurred to me before, but I said, yes, I should like that.

"Very good," said Steerforth. "You'll be glad to spend another shilling or so, in almond cakes, I dare say?"

I said, yes, I should like that, too.

"And another shilling or so in biscuits, and another in fruit, eh?" said Steerforth. "I say, young Copperfield, you're going it!"

I smiled because he smiled, but I was a little troubled in my mind, too.

"Well!" said Steerforth. "We must make it stretch as far as we can; that's all. I'll do the best in my power for you. I can go out when I like, and I'll smuggle the prog in."

He was as good as his word. When we went upstairs to bed, he produced the whole seven shillings' worth, and laid it out on my bed in the moonlight, saying:

"There you are, young Copperfield, and a royal spread you've got."

I couldn't think of doing the honours of the feast, at my time of life, while he was by; my hand shook at the very thought of it. I begged him to do me the favour of presiding; and my request being seconded by the other boys who were in that room, he acceded to it, and sat upon my pillow, handing round the viands—with perfect fairness, I must say—and dispensing the currant wine in a little glass without a foot, which was his own property.

As to me, I sat on his left hand, and the rest were grouped about us, on the nearest beds and on the floor.

I heard that Mr. Creakle had not preferred his claim to being a Tartar without reason; that he was the sternest and most severe of masters; that he laid about him, right and left, every day of his life, charging in among the boys like a trooper, and slashing away, unmercifully. That he knew nothing himself, being more ignorant (J. Steerforth said) than the lowest boy in the school; that he had been, a good many years ago, a small hop-dealer in the Borough, and had taken to the schooling business after being bankrupt in hops, and making away with Mrs. Creakle's money. With a good deal more of that sort, which I wondered how they knew.

I heard that the man with the wooden leg, whose name was Tungay, was an obstinate barbarian who had formerly assisted in the hop business, but had come into the scholastic line with Mr. Creakle, in consequence, as was supposed among the boys, of his having broken his leg in Mr. Creakle's service, and having done a deal of dishonest work for him, and knowing his secrets. I heard that Mr. Creakle had a son, who had not been Tungay's friend, and who, assisting in the school, had once held some remonstrance with his father on an occasion when its discipline was very cruelly exercised, and was supposed besides, to have protested against his father's usage of his mother. I heard that Mr. Creakle had turned him out of doors, in consequence, and that Mrs. and Miss Creakle had been in a sad way, ever since.

But the greatest wonder that I heard of Mr. Creakle was, there being one boy in the school on whom he never ventured to lay a hand, and that boy being J. Steerforth. Steerforth himself confirmed this when it was stated, and said that he should like to begin to see him do it.

The hearing of all this, and a good deal more, outlasted the banquet some time. At last we betook ourselves to bed, too.

"Good night, young Copperfield," said Steerforth. "I'll take care of you."

"You're very kind," I gratefully returned. "I am very much obliged to you."

"You haven't got a sister, have you?" said Steerforth, yawning.

"No," I answered.

"That's a pity," said Steerforth. "If you had had one, I should think she would have been a pretty, timid, little, bright-eyed sort of girl. I should have liked to know her. Good night, young Copperfield."

"Good night, sir," I replied.

I thought of him very much after I went to bed, and raised myself, I recollect, to look at him where he lay in the moonlight, with his handsome face turned up, and his head reclining easily on his arm. He was a person of great power in my eyes; that was, of course, the reason of my mind running on him. No veiled future dimly glanced upon him in the moonbeams. There was no shadowy picture of his footsteps, in the garden that I dreamed of walking in all night.

CHAPTER 7

My 'First Half' at Salem House

SCHOOL began in earnest next day. A profound impression was made upon me by the roar of voices in the schoolroom suddenly becoming hushed as death when Mr. Creakle entered after breakfast, and stood in the doorway looking round upon us like a giant surveying his captives.

Tungay stood at Mr. Creakle's elbow. He had no occasion, I thought, to cry out "Silence!" so ferociously, for the boys were all struck speechless and motionless.

Mr. Creakle was seen to speak, and Tungay was heard, to this effect.

"Now, boys, this is a new half. Take care what you're about, in this new half. Come fresh up to the lessons, I advise you, for I come fresh up to the punishment. I won't flinch. It will be of no use your rubbing yourselves; you won't rub the marks out that I shall give you. Now get to work, every boy!"

One day, Traddles (the most unfortunate boy in the world) breaks the window accidentally with a ball. I shudder at this moment with the tremendous sensation of seeing it done, and feeling that the ball has bounded on to Mr. Creakle's sacred head.

Poor Traddles! In a tight sky-blue suit that made his arms and legs like German sausages, or roly-poly puddings, he was the merriest and most miserable of all the boys. He was always being caned. After laying his head on the desk for a little while, he would cheer up somehow, begin to laugh again, and draw skeletons all over his slate, before his eyes were dry.

He was very honourable, Traddles was, and held it as a solemn duty in the boys to stand by one another. He suffered for this on several occasions; and particularly once, when Steerforth laughed in church, and the Beadle thought it was Traddles, and took him out. I see him now, going away in custody, despised by the congregation. He never said who was the real offender, though he smarted for it next day, and was imprisoned so many hours that he came forth with a whole churchyardful of skeletons swarming all over his Latin Dictionary. But he had his reward. Steerforth said there was nothing of the sneak in Traddles, and we all felt that to be the highest praise. For my part, I could have gone through a good deal (though I was much less brave than Traddles, and nothing like so old) to have won such a recompense.

To see Steerforth walk to church before us, arm-in-arm with Miss Creakle, was one of the great sights of my life. When Steerforth, in white trousers, carried her parasol for her, I felt proud to know him; and believed that she could not choose but adore him with all her heart.

Steerforth continued his protection of me, and proved a very useful friend, since nobody dared to annoy one whom he honoured with his countenance. He couldn't—or at all events he didn't—defend me from Mr. Creakle, who was very severe with me.

There was one advantage, and only one that I know of, in Mr. Creakle's severity. He found my placard in his way when he came up or down behind the form on which I sat, and wanted to make a cut at me in passing; for this reason it was soon taken off, and I saw it no more."

An accidental circumstance cemented the intimacy between Steerforth and me, in a manner that inspired me with great pride and satisfaction, though it sometimes led to inconvenience. It happened on one occasion, when he was doing me the honour of talking to me in the playground, that I hazarded the observation that something or somebody—I forget what now—was like something or somebody in Peregrine Pickle. He said nothing at the time; but when I was going to bed at night, asked me if I had got that book?

I told him no, and explained how it was that I had read it, and all those other books of which I have made mention.

"And do you recollect them?" Steerforth said.

"Oh, yes," I replied; I had a good memory, and I believed I recollected them very well.

"Then I tell you what, young Copperfield," said Steerforth, "you shall tell 'em to me. I can't get to sleep very early at night, and I generally wake rather early in the morning. We'll go over 'em one after another. We'll make some regular Arabian Nights of it."

The drawback was, that I was often sleepy at night, or out of spirits and indisposed to resume the story and then it was rather hard work, and it must be done; for to disappoint or to displease Steerforth was of course out of the question. In the morning too, when I felt weary, and should have enjoyed another hour's repose very much, it was a tiresome thing to be roused, like the Sultana Scheherazade, and forced into a long story before the getting-up bell rang; but Steerforth was resolute; and as he explained to me, in return, my sums and exercises, and anything in my tasks that was too hard for me, I was no loser by the transaction.

Steerforth was considerate too, and showed his consideration, in one particular instance, in an unflinching manner that was a little tantalising, I suspect, to poor Traddles and the rest. Peggotty's promised letter—what a comfortable letter it was!—arrived before 'the half' was many weeks old, and with it a cake in a perfect nest of oranges, and two bottles of cowslip wine. This treasure, as in duty bound, I laid at the feet of Steerforth, and begged him to dispense.

"Now, I'll tell you what, young Copperfield," said he: "the wine shall be kept to wet your whistle when you are story-telling."

I blushed at the idea, and begged him, in my modesty, not to think of it. But he said he had observed I was sometimes hoarse—a little ropy was his exact expression—and it should be, every drop, devoted to the purpose he had mentioned. Accordingly, it was locked up in his box, and drawn off by himself in a phial, and administered to me through a piece of quill in the cork, when I was supposed to be in want of a restorative.

We seem, to me, to have been months over Peregrine, and months more over the other stories. The institution never flagged for want of a story, I am certain, and the wine lasted out almost as well as the matter. Poor Traddles—I never think of that boy but with a strange disposition to laugh, and with tears in my eyes—was a sort of chorus, in general, and affected to be convulsed with mirth at the comic parts, and to be overcome with fear when there was any passage of an alarming character in the narrative.

In a school carried on by sheer cruelty, whether it is presided over by a dunce or not, there is not likely to be much learnt. I believe our boys were, generally, as ignorant a set as any schoolboys in existence; they were too much troubled and knocked about to learn. But Steerforth's help urged me on somehow; and without saving me from much, if anything, in the way of punishment, made me, for the time I was there, an exception to the general body, insomuch that I did steadily pick up some crumbs of knowledge.

In this I was much assisted by Mr. Mell, who had a liking for me that I am grateful to remember. It always gave me pain to observe that Steerforth treated him with systematic disparagement, and seldom lost an occasion of wounding his feelings, or inducing others to do so. This troubled me the more for a long time, because I had soon told Steerforth, from whom I could no more keep such a secret than I could keep a cake or any other tangible possesion, about the two old women Mr. Mell had taken me to see; and I was always afraid that Steerforth would let it out, and twit him with it.

One day when Mr. Creakle kept the house from indisposition, which naturally diffused a lively joy through the school, there was a good deal of noise in the course of the morning's work.

Boys started in and out of their places, playing at puss-in-the-corner with other boys; boys whirled about him, grinning, making faces, mimicking him behind his back and before his eyes; mimicking his poverty, his boots, his coat, his mother, everything belonging to him that they should have had consideration for.

"Silence!" cried Mr. Mell, suddenly rising up, and striking his desk with the book. "What does this mean? It's impossible to bear it. It's maddening. How can you do it to me, boys?"

It was my book that he struck his desk with; and as I stood beside him, following his eye as it glanced round the room, I saw the boys all stop, some suddenly surprised, some half afraid, and some sorry perhaps.

Steerforth's place was at the bottom of the school, at the opposite end of the long room. He was lounging with his back against the wall, and his hands in his pockets, and looked at Mr. Mell with his mouth shut up as if he were whistling, when Mr. Mell looked at him.

"Silence, Mr. Steerforth!" said Mr. Mell.

"Silence yourself," said Steerforth, turning red. "Whom are you talking to?"

"Sit down," said Mr. Mell.

"Sit down yourself," said Steerforth, "and mind your business."

There was a titter, and some applause; but Mr. Mell was so white, that silence immediately succeeded; and one boy, who had darted out behind him to imitate his mother again, changed his mind, and pretended to want a pen mended.

"If you think, Steerforth," said Mr. Mell, "that I am not acquainted with the power you can establish over any mind here"—he laid his hand, without considering what he did (as I supposed), upon my head—"or that I have not observed you, within a few minutes, urging your juniors on to every sort of outrage against me, you are mistaken."

"I don't give myself the trouble of thinking at all about you," said Steerforth, coolly; "so I'm not mistaken, as it happens."

"And when you make use of your position of favouritism here, sir," pursued Mr. Mell, with his lip trembling very much, "to insult a gentleman—"

"A what?—where is he?" said Steerforth.

Here somebody cried out, "Shame, J. Steerforth! Too bad!" It was Traddles; whom Mr. Mell instantly discomfited by bidding him hold his tongue.

—"To insult one who is not fortunate in life, sir, and who never gave you the least offence, and the many reasons for not insulting whom you are old enough and wise enough to understand," said Mr. Mell, with his lip trembling more and more, "you commit a mean and base action. You can sit down or stand up as you please, sir. Copperfield, go on."

"Young Copperfield," said Steerforth, coming forward up the room, "stop a bit. I tell you what, Mr. Mell, once for all. When you take the liberty of calling me mean or base, or anything of that sort, you are an impudent beggar. You are always a beggar, you know; but when you do that, you are an impudent beggar."

I am not clear whether he was going to strike Mr. Mell, or Mr. Mell was going to strike him, or there was any such intention on either side. I saw a rigidity come upon the whole school as if they had been turned into stone, and found Mr. Creakle in the midst of us, with Tungay at his side, and Mrs. and Miss Creakle looking in at the door as if they were frightened. Mr. Mell, with his elbows on his desk and his face in his hands, sat, for some moments, quite still.

"Mr. Mell," said Mr. Creakle, shaking him by the arm; and his whisper was audible now; "you have not forgotten yourself, I hope?"

"No, sir, no," returned the Master, showing his face, and shaking his head, and rubbing his hands in great agitation. "No, sir, no. I have remembered myself, I—no, Mr. Creakle, I have not forgotten myself, sir. I—I—could wish you had remembered me a little sooner, Mr. Creakle. It—it—would have been more kind, sir, more just, sir. It would have saved me something, sir."

Mr. Creakle, looking hard at Mr. Mell, put his hand on Tungay's shoulder, and got his feet upon the form close by, and sat upon the desk.

After still looking hard at Mr. Mell from this throne, as he shook his head, and rubbed his hands, and remained in the same state of agitation, Mr. Creakle turned to Steerforth, and said:

"Now, sir, as he don't condescend to tell me, what *is* this?"

Steerforth evaded the question for a little while; looking in scorn and anger on his opponent, and remaining silent. I could not help thinking even in that interval, I remember, what a noble fellow he was in appearance, and how homely and plain Mr. Mell looked opposed to him.

"What did he mean by talking about favourites, then?" said Steerforth, at length.

"And pray, what did you mean by that, sir?" demanded Mr. Creakle, turning angrily on his assistant.

"I meant, Mr. Creakle," he returned in a low voice, "as I said; that no pupil had a right to avail himself of his position of favouritism to degrade me."

"To degrade *you*?" said Mr. Creakle. "My stars! But give me leave to ask you, Mr. What's-your-name;" and here Mr. Creakle folded his arms, cane and all, upon his chest, and made such a knot of his brows that his little eyes were hardly visible below them; "whether, when you talk about favourites, you showed proper respect to me? To me, sir," said Mr. Creakle, darting his head at him suddenly, and drawing it back again, "the Principal of this establishment, and your employer."

"It was not judicious, sir, I am willing to admit," said Mr. Mell. "I should not have done so, if I had been cool."

Here Steerforth struck in.

"Then he said I was mean, and then he said I was base, and then I called him a beggar. If he is not a beggar himself, his near relation's one," said Steerforth. "It's all the same—what I have to say is, that his mother lives on charity in an alms-house."

Mr. Creakle turned to his assistant, with a severe frown and laboured politeness:

"Now you hear what this gentleman says, Mr. Mell. Have the goodness, if you please, to set him right before the assembled school."

"He is right, sir, without correction," returned Mr. Mell, in the midst of a dead silence; "what he has said is true."

"Be so good then as declare publicly, will you," said Mr. Creakle, putting his head on one side, and rolling his eyes round the school, "whether it ever came to my knowledge until this moment?"

"I apprehend you never supposed my worldly circumstances to be very good," replied the assistant. "You know what my position is, and always has been here."

"I apprehend, if you come to that," said Mr. Creakle, with his veins swelling again bigger than ever, "that you've been in a wrong position altogether, and mistook this for a charity school. Mr. Mell, we'll part, if you please. The sooner the better."

"There is no time," answered Mr. Mell, rising, "like the present."

"Sir, to you!" said Mr. Creakle.

"I take my leave of you, Mr. Creakle, and all of you," said Mr. Mell, again patting me gently on the shoulder. "James Steerforth, the best wish I can leave you is that you may come to be ashamed of what you have done to-day. At present I would prefer to see you anything rather than a friend, to me, or to any one in whom I feel an interest."

Once more he laid his hand upon my shoulder; and then taking his flute and a few books from his desk, and leaving the key in it for his successor, he went out of the school, with his property under his arm.

We were left to ourselves now, and looked very blank, I recollect, on one another. For myself, I felt so much self-reproach and contrition for my part in what had happened, that nothing would have enabled me to keep back my tears but the fear that Steerforth, who often looked at me, I saw, might think it unfriendly—or, I should rather say, considering our relative ages, and the feeling with which I regarded him, undutiful—if I showed the emotion which distressed me.

Traddles said Mr. Mell was ill-used.

"Who has ill-used him, you girl?" said Steerforth.

"Why, you have," returned Traddles.

"What have I done?" said Steerforth.

"What have you done?" retorted Traddles. "Hurt his feelings and lost him his situation."

"His feelings!" repeated Steerforth disdainfully. "His feelings will soon get the better of it, I'll be bound. His feelings are not like yours, Miss Traddles. As to his situation—which was a precious one, wasn't it?—do you suppose I am not going to write home, and take care that he gets some money? Polly?"

We thought this intention very noble in Steerforth, whose mother was a widow, and rich, and would do almost anything, it was said, that he asked her.

But I must say that when I was going on with a story in the dark that night, Mr. Mell's old flute seemed more than once to sound mournfully in my ears; and that when at last Steerforth was tired, and I lay down in my bed, I fancied it playing so sorrowfully somewhere, that I was quite wretched.

I soon forgot him in the contemplation of Steerforth, who, in an easy amateur way, and without any book (he seemed to me to know everything by heart), took some of his classes until a new master was found. The new master came from a grammar-school, and before he entered on his duties, dined in the parlour one day, to be introduced to Steerforth. Steerforth approved of him highly, and told us he was a Brick. Without exactly understanding what learned distinction was meant by this, I respected him greatly for it, and had no doubt whatever of his superior knowledge: though he never took the pains with me—not that *I* was anybody—that Mr. Mell had taken.

One afternoon, when we were all harassed into a state of dire confusion, and Mr. Creakle was laying about him dreadfully, Tungay came in, and called out in his usual strong way: "Visitors for Copperfield!"

A few words were interchanged between him and Mr. Creakle, as to who the visitors were, and what room they were to be shown into; and then I, who had, according to custom, stood up on the announcement being made, and felt quite faint with astonishment, was told to go by the back stairs and get a clean frill on, before I repaired to the dining-room. These orders

I obeyed, in such a flutter and hurry of my young spirits as I had never known before; and when I got to the parlour-door, and the thought came into my head that it might be my mother—I had only thought of Mr. or Miss Murdstone until then—I drew back my hand from the lock, and stopped to have a sob before I went in.

At first I saw nobody; but feeling a pressure against the door, I looked round it, and there, to my amazement, were Mr. Peggotty and Ham, ducking at me with their hats, and squeezing one another against the wall. We shook hands in a very cordial way; and I laughed and laughed.

Mr. Peggotty (who never shut his mouth once, I remember, during the visit) showed great concern when he saw me do this, and nudged Ham to say something.

"Cheer up, Mas'r Davy bor'!" said Ham, in his simpering way. "Why, how you have growed!"

"Do you know how mama is, Mr. Peggotty?" I said. "And how my dear, dear, old Peggotty is?"

"Oncommon," said Mr. Peggotty.

"And little Em'ly, and Mrs. Gummidge?"

"Oncommon," said Mr. Peggotty.

There was a silence. Mr. Peggotty, to relieve it, took two prodigious lobsters, and an enormous crab, and a large canvas bag of shrimps, out of his pockets, and piled them up in Ham's arms.

"You see," said Mr. Peggotty, "knowing as you was partial to a little relish with your wittles when you was along with us, we took the liberty."

I expressed my thanks. Mr. Peggotty, after looking at Ham, who stood smiling sheepishly over the shell-fish, without making any attempt to help him, said:

"We come, you see, the wind and tide making in our favour, in one of our Yarmouth lugs to Gravesen'. My sister she wrote to me the name of this here place, and wrote to me as if ever I chanced to come to Gravesen', I was to come over and inquire for Mas'r Davy, and give her dooty, humbly wishing him well, and reporting of the fam'ly as they was oncommon toe-be-sure. Little Em'ly, you see, she'll write to my sister when I go back as I see you, and as you was similarly oncommon, and so we make it quite a merry-go-rounder."

I thanked him heartily; and said, with a consciousness of reddening, that I supposed little Em'ly was altered too, since we used to pick up shells and pebbles on the beach.

"She's getting to be a woman, that's wot she's getting to be," said Mr. Peggotty. "Ask *him*."

He meant Ham, who beamed with delight and assent over the bag of shrimps.

"Her pretty face!" said Mr. Peggotty, with his own shining like a light.

"Her learning!" said Ham.

"Her writing!" said Mr. Peggotty. "Why it's as black as jet! And so large it is, you might see it anywheres."

It was perfectly delightful to behold with what enthusiasm Mr. Peggotty became inspired when he thought of his little favourite.

Ham was quite as earnest as he. I dare say they would have said much more about her, if they had not been abashed by the unexpected coming in of Steerforth, who, seeing me in a corner speaking with two strangers, stopped in a song he was singing, and said: "I didn't know you were here, young Copperfield!" (for it was not the usual visiting room) and crossed by us on his way out.

I am not sure whether it was in the pride of having such a friend as Steerforth, or in the desire to explain to him how I came to have such a friend as Mr. Peggotty, that I called to him as he was going away. But I said, modestly:

"Don't go, Steerforth, if you please. These are two Yarmouth boatmen —very kind, good people—who are relations of my nurse, and have come from Gravesend to see me."

"Aye, aye?" said Steerforth, returning. "I am glad to see them. How are you both?"

"You must let them know at home, if you please, Mr. Peggotty," I said, "when that letter is sent, that Mr. Steerforth is very kind to me, and that I don't know what I should ever do here without him."

"Nonsense!" said Steerforth, laughing. "You mustn't tell them anything of the sort."

"And if Mr. Steerforth ever comes into Norfolk or Suffolk, Mr. Peggotty," I said, "while I am here, you may depend upon it I shall bring him to Yarmouth, if he will let me, to see your house. You never saw such a good house, Steerforth. It's made out of a boat!"

"Made out of a boat, is it?" said Steerforth. "It's the right sort of house for such a thorough-built boatman."

"So 'tis, sir, so 'tis, sir," said Ham, grinning. "You're right, young gen'l'm'n. Mas'r Davy, bor', gen'l'm'n's right. A thorough-built boatman! Hor, hor! That's what he is, too!"

Mr. Peggotty was no less pleased than his nephew, though his modesty forbade him to claim a personal compliment so vociferously.

"Well, sir," he said, bowing and chuckling, and tucking in the ends of his neckerchief at his breast: "I thankee, sir, I thankee! I do my endeavours in my line of life, sir."

"The best of men can do no more, Mr. Peggotty," said Steerforth. He had got his name already.

"I'll pound it it's wot you do yourself, sir," said Mr. Peggotty, shaking his head, "and wot you do well—right well! I thankee, sir. I'm rough, sir, but I'm ready—least ways, I *hope* I'm ready, you unnerstand. My house ain't much for to see, sir, but it's hearty at your service if ever you should come along with Mas'r Davy to see it. I'm a reg'lar Dodman, I am," said Mr. Peggotty, by which he meant snail, and this was in allusion to his being slow to go, for he had attempted to go after every sentence, and had somehow or other come back again; "but I wish you both well, and I wish you happy!"

We transported the shell-fish, or the "relish" as Mr. Peggotty had modestly called it, up into our room unobserved, and made a great supper that evening. But Traddles couldn't get happily out of it. He was too unfortunate even to come through a supper like anybody else. He was taken ill in the night—quite prostrate he was—in consequence of Crab; and after being drugged with black draughts and blue pills, to an extent which Demple (whose father was a doctor) said was enough to undermine a horse's constitution, received a caning and six chapters of Greek Testament for refusing to confess.

I well remember though, how the distant idea of the holidays, after seeming for an immense time to be a stationary speck, began to come towards us, and to grow and grow. How from counting months, we came to weeks, and then to days; and how I then began to be afraid that I should not be sent for, and when I learnt from Steerforth that I *had* been sent for and was certainly to go home, had dim forebodings that I might break my leg first. How the breaking-up day changed its place fast, at last, from the week after next to next week, this week, the day after to-morrow, to-morrow, to-day, to-night—when I was inside the Yarmouth mail, and going home.

CHAPTER 8

My Holidays, Especially One Happy Afternoon

MR. BARKIS the carrier was to call for me in the morning at nine o'clock.

As soon as I and my box were in the cart, and the carrier was seated, the lazy horse walked away with us all at his accustomed pace.

"You look very well, Mr. Barkis," I said, thinking he would like to know it.

Mr. Barkis rubbed his cheek with his cuff, and then looked at his cuff as if he expected to find some of the bloom upon it; but made no other acknowledgment of the compliment.

"I gave your message, Mr. Barkis," I said: "I wrote to Peggotty."

"Nothing come of it," he explained, looking at me sideways. "No answer."

"There was an answer expected, was there, Mr. Barkis?" said I, opening my eyes. For this was a new light to me.

"When a man says he's willin'," said Mr. Barkis, turning his glance slowly on me again, "it's as much as to say, that man's a waitin' for a answer."

"Have you told her so, Mr. Barkis?"

"N—no," growled Mr. Barkis, reflecting about it. "I ain't got no call to go and tell her so. I never said six words to her myself. *I* ain't a goin' to tell her so."

"Would you like me to do it, Mr. Barkis?" said I, doubtfully.

"You might tell her, if you would," said Mr. Barkis, with another slow look at me, "that Barkis was a waitin' for an answer. Says you—what name is it?"

"Peggotty."

"Chrisen name? Or nat'ral name?" said Mr. Barkis.

"Oh, it's not her Christian name. Her Christian name is Clara."

"Well!" he resumed at length. "Says you, 'Peggotty! Barkis is a waitin' for a answer.' Says she, perhaps, 'Answer to what?' Says you, 'To what I told you.' 'What is that?' says she. 'Barkis is willin',' says you."

This extremely artful suggestion, Mr. Barkis accompanied with a nudge of his elbow that gave me quite a stitch in my side. After that, he slouched over his horse in his usual manner; and made no other reference to the subject except, half an hour afterwards, taking a piece of chalk from his pocket, and writing up, inside the tilt of the cart, "Clara Peggotty"— apparently as a private memorandum.

And soon I was at our house, where the bare old elm trees wrung their many hands in the bleak wintry air, and shreds of the old rooks' nests drifted away upon the wind.

The carrier put my box down at the garden gate, and left me. I walked along the path towards the house, glancing at the windows, and fearing at every step to see Mr. Murdstone or Miss Murdstone lowering out of one of them. No face appeared, however; and being come to the house, and knowing how to open the door, before dark, without knocking, I went in with a quiet, timid step.

My mother was singing in a low tone. The strain was new to me, and yet it was so old that it filled my heart brimful; like a friend come back from a long absence.

I believed, from the solitary and thoughtful way in which my mother murmured her song, that she was alone. And I went softly into the room. She was sitting by the fire, suckling an infant, whose tiny hand she held against her neck. Her eyes were looking down upon its face, and she sat singing to it. I was so far right, that she had no other companion.

Seeing me, she called me her dear Davy, her own boy! and coming half across the room to meet me, kneeled down upon the ground and kissed me, and laid my head down on her bosom near the little creature that was nestling there, and put its hand up to my lips.

"He is your brother," said my mother, fondling me. "Davy, my pretty boy! My poor child!" Then she kissed me more and more, and clasped me round the neck. This she was doing when Peggotty came running in, and bounced down on the ground beside us, and went mad about us both for a quarter of an hour.

It seemed that I had not been expected so soon, the carrier being much before his usual time. It seemed, too, that Mr. and Miss Murdstone had gone out upon a visit in the neighbourhood, and would not return before night.

We dined together by the fireside. Peggotty was in attendance to wait upon us, but my mother wouldn't let her do it, and made her dine with us.

While we were at table, I thought it a favourable occasion to tell Peggotty about Mr. Barkis, who, before I had finished what I had to tell her, began to laugh, and throw her apron over her face.

"Peggotty," said my mother. "What's the matter?"

"Oh, drat the man!" cried Peggotty. "He wants to marry me."

"It would be a very good match for you; wouldn't it?" said my mother.

"Oh! I don't know," said Peggotty. "Don't ask me. I wouldn't have him if he was made of gold. Nor I wouldn't have anybody."

"Then, why don't you tell him so, you ridiculous thing?" said my mother.

"Tell him so," retorted Peggotty, looking out of her apron. "He has never said a word to me about it. He knows better. If he was to make so bold as say a word to me, I should slap his face."

I remarked that my mother, though she smiled when Peggotty looked at her, became more serious and thoughtful. Her face was very pretty still, but it looked careworn, and too delicate; and her hand was so thin and white that it seemed to me to be almost transparent. But the real change was in her manner, which became anxious and fluttered. At last she said, putting out her hand, and laying it affectionately on the hand of her old servant:

"Peggotty dear, you are not going to be married?"

"Me, ma'am?" returned Peggotty, staring. "Lord bless you, no!"

"Don't leave me, Peggotty. Stay with me. It will not be for long, perhaps. What should I ever do without you!"

"Me leave you, my precious!" cried Peggotty. "Not for all the world and his wife. Why, what's put that in your silly little head?" For Peggotty had been used of old to talk to my mother sometimes, like a child.

But my mother made no answer, except to thank her, and Peggotty went running on in her own fashion.

We sat round the fire, and talked delightfully. I told them what a hard master Mr. Creakle was, and they pitied me very much. I told them what a fine fellow Steerforth was, and what a patron of mine, and Peggotty said she would walk a score of miles to see him.

Peggotty darned away at a stocking as long as she could see, and then sat with it drawn on her left hand like a glove, and her needle in her right, ready to take another stitch.

"I wonder," said Peggotty, who was sometimes seized with a fit of wondering on some most unexpected topic, "what's become of Davy's great-aunt?"

"What can have put such a person in your head?" inquired my mother. "Is there nobody else in the world to come there?"

"I don't know how it is," said Peggotty, "unless it's on account of being stupid, but my head never can pick and choose its people. They come and they go, and they don't come and they don't go, just as they like. I wonder what's become of her?"

"How absurd you are, Peggotty," returned my mother. "One would suppose you wanted a second visit from her. Miss Betsey is shut up in her cottage by the sea, no doubt, and will remain there. At all events, she is not likely ever to trouble us again."

"No!" mused Peggotty. "No, that ain't likely at all—I wonder, if she was to die, whether she'd leave Davy anything?"

"Good gracious me, Peggotty," returned my mother, "what a nonsensical woman you are! when you know that she took offence at the poor dear boy's ever being born at all!"

"I suppose she wouldn't be inclined to forgive him now?" hinted Peggotty.

"Why should she be inclined to forgive him now?" said my mother, rather sharply.

"Now that he's got a brother, I mean," said Peggotty.

My mother immediately began to cry, and wondered how Peggotty dared to say such a thing.

"There, Peggotty," said my mother, changing her tone, "don't let us fall out with one another, for I couldn't bear it. You are my true friend, and always have been, ever since the night when Mr. Copperfield first brought me home here, and you came out to the gate to meet me."

Peggotty was not slow to respond, and ratify the treaty of friendship by giving me one of her best hugs.

When we had had our tea, and the ashes were thrown up, and the candles snuffed, I read Peggotty a chapter out of the Crocodile Book, in remembrance of old times. We were very happy; and that evening, as the last of its race, and destined evermore to close that volume of my life, will never pass out of my memory.

It was almost ten o'clock before we heard the sound of wheels. We all got up then; and my mother said hurriedly that, as it was so late, and Mr. and Miss Murdstone approved of early hours for young people, perhaps I had better go to bed.

I felt uncomfortable about going down to breakfast in the morning, as I had never set eyes on Mr. Murdstone since the day when I committed my memorable offence. However, as it must be done, I went down, after two or three false starts half-way, and as many runs back on tiptoe to my own room, and presented myself in the parlour.

He was standing before the fire with his back to it, while Miss Murdstone made the tea. He looked at me steadily as I entered, but made no sign of recognition whatever.

I went up to him, after a moment of confusion, and said: "I beg your pardon, sir. I am very sorry for what I did, and I hope you will forgive me."

"I am glad to hear you are sorry, David," he replied.

The hand he gave me was the hand I had bitten. I could not restrain my eye from resting for an instant on a red spot upon it; but it was not so red as I turned, when I met that sinister expression in his face.

"How do you do, ma'am?" I said to Miss Murdstone.

"Ah, dear me!" sighed Miss Murdstone, giving me the tea-caddy scoop instead of her fingers. "How long are the holidays?"

"A month, ma'am."

"Counting from when?"

"From to-day, ma'am."

"Oh!" said Miss Murdstone. "Then here's *one* day off."

She kept a calendar of the holidays in this way, and every morning checked a day off in exactly the same manner. She did it gloomily, until she came to ten, but when she got into two figures she became more hopeful, and, as the time advanced, even jocular.

In short, I was not a favourite with Miss Murdstone. In short, I was not a favourite there with anybody, not even with myself; for those who did like me could not show it, and those who did not showed it so plainly that I had a sensitive consciousness of always appearing constrained, boorish, and dull.

I was still held to be necessary to my poor mother's training, and, as one of her trials, could not be suffered to absent myself.

"David," said Mr. Murdstone, one day after dinner when I was going to leave the room as usual; "I am sorry to observe that you are of a sullen disposition. This is not a character that I can suffer to develop itself beneath my eyes without an effort at improvement. You must endeavour, sir, to change it. We must endeavour to change it for you."

"I will have a respectful, prompt, and ready bearing towards myself," he continued, "and towards Jane Murdstone, and towards your mother. I will not have this room shunned as if it were infected, at the pleasure of a child. Sit down."

He ordered me like a dog, and I obeyed like a dog.

"One thing more," he said. "I observe that you have an attachment to low and common company. You are not to associate with servants. The kitchen will not improve you, in the many respects in which you need improvement. I disapprove of your preferring such company as Mistress Peggotty, and it is to be abandoned. Now, David, you understand me, and you know what will be the consequence if you fail to obey me to the letter."

I knew well—better perhaps than he thought, as far as my poor mother was concerned—and I obeyed him to the letter. I retreated to my own room no more; I took refuge with Peggotty no more; but sat wearily in the parlour day after day looking forward to night, and bedtime.

Thus the holidays lagged away, until the morning came when Miss Murdstone said: "Here's the last day off!" and gave me the closing cup of tea of the vacation.

I was not sorry to go. I had lapsed into a stupid state; but I was recovering a little and looking forward to Steerforth, albeit Mr. Creakle loomed behind him. Again Mr. Barkis appeared at the gate, and again Miss Murdstone in her warning voice, said: "Clara!" when my mother bent over me, to bid me farewell.

I kissed her, and my baby brother, and was very sorry then; but not sorry to go away, for the gulf between us was there, and the parting was there, every day. And it is not so much the embrace she gave me, that lives in my mind, though it was as fervent as could be, as what followed the embrace.

I was in the carrier's cart when I heard her calling to me. I looked out, and she stood at the garden-gate alone, holding her baby up in her arms for me to see. It was cold still weather; and not a hair of her head, nor a fold of her dress, was stirred, as she looked intently at me, holding up her child.

So I lost her. So I saw her afterwards, in my sleep at school—a silent presence near my bed—looking at me with the same intent face—holding up her baby in her arms.

CHAPTER 9

I Have a Memorable Birthday

I PASS over all that happened at school, until the anniversary of my birthday came round in March. Except that Steerforth was more to be admired than ever, I remember nothing. He was going away at the end of the half-year, if not sooner, and was more spirited and independent than before in my eyes, and therefore more engaging than before.

It is even difficult for me to believe that there was a gap of full two months between my return to Salem House and the arrival of that birthday. I can only understand that the fact was so, because I know it must have been so; otherwise I should feel convinced that there was no interval, and that the one occasion trod upon the other's heels.

It was after breakfast, and we had been summoned in from the playground, when Mr. Sharp entered and said:

"David Copperfield is to go into the parlour."

I expected a hamper from Peggotty, and brightened at the order. Some of the boys about me put in their claim not to be forgotten in the distribution of the good things, as I got out of my seat with great alacrity.

"Don't hurry, David," said Mr. Sharp. "There's time enough, my boy, don't hurry."

I might have been surprised by the feeling tone in which he spoke, if I had given it a thought; but I gave it none until afterwards. I hurried away to the parlour; and there I found Mr. Creakle, sitting at his breakfast with the cane and a newspaper before him, and Mrs. Creakle with an

54

opened letter in her hand. But no hamper.

"David Copperfield," said Mrs. Creakle, leading me to a sofa, and sitting down beside me. "I want to speak to you very particularly. I have something to tell you, my child."

Mr. Creakle, at whom of course I looked, shook his head without looking at me, and stopped up a sigh with a very large piece of buttered toast.

"You are too young to know how the world changes every day," said Mrs. Creakle, "and how the people in it pass away. But we all have to learn it, David; some of us when we are young, some of us when we are old, some of us at all times of our lives."

I looked at her earnestly.

"When you came away from home at the end of the vacation," said Mrs. Creakle, after a pause, "were they all well?" After another pause, "Was your mama well?"

I trembled without distinctly knowing why, and still looked at her earnestly, making no attempt to answer.

"Because," said she, "I grieve to tell you that I hear this morning your mama is very ill."

A mist rose between Mrs. Creakle and me; and her figure seemed to move in it for an instant. Then I felt the burning tears run down my face, and it was steady again.

"She is very dangerously ill," she added.

I knew all now.

"She is dead."

There was no need to tell me so. I had already broken out into a desolate cry, and felt an orphan in the wide world.

She was very kind to me. She kept me there all day, and left me alone sometimes; and I cried, and wore myself to sleep, and awoke and cried again. When I could cry no more, I began to think; and then the oppression on my breast was heaviest, and my grief a dull pain that there was no ease for.

I left Salem House upon the morrow afternoon. I little thought then that I left it, never to return.

I was in Peggotty's arms before I got to the door, and she took me into the house. Her grief burst out when she first saw me; but she controlled it soon, and spoke in whispers, and walked softly, as if the dead could be disturbed. She had not been in bed, I found, for a long time. She sat up at night still, and watched. As long as her poor dear pretty was above the ground, she said, she would never desert her.

Mr. Murdstone took no heed of me when I went into the parlour, where he was, but sat by the fireside, weeping silently, and pondering in his elbow-chair. Miss Murdstone, who was busy at her writing-desk, which was covered with letters and papers, gave me her cold finger-nails, and asked me, in an iron whisper, if I had been measured for my mourning.

I said: "Yes."

"And your shirts," said Miss Murdstone; "have you brought 'em home?"

"Yes, ma'am. I have brought home all my clothes."

Her brother took a book sometimes, but never read it that I saw. He would open it and look at it as if he were reading, but would remain for a whole hour without turning the leaf, and then put it down and walk to and fro in the room.

In these days before the funeral, I saw but little of Peggotty, except that, in passing up or down stairs, I always found her close to the room where my mother and her baby lay, and except that she came to me every night, and sat by my bed's head while I went to sleep.

And now the bell begins to sound, and Mr. Omer and another come to make us ready. As Peggotty was wont to tell me, long ago, the followers of my father to the same grave were made ready in the same room.

We stand around the grave. The day seems different to me from every other day, and the light not of the same colour—of a sadder colour. Now there is a solemn hush, which we have brought from home with what is resting in the mould; and while we stand bare-headed, I hear the voice of the clergyman, sounding remote in the open air, and yet distinct and plain, saying: "I am the Resurrection and the Life, saith the Lord!" Then I hear sobs; and, standing apart among the lookers-on, I see that good and faithful servant, whom of all the people upon earth I love the best, and unto whom my childish heart is certain that the Lord will one day say: "Well done."

It is over, and the earth is filled in, and we turn to come away. Before us stands our house, so pretty and unchanged, so linked in my mind with the young idea of what is gone, that all my sorrow has been nothing to the sorrow it calls forth.

I knew that Peggotty would come to me in my room. She sat down by my side upon my little bed; "She was never well," said Peggotty, "for a long time. She was uncertain in her mind, and not happy. When her baby was born, I thought at first she would get better, but she was more delicate, and sunk a little every day.

"I think she got to be more timid, and more frightened-like of late; and that a hard word was like a blow to her. But she was always the same to me. She never changed to her foolish Peggotty, didn't my sweet girl.

"The last time that I saw her like her own old self, was the night when you came home, my dear. The day you went away, she said to me, 'I never shall see my pretty darling again.'

She never told her husband what she had told me—she was afraid of saying it to anybody else—till one night, a little more than a week before it happened, when she said to him: 'My dear, I think I am dying.'

" 'It's off my mind now, Peggotty,' she told me, when I laid her in her bed that night. 'He will believe it more, and more, poor fellow, every day for a few days to come; and then it will be past. I am very tired. If this is sleep, sit by me while I sleep: don't leave me. God bless both my children! God protect and keep my fatherless boy!' "

CHAPTER 10

I Become Neglected, and Am Provided For

THE first act of business Miss Murdstone performed when the day of the solemnity was over, and light was freely admitted into the house, was to give Peggotty a month's warning. Much as Peggotty would have disliked such a service, I believe she would have retained it, for my sake, in preference to the best upon earth. She told me we must part, and told me why; and we condoled with one another, in all sincerity.

As to me or my future, not a word was said, or a step taken. Happy they would have been, I dare say, if they could have dismissed me at a month's warning too. I mustered courage once, to ask Miss Murdstone when I was going back to school; and she answered drily, she believed I was not going back at all. I was told nothing more. I was very anxious to know what was going to be done with me, and so was Peggotty; but neither she nor I could pick up any information on the subject.

"And what do you mean to do, Peggotty," says I, wistfully. "Do you mean to go and seek your fortune?"

"I expect I shall be forced to go to Yarmouth," replied Peggotty, "and live there."

"You might have gone farther off," I said, brightening a little, "and been as bad as lost. I shall see you sometimes, my dear old Peggotty, there. You won't be quite at the other end of the world, will you?"

"Contrary ways, please God!" cried Peggotty, with great animation. "As long as you are here, my pet, I shall come over every week of my life to see you. One day every week of my life!"

I felt a great weight taken off my mind by this promise; but even this was not all, for Peggotty went on to say:

"I'm a going, Davy, you see, to my brother's, first, for another fortnight's visit—just till I have had time to look about me, and get to be something like myself again. Now, I have been thinking, that perhaps, as they don't want you here at present, you might be let to go along with me."

"The boy will be idle there," said Miss Murdstone, looking into a pickle-jar, "and idleness is the root of all evil. But, to be sure, he would be idle here—or anywhere, in my opinion."

Peggotty had an angry answer ready, I could see, but she swallowed it for my sake, and remained silent.

"Humph!" said Miss Murdstone, still keeping her eye on the pickles; "it is of more importance than anything else—it is of paramount importance—that my brother should not be disturbed or made uncomfortable. I suppose I had better say yes."

I thanked her, without making any demonstration of joy, lest it should induce her to withdraw her assent.

Mr. Barkis came into the house for Peggotty's boxes. I had never known

57

him to pass the garden-gate before, but on this occasion he came into the house. And he gave me a look as he shouldered the largest box and went out, which I thought had meaning in it, if meaning could ever be said to find its way into Mr. Barkis's visage.

Peggotty was naturally in low spirits at leaving what had been her home so many years, and she got into the cart, and sat in it with her handkerchief at her eyes.

So long as she remained in this condition, Mr. Barkis gave no sign of life whatever. He sat in his usual place and attitude like a great stuffed figure. But when she began to look about her, and to speak to me, he nodded his head and grinned several times. I have not the least notion at whom, or what he meant by it.

"Peggotty is quite comfortable now, Mr. Barkis," I remarked, for his satisfaction.

"Is she, though?" said Mr. Barkis.

After reflecting about it, with a sagacious air, Mr. Barkis eyed her, and said:

"*Are* you pretty comfortable?"

Peggotty laughed, and answered in the affirmative.

Mr. Peggotty and Ham waited for us at the old place. They received me and Peggotty in an affectionate manner, and shook hands with Mr. Barkis, who, with his hat on the very back of his head, and a shamefaced leer upon his countenance, and pervading his very legs, presented but a vacant appearance, I thought. They each took one of Peggotty's trunks, and we were going away, when Mr. Barkis solemnly made a sign to me with his forefinger to come under an archway.

"It didn't come to a end there," said Mr. Barkis, nodding confidentially. "It was all right."

Again I answered, "Oh!"

"It's all right," said Mr. Barkis, shaking hands; "I'm a friend of your'n. You made it all right, first. It's all right."

In his attempts to be particularly lucid, Mr. Barkis was so extremely mysterious that I might have stood looking in his face for an hour, but for Peggotty's calling me away. As we were going along, she asked me what he had said; and I told her he had said it was all right.

"Like his impudence," said Peggotty, "but I don't mind that! Davy dear, what should you think if I was to think of being married?"

"If you were thinking of being married—to Mr. Barkis, Peggotty?"

"Yes," said Peggotty.

"I should think it would be a very good thing. For then you know, Peggotty, you would always have the horse and cart to bring you over to see me, and could come for nothing, and be sure of coming."

"The sense of the dear!" cried Peggotty. "What I have been thinking of, this month back! Yes, my precious; and I think I should be more independent altogether, you see; let alone my working with a better heart in my own house, than I could in anybody else's now."

"But I wouldn't so much as give it another thought," said Peggotty, cheerily, "if my Davy was anyways against it."

"Look at me, Peggotty," I replied; "and see if I am not really glad, and don't truly wish it!" As indeed I did, with all my heart.

"Barkis is a good plain creatur," said Peggotty, "and if I tried to do my duty by him, I think it would be my fault if I wasn't—if I wasn't pretty comfortable," said Peggotty, laughing heartily.

This quotation from Mr. Barkis was so appropriate, and tickled us both so much, that we laughed again and again, and were quite in a pleasant humour when we came within view of Mr. Peggotty's cottage.

It looked just the same, except that it may, perhaps, have shrunk a little in my eyes.

But there was no little Em'ly to be seen, so I asked Mr. Peggotty where she was.

"She's at school, sir," said Mr. Peggotty, wiping the heat consequent on the porterage of Peggotty's box from his forehead; "she'll be home," looking at the Dutch clock, "in from twenty minutes to half-an-hour's time. We all on us feel the loss of her, bless ye!"

Mrs. Gummidge moaned.

"Cheer up, Mawther!" cried Mr. Peggotty.

"I feel it more than anybody else," said Mrs. Gummidge: "I'm a lone lorn creetur', and she used to be a'most the only thing that didn't go contrairy with me."

A figure appeared in the distance before long, and I soon knew it to be Em'ly, who was a little creature still in stature, though she was grown. But then she drew nearer, and I saw her blue eyes looking bluer, and her dimpled face looking brighter, and her whole self prettier and gayer.

Little Em'ly didn't care a bit. She saw me well enough; but instead of turning round and calling after me, ran away laughing. This obliged me to run after her, and she ran so fast that we were very near the cottage before I caught her.

The tea-table was ready, and our little locker was put out in its old place, but instead of coming to sit by me, she went and bestowed her company upon that grumbling Mrs. Gummidge: and on Mr. Peggotty's inquiring why, rumpled her hair all over her face to hide it, and would do nothing but laugh.

"A little puss it is!" said Mr. Peggotty, patting her with his great hand.

"So sh' is! so sh' is!" cried Ham. "Mas'r Davy bor, so sh' is!" and he sat and chuckled at her for some time, in a state of mingled admiration and delight, that made his face a burning red.

Little Em'ly was spoiled by them all, in fact; and by no one more than Mr. Peggotty himself, whom she could have coaxed into anything by only going and laying her cheek against his rough whisker. But she was so affectionate and sweet-natured, and had such a pleasant manner of being both sly and shy at once, that she captivated me more than ever.

She was tender-hearted, too; for when, as we sat round the fire after tea, an allusion was made by Mr. Peggotty over his pipe to the loss I had sustained, the tears stood in her eyes, and she looked at me so kindly across the table, that I felt quite thankful to her.

"And how's your friend, sir?" said Mr. Peggotty to me.

"Steerforth?" said I.

"There's a friend!" said Mr. Peggotty, stretching out his pipe. "There's a friend, if you talk of friends! Why, Lord love my heart alive, if it ain't a treat to look at him!"

"He is very handsome, is he not?" said I, my heart warming with this praise.

"Handsome!" cried Mr. Peggotty. "He stands up to you like—like a— why I don't know what he *don't* stand up to you like. He's so bold!"

"Yes! That's just his character," said I. "He's as brave as a lion, and you can't think how frank he is, Mr. Peggotty."

"And I do suppose, now," said Mr. Peggotty, looking at me through the smoke of his pipe, "that in the way of book-larning he'd take the wind out of a'most anything."

"Yes," said I, delighted; "he knows everything. He is astonishingly clever."

I was running on, very fast indeed, when my eyes rested on little Em'ly's face, which was bent forward over the table, listening with the deepest attention, her breath held, her blue eyes sparkling like jewels, and the colour mantling in her cheeks. She looked so extraordinarily earnest and pretty, that I stopped in a sort of wonder; and they all observed her at the same time, for as I stopped, they laughed and looked at her.

"Em'ly is like me," said Peggotty, "and would like to see him."

Em'ly was confused by our all observing her, and hung down her head, and her face was covered with blushes. Glancing up presently through her stray curls, and seeing that we were all looking at her still (I am sure I, for one, could have looked at her for hours), she ran away, and kept away till it was nearly bedtime.

Wild and full of childish whims as Em'ly was, she was more of a little woman than I had supposed. She seemed to have got a great distance away from me, in little more than a year. She liked me, but she laughed at me, and tormented me; and when I went to meet her, stole home another way, and was laughing at the door when I came back, disappointed. The best times were when she sat quietly at work in the doorway, and I sat on the wooden steps at her feet, reading to her.

On the very first evening after our arrival, Mr. Barkis appeared with a bundle of oranges tied up in a handkerchief. As he made no allusion of any kind to this property, he was supposed to have left it behind him by accident when he went away; until Ham, running after him to restore it, came back with the information that it was intended for Peggotty. After that occasion he appeared every evening at exactly the same hour, and always with a little bundle, to which he never alluded, and which he regularly put behind the door, and left there.

Mr. Barkis's wooing, as I remember it, was altogether of a peculiar kind. He very seldom said anything; but would sit by the fire in much the same attitude as he sat in his cart, and stare heavily at Peggotty, who was opposite. Even when he took Peggotty out for a walk on the flats, he had no uneasiness on that head, I believe; contenting himself with now and then asking her if she was pretty comfortable.

At length, when the term of my visit was nearly expired, it was given out that Peggotty and Mr. Barkis were going to make a day's holiday together, and that little Em'ly and I were to accompany them. I had but a broken sleep the night before, in anticipation of the pleasure of a whole day with Em'ly. We were all astir betimes in the morning; and while we were yet at breakfast, Mr. Barkis appeared in the distance, driving a chaise-cart towards the object of his affections.

Peggotty was dressed as usual, in her neat and quiet mourning; but Mr. Barkis bloomed in a new blue coat, of which the tailor had given him such good measure, that the cuffs would have rendered gloves unnecessary in the coldest weather, while the collar was so high that it pushed his hair up on end on the top of his head. His bright buttons, too, were of the largest size. Rendered complete by drab pantaloons and a buff waistcoat, I thought Mr. Barkis a phenomenon of respectability.

When we were all in a bustle outside the door, I found that Mr. Peggotty was prepared with an old shoe, which was to be thrown after us for luck, and which he offered to Mrs. Gummidge for that purpose.

"No. It had better be done by somebody else, Dan'l," said Mrs. Gummidge. "I'm a lone lorn creetur' myself, and everythink that reminds me of creeturs that ain't lone and lorn, goes contrairy with me."

But here Peggotty called out from the cart, in which we all were by this time (Em'ly and I on two little chairs, side by side), that Mrs. Gummidge must do it. So Mrs. Gummidge did it; and, I am sorry to relate, cast a damp upon the festive character of our departure, by immediately bursting into tears, and sinking subdued into the arms of Ham.

Away we went, however, on our holiday excursion; and the first thing we did was to stop at a church, were Mr. Barkis tied the horse to some rails, and went in with Peggotty, leaving little Em'ly and me alone in the chaise. I took that occasion to put my arm round Em'ly's waist, and propose that as I was going away so very soon now, we should determine to be very affectionate to one another, and very happy, all day. Little Em'ly consenting, and allowing me to kiss her, I became desperate; informing her, I recollect, that I never could love another, and that I was prepared to shed the blood of anybody who should aspire to her affections.

Mr. Barkis and Peggotty were a good while in the church, but came out at last, and then we drove away into the country. As we were going along, Mr. Barkis turned to me, and said, with a wink:

"What name was it as I wrote up in the cart?"

"Clara Peggotty," I answered.

"Clara Peggotty BARKIS!" he returned, and burst into a roar of laughter.

In a word, they were married, and had gone into the church for no other purpose. Peggotty was resolved that it should be quietly done; and the clerk had given her away, and there had been no witnesses of the ceremony. She was a little confused when Mr. Barkis made this abrupt announcement of their union, and could not hug me enough in token of her unimpaired affection; but she soon became herself again, and said she was very glad it was over.

I drove cosily back, looking up at the stars. Little Em'ly and I made a cloak of an old wrapper, and sat under it for the rest of the journey. Ah, how I loved her! What happiness (I thought) if we were married, and were going away anywhere to live among the trees and in the fields, never growing older, never growing wiser, children ever rambling hand in hand through sunshine and among flowery meadows.

Well, we came to the old boat again in good time at night; and there Mr. and Mrs. Barkis bade us good-bye, and drove away snugly to their own home.

I felt then, for the first time, that I had lost Peggotty. I should have gone to bed with a sore heart indeed under any other roof but that which sheltered little Em'ly's head.

Mr. Peggotty and Ham knew what was in my thoughts as well as I did, and were ready with some supper and their hospitable faces to drive it away. Little Em'ly came and sat beside me on the locker for the only time in all that visit; and it was altogether a wonderful close to a wonderful day.

With morning came Peggotty. After breakfast she took me to her own home, and a beautiful little home it was.

I took leave of Mr. Peggotty, and Ham, and Mrs. Gummidge, and little Em'ly that day; and passed the night at Peggotty's in a little room in the roof, which was to be always mine, Peggotty said, and should always be kept for me in exactly the same state.

"Young or old, Davy dear, as long as I am alive and have this house over my head," said Peggotty, "you shall find it as if I expected you here directly. I shall keep it every day, as I used to keep your old little room, my darling; and if you was to go to China, you might think of it as being kept just the same, all the time you were away."

I felt the truth and constancy of my dear old nurse, with all my heart, and thanked her as well as I could. I went home in the morning, with herself and Mr. Barkis in the cart. They left me at the gate, not easily or lightly; and it was a strange sight to me to see the cart go on, taking Peggotty away, and leaving me under the old elm-trees looking at the house in which there was no face to look on mine with love or liking any more.

I was not actively ill-used. I was not beaten, or starved; but the wrong that was done to me had no intervals of relenting, and was done in a systematic, passionless manner. Day after day, week after week, month after month, I was coldly neglected. I wonder sometimes, when I think of it, what they would have done if I had been taken with an illness; whether I should have lain down in my lonely room, and languished through it in my usual solitary way, or whether anybody would have helped me out.

When Mr. and Miss Murdstone were at home, I took my meals with them; in their absence, I ate and drank by myself. At all times I lounged about the house and neighbourhood quite disregarded, except that they were jealous of my making any friends: thinking, perhaps, that if I did, I might complain to some one.

For the same reason, added no doubt to the old dislike of her, I was seldom allowed to visit Peggotty. Faithful to her promise, she either came to see me, or met me somewhere near, once every week, and never empty-handed; but many and bitter were the disappointments I had, in being refused permission to pay a visit to her at her house.

I had been out, one day, loitering somewhere, in the listless meditative manner that my way of life engendered, when, turning the corner of a lane near our house, I came upon Mr. Murdstone walking with a gentleman.

I observed the gentleman more attentively. I knew him to be Mr. Quinion, whom I had gone over to Lowestoft with Mr. Murdstone to see.

"And how do you get on, and where are you being educated?" said Mr. Quinion.

He had put his hand upon my shoulder, and turned me about, to walk with them. I did not know what to reply, and glanced dubiously at Mr. Murdstone.

"He is at home at present," said the latter. "He is not being educated anywhere. I don't know what to do with him. He is a difficult subject."

That old, double look was on me for a moment; and then his eye darkened with a frown, as it turned, in its aversion, elsewhere.

"Humph!" said Mr. Quinion, looking at us both, I thought. "Fine weather."

Silence ensued, and I was considering how I could best disengage my shoulder from his hand, and go away, when he said:

"I suppose you are a pretty sharp fellow?"

"Ay! He is sharp enough," said Mr. Murdstone, impatiently. "You had better let him go. He will not thank you for troubling him."

Mr. Quinion lay at our house that night. After breakfast, the next morning, I had put my chair away, and was going out of the room, when Mr. Murdstone called me back. He then gravely repaired to another table, where his sister sat herself at her desk. Mr. Quinion, with his hands in his pockets, stood looking out of window; and I stood looking at them all.

"David," said Mr. Murdstone, "to the young this is a world for action; not for moping and droning in."

"It is especially so for a young boy of your disposition, which requires a great deal of correcting; and to which no greater service can be done than to force it to conform to the ways of the working world."

"For stubbornness won't do here," said his sister. "What it wants is, to be crushed. And crushed it must be. Shall be, too!"

He gave her a look, half in remonstrance, half in approval, and went on:

"I suppose you know, David, that I am not rich. At any rate, you know it now. You have received some considerable education already. Education is costly; and even if it were not, and I could afford it, I am of opinion that it would not be at all advantageous to you to be kept at a school. What is before you, is a fight with the world; and the sooner you begin it, the better."

I think it occurred to me that I had already begun it, in my poor way: but it occurs to me now, whether or no.

"You have heard the 'counting-house' mentioned, or the business, or the cellars, or the wharf, or something about it."

"Mr. Quinion manages that business."

I glanced at the latter deferentially as he stood looking out of the window.

"Mr. Quinion suggests that it gives employment to some other boys, and that he sees no reason why it shouldn't, on the same terms, give employment to you. Those terms are, that you will earn enough for yourself to provide for your eating and drinking, and pocket-money. Your lodging (which I have arranged for) will be paid by me. So will your washing."

"Which will be kept down to my estimate," said his sister.

"Your clothes will be looked after for you, too," said Mr. Murdstone; "as you will not be able, yet awhile, to get them for yourself. So you are now going to London, David, with Mr. Quinion, to begin the world on your own account."

"In short, you are provided for," observed his sister; "and will please to do your duty."

CHAPTER 11

I Begin Life On My Own Account, and Don't Like It

MURDSTONE and Grinby's warehouse was at the water side. It was a crazy old house with a wharf of its own, abutting on the water when the tide was in, and on the mud when the tide was out, and literally overrun with rats.

Murdstone and Grinby's trade was among a good many kinds of people, but an important branch of it was the supply of wines and spirits to certain packet ships. When the empty bottles ran short, there were labels to be pasted on full ones, or corks to be fitted to them, or seals to be put upon the corks, or finished bottles to be packed in casks. All this work was my work, and of the boys employed upon it I was one.

There were three or four of us, counting me. My working place was established in a corner of the warehouse. Hither, on the first morning of my so auspiciously beginning life on my own account, the oldest of the regular boys was summoned to show me my business. His name was Mick Walker, and he wore a ragged apron and a paper cap. He informed me that his father was a bargeman, and walked, in a black velvet head-dress, in the Lord Mayor's Show. He also informed me that our principal associate would be another boy whom he introduced by the—to me—extraordinary name of Mealy Potatoes. I discovered, however, that this youth had not been christened by that name, but that it had been bestowed upon him in the warehouse, on account of his complexion, which was pale or mealy. Mealy's father was a waterman, who had the additional distinction of being a fireman, and was engaged as such at one of the large theatres; where some young relation of Mealy's—I think his little sister—did Imps in the Pantomimes.

No words can express the secret agony of my soul as I sunk into this companionship; compared these henceforth every-day associates with those of my happier childhood—not to say with Steerforth, Traddles, and the rest of those boys; and felt my hopes of growing up to be a learned and distinguished man crushed in my bosom.

The counting-house clock was at half-past twelve, and there was general preparation for going to dinner, when Mr. Quinion tapped at the counting-house window, and beckoned to me to go in. I went in, and found there a stoutish, middle-aged person, in a brown surtout and black tights and shoes, with no more hair upon his head (which was a large one, and very shining) than there is upon an egg, and with a very extensive face, which he turned full upon me. His clothes were shabby, but he had an imposing shirt-collar on. He carried a jaunty sort of a stick, with a large pair of rusty tassels to it; and a quizzing-glass hung outside his coat—for ornament, I afterwards found, as he very seldom looked through it, and couldn't see anything when he did.

"This," said Mr. Quinion, in allusion to myself, "is he."

"This," said the stranger, with a certain condescending roll in his voice, and a certain indescribable air of doing something genteel, which impressed me very much, "is Master Copperfield. I hope I see you well, sir?"

I said I was very well, and hoped he was. I was sufficiently ill at ease, Heaven knows; but it was not in my nature to complain much at that time of my life, so I said I was very well, and hoped he was.

"I am," said the stranger, "thank Heaven, quite well. I have received a letter from Mr. Murdstone, in which he mentions that he would desire me to receive into an apartment in the rear of my house, which is at present unoccupied—and is, in short, to be let as a—in short," said the stranger, with a smile and in a burst of confidence, "as a bedroom—the young beginner whom I have now the pleasure to—" and the stranger waved his hand, and settled his chin in his shirt collar.

"This is Mr. Micawber," said Mr. Quinion to me.

"Mr. Micawber," said Mr. Quinion, "is known to Mr. Murdstone. He takes orders for us on commission, when he can get any. He has been written to by Mr. Murdstone, on the subject of your lodgings, and he will receive you as a lodger."

"My address," said Mr. Micawber, "is Windsor Terrace, City Road. I—in short," said Mr. Micawber, with the same genteel air, and in another burst of confidence—"I live there."

I made him a bow.

"Under the impression," said Mr. Micawber, "that your peregrinations in this metropolis have not as yet been extensive, and that you might have some difficulty in penetrating the arcana of the Modern Babylon in the direction of the City Road—in short," said Mr. Micawber, in another burst of confidence, "that you might lose yourself—I shall be happy to call this evening, and install you in the knowledge of the nearest way."

I thanked him with all my heart, for it was friendly in him to offer to take that trouble.

"At what hour," said Mr. Micawber, "shall I——"

"At about eight," said Mr. Quinion.

"At about eight," said Mr. Micawber. "I beg to wish you good day, Mr. Quinion. I will intrude no longer."

So he put on his hat, and went out with his cane under his arm; very upright, and humming a tune when he was clear of the counting-house.

Mr. Quinion then formally engaged me to be as useful as I could in the warehouse of Murdstone and Grinby, at a salary, I think, of six shillings a week. He paid me a week down (from his own pocket, I believe), and I gave Mealy sixpence out of it to get my trunk carried to Windsor Terrace at night: it being too heavy for my strength, small as it was. I paid sixpence more for my dinner, which was a meat pie and a turn at a neighbouring pump; and passed the hour which was allowed for that meal, in walking about the streets.

At the appointed time in the evening, Mr. Micawber reappeared. I washed my hands and face, to do the greater honour to his gentility, and we walked to our house, as I suppose I must now call it, together; Mr. Micawber impressing the names of streets, and the shapes of corner houses upon me, as we went along, that I might find my way back, easily, in the morning.

Arrived at his house in Windsor Terrace (which I noticed was shabby like himself, but also, like himself, made all the show it could), he presented me to Mrs. Micawber, a thin and faded lady, not at all young, who was sitting in the parlour (the first floor was altogether unfurnished, and the blinds were kept down to delude the neighbours), with a baby at her breast.

There were two other children; Master Micawber, aged about four, and Miss Micawber, aged about three. My room was at the top of the house, at the back: a close chamber; stencilled all over with an ornament which my young imagination represented as a blue muffin; and very scantily furnished.

"I never thought," said Mrs. Micawber, when she came up, to show me the apartment, and sat down to take breath, "before I was married, when I lived with papa and mama, that I should ever find it necessary to take a lodger. But Mr. Micawber being in difficulties, all considerations of private feeling must give way."

I said: "Yes, ma'am."

"Mr. Micawber's difficulties are almost overwhelming just at present," said Mrs. Micawber; "and whether it is possible to bring him through them, I don't know. "If Mr. Micawber's creditors *will not* give him time," said Mrs. Micawber, "they must take the consequences; and the sooner they bring it to an issue the better. Blood cannot be obtained from a stone, neither can anything on account be obtained at present (not to mention law expenses) from Mr. Micawber."

I thought them quite ferocious. One dirty-faced man, I think he was a bootmaker, used to edge himself into the passage as early as seven o'clock in the morning, and call up the stairs to Mr. Micawber—Receiving no answer to these taunts, he would mount in his wrath to the words "swindlers" and "robbers"; and these being ineffectual too, would sometimes go to the extremity of crossing the street, and roaring up at the windows of the second floor, where he knew Mr. Micawber was.

In this house, and with this family, I passed my leisure time. My own exclusive breakfast of a penny loaf and a pennyworth of milk, I provided myself, I kept another small loaf, and a modicum of cheese, on a particular shelf of a particular cupboard, to make my supper on when I came back at night. From Monday morning until Saturday night, I had no assistance, no support, of any kind, from any one.

I was so young and childish, and so little qualified—to undertake the whole charge of my own existence, that often, in going to Murdstone and Grinby's, of a morning, I could not resist the stale pastry put out for sale at half-price at the pastrycooks' doors, and spent in that, the money I should have kept for my dinner. Then, I went without my dinner, or bought a roll or a slice of pudding. It was a stout pale pudding, heavy and flabby, and with great flat raisins in it, stuck in whole at wide distances apart. It came up hot at about my time every day, and many a day did I dine off it. When I dined regularly and handsomely, I had a saveloy and a penny loaf, or a fourpenny plate of red beef from a cook's shop; or a plate of bread and cheese and a glass of beer, from a miserable old public-house opposite our place of business, called the Lion, or the Lion and something else that I have forgotten.

I was such a child, and so little, that frequently when I went into the bar of a strange public-house for a glass of ale or porter, to moisten what I had had for dinner, they were afraid to give it me. I remember one hot evening I went into the bar of a public-house and said to the landlord:

"What is your best—your *very best*—ale a glass?" For it was a special occasion, I don't know what. It may have been my birth-day.

"Twopence-halfpenny," says the landlord, "is the price of the Genuine Stunning ale."

"Then," says I, producing the money, "just draw me a glass of the

Genuine Stunning, if you please, with a good head to it."

The landlord looked at me in return over the bar, from head to foot, with a strange smile on his face; and instead of drawing the beer, looked round the screen and said something to his wife. She came out from behind it, with her work in her hand, and joined him in surveying me. They asked me a good many questions; as, what my name was, how old I was, where I lived, how I was employed, and how I came there. To all of which, that I might commit nobody, I invented, I am afraid, appropriate answers. They served me with the ale, though I suspect it was not the Genuine Stunning: and the landlord's wife, opening the little half-door of the bar, and bending down, gave me my money back, and gave me a kiss that was half admiring, and half compassionate, but all womanly and good, I am sure.

My rescue from this kind of existence I considered quite hopeless, and abandoned, as such, altogether. But I bore it; and even to Peggotty, partly for the love of her and partly for shame, never in any letter (though many passed between us) revealed the truth.

A curious equality of friendship, originating, I suppose, in our respective circumstances, sprung up between me and the Micawbers notwithstanding the ludicrous disparity in our years.

"Master Copperfield," said Mrs. Micawber, "I make no stranger of you, and therefore do not hesitate to say that Mr. Micawber's difficulties are coming to a crisis."

"With the exception of the heel of a Dutch cheese," said Mrs. Micawber, "there is really not a scrap of anything in the larder. What I mean to express is, that there is nothing to eat in the house."

"Dear me!" I said, in great concern.

I had two or three shillings of my week's money in my pocket—and I hastily produced them, and with heartfelt emotion begged Mrs. Micawber to accept of them as a loan. But that lady, kissing me, and making me put them back in my pocket, replied that she couldn't think of it.

"No, my dear Master Copperfield," said she, "far be it from my thoughts! But you have a discretion beyond your years, and can render me another kind of service, if you will; and a service I will thankfully accept of."

I begged Mrs. Micawber to name it.

"I have parted with the plate myself," said Mrs. Micawber. "Six tea, two salt, and a pair of sugars, I have at different times borrowed money on, in secret, with my own hands. There are still a few trifles that we could part with. Mr. Micawber's feelings would never allow *him* to dispose of them. Master Copperfield, if I might ask you"—

I understood Mrs. Micawber now, and begged her to make use of me to any extent. I began to dispose of the more portable articles of property that very evening; and went out on a similar expedition almost every morning, before I went to Murdstone and Grinby's.

At the pawnbroker's shop, I began to be very well known. The principal gentleman who officiated behind the counter, took a good deal of notice of me; and often got me, I recollect, to decline a Latin noun or adjective, or to conjugate a Latin verb, in his ear, while he transacted my business. After all these occasions Mrs. Micawber made a little treat, which was generally a supper; and there was a peculiar relish in these meals which I well remember.

At last Mr. Micawber's difficulties came to a crisis, and he was arrested early one morning, and carried over to the King's Bench Prison in the Borough. He told me, as he went out of the house, that the God of day had now gone down upon him—and I really thought his heart was broken and mine too. But I heard, afterwards, that he was seen to play a lively game at skittles, before noon.

All this time I was working at Murdstone and Grinby's in the same common way, and with the same common companions, and with the same sense of unmerited degradation as at first. I led the same secretly unhappy life; but I led it in the same lonely, self-reliant manner. The only changes I am conscious of are, firstly, that I had grown more shabby, and secondly, that I was now relieved of much of the weight of Mr. and Mrs. Micawber's cares; for some relatives or friends had engaged to help them at their present pass, and they lived more comfortably in the prison than they had lived for a long while out of it. I used to breakfast with them now, in virtue of some arrangement, of which I have forgotten the details. In the evening I used to go back to the prison, and walk up and down the parade with Mr. Micawber; or play casino with Mrs. Micawber, and hear reminiscences of her papa and mama. Whether Mr. Murdstone knew where I was, I am unable to say. I never told them at Murdstone and Grinby's.

Mr. Micawber's affairs, although past their crisis, were very much involved by reason of a certain "Deed," of which I used to hear a great deal, and which I suppose, now, to have been some former composition with his creditors. At last this document appeared to be got out of the way, somehow; and Mrs. Micawber informed me that "her family" had decided that Mr. Micawber should apply for his release under the Insolvent Debtors' Act, which would set him free, she expected, in about six weeks.

"And then," said Mr. Micawber, who was present, "I have no doubt I shall, please Heaven, begin to be beforehand with the world, and to live in a perfectly new manner, if—in short, if anything turns up."

CHAPTER 12

Liking Life On My Own Account No Better, I Form a Great Resolution

IN due time, Mr. Micawber's petition was ripe for hearing; and that gentleman was ordered to be discharged under the act, to my great joy. His creditors were not implacable; and Mrs. Micawber informed me that even the revengeful boot-maker had declared in open court that he bore him no malice, but that when money was owing to him he liked to be paid. He said he thought it was human nature.

Mr. Micawber returned to the King's Bench when his case was over, as some fees were to be settled, and some formalities observed, before he could be actually released.

As I could hardly hope for a more favourable opportunity of putting a question in which I had a near interest, I said to Mrs. Micawber:

"May I ask, ma'am, what you and Mr. Micawber intend to do, now that Mr. Micawber is out of his difficulties, and at liberty? Have you settled yet?"

"My family," said Mrs. Micawber, "are of opinion that Mr. Micawber should quit London, and exert his talents in the country. Mr. Micawber is a man of great talent, Master Copperfield."

I said I was sure of that.

Mrs. Micawber had not spoken of their going away without warrant. They took a lodging in the house where I lived, for a week; at the expiration of which time they were to start for Plymouth. Mr. Micawber himself came down to the counting-house, in the afternoon, to tell Mr. Quinion that he must relinquish me on the day of his departure, and to give me a high character, which I am sure I deserved. And Mr. Quinion, calling in Tipp the carman, who was a married man, and had a room to let, quartered me prospectively on him—by our mutual consent, as he had every reason to think; for I said nothing, though my resolution was now taken.

I passed my evenings with Mr. and Mrs. Micawber, during the remaining term of our residence under the same roof; and I think we became fonder of one another as the time went on.

"I shall never, Master Copperfield," said Mrs. Micawber, "revert to the period when Mr. Micawber was in difficulties, without thinking of you. Your conduct has always been of the most delicate and obliging description. You have never been a lodger. You have been a friend."

I expressed my sense of this commendation, and said I was very sorry we were going to lose one another.

"My dear young friend," said Mr. Micawber, "I am older than you; a man of some experience in life, and—and of some experience, in short, in difficulties, generally speaking. At present, and until something turns up, I have nothing to bestow but advice. My advice is, never do to-morrow what you can do to-day. Procrastination is the thief of time. Collar him!"

"My other piece of advice, Copperfield," said Mr. Micawber, "you know. Annual income twenty pounds, annual expenditure nineteen nineteen six, result happiness. Annual income twenty pounds, annual expenditure twenty pounds ought and six, result misery. The blossom is blighted, the leaf is withered, the God of day goes down upon the dreary scene, and—and in short you are for ever floored. As I am!"

Next morning I met the whole family at the coach office, and saw them, with a desolate heart, take their places outside, at the back.

"Master Copperfield," said Mrs. Micawber, "God bless you! I never can forget all that, you know, and I never would if I could."

"Copperfield," said Mr. Micawber, "farewell! In case of anything turning up (of which I am rather confident), I shall be extremely happy if it should be in my power to improve your prospects."

The coach started, and I could hardly see the family for the handkerchiefs they waved. It was gone in a minute. I went to begin my weary day at Murdstone and Grinby's.

But with no intention of passing many more weary days there. No.

I had resolved to run away.—To go, by some means or other, down into the country, to the only relation I had in the world, and tell my story to my aunt, Miss Betsey.

Again, and again, and a hundred times again, since the night when the thought had first occured to me and banished sleep, I had gone over that old story of my poor mother's about my birth, which it had been one of my great delights in the old time to hear her tell.

As I did not even know where Miss Betsey lived, I wrote a long letter to Peggotty. In the course of that letter, I told Peggotty that I had a particular occasion for half a guinea; and that if she could lend me that sum until I could repay it, I should be very much obliged to her, and would tell her afterwards what I had wanted it for.

Peggotty's answer soon arrived, and was, as usual, full of affectionate devotion. She enclosed the half guinea and told me that Miss Betsey lived near Dover, but whether at Dover itself, at Hythe, Sandgate, or Folkestone, she could not say. One of our men, however, informing me on my asking him about these places, that they were all close together, I deemed this enough for my object, and resolved to set out at the end of that week.

My box was at my old lodging over the water, and I had written a direction for it on the back of one of our address cards that we nailed on the casks: "Master David, to be left till called for, at the Coach Office, Dover." This I had in my pocket ready to put on the box, after I should have got it out of the house; and as I went towards my lodging, I looked about me for some one who would help me to carry it to the booking-office.

There was a long-legged young man, with a very little empty donkey-cart, standing near the Obelisk, in the Blackfriars Road, whose eye I caught.

I told him my box was down that street there, and which I wanted him to take to the Dover coach-office for sixpence.

"Done with you for a tanner!" said the long-legged young man, and directly got upon his cart, which was nothing but a large wooden tray on wheels, and rattled away at such a rate, that it was as much as I could do to keep pace with the donkey.

There was a defiant manner about this young man, and particularly about the way in which he chewed straw as he spoke to me, that I did not much like; as the bargain was made, however, I took him up-stairs to the room I was leaving, and we brought the box down, and put it on his cart.

They rattled away as if he, my box, the cart, and the donkey, were all equally mad; and I was quite out of breath with running and calling after him, when I caught him at the place appointed.

Being much flushed and excited, I tumbled my half-guinea out of my pocket. I put it in my mouth for safety, when I felt myself violently chucked under the chin by the long-legged young man, and saw my half-guinea fly out of my mouth into his hand.

"Wot!" said the young man, seizing me by my jacket collar, with a frightful grin. "This is a pollis case, is it? You're a going to bolt, are you? Come to the pollis, you young warmin, come to the pollis!"

"You give me my money back, if you please," said I, very much frightened; "and leave me alone."

The young man still replied: "Come to the pollis!" and was dragging me against the donkey in a violent manner, as if there were any affinity between that animal and a magistrate, when he changed his mind, jumped into the cart, sat upon my box, and, exclaiming that he would drive to the pollis straight, rattled away harder than ever.

I ran after him as fast as I could, but I had no breath to call out with, and should not have dared to call out, now, if I had. Now I saw him, now I lost him, now I was cut at with a whip, now shouted at, now running headlong at a post. At length, confused by fright and heat, and doubting whether half London might not by this time be turning out for my apprehension, I left the young man to go where he would with my box and money; and, panting and crying, but never stopping, faced about for Greenwich, which I had understood was on the Dover Road: taking very little more out of the world, towards the retreat of my aunt, Miss Betsey, than I had brought into it, on the night when my arrival gave her so much umbrage.

CHAPTER 13

The Sequel of My Resolution

MY standing possessions of only three-halfpence in the world troubled me none the less because I trudged on miserably, though as fast as I could, until I happened to pass a little shop, where it was written up that ladies' and gentlemen's wardrobes were bought.

My late experiences with Mr. and Mrs. Micawber suggested to me that here might be a means of keeping off the wolf for a little while. I went up the next bye-street, took off my waistcoat, rolled it neatly under my arm, and came back to the shop-door. "If you please, sir," I said, "I am to sell this for a fair price."

"What do you call a price, now, for this here little weskit?"

"Would eighteenpence be?"—I hinted, after some hesitation.

Mr. Dolloby rolled it up again, and gave it me back. "I should rob my family," he said, "if I was to offer ninepence for it."

My circumstances being so, I said I would take ninepence for it, if he pleased.

Indeed, I foresaw pretty clearly that my jacket would go next, and that I should have to make the best of my way to Dover in a shirt and a pair of trousers, and might deem myself lucky if I got there even in that trim.

I had had a hard day's work, and was pretty well jaded when I came climbing out, at last, upon the level of Blackheath. I found a haystack in the corner, and I lay down by it. Never shall I forget the lonely sensation of first lying down, without a roof above my head!

What a different Sunday morning from the old Sunday morning at Yarmouth! In due time I heard the church-bells ringing, as I plodded on; and I met people who were going to church.

I got, that Sunday, through three-and-twenty miles on the straight road, though not very easily, for I was new to that kind of toil. I see myself, as evening closes in, coming over the bridge at Rochester, footsore and tired, and eating bread that I had bought for supper. I sought no shelter, therefore, but the sky; and toiling into Chatham—crept, at last, upon a sort of grass-grown battery overhanging a lane, where a sentry was walking to and fro. Here I lay down, near a cannon; and, happy in the society of the sentry's footsteps.

Very stiff and sore of foot I was in the morning. Feeling that I could go but a very little way that day, if I were to reserve any strength for getting to my journey's end, I resolved to make the sale of my jacket its principal business.

I directed my attention to the marine-store shops, in preference to the regular dealers. At last I found one that I thought looked promising.

I went with a palpitating heart; which was not relieved when an ugly old man, with the lower part of his face all covered with a stubbly grey beard, rushed out of a dirty den behind it, and seized me by the hair of my head. He was a dreadful old man to look at, in a filthy flannel waistcoat, and smelling terribly of rum.

"Oh, what do you want?" grinned this old man, in a fierce, monotonous whine. "Oh, my eyes and limbs, what do you want? Oh, my lungs and liver, what do you want? Oh, goroo, goroo!"

"I wanted to know," I said, trembling, "if you would buy a jacket."

"Oh, how much for the jacket?" cried the old man, after examining it. "Oh—goroo!—how much for the jacket?"

"Half-a-crown," I answered, recovering myself.

"Oh, my lungs and liver," cried the old man, "no! Oh, my eyes, no! Oh, my limbs, no! Eighteenpence. Goroo!"

"Well," said I, glad to have closed the bargain, "I'll take eighteenpence."

"Oh, my liver!" cried the old man, throwing the jacket on a shelf. "Get out of the shop! Oh, my lungs, get out of the shop! Oh, my eyes and limbs —goroo!—don't ask for money; make it an exchange."

He made many attempts to induce me to consent to an exchange; at one time coming out with a fishing-rod, at another with a fiddle. But I resisted all these overtures. At last he began to pay me in halfpence at a time; and was full two hours getting by easy stages to a shilling.

"Oh, go—roo; will you go for fourpence?"

I was so faint and weary that I closed with this offer; and taking the money out of his claw, not without trembling, went away more hungry and thirsty than I had ever been, a little before sunset. But at an expense of threepence I soon refreshed myself completely; and, being in better spirits then, limped seven miles upon my road.

My bed at night was under another haystack, where I rested comfortably, after having washed my blistered feet in a stream, and dressed them as well as I was able, with some cool leaves. When I took the road again next morning, I found that it lay through a succession of hop grounds and orchards. It was sufficiently late in the year for the orchards to be ruddy with ripe apples; and in a few places the hop-pickers were already at work. I thought it all extremely beautiful, and made up my mind to sleep among the hops that night.

I came, at last, upon the bare, wide downs near Dover, then, I stood with my ragged shoes, and my dusty, sunburnt, half-clothed figure, in the place so long desired.

I inquired about my aunt among the boatman first, and received various answers. The fly-drivers, among whom I inquired next, were equally jocose and equally disrespectful; and the shopkeepers, not liking my appearance, generally replied, without hearing what I had to say, that they had got nothing for me.

The morning had worn away in these inquiries, and I was sitting on the step of an empty shop at a street corner, when a fly-driver, coming by with his carriage, dropped a horsecloth. Something good-natured in the man's face, as I handed it up, encouraged me to ask him if he could tell me where Miss Trotwood lived.

"Trotwood," said he. "Let me see. I know the name, too. Old lady? Pretty stiff in the back?" said he, making himself upright. "Carries a bag?" said he: "bag with a good deal of room in it: is gruffish, and comes down upon you, sharp?"

My heart sank within me as I acknowledged the undoubted accuracy of this description.

"Why then, I tell you what," said he. "If you go up there," pointing with his whip towards the heights, "and keep right on till you come to some houses facing the sea, I think you'll hear of her. My opinion is, she won't stand anything, so here's a penny for you."

I accepted the gift thankfully, and bought a loaf with it. Dispatching this refreshment by the way, I walked on a good distance without coming to the houses he had mentioned. At length I saw some before me; and approaching them, went into a little shop, and inquired if they could have the goodness to tell me where Miss Trotwood lived. I addressed myself to a man behind the counter, who was weighing some rice for a young woman; but the latter, taking the inquiry to herself, turned round quickly.

"My mistress?" she said. "What do you want with her, boy?"

"I want," I replied, "to speak to her, if you please."

"To beg of her, you mean," retorted the damsel.

"No," I said, "indeed."

My aunt's handmaid, as I supposed she was from what she had said, put her rice in a little basket and walked out of the shop; telling me that I could follow her, if I wanted to know where Miss Trotwood lived. I followed the young woman, and we soon came to a very neat little cottage with cheerful bow-windows: in front of it, a small square gravelled court or garden full of flowers, carefully tended, and smelling deliciously.

"This is Miss Trotwood's," said the young woman. "Now you know; and that's all I have got to say." With which words she hurried into the house.

My shoes were by this time in a woeful condition. The soles had shed themselves bit by bit, and the upper leathers had broken and burst until the very shape and form of shoes had departed from them. My hat (which had served me for a nightcap, too) was so crushed and bent, that no old battered handleless saucepan on a dunghill need have been ashamed to vie with it. My shirt and trousers, stained with heat, dew, grass, and the Kentish soil on which I had slept—and torn besides. My hair had known no comb or brush since I left London. From head to foot I was powdered almost as white with chalk and dust, as if I had come out of a limekiln. In this plight, and with a strong consciousness of it, I waited to introduce myself to, and make my first impression on, my formidable aunt.

I was on the point of slinking off, to think how I had best proceed, when there came out of the house a lady with her handkerchief tied over her cap, and a pair of gardening gloves on her hands, wearing a gardening pocket like a toll-man's apron, and carrying a great knife. I knew her immediately to be Miss Betsey, for she came stalking out of the house exactly as my poor mother had often described her stalking up our garden at Blunderstone Rookery.

"Go away!" said Miss Betsey, shaking her head, and making a distant chop in the air with her knife. "Go along! No boys here!"

"If you please, ma'am," I began.

She started and looked up.

"If you please, aunt."

"Eh?" exclaimed Miss Betsey, in a tone of amazement I have never heard approached.

"If you please, aunt, I am your nephew."

"Oh, Lord!" said my aunt. And sat flat down in the garden-path.

"I am David Copperfield, of Blunderstone, in Suffolk—where you came, on the night when I was born, and saw my dear mama. I have been very unhappy since she died. I have been slighted, and taught nothing, and thrown upon myself, and put to work not fit for me. It made me run away to you. I was robbed at first setting out, and have walked all the way, and have never slept in a bed since I began the journey." Here my self-support gave way all at once; and with a movement of my hands, intended to show her my ragged state, and call it to witness that I had suffered something, I broke into a passion of crying, which I suppose had been pent up within me all the week.

My aunt got up in a great hurry, collared me, and took me into the parlour. Her first proceeding there was to unlock a tall press, bring out several bottles, and pour some of the contents of each into my mouth. When she had administered these restoratives, she put me on the sofa, with a shawl under my head, and the handkerchief from her own head under my feet, lest I should sully the cover.

After a time she rang the bell. "Janet," said my aunt, when her servant came in. "Go up-stairs, give my compliments to Mr. Dick, and say I wish to speak to him."

My aunt, with her hands behind her, walked up and down the room, until the gentleman who had squinted at me from the upper window came in laughing.

"Mr. Dick," said my aunt, "you have heard me mention David Copperfield? Now don't pretend not to have a memory, because you and I know better."

"David Copperfield?" said Mr. Dick, who did not appear to me to remember much about it. "*David* Copperfield? Oh yes, to be sure. David, certainly."

"Well," said my aunt, "this is his boy, his son. He would be as like his father as it's possible to be, if he was not so like his mother, too."

"His son?" said Mr. Dick. "David's son? Indeed!"

"Yes," pursued my aunt, "and he has done a pretty piece of business. He has run away. Now, here you see young David Copperfield, and the question I put to you is, what shall I do with him?"

"Why, if I was you," said Mr. Dick, considering, and looking vacantly at me, "I should——" The contemplation of me seemed to inspire him with a sudden idea, and he added, briskly, "—I should wash him!"

"Janet," said my aunt, turning round with a quiet triumph, which I did not then understand, "Mr. Dick sets us all right. Heat the bath!"

My aunt was a tall, hard-featured lady, but by no means ill-looking. There was an inflexibility in her face, in her voice, in her gait and carriage, amply sufficient to account for the effect she had made upon a gentle creature like my mother.

Mr. Dick, was grey-headed and florid: and his grey eyes prominent and large, with a strange kind of watery brightness in them, in combination with his vacant manner. He was dressed like any other ordinary gentleman, in a loose grey morning coat and waistcoat, and white trousers; and had his watch in his fob, and his money in his pockets: which he rattled as if he were very proud of it.

The bath was a great comfort. When I had bathed, they enrobed me in a shirt and a pair of trousers belonging to Mr. Dick, and tied me up in two or three great shawls. Feeling very faint and drowsy, I soon lay down on the sofa again and fell asleep.

We dined soon after I awoke, off a roast fowl and a pudding; I sitting at table, not unlike a trussed bird myself, and moving my arms with considerable difficulty. But as my aunt had swathed me up, I made no complaint of being inconvenienced.

All this time, I was deeply anxious to know what she was going to do with me; but she took her dinner in profound silence, except when she occasionally fixed her eyes on me sitting opposite, and said, "Mercy upon us!" which did not by any means relieve my anxiety.

The cloth being drawn, and some sherry put upon the table (of which I had a glass), my aunt sent up for Mr. Dick again, who joined us, and looked as wise as he could when she requested him to attend to my story, which she elicited from me, gradually, by a course of questions. During my recital, she kept her eyes on Mr. Dick, who I thought would have gone to sleep but for that, and who, whensoever he lapsed into a smile, was checked by a frown from my aunt.

"Whatever possessed that poor unfortunate Baby, that she must go and be married again," said my aunt, when I had finished, "*I* can't conceive. And then, as if this was not enough, goes and marries a Murderer—or a man with a name like it—and stands in *this* child's light! And the natural consequence is, as anybody but a baby might have foreseen, that he prowls and wanders. He's as like Cain before he was grown up, as he can be. Now, Mr. Dick," said my aunt, with her grave look, and her forefinger up as before, "I am going to ask you another question. Look at this child."

"David's son?" said Mr. Dick, with an attentive, puzzled face.

"Exactly so," returned my aunt. "What would you do with him, now?"

"Oh!" said Mr. Dick. "Yes. Do with—I should put him to bed."

Janet reporting it to be quite ready, I was taken up to it; kindly, but in some sort like a prisoner; my aunt going in front, and Janet bringing up the rear.

I thought of all the solitary places under the night sky where I had slept, and how I prayed that I never might be houseless any more, and never might forget the houseless.

CHAPTER 14

My Aunt Makes Her Mind Up About Me

On going down in the morning, I found my aunt musing so profoundly over the breakfast-table, with her elbow on the tray, that the contents of the urn had over-flowed the teapot and were laying the whole tablecloth under water, when my entrance put her meditations to flight.

"Hallo!" said my aunt, after a long time. "I have written to him," said my aunt. "To your father-in-law," said my aunt. "I have sent him a letter that I'll trouble him to attend to, or he and I will fall out, I can tell him!"

"Does he know where I am, aunt?" I inquired, alarmed.

"I have told him," said my aunt, with a nod.

"Oh! I can't think what I shall do," I exclaimed, "if I have to go back to Mr. Murdstone!"

"I don't know anything about it," said my aunt, shaking her head. "I can't say, I am sure. We shall see."

"I wish you'd go upstairs," said my aunt, as she threaded her needle, "and give my compliments to Mr. Dick, and I'll be glad to know how he gets on with his Memorial."

I rose with all alacrity, to acquit myself of this commission.

I went up-stairs with my message; I found him still driving at it with a long pen, and his head almost laid upon the paper. He was so intent upon it, that I had ample leisure to observe the large paper kite in a corner.

"Ha! Phœbus!" said Mr. Dick, laying down his pen. "How does the world go?"

Without presuming to give my opinion on this question, I delivered my message.

"Well," said Mr. Dick, in answer, "my compliments to her, and I—I believe I have made a start. I," said Mr. Dick, passing his hand among his grey hair, and casting anything but a confident look at his manuscript.

"Do you recollect the date," said Mr. Dick, looking earnestly at me, and taking up his pen to note it down, "when King Charles the First had his head cut off?"

I said I believed it happened in the year sixteen hundred and forty-nine.

"It's very strange," said Mr. Dick, with a despondent look upon his papers, and with his hand among his hair again, "that I never can get that quite right. I never can make that perfectly clear. But no matter, no matter!" he said cheerfully, and rousing himself, "there's time enough! My compliments to Miss Trotwood, I am getting on very well indeed."

I was going away, when he directed my attention to the kite.

"What do you think of that for a kite?" he said.

I answered that it was a beautiful one. I should think it must have been as much as seven feet high.

"I made it. We'll go and fly it, you and I," said Mr. Dick. "Do you see this?"

He showed me that it was covered with manuscript, very closely and laboriously written; but so plainly, that as I looked along the lines, I thought I saw some allusion to King Charles the First's head again, in one or two places.

"Well, child," said my aunt, when I went down-stairs. "And what of Mr. Dick, this morning?"

I informed her that he sent his compliments, and was getting on well.

"What do you think of him?" said my aunt.

"Is he—is Mr. Dick—I ask because I don't know, aunt—is he at all out of his mind?" I stammered.

"If there is anything in the world," said my aunt, with great decision and force of manner, "that Mr. Dick is not, it's that. He has been *called* mad," said my aunt. "And nice people they were, who had the audacity to call him mad," pursued my aunt. "Mr. Dick is a sort of distant connexion of mine; it doesn't matter how; I needn't enter into that. If it hadn't been for me, his own brother would have shut him up for life. That's all."

CHAPTER 15

I Make Another Beginning

Mr. Dick and I soon became the best of friends, and very often, when his day's work was done, went out together to fly the great kite.

While I advanced in friendship and intimacy with Mr. Dick, I did not go backward in the favour of his staunch friend, my aunt. She took so kindly to me, that, in the course of a few weeks, she shortened my adopted name of Trotwood into Trot; and even encouraged me to hope, that if I went on as I had begun, I might take equal rank in her affections with my mother.

"Trot," said my aunt one evening, when the backgammon-board was placed as usual for herself and Mr. Dick, "we must not forget your education. Should you like to go to school at Canterbury?" said my aunt.

I replied that I should like it very much, as it was so near her.

"Good," said my aunt. "Should you like to go to-morrow?"

Being already no stranger to the general rapidity of my aunt's evolutions, I was not surprised by the suddenness of the proposal, and said: "Yes."

"Good," said my aunt again. "Janet, hire the grey pony and chaise to-morrow morning at ten o'clock, and pack up Master Trotwood's clothes to-night."

"Is it a large school, aunt?" I asked.

"Why, I don't know," said my aunt. "We are going to Mr. Wickfield's first."

"Does *he* keep a school?" I asked.

"No, Trot," said my aunt. "He keeps an office."

We came to Canterbury, where, as it was market-day, my aunt had a great opportunity of insinuating the grey pony among carts, baskets, vegetables, and hucksters' goods. The hair-breadth turns and twists we made, drew down upon us a variety of speeches from the people standing about, which were not always complimentary; but my aunt drove on with perfect indifference, and I dare say would have taken her own way with as much coolness through an enemy's country.

At length we stopped before a very old house bulging out over the road.

When the pony-chaise stopped at the door, I saw a cadaverous face appear at a small window on the ground floor and quickly disappear. It belonged to a red-haired person—a youth of fifteen, as I take it now, but looking much older—whose hair was cropped as close as the closest stubble; who had hardly any eyebrows, and no eyelashes, and eyes of a red-brown, so unsheltered and unshaded, that I remember wondering how he went to sleep. He was high-shouldered and bony; dressed in decent black, with a white wisp of a neck-cloth; buttoned up to the throat; and had a long, lank, skeleton hand, which particularly attracted my attention, as he stood at the pony's head, rubbing his chin with it, and looking up at us in the chaise.

"Is Mr. Wickfield at home, Uriah Heep?" said my aunt.

"Mr. Wickfield's at home, ma'am," said Uriah Heep, "if you'll please to walk in there": pointing with his long hand to the room he meant.

We got out; and went into a long low parlour looking towards the street.

A gentleman entered. "Miss Betsey Trotwood," said the gentleman, "pray walk in. I was engaged for a moment, but you'll excuse my being busy. You know my motive. I have but one in life."

Miss Betsey thanked him, and we went into his room.

"Well, Miss Trotwood," said Mr. Wickfield; for I soon found that it was he, and that he was a lawyer, and steward of the estates of a rich gentleman of the county; "what wind blows you here? Not an ill wind, I hope?"

"No," replied my aunt, "I have not come for any law."

"This is my grand-nephew," observed my aunt.

"Wasn't aware you had a grand-nephew, I give you my word," said Mr. Wickfield.

"I have adopted him," said my aunt, with a wave of her hand, importing that his knowledge and his ignorance were all one to her, "and I have brought him here, to put him to a school where he may be thoroughly well taught, and well treated. Now tell me where that school is, and what it is, and all about it."

"At the best we have," said Mr. Wickfield, considering, "your nephew couldn't board just now."

"But he could board somewhere else, I suppose?" suggested my aunt.

Mr. Wickfield thought I could. After a little discussion, he proposed to take my aunt to the school, that she might see it and judge for herself.

I said I would gladly remain behind, if they pleased; and returned into Mr. Wickfield's office, where I sat down again, in the chair I had first occupied, to await their return.

At length, my aunt and Mr. Wickfield came back, after a pretty long absence. They were not so successful as I could have wished; for though the advantages of the school were undeniable, my aunt had not approved of any of the boarding-houses proposed for me.

"It's very unfortunate," said my aunt. "I don't know what to do, Trot."

"It *does* happen unfortunately," said Mr. Wickfield. "But I'll tell you what you can do, Miss Trotwood."

"What's that?" inquired my aunt.

"Leave your nephew here, for the present. He won't disturb me at all. It's a capital house for study. As quiet as a monastery, and almost as roomy. Leave him here."

My aunt evidently liked the offer, though she was delicate of accepting it. So did I.

"Come, Miss Trotwood," said Mr. Wickfield. "It's only a temporary arrangement, you know. There will be time to find some better place for him in the meanwhile."

"I am very much obliged to you," said my aunt; "and so is he, I see; but—"

"Come!" cried Mr. Wickfield. "You may pay for him, if you like. We won't be hard about terms, but you shall pay if you will."

"On that understanding," said my aunt, "though it doesn't lessen the real obligation, I shall be very glad to leave him."

"Then come and see my little housekeeper," said Mr. Wickfield.

We accordingly went up a wonderful old staircase; and into a shady old drawing-room.

Mr. Wickfield tapped at a door in a corner of the panelled wall, and a girl of about my own age came quickly out and kissed him. Although her face was quite bright and happy, there was a tranquillity about it, and about her—a quiet, good, calm spirit,—that I never have forgotten; that I never shall forget.

This was his little housekeeper, his daughter Agnes, Mr. Wickfield said. When I heard how he said it, and saw how he held her hand, I guessed what the one motive of his life was.

My aunt was as happy as I was, in the arrangement made for me, and we went down to the drawing-room again, well pleased and gratified.

She embraced me hastily, and went out of the room, shutting the door after her. At first I was startled by so abrupt a departure, and almost feared I had displeased her; but when I looked into the street, and saw how dejectedly she got into the chaise, and drove away without looking up, I understood her better, and did not do her that injustice.

By five o'clock, which was Mr. Wickfield's dinner-hour, I had mustered up my spirits again, and was ready for my knife and fork.

After dinner, up-stairs into the drawing-room again: Agnes set glasses for her father, and a decanter of port wine.

There he sat, taking his wine, and taking a good deal of it, for two hours; while Agnes played on the piano, worked, and talked to him and me. He was, for the most part, gay and cheerful with us; but sometimes his eyes rested on her, and he fell into a brooding state, and was silent. Then he came out of his meditation, and drank more wine.

CHAPTER 16

I Am a New Boy in More Senses Than One

NEXT morning, after breakfast, I entered on school life again. I went, accompanied by Mr. Wickfield, to the scene of my future studies—and was introduced to my new master, Doctor Strong.

Doctor Strong looked almost as rusty, to my thinking, as the tall iron rails and gates outside the house. He was in his library, with his clothes not particularly well brushed, and his hair not particularly well combed; his knee-smalls unbraced; his long black gaiters unbuttoned; and his shoes yawning like two caverns on the hearth rug.

But, sitting at work, not far off from Doctor Strong, was a very pretty young lady—whom he called Annie,—who got down to put Doctor Strong's shoes on, and button his gaiters, which she did with great cheerfulness and quickness. When she had finished, and we were going out to the schoolroom, I was much surprised to hear Mr. Wickfield, in bidding her good morning, address her as "Mrs. Strong".

"By-the-by, Wickfield," the Doctor said, stopping in a passage with his hand on my shoulder; "you have not found any suitable provision for my wife's cousin yet?"

"No," said Mr. Wickfield. "No. Not yet."

"I could wish it done as soon as it *can* be done, Wickfield," said Doctor Strong, "for Jack Maldon is needy, and idle; and of those two bad things, worse things sometimes come."

The school-room was a pretty large hall, on the quietest side of the house. About five-and-twenty boys were studiously engaged at their books when we went in, but they rose to give the Doctor good morning, and remained standing when they saw Mr. Wickfield and me.

"A new boy, young gentlemen," said the Doctor; "Trotwood Copperfield."

One Adams, who was the head-boy, then stepped out of his place and welcomed me. He looked like a young clergyman, in his white cravat, but he was very affable and good-humoured; and he showed me my place, and presented me to the masters, in a gentlemanly way that would have put me at my ease, if anything could.

In Mr. Wickfield's old house, I sat, sturdily conning my books, until dinner-time (we were out of school for good at three).

Agnes was in the drawing-room, waiting for her father, who was detained by some one in his office.

"Hark! That's papa now!"

Her bright calm face lighted up with pleasure as she went to meet him, and as they came in, hand in hand. He greeted me cordially, and told me I should certainly be happy under Doctor Strong, who was one of the gentlest of men.

"There may be some, perhaps—I don't know that there are—who abuse his kindness," said Mr. Wickfield. "Never be one of those, Trotwood, in anything. He is the least suspicious of mankind; and whether that's a merit, or whether it's a blemish, it deserves consideration in all dealings with the Doctor, great or small."

He spoke, I thought, as if he were weary, or dissatisfied with something; but I did not pursue the question in my mind, for dinner was just then announced, and we went down and took the same seats as before.

We had scarcely done so, when Uriah Heep put in his red head and his lank hand at the door, and said:

"Here's Mr. Maldon begs the favour of a word, sir."

"I am but this moment quit of Mr. Maldon," said his master.

"Yes, sir," returned Uriah; "but Mr. Maldon has come back, and he begs the favour of a word."

"I beg your pardon. It's only to say, on reflection," observed a voice behind Uriah, as Uriah's head was pushed away, and the speaker's substituted—"pray excuse me for this intrusion—that as it seems I have no choice in the matter, the sooner I go abroad the better. My cousin Annie did say, when we talked of it, that she liked to have her friends within reach rather than to have them banished, and the old Doctor——"

"Doctor Strong, was that?" Mr. Wickfield interposed, gravely.

"Well, Doctor Strong," said the other. "Doctor Strong was of the same mind, I believed. But as it appears from the course you take with me, that he has changed his mind, why there's no more to be said, except that the sooner I am off, the better. Of course I shall observe your directions, in considering the matter as one to be arranged between you and me solely, and not to be referred to, up at the Doctor's."

"Have you dined?" asked Mr. Wickfield, with a motion of his hand towards the table.

"Thank'ee. I am going to dine," said Mr. Maldon, "with my cousin Annie. Goodbye!"

Mr. Wickfield, without rising, looked after him thoughtfully as he went out. He was rather a shallow sort of young gentleman, I thought, with a handsome face, a rapid utterance, and a confident bold air. And this was the first I ever saw of Mr. Jack Maldon; whom I had not expected to see so soon, when I heard the Doctor speak of him that morning.

When we had dined, we went up-stairs again, where everything went on exactly as on the previous day. Agnes set the glasses and decanters in the same corner, and Mr. Wickfield sat down to drink, and drank a good deal.

Mr. Wickfield said: "Should you like to stay with us, Trotwood, or to go elsewhere?"

"To stay," I answered, quickly.

"You are sure?"

"If you please. If I may!"

He had drunk wine that evening (or I fancied it), until his eyes were bloodshot. Not that I could see them now, for they were cast down, and shaded by his hand; but I had noticed them a little while before.

"Stay with us, Trotwood, eh?" he said in his usual manner. "I am glad of it. You are company to us both. It is wholesome to have you here."

"I am sure it is for me, sir," I said. "I am so glad to be here."

"That's a fine fellow!" said Mr. Wickfield. "As long as you are glad to be here, you shall stay here."

Doctor Strong's was an excellent school; as different from Mr. Creakle's as good is from evil. It was very gravely and decorously ordered, and on a sound system; with an appeal, in everything, to the honour and good faith of the boys, and an avowed intention to rely on their possession of those qualities unless they proved themselves unworthy of it, which worked wonders.

It was very pleasant to see the Doctor with his pretty young wife. He had a fatherly, benignant way of showing his fondness for her, which seemed in itself to express a good man.

I saw a good deal of Mrs. Strong, both because she had taken a liking to me on the morning of my introduction to the Doctor, and was always afterwards kind to me, and interested in me; and because she was very fond of Agnes, and was often backwards and forwards at our house. There was a curious constraint between her and Mr. Wickfield, I thought (of whom she seemed to be afraid), that never wore off.

Mrs. Strong's mama was a lady I took great delight in. Her name was Mrs. Markleham: but our boys used to call her the Old Soldier.

I observed the Old Soldier—to pretty good advantage, on the night of a little party at the Doctor's, which was given on the occasion of Mr. Jack Maldon's departure for India, whither he was going as a cadet, or something of that kind: Mr. Wickfield having at length arranged the business. It happened to be the Doctor's birthday, too. In the evening, Mr. Wickfield, Agnes, and I, went to have tea with him in his private capacity.

Mr. Jack Maldon was there, before us. Mrs. Strong, dressed in white, with cherry-coloured ribbons, was playing the piano, when we went in; and he was leaning over her to turn the leaves. The clear red and white of her complexion was not so blooming and flower-like as usual, I thought, when she turned round; but she looked very pretty, wonderfully pretty.

"I have forgotten, Doctor," said Mrs. Strong's mama, when we were seated, "to pay you the compliments of the day: though they are, as you may suppose, very far from being mere compliments in my case. Allow me to wish you many happy returns."

"I thank you, ma'am," replied the Doctor.

"Many, many, many, happy returns," said the Old Soldier. "Not only for your own sake, but for Annie's and John Maldon's, and many other people's. It seems but yesterday to me, John, when you were a little creature, a head shorter than Master Copperfield, making baby love to Annie behind the gooseberry bushes in the back-garden."

Some more company coming in, among whom were the two masters and Adams, the talk became general; and it naturally turned on Mr. Jack Maldon, and his voyage, and the country he was going to, and his various plans and prospects. He was to leave that night, after supper, in a post-chaise, for Gravesend; where the ship, in which he was to make the voyage, lay; and was to be gone—unless he came home on leave, or for his health— I don't know how many years.

We had a merry game at cards. Mrs. Strong had declined to play, on the ground of not feeling very well; and her cousin Maldon had excused himself because he had some packing to do. When he had done it, however, he returned, and they sat together, talking, on the sofa.

At supper, we were hardly so gay. Every one appeared to feel that a parting of that sort was an awkward thing, and that the nearer it approached, the more awkward it was.

"It's an affecting thing," said Mrs. Markleham, "however it's viewed, it's affecting, to see a fine young man one has known from an infant, going away to the other end of the world, leaving all he knows behind, and not knowing what's before him."

"Time will go fast with you, Mr. Jack Maldon," pursued the Doctor, "and fast with all of us. Some of us can hardly expect, perhaps, in the natural course of things, to greet you on your return. The next best thing is to hope to do it, and that's my case. I shall not weary you with good advice. You have long had a good model before you, in your cousin Annie. Imitate her virtues as nearly as you can."

Mrs. Markleham fanned herself, and shook her head.

"Farewell, Mr. Jack," said the Doctor, standing up; on which we all stood up. "A prosperous voyage out, a thriving career abroad, and a happy return home!"

We all drank the toast. Mr. Jack Maldon hurried to the door, where he was received, as he got into the chaise, with a tremendous broadside of cheers discharged by our boys. Running in among them to swell the ranks, I was very near the chaise when it rolled away; and I had a lively impression of having seen Mr. Jack Maldon rattle past with an agitated face, and something cherry-coloured in his hand.

I went back into the house, where I found the guests all standing in a group about the Doctor, discussing how Mr. Jack Maldon had gone away. In the midst of these remarks, Mrs. Markleham cried: "Where's Annie?"

We found her lying on the hall floor. There was great alarm at first, until it was found that she was in a swoon. The Doctor, who had lifted her head upon his knee, put her curls aside with his hand, and said, looking around:

"Poor Annie! She's so faithful and tender-hearted! It's the parting from her old playfellow and friend."

We went into the drawing-room, to leave her with the Doctor and her mother; but it seemed that she would rather be brought among us; so they brought her in, looking very white and weak, I thought, and sat her on a sofa.

"Annie, my dear," said her mother, doing something to her dress. "You have lost a bow. Will anybody be so good as find a ribbon; a cherry-coloured ribbon?"

We all looked for it; I myself looked everywhere, I am certain; but nobody could find it.

We walked very slowly home, Mr. Wickfield, Agnes, and I; Agnes and I admiring the moonlight, and Mr. Wickfield scarcely raising his eyes from the ground. When we, at last, reached our own door, Agnes discovered that she had left her little reticule behind. Delighted to be of any service to her, I ran back to fetch it.

The Doctor was sitting in his easy-chair by the fireside, and his young wife was on a stool at his feet. The Doctor, was reading aloud some manuscript, and she was looking up at him. But, with such a face as I never saw. It was so beautiful in its form, it was so ashy pale, it was so fixed in its abstraction, it was so full of a wild, sleep-walking, dreamy horror of I don't know what. The eyes were wide open, and her brown hair fell in two rich clusters on her shoulders, and on her white dress, disordered by the want of the lost ribbon. Distinctly, I recollect her look. Penitence, humiliation, shame, pride, love, and trustfulness, I see them all; and in them all, I see that horror of I don't know what.

My entrance roused her. It disturbed the Doctor too; he was patting her head, in his fatherly way, saying he would have her go to bed.

But she asked him, in a rapid, urgent manner, to let her stay. To let her feel assured that she was in his confidence that night. And, as she turned again towards him, after glancing at me as I left the room and went out at the door, I saw her cross her hands upon his knee, and look up at him with the same face, something quieted, as he resumed his reading.

It made a great impression on me, and I remembered it a long time afterwards, as I shall have occasion to narrate when the time comes.

CHAPTER 17

Somebody Turns Up

IT has not occurred to me to mention Peggotty since I ran away; but, of course, I wrote her a letter almost as soon as I was housed at Dover, and another and a longer letter, containing all particulars fully related, when my aunt took me formally under her protection.

Peggotty replied as promptly.

Mr. Barkis was an excellent husband, she said, though still a little near; but we all had our faults, and she had plenty (though I am sure I don't know what they were); and he sent his duty, and my little bedroom was always ready for me. Mr. Peggotty was well, and Ham was well, and Mrs. Gummidge was but poorly, and little Em'ly wouldn't send her love, but said that Peggotty might send it.

My aunt made several excursions over to Canterbury to see me, and always at unseasonable hours: with the view, I suppose, of taking me by surprise. But, finding me well employed, and bearing a good character, and hearing on all hands that I rose fast in the school, she soon discontinued these visits. I saw her on a Saturday, every third or fourth week, when I went over to Dover for a treat; and I saw Mr. Dick every alternate Wednesday, when he arrived by stage-coach at noon, to stay until next morning.

"Trotwood," said Mr. Dick, with an air of mystery, one Wednesday; "who's the man that hides near our house and frightens her?"

"Frightens my aunt, sir?"

"The first time he came," said Mr. Dick, "was—let me see—sixteen hundred and forty-nine was the date of King Charles's execution. I think you said sixteen hundred and forty-nine?"

"Yes, sir."

"I can't make it out," said Mr. Dick, shaking his head. "There's something wrong, somewhere. However, it was very soon after the mistake was made of putting some of the trouble out of King Charles's head into my head, that the man first came. I was walking out with Miss Trotwood after tea, just at dark, and there he was, close to our house."

"Walking about?" I inquired.

"Walking about?" repeated Mr. Dick. "Let me see. I must recollect a bit. N—no, no; he was not walking about."

I asked, as the shortest way to get at it, what he *was* doing.

"Well, he wasn't there at all," said Mr. Dick, "until he came up behind her, and whispered. Then she turned round and fainted, and I stood still and looked at him, and he walked away; but that he should have been hiding ever since (in the ground or somewhere), is the most extraordinary thing!"

"*Has* he been hiding ever since?" I asked.

"To be sure he has," retorted Mr. Dick, nodding his head gravely. "Never came out, till last night! We were walking last night, and he came up behind her again, and I knew him again."

"And did he frighten my aunt again?"

"All of a shiver," said Mr. Dick, counterfeiting that affection and making his teeth chatter. "Held by the palings. Cried. But Trotwood, come here," getting me close to him, that he might whisper very softly; "why did she give him money, boy, in the moonlight?"

"He was a beggar, perhaps."

Mr. Dick shook his head, as utterly renouncing the suggestion; and having replied a great many times, and with great confidence, "No beggar, no beggar, no beggar, sir!" went on to say, that from his window he had afterwards, and late at night, seen my aunt give this person money outside the garden rails in the moonlight, who then slunk away—into the ground again, as he thought probable—and was seen no more: while my aunt came hurriedly and secretly back into the house, and had, even that morning, been quite different from her usual self; which preyed on Mr. Dick's mind.

After a few Wednesdays, Doctor Strong himself made some inquiries of me about Mr. Dick, and I told him all my aunt had told me; which interested the Doctor so much that he requested, on the occasion of his next visit, to be presented to him. This ceremony I performed; and the Doctor begging Mr. Dick, whensoever he should not find me at the coach-office to come on there, and rest himself until our morning's work was over.

One Thursday morning, Uriah reminded me of the promise I had made to take tea with himself and his mother: adding, with a writhe, "But I didn't expect you to keep it, Master Copperfield, we're so very umble."

I really had not yet been able to make up my mind whether I liked Uriah or detested him; and I was very doubtful about it still, as I stood looking him in the face in the street. But I felt it quite an affront to be supposed proud, and said I only wanted to be asked.

"Oh, if that's all, Master Copperfield," said Uriah, "and it really isn't our umbleness that prevents you, will you come this evening? But if it is our umbleness, I hope you won't mind owning to it, Master Copperfield; for we are all well aware of our condition."

I said I would mention it to Mr. Wickfield, and if he approved, as I had no doubt he would, I would come with pleasure. So, at six o'clock that evening, which was one of the early office evenings, I announced myself as ready, to Uriah.

"Mother will be proud, indeed," he said, as we walked away together, "because we are so very umble."

"Have you been studying much law lately?" I asked, to change the subject.

"Oh, Master Copperfield," he said, with an air of self-denial, "my reading is hardly to be called study. I have passed an hour or two in the evening, sometimes, with Mr. Tidd."

After beating a little tune on his chin as he walked on, with the two forefingers of his skeleton right hand, he added:

"There are expressions, Master Copperfield—Latin words and terms—in Mr. Tidd, that are trying to a reader of my umble attainments."

I said, briskly. "I will teach you Latin with pleasure, as I learn it."

"I am sure it's very kind of you to make the offer, but I am much too umble to accept it. There are people enough to tread upon me in my lowly state, without my doing outrage to their feelings by possessing learning. A person like myself must get on umbly, Master Copperfield."

"I think you are wrong, Uriah," I said. "I dare say there are several things that I could teach you, if you would like to learn them."

"Oh, I don't doubt that, Master Copperfield," he answered; "I won't provoke my betters with knowledge, thank you. I'm much too umble. Here is my umble dwelling, Master Copperfield!"

We entered a low, old-fashioned room, walked straight into from the street, and found there Mrs. Heep, who was the dead image of Uriah, only short. She received me with the utmost humility.

It was perhaps a part of Mrs. Heep's humility, that she still wore weeds.

"This is a day to be remembered, my Uriah, I am sure," said Mrs. Heep, making the tea, "when Master Copperfield pays us a visit."

I was sensible, of being entertained as an honoured guest, and I thought Mrs. Heep an agreeable woman.

"My Uriah," said Mrs. Heep, "has looked forward to this, sir, a long while. He had his fears that our umbleness stood in the way, and I joined in them myself. Umble we are, umble we have been, umble we shall ever be," said Mrs. Heep.

"I am sure you have no occasion to be so, ma'am," I said, "unless you like."

"Thank you, sir," retorted Mrs. Heep. "We know our station and are thankful in it."

Presently they began to talk about aunts, and then I told them about mine; and about fathers and mothers, and then I told them about mine; and then Mrs. Heep began to talk about stepfathers, and then I began to tell her about mine; but stopped, because my aunt had advised me to observe a silence on that subject. A tender young cork, however, would have had no more chance against a pair corkscrews, than I had against Uriah and Mrs. Heep.

I had begun to be a little uncomfortable, and to wish myself well out of the visit, when a figure coming down the street passed the door—it stood open to air the room, which was warm, the weather being close for the time of year—came back again, looked in, and walked in, exclaiming loudly, "Copperfield! Is it possible?"

It was Mr. Micawber! It was Mr. Micawber, with his eyeglass and his walking stick, and his shirt-collar, and his genteel air, and the condescending roll in his voice, all complete!

"My dear Copperfield," said Mr. Micawber, putting out his hand. "Walking along the street, reflecting upon the probability of something turning up, I find a young but valued friend turn up, who is connected with the most eventful period of my life; I may say, with the turning-point of my existence. Copperfield, my dear fellow, how do you do?"

I was glad to see him, and shook hands with him heartily, inquiring how Mrs. Micawber was.

"Thank you," said Mr. Micawber, waving his hand as of old, and settling his chin in his shirt-collar. "She is tolerably convalescent. She will be rejoiced, Copperfield, to renew her acquaintance with one who has proved himself in all respects a worthy minister at the sacred altar of friendship."

I said I should be delighted to see her.

Mr. Micawber then smiled, settled his chin again, and looked about him.

"I have discovered my friend Copperfield, partaking of a social meal in company with a widow lady, and one who is apparently her son. I shall esteem it an honour to be presented."

I could do no less, under these circumstances, than make Mr. Micawber known to Uriah Heep and his mother; which I accordingly did. As they abased themselves before him, Mr. Micawber took a seat, and waved his hand in his most courtly manner.

"Any friend of my friend Copperfield's," said Mr. Micawber, "has a personal claim upon myself."

"We are too umble, sir," said Mrs. Heep, "my son and me, to be the friends of Master Copperfield. He has been so good as to take his tea with us, and we are thankful to him for his company; also to you, sir, for your notice."

"Ma'am," returned Mr. Micawber, with a bow, "you are very obliging: and what are you doing, Copperfield?"

"I am a pupil at Doctor Strong's," I replied.

"A pupil?" said Mr. Micawber, raising his eyebrows. "I am extremely happy to hear it. Although a mind like my friend Copperfield's", (to Uriah and Mrs. Heep) "it is an intellect capable of getting up the classics to any extent."

Uriah, with his long hands slowly twining over one another, made a ghastly writhe from the waist upwards, to express his concurrence in this estimation of me.

"Shall we go and see Mrs. Micawber, sir?" I said, to get Mr. Micawber away.

"If you will do her that favour, Copperfield," replied Mr. Micawber, rising.

It was a little inn where Mr. Micawber occupied a little room. Here, recumbent on a small sofa was Mrs. Micawber.

Mrs. Micawber was amazed, but very glad to see me. I was very glad to see her too, and, after an affectionate greeting on both sides, sat down on the small sofa near her.

When I took my leave of them, they both pressed me so much to come and dine before they went away. Accordingly I was called out of school next forenoon, and found Mr. Micawber in the parlour; who had called to say that the dinner would take place as proposed.

As I was looking out of the window that same evening, it surprised me, and made me rather uneasy, to see Mr. Micawber and Uriah Heep walk past, arm in arm:

"And I'll tell you what, my dear Copperfield," said Mr. Micawber, "your friend Heep is a young fellow who might be attorney-general. If I had known that young man, at the period when my difficulties came to a crisis, all I can say is, that I believe my creditors would have been a great deal better managed than they were."

I hardly understood how this could have been, seeing that Mr. Micawber had paid them nothing at all as it was; but I was uncomfortable about it, too, and often thought about it afterwards.

We had a beautiful little dinner. Quite an elegant dish of fish; the kidney-end of a loin of veal, roasted; fried sausage-meat; a partridge, and a pudding. There was wine, and there was strong ale; and after dinner

Mrs. Micawber made us a bowl of hot punch with her own hands.

I never saw anybody so thoroughly jovial as Mr. Micawber was, down to the very last moment of the evening, when I took a hearty farewell of himself and his amiable wife. Consequently, I was not prepared, at seven o'clock next morning, to receive the following communication, dated half-past nine in the evening; a quarter of an hour after I had left him:—

"MY DEAR YOUNG FRIEND,

"The die is cast—all is over. Under these circumstances, alike humiliating to endure, humiliating to contemplate, and humiliating to relate, I have discharged the pecuniary liability contracted at this establishment, by giving a note of hand, made payable fourteen days after date, at my residence, Pentonville, London. When it becomes due, it will not be taken up. The result is destruction. The bolt is impending, and the tree must fall.

"This is the last communication, my dear Copperfield, you will ever receive "From

"WILKINS MICAWBER."

I was so shocked by the contents of this heartrending letter, that I ran off directly towards the little hotel. But, half way there, I met the London coach with Mr. and Mrs. Micawber up behind; Mr. Micawber, the very picture of tranquil enjoyment, smiling at Mrs. Micawber's conversation, eating walnuts out of a paper bag, with a bottle sticking out of his breast pocket. So, with a great weight taken off my mind, I turned into a by-street that was the nearest way to school, and felt, upon the whole, relieved that they were gone: though I still liked them very much, nevertheless.

CHAPTER 18

I Look About Me, and Make a Discovery

MY aunt and I had held many grave deliberations on the calling to which I should be devoted. For a year or more I had endeavoured to find a satisfactory answer to her often-repeated question, what would I like to be? But I had no particular liking, that I could discover, for anything.

"It has occurred to me," pursued my aunt, "that a little change, and a glimpse of life out of doors, may be useful, in helping you to know your own mind, and form a cooler judgment. Suppose you were to go down into the old part of the country again, for instance, and see that—that out-of-the-way woman with the savagest of names," said my aunt, rubbing her nose, for she could never thoroughly forgive Peggotty for being so called.

I was shortly afterwards fitted out with a handsome purse of money, and a portmanteau, and tenderly dismissed upon my expedition. At parting, my aunt said that as her object was that I should look about me, and should think a little, she would recommend me to stay a few days in London, if I liked it, either on my way down into Suffolk, or in coming back.

I went to Canterbury first, that I might take leave of Agnes and Mr. Wickfield and also of the good Doctor.

Agnes was very glad to see me. We had gone on, so far, in a mixture of confidential jest and earnest, that had long grown naturally out of our familiar relations, begun as mere children. But Agnes, now suddenly lifting up her eyes to mine, and speaking in a different manner, said:

"Trotwood, there is something that I want to ask you. Have you observed any gradual alteration in Papa?"

I had observed it, and had often wondered whether she had too.

"I think he does himself no good by the habit that has increased upon him since I first came here. He is often very nervous, or I fancy so."

"It is not fancy," said Agnes, shaking her head.

"His hand trembles, his speech is not plain, and his eyes look wild. I have remarked that at those times, and when he is least like himself, he is most certain to be wanted on some business."

"By Uriah," said Agnes.

"Yes; and the sense of being unfit for it, or of not having understood it, or of having shown his condition in spite of himself, seems to make him so uneasy, that next day he is worse, and next day worse, and so he becomes jaded and haggard."

Her hand passed softly before my lips while I was yet speaking, and in a moment she had met her father at the door of the room, and was hanging on his shoulder. She was, at once, so proud of him and devoted to him, yet so compassionate and sorry, and so reliant upon me to be so, too; that nothing she could have said would have expressed more to me, or moved me more.

We were to drink tea at the Doctor's. We went there at the usual hour; and round the study-fireside found the Doctor, and his young wife, and her mother.

"I shall not see many more new faces in Trotwood's stead, Wickfield," said the Doctor, warming his hands; "I am getting lazy, and want ease. I shall relinquish all my young people in another six months, and lead a quieter life. I shall have nothing to think of, then, but my Dictionary; and this other contract-bargain—Annie."

Mr. Wickfield glanced towards her, sitting at the tea-table by Agnes.

"There is a post come in from India, I observe," he said, after a short silence.

"By-the-by! and letters from Mr. Jack Maldon!" said the Doctor.

"Poor dear Jack!" said Mrs. Markleham, shaking her head. "That trying climate! He looked strong, but he wasn't. My dear Doctor, it was his spirit, not his constitution, that he ventured on so boldly."

"Do I gather that Mr. Maldon is ill?" asked Mr. Wickfield.

"I'll!" replied the Old Soldier.

"He has had dreadful strokes of the sun, no doubt, and jungle fevers and agues, and every kind of thing you can mention."

"Does he say all this?" asked Mr. Wickfield.

"Say? My dear sir," returned Mrs. Markleham. "Not he. You might drag him at the heels of four wild horses first."

"Mama!" said Mrs. Strong.

"Annie, my dear," returned her mother, "you know as well as I do, that your cousin Maldon would be dragged at the heels of any number of wild horses—rather than say anything calculated to overturn the Doctor's plans."

"Wickfield's plans," said the Doctor, stroking his face, and looking penitently at his adviser. "That is to say, our joint plans for him; I said myself, abroad or at home."

"And I said," added Mr. Wickfield gravely, "abroad. I was the means of sending him abroad. It's my responsibility."

"Oh! Responsibility!" said the Old Soldier.

"Well, well, ma'am," said the Doctor cheerfully. "If Mr. Jack Maldon comes home on account of ill health, he must not be allowed to go back, and we must endeavour to make some more suitable and fortunate provision for him in this country."

Mrs. Markleham was overcome by this generous speech. She gently chid her daughter Annie, for not being more demonstrative when such kindnesses were showered, for her sake, on her old playfellow.

All this time, her daughter Annie never once spoke, or lifted up her eyes on the coffee-room fire. All this time, Mr. Wickfield had his glance upon her as she sat by his own daughter's side. He now asked what Mr. Jack Maldon had actually written in reference to himself, and to whom he had written it?

"Why, here," said Mrs. Markleham, taking a letter from the chimney-piece above the Doctor's head, "the dear fellow says to the Doctor himself—where is it? Oh!—'I am sorry to inform you that my health is suffering severely, and that I fear I may be reduced to the necessity of returning home for a time, as the only hope of restoration.' That's pretty plain, poor fellow! His only hope of restoration! But Annie's letter is plainer still. Annie, show me that letter again."

"Not now, mama," she pleaded in a low tone.

The letter was reluctantly produced; and as I handed it to the old lady, I saw how the unwilling hand from which I took it, trembled.

"Now let us see," said Mrs. Markleham, putting her glass to her eye, "where the passage is. 'The amiable old Proctor'—who's he? Dear me, Annie, how illegibly your cousin Maldon writes, and how stupid I am! 'Doctor,' of course. Ah, amiable indeed! Now I have found it. 'You may not be surprised to hear, Annie,'— 'that I have undergone so much in this distant place, as to have decided to leave it at all hazards; on sick leave, if I can; on total resignation, if that is not to be obtained. What I have endured, and do endure here, is insupportable.' "

Mr. Wickfield said not one word, but sat severely silent, with his eyes fixed on the ground, long after the subject was dismissed.

The evening closed in an incident which I well remember. They were taking leave of each other, and Agnes was going to embrace her and kiss her, when Mr. Wickfield stepped between them, as if by accident, and drew Agnes quickly away. Then I saw, as though all the intervening time had been cancelled, and I were still standing in the doorway on the night of the departure, the expression of that night in the face of Mrs. Strong, as it confronted his.

Now impossible I found it, when I thought of her afterwards, to separate her from this look, and remember her face in its innocent loveliness again. It haunted me when I got home. I seemed to have left the Doctor's roof with a dark cloud lowering on it. The reverence that I had for his grey head, was mingled with commiseration for his faith in those who were treacherous to him, and with resentment against those who injured him. The impending shadow of great affliction, and a great disgrace that had no distinct form in it yet, fell like a stain upon the quiet place where I had worked and played as a boy, and did it a cruel wrong.

I got away from Agnes and her father, somehow, with an indifferent show of being very manly, and took my seat upon the box of the London coach.

We went to the Golden Cross, at Charing Cross, then a mouldy sort of establishment in a close neighbourhood. A waiter showed me into the coffee-room; and a chambermaid introduced me to my small bedchamber, which smelt like a hackney-coach, and was shut up like a family vault.

Then I resolved to go to the play. It was Covent Garden Theatre that I chose; and there, from the back of a centre box, I saw Julius Cæsar and the new Pantomime.

When I came out into the rainy street, at twelve o'clock at night, I felt as if I had come from the clouds, where I had been leading a romantic life for ages, to a bawling, splashing, link-lighted, umbrella-struggling, hackney-coach-jostling, patten-clinking, muddy, miserable world.

I had emerged by another door, but the unceremonious pushing and hustling that I received, soon recalled me to myself, and put me in the road back to the hotel; where after some porter and oysters, I sat, with my eyes on the coffee-room fire.

I was so filled with the play, that I don't know when the figure of a handsome well-formed young man, dressed with a tasteful easy negligence which I have reason to remember very well, became a real presence to me. But I recollect being conscious of his company.

At last I rose to go to bed. In going towards the door, I passed the person who had come in, and saw him plainly.

"Steerforth! won't you speak to me?"

He looked at me—but I saw no recognition in his face.

"You don't remember me, I am afraid," said I.

"My God!" he suddenly exclaimed. "It's little Copperfield!"

I grasped him by both hands, and could not let them go. But for very shame, and the fear that it might displease him, I could have held him round the neck and cried.

"My dear Steerforth, I am so overjoyed to see you!"

"And I am rejoiced to see you, too!" he said, shaking my hands heartily.

"Why, how do you come to be here?" and he clapped me on the shoulder.

"I came here by the Canterbury coach, to-day. I have been adopted by an aunt down in that part of the country, and have just finished my education there. How do *you* come to be here, Steerforth?"

"Well, I am what they call an Oxford man," he returned; "that is to say, I get bored to death down there, periodically—and I am on my way now to my mother's. You're a devilish amiable-looking fellow, Copperfield. Just what you used to be, now I look at you! Not altered in the least!"

"I knew you immediately," I said; "but you are more easily remembered."

"I have been at the play," said I. "At Covent Garden. What a delightful and magnificent entertainment, Steerforth!"

Steerforth laughed heartily.

"My dear young Davy," he said, clapping me on the shoulder again, "I have been at Covent Garden, too, and there never was a more miserable business. Holloa, you sir!"

This was addressed to the waiter, who now came forward deferentially.

"Where have you put my friend, Mr. Copperfield?" said Steerforth. "What's his number? You know what I mean," said Steerforth.

"Well, sir," said the waiter, with an apologetic air. "Mr. Copperfield is at present in forty-four, sir."

"And what the devil do you mean," retorted Steerforth, "by putting Mr. Copperfield into a little loft over a stable?"

"Why, you see we wasn't aware, sir," returned the waiter, still apologetically, "as Mr. Copperfield was anyways particular. We can give Mr. Copperfield seventy-two, sir, if it would be preferred. Next you, sir."

"Of course it would be preferred," said Steerforth. "And do it at once."

The waiter immediately withdrew to make the exchange. Steerforth, very much amused at my having been put into forty-four, laughed again, and clapped me on the shoulder again, and invited me to breakfast with him the following morning at ten o'clock.

CHAPTER 19

Steerforth's Home

IT was not in the coffee-room that I found Steerforth expecting me, but in a snug private apartment, red-curtained and Turkey-carpeted, where the fire burnt bright, and a fine hot breakfast was set forth on a table covered with a clean cloth.

"Now, Copperfield," said Steerforth, when we were alone, "I should like to hear what you are doing, and where you are going, and all about you. I feel as if you were my property."

Glowing with pleasure to find that he had still this interest in me, I told him how my aunt had proposed the little expedition that I had before me, and whither it tended.

"As you are in no hurry, then," said Steerforth, "come home with me to Highgate, and stay a day or two. You will be pleased with my mother—she is a little vain and prosy about me, but that you can forgive her—and she will be pleased with you."

After I had written to my aunt and told her of my fortunate meeting with my admired old school-fellow, and my acceptance of his invitation, we went out in a hackney-chariot, and saw a Panorama and some other sights, and took a walk through the Museum, where I could not help observing how much Steerforth knew.

"You'll take a high degree at college, Steerforth," said I, "if you have not done so already."

"Not I! My dear Daisy—will you mind my calling you Daisy? That's a good fellow! My dear Daisy," said Steerforth, laughing, "I have not the least desire or intention to distinguish myself in that way. I have done quite sufficient for my purpose."

I was abashed at having made so great a mistake, and was glad to change the subject. Fortunately it was not difficult to do, for Steerforth could always pass from one subject to another with a carelessness and lightness that were his own.

Lunch succeeded to our sight-seeing, and the short winter day wore away so fast, that it was dusk when the stage-coach stopped with us at an old brick house at Highgate on the summit of the hill. An elderly lady, though not very far advanced in years, with a proud carriage and a handsome face, was in the doorway as we alighted; and greeting Steerforth as "My dearest James," folded him in her arms. To this lady he presented me as his mother, and she gave me a stately welcome.

There was a second lady in the dining-room, of a slight short figure, dark, but with some appearance of good looks too. She had black hair and eager black eyes, and was thin, and had a scar upon her lip. It was an old scar—I should rather call it, seam, for it was not discoloured, and had healed years ago—which had once cut through her mouth, downward towards the chin, but was now barely visible across the table, except above and on her upper lip, the shape of which it had altered. I concluded in my own mind that she was about thirty years of age, and that she wished to be married. Her thinness seemed to be the effect of some wasting fire within her, which found a vent in her gaunt eyes.

She was introduced as Miss Dartle, and both Steerforth and his mother called her Rosa. I found that she lived there, and had been for a long time Mrs. Steerforth's companion.

When the evening was pretty far spent, and a tray of glasses and decanters came in, Steerforth promised, over the fire, that he would seriously think of going down into the country with me. There was no hurry, he said; a week hence would do; and his mother hospitably said the same.

While we were talking, he more than once called me Daisy; which brought Miss Dartle out again.

"But really, Mr. Copperfield," she asked, "is it a nickname? And why does he give it you? Is it—eh?—because he thinks you young and innocent? I am so stupid in these things."

I coloured in replying that I believed it was.

"Oh!" said Miss Dartle. "Now I am glad to know that! I ask for information, and I am glad to know it. He thinks you young and innocent; and so you are his friend? Well, that's quite delightful!"

She went to bed soon after this, and Mrs. Steerforth retired too. Steerforth and I, after lingering for half an hour over the fire, talking about Traddles and all the rest of them at old Salem House, went up-stairs together.

CHAPTER 20

Little Em'ly

THERE was a servant in that house, a man who, I understood, was usually with Steerforth, and had come into his service at the University, who was in appearance a pattern of respectability. He was taciturn, soft-footed, very quiet in his manner, deferential, observant, always at hand when wanted.

Such a self-contained man I never saw. Even the fact that no one knew his Christian name, seemed to form a part of his respectability. Nothing could be objected against his surname, Littimer, by which he was known.

Littimer was in my room in the morning before I was up, to bring me that reproachful shaving-water, and to put out my clothes.

"Is there anything more I can have the honour of doing for you, sir? The warning-bell will ring at nine; the family take breakfast at half-past nine."

"Nothing, I thank you."

"I thank *you*, sir, if you please"; and with that, and with a little inclination of his head, as an apology for correcting me, he went out.

Every morning we held exactly this conversation: never any more, and never any less.

He got horses for us; Steerforth gave me lessons in riding. He provided foils for us. Steerforth gave me lessons in fencing—gloves, and I began, of the same master, to improve in boxing.

But I never could bear to show my want of skill before the respectable Littimer. I had no reason to believe that Littimer understood such arts himself; yet whenever he was by, while we were practising, I felt myself the greenest and most inexperienced of mortals.

I am particular about this man, because he made a particular effect on me at that time, and because of what took place thereafter.

The week passed away in a most delightful manner. Steerforth at its close made up his mind to go with me into the country, and the day arrived for our departure. We went down by the Mail.

I gave Steerforth minute directions for finding the residence of Mr. Barkis, carrier to Blunderstone and elsewhere; and, on this understanding, went out alone when we arrived at Yarmouth, and went to my dear old Peggotty's.

Here she was, in the tiled kitchen, cooking dinner! The moment I knocked at the door she opened it, and asked me what I pleased to want. I looked at her with a smile, but she gave me no smile in return. I had never ceased to write to her, but it must have been seven years since we had met.

"Is Mr. Barkis at home, ma'am?" I said, feigning to speak roughly to her.

"He's at home, sir," returned Peggotty, "but he's bad abed with the rheumatics."

"Don't he go over to Blunderstone now?" I asked.

"When he's well he do," she answered.

"Do *you* ever go there, Mrs. Barkis? Because I want to ask a question about a house there, that they call the—what is it?—the Rookery," said I.

She took a step backward, and put out her hands in an undecided frightened way, as if to keep me off.

"Peggotty!" I cried to her.

She cried, "My darling boy!" and we both burst into tears, and were locked in one another's arms.

What extravagancies she committed; what laughing and crying over me.

"Barkis will be so glad," said Peggotty, wiping her eyes with her apron, "that it'll do him more good than pints of liniment."

He received me with enthusiasm. He was too rheumatic to be shaken hands with, but he begged me to shake the tassel on the top of his nightcap, which I did most cordially. As he lay in bed, face upward, and so covered, with that exception, that he seemed to be nothing but a face—like a conventional cherubim—he looked the queerest object I ever beheld.

"What name was it as I wrote up in the cart, sir?" said Mr. Barkis, with a slow rheumatic smile.

"Ah! Mr. Barkis, we had some grave talks about that matter, didn't we?"

"I was willin' a long time, sir?" said Mr. Barkis.

"A long time," said I.

"And I don't regret it," said Mr. Barkis.

I prepared Peggotty for Steerforth's arrival, and it was not long before he came. His manner to me, alone, would have won her. But he bound her to him wholly in five minutes. I sincerely believe she had a kind of adoration for him before he left the house that night.

"Of course," he said. "You'll sleep here, while we stay, and I shall sleep at the hotel."

He maintained all his delightful qualities to the last, until we started forth, at eight o'clock, for Mr. Peggotty's boat. Indeed, they were more and more brightly exhibited as the hours went on. If any one had told me, then, that all this was a brilliant game, played for the excitement of the moment, in the thoughtless love of superiority, in a careless course of winning, what was worthless to him, and next minute thrown away, I wonder in what manner of receiving it my indignation would have found a vent!

Approaching the light, we made softly for the door. I laid my hand upon the latch; and whispering Steerforth to keep close to me, went in.

A murmur of voices had been audible on the outside, and, at the moment of our entrance, a clapping of hands: which latter noise, I was surprised to see, proceeded from the generally disconsolate Mrs. Gummidge. Mr. Peggotty, his face lighted up with uncommon satisfaction, and laughing with all his might, held his rough arms wide open, as if for little Em'ly to run into them; Ham, with a mixed expression in his face of admiration, exultation, and a lumbering sort of bashfulness that sat upon him very well, held little Em'ly by the hand, as if he were presenting her to Mr. Peggotty; little Em'ly herself, blushing and shy, but delighted with Mr. Peggotty's delight, as her joyous eyes expressed, was stopped by our entrance in the very act of springing from Ham to nestle in Mr. Peggotty's embrace.

The little picture was instantaneously dissolved by our going in. I was in the midst of the astonished family, face to face with Mr. Peggotty, and holding out my hand to him, when Ham shouted:

"Mas'r Davy! It's Mas'r Davy!"

In a moment we were all shaking hands with one another, and asking one another how we did. Mr. Peggotty was so proud and joyful to see us, that he did not know what to say or do, but kept over and over again shaking hands with me, and then with Steerforth.

"Why, that you two gent'lmen—gent'lmen growed—should come to this here roof to-night, of all nights in my life," said Mr. Peggotty. "Em'ly, my darling, come here! There's Mas'r Davy's friend, my dear! There's the gent'lman as you've heerd on, Em'ly. He comes to see you, along with Mas'r Davy, on the brightest night of your uncle's life."

"There was a certain person as had know'd our Em'ly, from the time when her father was drownded; as had seen her constant; when a babby, when a young gal, when a woman. Not much of a person to look at, he warn't," said Mr. Peggotty, "him—wery salt—but, on the whole, a honest sort of a chap, with his art in the right place."

"What does this here blessed tarpaulin go and do," said Mr. Peggotty, with his face one high noon of enjoyment, "but he loses that there art of his to our little Em'ly. Now I could wish, that our little Em'ly was in a fair way of being married to a honest man as had a right to defend her. I know that if I was capsized, any night, in a gale of wind in Yarmouth Roads here, I could go down quieter for thinking 'There's a man ashore there, irontrue to my little Em'ly.' "

So *I* speak. "What! *Him!*" says Em'ly. "Oh, Uncle! I never can have *him*. He's such a good fellow!"

"All of a sudden, one evening—this tarpaulin chap, he takes hold of her hand, and he cries out to me, joyful, 'Look here! This is to be my little wife!' And she says, half bold and half shy, and half a laughing and a half a crying, 'Yes, Uncle! If you please. I am steadier now, and I have thought better of it, and I'll be as good a little wife as I can to him, for he's a dear, good fellow!' Then you come in! It took place this here present hour; and here's the man that'll marry her."

Ham said, with much faltering and great difficulty:

"I—I love her true. There ain't a gent'lman in all the land—nor yet sailing upon all the sea—that can love his lady more than I love her."

If it had depended upon me to touch the prevailing chord among them with any skill, I should have made a poor hand of it. But it depended upon Steerforth.

"Mr. Peggotty," he said, "you are a thoroughly good fellow, and deserve to be as happy as you are to-night. Ham, I give you joy, my boy. Mr. Peggotty, induce your gentle niece to come back."

So Mr. Peggotty went into my old room to fetch little Em'ly very much confused, and very shy—but she soon became more assured when she found how gently and respectfully Steerforth spoke to her.

It was almost midnight when we took our leave. We parted merrily and they all stood crowded round the door to light us as far as they could upon our road.

"A most engaging little Beauty!" said Steerforth, taking my arm. "Well! It's a quaint place, and they are quaint company; and it's quite a new sensation to mix with them. That's rather a chuckle-headed fellow for the girl; isn't he?"

"Ah, Steerforth! When I see how perfectly you can enter into happiness like this plain fisherman's, or humour a love like my old nurse's, I know that there is not an emotion, of such people, that can be indifferent to you.

100

And I admire you and love you for it."

He stopped, and looking in my face, said: "Daisy, I believe you are in earnest, and are good. I wish we all were!"

CHAPTER 21

Some Old Scenes, and Some New People

STEERFORTH and I stayed for more than a fortnight in that part of the country. We were very much together, I need not say; but occasionally we were asunder for some hours at a time. He was a good sailor, and I was but an indifferent one; and when he went out boating with Mr. Peggotty, which was a favourite amusement of his, I generally remained ashore.

On three or four days that I can at once recall, we went our several ways after an early breakfast, and met again at a late dinner. I had no idea how he employed his time, beyond a general knowledge that he was very popular in the place.

One dark evening, when I was later than usual—for I had, that day, been making my parting visit to Blunderstone, as we were now about to return home—I found him alone in Mr. Peggotty's house, sitting thoughtfully before the fire. He was so intent upon his own reflections that he was quite unconscious of my approach.

He gave such a start when I put my hand upon his shoulder, that he made me start too.

"You come upon me," he said, almost angrily, "like a reproachful ghost!"

"I was obliged to announce myself, somehow," I replied.

"I have been sitting here," said Steerforth, glancing round the room, "thinking after strolling to the ferry looking for you. I strolled in here and found the place deserted. That set me thinking, and you found me thinking. And so," he said, "we abandon this buccaneer life to-morrow, do we?"

"So we agreed," I returned. "And our places by the coach are taken, you know."

"Ay! there's no help for it, I suppose," said Steerforth. "I have almost forgotten that there is anything to do in the world but to go out tossing on the sea here. I wish there was not."

"That amazes me most in you, Steerforth—that you should be contented with such fitful uses of your powers."

"Contented?" he answered merrily. "I am never contented, except with your freshness, my gentle Daisy. You know I have bought a boat down here?"

"What an extraordinary fellow you are, Steerforth!" I exclaimed, stopping—for this was the first I had heard of it. "When you may never care to come near the place again!"

"I have taken a fancy to the place. I have bought a boat that was for sale—and Mr. Peggotty will be master of her in my absence."

"Steerforth!" said I, exultingly. "You pretend to have bought it for yourself, but you have really done so to confer a benefit on him."

"She must be newly rigged," said Steerforth, "and I shall leave Littimer behind to see it done. Did I tell you Littimer had come down this morning, with a letter from my mother?"

"The same as ever?" said I.

"The same as ever," said Steerforth. "Distant and quiet as the North Pole. He shall see to the boat being fresh named. I'll have her christened again."

"By what name?" I asked.

"The Little Em'ly."

"But see here," he said, looking before us, "where the original little Em'ly comes! And that fellow with her, eh? Upon my soul, he's a true knight. He never leaves her!"

Ham looked rugged enough, but manly withal, and a very fit protector for the blooming little creature at his side. Indeed, there was a frankness in his face, an honesty, and an undisguised show of his pride in her, and his love for her.

She withdrew her hand timidly from his arm as we stopped to speak to them, and blushed as she gave it to Steerforth and to me. Then they passed on.

Suddenly there passed us—evidently following them—a young woman whose approach we had not observed, but whose face I saw as she went by, and thought I had a faint remembrance of.

"That is a black shadow to be following the girl," said Steerforth, standing still; "what does it mean?"

He spoke in a low voice that sounded almost strange to me.

"She must have it in her mind to beg of them, I think," said I.

"A beggar would be no novelty," said Steerforth; "but it is a strange thing that the beggar should take that shape to-night."

"Why?" I asked him.

"For no better reason, truly, than because I was thinking," he said, after a pause, "of something like it, when it came by. Where the Devil did it come from, I wonder!"

"From the shadow of this wall, I think," said I, as we emerged upon a road on which a wall abutted.

"It's gone!" he returned, looking over his shoulder. "And all ill go with it. Now for our dinner!"

She was the principal theme of our conversation during the evening; until we parted for the night.

I was surprised, when I came to Mr. Barkis's house, to find Ham walking up and down in front of it.

"Why, you see, Mas'r Davy," he rejoined, in a hesitating manner,

"Em'ly, she's talking to some 'un in here. It's a young woman, sir—a young woman, that Em'ly knowed once, and doen't ought to know no more."

When I heard these words, a light began to fall upon the figure I had seen following them, some hours ago.

"It's a poor woman, Mas'r Davy," said Ham, "as is trod under foot by all the town."

"Did I see her to-night, Ham, on the sands, after we met you?"

"It's like you did, Mas'r Davy. Not that I know'd then, she was theer, sir, but along of her creeping soon arterwards under Em'ly's little winder, when she see the light come, and whisp'ring 'Em'ly, Em'ly, for Christ's sake, have a woman's heart towards me. I was once like you!' "

"What did Em'ly do?"

"Says Em'ly, 'Martha, is it you? Oh, Martha, can it be you!' Martha Endell," said Ham. "Two or three year older than Em'ly, but was at the school with her.

"She wanted to speak to Em'ly. Em'ly couldn't speak to her theer, for her loving uncle was come home. He couldn't, kind-natured, tender-hearted as he is, see them two together, side by side, for all the treasures that's wrecked in the sea."

I felt how true this was. I knew it, on the instant, quite as well as Ham.

"So Em'ly writes in pencil on a bit of paper," he pursued, "and gives it to her out o' window to bring here. 'Show that,' she says, 'to my aunt, Mrs. Barkis, and she'll set you down by her fire, for the love of me, till uncle is gone out, and I can come.' By-and-by she tells me, and asks me to bring her. She doesn't ought to know any such, but I can't deny her, when the tears is on her face."

He put his hand into the breast of his shaggy jacket, and took out with great care a pretty little purse.

"And how could I deny her when she give me this to carry for her—knowing what she brought it for?" said Ham, thoughtfully looking on it. "With such a little money in it, Em'ly my dear!"

The door opened then, and Peggotty appeared, beckoning to Ham to come in. I would have kept away, but she came after me, entreating me to come in too.

The girl—the same I had seen upon the sands—was near the fire. I saw but little of the girl's face, over which her hair fell loose and scattered, as if she had been disordering it with her own hands; but I saw that she was young, and of a fair complexion. Peggotty had been crying. So had little Em'ly.

Em'ly spoke first.

"Martha wants," she said to Ham, "to go to London."

"Why to London?" returned Ham.

They both spoke in a soft, suppressed tone that was plainly heard, although it hardly rose above a whisper.

"Better there than here," said a third voice aloud—Martha's, though she did not move. "Everybody knows me here."

"What will she do there?" inquired Ham.

"She will try to do well," said little Em'ly.

"I'll try," said Martha, "if you'll help me away. I never can do worse than I have done here." With a dreadful shiver, "Take me out of these streets, where the whole town knows me from a child!"

As Em'ly held out her hand to Ham, I saw him put in it a little canvas bag.

"It's all yourn, Em'ly," I could hear him say. "I haven't nowt in all the wureld that ain't yourn, my dear."

The tears rose freshly in her eyes, but she turned away and went to Martha. I saw her stooping over her, and putting money in her bosom. She asked was that enough? "More than enough," the other said, and took her hand and kissed it.

Then Martha arose, and gathering her shawl about her, covering her face with it, and weeping aloud, went slowly to the door. Making the same low, dreary, wretched moaning in her shawl, she went away.

As the door closed, little Em'ly looked at us three in a hurried manner, and then hid her face in her hands, and fell to sobbing.

"Doen't Em'ly!" said Ham, tapping her gently on the shoulder.

"Oh, Ham!" she exclaimed, still weeping pitifully, "I am not as good a girl as I ought to be! And still she cried, as if her heart would break.

CHAPTER 22

I Corroborate Mr. Dick, and Choose a Profession

WHILE we were at breakfast, a letter was delivered to me from my aunt. As it contained matter on which I thought Steerforth could advise me as well as anyone, and on which I knew I should be delighted to consult him, I resolved to make it a subject of discussion on our journey home. We departed to the regret and admiration of all concerned, and left a great many people very sorry behind us.

"Do you stay long here, Littimer?" said I, as he stood waiting to see the coach start.

"No, sir," he replied; "probably not very long, sir."

"He can hardly say, just now," observed Steerforth, carelessly. "He knows what he has to do, and he'll do it."

"That I am sure he will," said I.

For some little time we held no conversation, Steerforth being unusually silent. At length, Steerforth pulled me by the arm:

"Find a voice, David. What about the letter you were speaking of at breakfast?"

"Oh!" said I, taking it out of my pocket. "It's from my aunt."

"She reminds me, Steerforth," said I, "that I came out on this expedition to look about me, and to think a little. To tell you the truth, I am afraid I had forgotten it."

"What says your aunt on the subject?" inquired Steerforth, glancing at the letter in my hand. "Does she suggest anything?"

"She asks me here, if I think I should like to be a proctor."

"That's a proceeding," said Steerforth, "deserving of all encouragement. My advice is that you take kindly to Doctors' Commons."

I quite made up my mind to do so. My aunt was in town awaiting me. She had taken lodgings for a week at a kind of private hotel in Lincoln's Inn Fields.

When we came to our journey's end, Steerforth went home, engaging to call upon me next day but one; and I drove to Lincoln's Inn Fields. My aunt cried outright as she embraced me.

"So you have left Mr. Dick behind, aunt?" said I. "I am sorry for that."

Supper consisted of a roast fowl, a steak, and some vegetables, to all of which I did ample justice. When the table was cleared, my aunt sat opposite me.

"Well, Trot," she began, "what do you think of the proctor plan?"

"I have thought a good deal about it, my dear aunt. I like it very much indeed. I have only one difficulty, aunt."

"Say what it is, Trot," she returned.

"Why whether my entrance would not be very expensive?"

"It will cost, to article you, just a thousand pounds."

"Now, my dear aunt," said I, drawing my chair nearer, "I am uneasy in my mind about that. It's a large sum of money. You have been the soul of generosity. Are you certain that you can afford to part with so much money?"

"Trot, my child, if I have any object in life, it is to provide for your being a good, a sensible, and a happy man. I have no other claim upon my means; at least"—here to my surprise she hesitated, and was confused—"no, I have *no* other claim upon my means—and you are my adopted child."

At about mid-day, we set out for the office of Messrs. Spenlow and Jorkins, in Doctors' Commons. My aunt, who had the opinion that every man was a pick-pocket, gave me her purse to carry, which had ten guineas in it and some silver.

We made a pause in Fleet Street—and then went on towards Ludgate Hill and St. Paul's Churchyard. We were crossing to the former place, when I found that my aunt greatly accelerated her speed, and looked frightened. At the same time, a glowering ill-dressed man, was coming so close after us, as to brush against her.

"Trot!" cried my aunt, in a terrified whisper. "What am I to do?"

"Don't be alarmed," said I. "I'll soon get rid of this fellow."

"No, no, child. Don't speak to him for the world."

"Good Heaven, aunt!" said I. "He is nothing but a sturdy beggar."

"You don't know who he is! You don't know what you say! Get me a coach, and wait for me in St. Paul's Churchyard."

"Wait for you?" I repeated.

"Yes," rejoined my aunt. "I must go alone. I must go with him."

I called a hackney chariot which was passing empty. Almost before I could let down the steps, my aunt sprang in, and the man followed. Confounded as I was, I turned from them. In doing so, I heard her say, "Drive anywhere! Drive straight on!"

What Mr. Dick had told me, now came into my mind. I could not doubt that this was the person of whom he had made such mysterious mention. After half an hour I saw the chariot coming back. My aunt was sitting in it alone.

She said no more, except, "My dear child, never ask me what it was, and don't refer to it." On her giving me her purse, to pay the driver, I found that all the guineas were gone, and only the loose silver remained.

Doctors' Commons was approached by a little low archway. A few dull courts and narrow ways brought us to the sky-lighted offices of Spenlow and Jorkins. A little dry man, who wore a stiff brown wig that looked as if it were made of gingerbread, rose to show us into Mr. Spenlow's room.

"Mr. Spenlow's in Court, ma'am," said the dry man; "it's an Arches day; but it's close by, and I'll send for him directly."

We were left to look about us while Mr. Spenlow was fetched. I was casting my eyes over many objects, when hasty footsteps were heard in the room outside, and Mr. Spenlow, in a black gown trimmed with white fur, came hurrying in, taking off his hat as he came.

He was a little light-haired gentleman, with the stiffest of white cravats and shirt-collars. He was buttoned up mighty trim and tight. He now said:

"And so, Mr. Copperfield, I casually mentioned to Miss Trotwood—that there was a vacancy here. Miss Trotwood was good enough to mention that she had a nephew for whom she was seeking to provide genteelly in life. That nephew, I believe, I have now the pleasure of"—

I bowed my acknowledgements, and said my aunt had mentioned to me that there was that opening, and that I believed I should like it very much.

"We always, in this house, propose a month—an initiatory month. I should be happy, myself, to propose two months—three—an indefinite period, in fact—but I have a partner. Mr. Jorkins."

"And the premium, sir," I returned, "is a thousand pounds."

It was settled that I should begin my month's probation as soon as I pleased.

We arrived at Lincoln's Inn Fields without any new adventures. We had another long talk about my plans.

"There is a furnished little set of chambers to be let in the Adelphi, Trot, which ought to suit you to a marvel."

She produced from her pocket an advertisement, setting forth that in Buckingham Street in the Adelphi there was to be let furnished, with a view of the river, a singularly desirable and compact set of chambers, forming a genteel residence for a young gentleman.

"Why, this is the very thing, aunt!" said I, flushed with the possible dignity of living in chambers.

"Then come," replied my aunt, immediately resuming the bonnet she had a minute before laid aside. "We'll go and look at 'em."

They were on the top of the house—and consisted of a little half-blind pantry, a sitting-room and a bed-room. The furniture was rather faded; and, sure enough, the river was outside the windows.

My aunt, seeing how enraptured I was with the premises, took them for a month, with leave to remain for twelve months when that time was out.

On our way back, my aunt informed me how she confidently trusted that the life I was now to lead would make me firm and self-reliant, and that she had made a handsome provision for all my possible wants during my month of trial.

CHAPTER 23

My First Dissipation

AFTER two days and nights, I felt as if I had lived there for a year.

Steerforth not yet appearing, which induced me to apprehend that he must be ill, I left the Commons early on the third day, and walked out to Highgate. Mrs. Steerforth was very glad to see me, and said that he had gone away with one of his Oxford friends to see another who lived near St. Albans, but that she expected him to return to-morrow.

As she pressed me to stay to dinner, I remained. I told her how much the people liked him at Yarmouth, and what a delightful companion he had been. Miss Dartle was full of hints and mysterious questions, but took a great interest in all our proceedings there.

I was taking my coffee and roll in the morning, before going to the Commons—when Steerforth himself walked in.

I showed him over the establishment. "I tell you what, old boy," he said, "I shall make quite a town-house of this place, unless you give me notice to quit."

This was a delightful hearing.

"But you shall have some breakfast!" said I, with my hand on the bell-rope.

"No, no!" said Steerforth. "I am going to breakfast with one of these fellows who is at the Piazza Hotel, in Covent Garden."

"But you'll come back to dinner?" said I.

"There's nothing I should like better, but I *must* remain with these two fellows. We are all off tomorrow morning."

"Then bring them here to dinner," I returned. "Do you think they would come?"

"You had better come and dine with us somewhere."

I would not by any means consent to this, for it occurred to me that I really ought to have a little house-warming. I therefore made him promise positively in the names of his two friends, and we appointed six o'clock as the dinner-hour.

They were both very gay and lively fellows. Being a little embarrassed at first, I made Steerforth take the head of the table when dinner was announced, and seated myself opposite to him. Everything was very good; we did not spare the wine; and he exerted himself so brilliantly to make the thing pass off well, that there was no pause in our festivity.

I went on, passing the wine faster and faster yet, and continually starting up with a corkscrew to open more wine, long before any was needed.

Somebody was leaning out of my bed-room window, refreshing his forehead against the cool stone of the parapet, and feeling the air upon his face. It was myself. Now, somebody was unsteadily contemplating his features in the looking-glass. That was I too.

Somebody said to me, "Let us go to the theatre, Copperfield!"

Shortly afterwards, we were very high up in a very hot theatre, looking down into a large pit, that seemed to me to smoke; the people with whom it was crammed were so indistinct.

On somebody's motion, we resolved to go down-stairs to the dress-boxes, where the ladies were. Then I was being ushered into one of these boxes, and found myself saying something as I sat down, and people about me crying "Silence!" to somebody, and ladies casting indignant glances at me, and—what! yes!—Agnes, sitting on the seat before me, in the same box, with a lady and gentleman beside her, whom I didn't know.

"Agnes!" I said, thickly, "Lorblessmer! Agnes!"

"Hush! Pray!" she answered, I could not conceive why. "You disturb the company. Look at the stage!"

I tried, on her injunction, to fix it, and to hear something of what was going on there, but quite in vain. I looked at her again by-and-by, and saw her shrink into her corner, and put her gloved hand to her forehead.

"I know you will do as I ask you, if I tell you I am very earnest in it. Go away now, Trotwood, for my sake, and ask your friends to take you home."

I felt ashamed, and with a short "Goori!" (which I intended for "Goodnight!") got up and went away.

They followed, and I stepped at once out of the box-door into my bedroom, where only Steerforth was with me, helping me to undress, and where I was by turns telling him that Agnes was my sister, and adjuring him to bring the corkscrew, that I might open another bottle of wine.

But the agony of mind, the remorse I felt, when I became conscious next day! My disgust at the very sight of the room where the revel had been held—my racking head—the smell of smoke, the sight of glasses, the impossibility of going out, or even getting up! Oh, what a day it was!

CHAPTER 24

Good and Bad Angels

I WAS going out at my door on the morning after that deplorable day, when I saw a ticket-porter coming up-stairs, with a letter in his hand.

"T. Copperfield, Esquire," said the ticket-porter, touching his hat with his little cane.

I told him I was T. Copperfield, Esquire, and he believed it, and gave me the letter, which he said required an answer.

All it said was, "My dear Trotwood. I am staying at the house of papa's agent, Mr. Waterbrook, in Ely Place, Holborn. Will you come and see me to-day, at any time you like to appoint? Ever yours affectionately, AGNES."

The professional business of Mr. Waterbrook's establishment was done on the ground floor. I was shown into a pretty but rather close drawing-room, and there sat Agnes.

"If it had been any one but you, Agnes," said I, turning away my head, "I should not have minded it half so much. But that it should have been you who saw me! I almost wish I had been dead, first."

"Sit down," said Agnes, cheerfully. "Don't be unhappy, Trotwood. If you cannot confidently trust me, whom will you trust?"

"Ah, Agnes!" I returned. "You are my good Angel!"

"If I were, Trotwood," she returned, "there is one thing that I should set my heart on: warning you," said Agnes with a steady glance, "against your bad Angel."

"My dear Agnes," I began, "if you mean Steerforth—is it not unjust, and unlike you, to judge him from what you saw of me the other night?"

I saw a passing shadow on her face when I made this mention of him, but she returned my smile, and we were again as unreserved in our mutual confidence as of old.

"And when, Agnes," said I, "will you forgive me the other night?"

"When I recall it," said Agnes.

Then she asked me if I had seen Uriah.

"Uriah Heep?" said I. "No. Is he in London?"

"He comes to the office down-stairs, every day," returned Agnes. "He was in London a week before me, I am afraid on disagreeable business, Trotwood."

"On some business that makes you uneasy, Agnes, I see," said I. "What can that be?"

"I believe he is going to enter into partnership with papa."

"What? Uriah? That mean, fawning fellow, worm himself into such promotion!" I cried, indignantly.

"Let me earnestly entreat you, Trotwood, to be friendly to Uriah. Don't resent what may be uncongenial to you in him. He may not deserve it, for we know no certain ill of him. In any case, think first of papa and me!"

Agnes had no time to say more, for the room-door opened, and Mrs. Waterbrook came in. I had a dim recollection of having seen her at the theatre; but she appeared to remember me perfectly, and still to suspect me of being in a state of intoxication.

Finding by degrees, however, that I was sober, Mrs. Waterbrook softened towards me considerably, and invited me to dinner next day.

I accepted the invitation, and took my leave, making a call on Uriah in the office as I went out, and leaving a card for him in his absence.

I found Uriah Heep among the company, in a suit of black, and in deep humility. He told me, when I shook hands with him, that he was proud to be noticed by me, and that he really felt obliged to me for my condescension.

There were other guests.—But, there was one who attracted my attention before he came in, on account of my hearing him announced as Mr. Traddles! Could it be Tommy, who used to draw the skeletons!

I looked for Mr. Traddles with unusual interest. He was a sober, steady-looking young man of retiring manners and either my vision deceived me, or it was the old unfortunate Tommy.

When dinner was announced. Uriah, Traddles, and I, as the junior part of the company, went down last. I was not so vexed at losing Agnes as I might have been, since it gave me an opportunity of making myself known to Traddles on the stairs, who greeted me with great fervour.

As she was not among people with whom I believed she could be very much at home, I was almost glad to hear that she was going away within a few days, though I was sorry at the prospect of parting from her again so soon. This caused me to remain until all the company were gone. Conversing with her, and hearing her sing, was such a delightful reminder to me of my happy life in the grave old house she had made so beautiful, that I could have remained there half the night; but, having no excuse for staying any longer, I took my leave very much against my inclination. I felt then, more than ever, that she was my better Angel.

The company were all gone except Uriah, who had never ceased to hover near us. He was close behind me when I went down-stairs. He was close beside me, when I walked away from the house.

In remembrance of the entreaty Agnes had made I asked him if he would come home to my rooms, and have some coffee.

"I beg your pardon, Mister Copperfield, I don't like that you should put a constraint upon yourself to ask a numble person like me to your ouse."

"There is no constraint in the case," said I. "Will you come?"

"I should like to very much," replied Uriah, with a writhe.

"Well, then, come along!" said I.

We went the nearest way, without conversing much upon the road.

I led him up the stairs, and conducted him to my fireside. When I lighted my candles, he fell into meek transports with the room that was revealed to him; and when I heated the coffee in an unassuming block-tin vessel, he professed so much emotion, that I could joyfully have scalded him.

"Oh, really, Master Copperfield—I mean Mister Copperfield," said Uriah, "to see you waiting upon me is what I never could have expected! But, one way and another, so many things happen to me which I never could have expected, I am sure, in my umble station, that it seems to rain blessings on my ed."

As he sat on my sofa, a snaky undulation pervading his frame from his chin to his boots, I decided in my own mind that I disliked him intensely. It made me very uncomfortable to have him for a guest, for I was young then, and unused to disguise what I so strongly felt.

"You have heard something, I des-say, of a change in my expectations, Mister Copperfield?" observed Uriah.

"Yes," said I, "something."

"Ah! I thought Miss Agnes would know of it!" he quietly returned. "I'm glad to find Miss Agnes knows of it. What a prophet you have shown yourself, Mister Copperfield!" pursued Uriah. "Don't you remember saying to me once, that perhaps I should be a partner in Mr. Wickfield's business, and perhaps it might be Wickfield and Heep?"

He sat, with that carved grin on his face, looking at the fire, as I looked at him.

"But the umblest persons, Master Copperfield," he presently resumed, "may be the instruments of good. I am glad to think I have been the instrument of good to Mr. Wickfield, Mister Copperfield, but how imprudent he has been!"

"So, Mr. Wickfield," said I, at last, "who is worth five hundred of you—or me"; for my life, I think, I could not have helped dividing that part of the sentence with an awkward jerk; "has been imprudent, has he, Mr. Heep?"

"Oh dear, yes, Master Copperfield," he proceeded, in a soft voice, "there's no doubt of it. There would have been loss, disgrace, I don't know what all. You will not think the worse of my umbleness, if I make a little confidence to you, Master Copperfield? Will you?"

"Oh no," said I, with an effort.

He took out his pocket-handkerchief, and began wiping the palms of his hands. "Miss Agnes, Master Copperfield——"

"Well, Uriah?"

"Umble as I am," he wiped his hands harder, and looked at them and at the fire by turns, "umble as my mother is, and lowly as our poor but honest roof has ever been, the image of Miss Agnes has been in my breast for years. Oh, Master Copperfield, with what a pure affection do I love the ground my Agnes walks on!"

I asked him, whether he had made his feelings known to Agnes.

"Oh no, Master Copperfield!" he returned; "I rest a good deal of hope on her observing how useful I am to her father and how I smooth the way for him, and keep him straight. She's so much attached to her father, Master Copperfield, that I think she may come, on his account, to be kind to me."

I fathomed the depth of the rascal's whole scheme.

"If you'll have the goodness to keep my secret, Master Copperfield," he pursued, "I shall take it as a particular favour. Having only known me on my umble footing you might, unbeknown, go against me rather, with my Agnes. I call her mine, you see Master Copperfield. I hope to do it, one of these days."

Dear Agnes! Was it possible that she was reserved to be the wife of such a wretch as this!

He took the hand which I dared not withhold, and having given it a damp squeeze, referred to his pale-faced watch.

"Dear me!" he said, "it's past one."

I answered that I had thought it was later.

"Dear me!" he said, considering. "The ouse that I am stopping at—will have gone to bed these two hours."

"I am sorry," I returned, "that there is only one bed here."

"Oh, don't think of mentioning beds, Master Copperfield!" he rejoined ecstatically, drawing up one leg. "But *would* you have any objections to my laying down before the fire?"

"Pray take my bed, and I'll lie down, before the fire."

As no arguments I could urge, in my bewildered condition, had the least effect upon his modesty in inducing him to accept my bed-room, I was obliged to make the best arrangements I could, for his repose before the fire.

When I saw him going down-stairs early in the morning (for, thank Heaven! he would not stay to breakfast), it appeared to me as if the night was going away in his person. When I went out to the Commons, I charged Mrs. Crupp with particular directions to leave the windows open, that my sitting-room might be aired, and purged of his presence.

CHAPTER 25

I Fall Into Captivity

DAYS and weeks slipped away. I was articled to Spenlow and Jorkins. I had ninety pounds a year (exclusive of my house-rent and sundry collateral matters) from my aunt.

On the day when I was articled, Mr. Spenlow remarked, that he should have been happy to have seen me at his house at Norwood, but for his domestic arrangements being in some disorder, on account of the expected return of his daughter from finishing her education at Paris. But, when she came home he should hope to have the pleasure of entertaining me.

In a week or two, he referred to this engagement, and said, that if I would do him the favour to come down next Saturday, and stay till Monday, he would be extremely happy to see me.

We went into the house, which was cheerfully lighted up, and into a hall where there were all sorts of hats, caps, great-coats, plaids, gloves, whips, and walking-sticks.

"Where is Miss Dora?" said Mr. Spenlow to the servant. "Dora!" I thought. "What a beautiful name!"

We turned into a room near at hand.

"Mr. Copperfield, my daughter Dora, and my daughter Dora's confidential friend!"

All was over in a moment. I had fulfilled my destiny. I was a captive and a slave. I loved Dora Spenlow to distraction!

"*I*", observed a well-remembered voice, when I had bowed and murmured something, "have seen Mr. Copperfield before."

The speaker was not Dora. No; the confidential friend, Miss Murdstone!

I said, "How do you do, Miss Murdstone? I hope you are well." She answered, "Very well." I said, "How is Mr. Murdstone?" She replied, "My brother is robust, I am obliged to you."

Mr. Spenlow, who, I suppose, had been surprised to see us recognise each other, then put in his word.

"I am glad to find," he said, "Copperfield, that you and Miss Murdstone are already acquainted."

"Mr. Copperfield and myself," said Miss Murdstone, with severe composure, "are connexions. We were once slightly acquainted. It was in his childish days. Circumstances have separated us since. I should not have known him."

I replied that I should have known her, anywhere. Which was true enough.

"Miss Murdstone has had the goodness," said Mr. Spenlow to me, "to accept the office—if I may so describe it—of my daughter Dora's confidential friend. My daughter Dora having, unhappily, no mother, Miss Murdstone is obliging enough to become her companion and protector."

As I had none but passing thoughts for any subject save Dora, I glanced at her, directly afterwards, and was thinking that I saw, in her prettily pettish manner, that she was not very much inclined to be particularly confidential to her companion and protector.

I sat next to her. I talked to her. She had the most delightful little voice, the gayest little laugh, the pleasantest and most fascinating little ways, that ever led a lost youth into hopeless slavery.

I retired to bed in a most maudlin state of mind, and got up in a crisis of feeble infatuation.

It was a fine morning, and early, and I thought I would go and take a stroll down one of those wire-arched walks. On my way through the hall, I encountered her little dog, who was called Jip—short for Gipsy. I approached him tenderly, for I loved even him; but he showed his whole set of teeth, got under a chair expressly to snarl, and wouldn't hear of the least familiarity.

I had not been walking long, when I turned a corner, and met her.

"You—are—out early, Miss Spenlow," said I.

"It's so stupid at home," she replied, "and Miss Murdstone is so absurd! She talks such nonsense about its being necessary for the day to be aired, before I come out. Aired!" (She laughed, here, in the most melodious manner.)

I hazarded a bold flight, and said (not without stammering) that it was very bright to me then, though it had been very dark to me a minute before.

I never saw such curls—how could I, for there never were such curls!—as those she shook out to hide her blushes. As to the straw hat with blue ribbons which was on the top of the curls, if I could only have hung it up in my room in Buckingham Street, what a priceless possession it would have been!

But, by good fortune the greenhouse was not far off, and these words brought us to it.

It contained quite a show of beautiful geraniums. We loitered along in front of them, and Dora often stopped to admire this one or that one, and I stopped to admire the same one, and Dora, laughing, held the dog up childishly, to smell the flowers; and if we were not all three in Fairyland, certainly *I* was.

Miss Murdstone had been looking for us. She found us here; and presented her uncongenial cheek, the little wrinkles in it filled with hair powder, to Dora to be kissed. Then she took Dora's arm in hers, and marched us into breakfast as if it were a soldier's funeral.

We had a quiet day. No company, a walk, a family dinner of four, and an evening of looking over books and pictures; Miss Murdstone with a homily before her, and her eye upon us, keeping guard vigilantly. Ah! little did Mr. Spenlow imagine, when he sat opposite to me after dinner that day, with his pocket-handkerchief over his head, how fervently I was embracing him, in my fancy, as his son-in-law! Little did he think, when I took leave of him at night, that he had just given his full consent to my being engaged to Dora, and that I was invoking blessings on his head!

CHAPTER 26

Tommy Traddles

IT came into my head, one day, to go and look after Traddles. The time he had mentioned was more than out, and he lived in a little street near the Veterinary College at Camden Town.

When I got to the top of the stairs—the house was only a storey high above the ground floor—Traddles was on the landing to meet me. He was delighted to see me, and gave me welcome to his little room. It was in the front of the house, and extremely neat, though sparely furnished.

"Traddles," said I, "I am delighted to see you."

"I am delighted to see *you*, Copperfield," he returned. "It was because I was sure you were thoroughly glad to see me, that I gave you this address instead of my address at chambers."

"Oh! You have chambers?" said I.

"Why, I have the fourth of a room and a passage, and the fourth of a clerk," returned Traddles. "Three others and myself unite to have a set of chambers—to look business-like—and we quarter the clerk too. Half-a-crown a week he costs me."

His old simple character, smiled at me in the smile with which he made this explanation.

"I don't usually give my address here. I am fighting my way on in the world against difficulties, and it would be ridiculous if I made a pretence of doing anything else."

"You are reading for the bar?" said I.

"Why, yes," said Traddles, rubbing his hands, slowly over one another, "I have just begun to keep my terms, after rather a long delay. It's some time since I was articled, but the payment of that hundred pounds was a great pull. Now Copperfield, I sha'n't conceal anything. Therefore you must know that I am engaged."

Engaged! Oh Dora!

"She is a curate's daughter," said Traddles; "one of ten, down in Devonshire. She is such a dear girl!" said Traddles; "a little older than me, but the dearest girl! I dare say ours is likely to be a rather long engagement. And she would wait, Copperfield, till she was sixty—any age you can mention—for me!"

"I am quite certain of it," said I.

"In the meantime," said Traddles, coming back to his chair; "I get on as well as I can. In general, I board with the people down-stairs. Both Mr. and Mrs. Micawber have seen a good deal of life, and are excellent company."

"Mr. and Mrs. Micawber!" I repeated. "Why, I am intimately acquainted with them!"

An opportune double knock at the door, resolved any doubt in my mind as to their being my old friends.

I begged Traddles to ask his landlord to walk up.

"I beg your pardon, Mr. Traddles," said Mr. Micawber, with the old roll in his voice, as he checked himself in humming a soft tune. "I was not aware that there was any individual, alien to this tenement, in your sanctum."

Mr. Micawber slightly bowed to me, and pulled up his shirt-collar.

"How do you do, Mr. Micawber?" said I.

He examined my features with more attention, "Is it possible! Have I the pleasure of again beholding Copperfield!" and shook me by both hands with the utmost fervour.

"My dear Copperfield," said Mr. Micawber, "I need hardly tell you that to have beneath our roof, a mind like that which gleams—if in your friend Traddles, is an unspeakable comfort. I am, however, delighted to add that I have now an immediate prospect of something turning up which I trust will enable me to provide, permanently, both for myself and for your friend Traddles, in whom I have an unaffected interest."

Mr. Micawber than shook hands with me again, and left me.

I returned to my fireside, and was musing, on the character of Mr. Micawber, when I heard a quick step ascending the stairs. As the step approached, I knew it, for it was Steerforth's.

"Why, Daisy, here's a supper for a king!" he exclaimed, taking his seat at the table. "I shall do it justice, for I have come from Yarmouth."

"I thought you came from Oxford?" I returned.

"Not I," said Steerforth. "I have been to Yarmouth."

I moved my chair to the table. "So you have been at Yarmouth, Steerforth! I'm interested to know all about it. And how are they all? Of course, little Emily is not married yet?"

"Not yet. Going to be, I believe—in so many weeks, or months, or something or other. By-the-bye"; he laid down his knife and fork, which he had been using with great diligence, and began feeling in his pockets; "I have a letter for you."

"From whom?"

"Why, from your old nurse," he returned, taking some papers out of his breast pocket. "Old what's-his-name's in a bad way, and it's about that, I believe."

"Barkis, do you mean?"

"Yes! It's all over with poor Barkis, I am afraid. Put your hand into the breast pocket of my great-coat on the chair yonder, and I think you'll find the letter."

It was from Peggotty. It informed me of her husband's hopeless state, and hinted at his being "a little nearer" than heretofore, and consequently more difficult to manage for his own comfort. It was written with a plain, unaffected, homely piety and ended with "my duty to my ever darling"—meaning myself.

"I tell you what, Steerforth. I think I will go down and see my old nurse. It is not that I can do her any good, or render her any real service; but she is so attached to me that my visit will have as much effect on her, as if I could do both. Wouldn't you go a day's journey, if you were in my place?"

His face was thoughtful. "Well! Go. You can do no harm."

He put on his great-coat and lighted his cigar, and set off to walk home.

CHAPTER 27

A Loss

I GOT down to Yarmouth in the evening.

My low tap at the door was answered by Mr. Peggotty.

I shook hands with Mr. Peggotty, and passed into the kitchen, while he softly closed the door. Little Emily was sitting by the fire, with her hands before her face.

"This is very kind of you, Mas'r Davy," said Mr. Peggotty.

"Em'ly, my dear," cried Mr. Peggotty. "See here! Here's Mas'r Davy come! What, cheer up, pretty! Not a wured to Mas'r Davy?"

There was a trembling upon her, that I can see now. The coldness of her hand when I touched it, I can feel yet. Its only sign of animation was to shrink from mine; and then she glided from the chair, and, creeping to the other side of her uncle, bowed herself, silently and trembling still, upon his breast.

"Now, I'm a going up-stairs, to tell your aunt as Mas'r Davy's here, and that'll cheer her up a bit," he said.

Peggotty took me in her arms, and blessed and thanked me over and over again for being such a comfort to her (that was what she said) in her distress. She then entreated me to come up-stairs, sobbing that Mr. Barkis had always liked me and admired me; that he had often talked of me, before he fell into a stupor.

"Barkis, my dear!" said Peggotty, almost cheerfully: bending over him, while her brother and I stood at the bed's foot. "Here's my dear boy—my dear boy, Master Davy, who brought us together, Barkis! That you sent messages by, you know! Won't you speak to Master Davy?"

"He's a going out with the tide," said Mr. Peggotty. "People can't die, along the coast," said Mr. Peggotty, "except when the tide's pretty nigh out."

What mysterious influence my presence had upon him in that state of his senses, I shall not pretend to say; but when he at last began to wander feebly, it is certain he was muttering about driving me to school.

"He's coming to himself," said Peggotty.

"Barkis, my dear!" said Peggotty. "Look! Here's Master Davy!" For he now opened his eyes.

He tried to stretch out his arm, and said to me, distinctly, with a pleasant smile:

"Barkis is willin'!"

And, it being low water, he went out with the tide.

CHAPTER 28

A Greater Loss

My old nurse was to go to London with me next day, on the business of the will. We were all to meet in the old boathouse that night. Ham would bring Emily at the usual hour. I would walk back at my leisure.

I turned, and walked back towards Yarmouth. I stayed to dine at a decent alehouse, some mile or two from the Ferry, and it was evening when I reached it.

I was soon within sight of Mr. Peggotty's house.

It looked very comfortable indeed. Mr. Peggotty had smoked his evening pipe. The fire was bright. In her own old place, sat Peggotty, once more, looking as if she had never left it.

"Sit ye down, sir. It ain't o' no use saying welcome to you, but you're welcome, kind and hearty."

"Thank you, Mr. Peggotty, I am sure of that. Well, Peggotty!" said I, giving her a kiss, "and how are you, old woman?"

"Ha, ha!" laughed Mr. Peggotty; "there's not a woman in the wureld, sir—as I tell her—that need to feel more easy in her mind than her!"

Mrs. Gummidge groaned.

"Cheer up, my pretty mawther!" said Mr. Peggotty. (But he shook his head aside at us, evidently sensible of the tendency of the late occurrences to recall the memory of the old one.) "Doen't be down! Cheer up, for your own self, on'y a little bit, and see if a good deal more doen't come nat'ral!"

"Not to me, Dan'l," returned Mrs. Gummidge. "Nothink's nat'ral to me but to be lone and lorn. I ain't a person to live with them as has had money left. Thinks go too contrairy with me. I had better be a riddance."

"Why, how should I ever spend it without you?" said Mr. Peggotty, with an air of serious remonstrance. "What are you a talking on? Doen't I want you more now, than ever I did?"

"Theer!" said Mr. Peggotty, cheerily. "Theer we are! You're a wonderin' what that's fur, sir! Well, it's fur our little Em'ly. You see, the path ain't over light or cheerful arter dark; and when I'm here at the hour as she's a comin' home, I puts the light in the winder," said Mr. Peggotty smiting his hands together; "fur here she is!"

It was only Ham. He had a large sou-wester hat on, slouched over his face.

"Where's Em'ly?" said Mr. Peggotty.

Ham made a motion with his head, as if she were outside. Mr. Peggotty took the light from the window, trimmed it, put it on the table, and was busily stirring the fire, when Ham, who had not moved, said:

"Mas'r Davy, will you come out a minute, and see what Em'ly and me has got to show you?"

We went out. His face was deadly pale. He pushed me hastily into the open air, and closed the door upon us.

"Ham! what's the matter?"

"Mas'r Davy!—" Oh, for his broken heart, how dreadfully he wept! I was paralyzed by the sight of such grief.

"Ham! For Heaven's sake, tell me what's the matter!"

"My love, Mas'r Davy—her that I'd have died for, and would die for now—she's gone!"

"Gone!"

"Em'ly's run away! I pray my good and gracious God to kill her sooner than let her come to ruin and disgrace!"

"You're a scholar," he said, hurriedly. "What am I to say, indoors? How am I ever to break it to him, Mas'r Davy?"

I saw the door move. It was too late. Mr. Peggotty thrust forth his face; and never could I forget the change that came upon it when he saw us, if I were to live five hundred years.

I remember a great wail and cry, and the women hanging about him, and we all standing in the room; I with a paper in my hand, which Ham had given me; Mr. Peggotty, with his vest torn open, his hair wild, his face and lips quite white, and blood trickling down his bosom (it had sprung from his mouth, I think), looking fixedly at me.

"Read it, sir," he said, in a low shivering voice. "Slow, please. I doen't know as I can understand."

"When you, who love me so much better than I ever have deserved see this, I shall be far away."

"When I leave my dear home—in the morning."

"—it will be never to come back, unless he brings me back a lady. This will be found at night, many hours after, instead of me. Oh, if even you, that I have wronged so much, could only know what I suffer! I am too wicked to write about myself. Oh, for mercy's sake, tell uncle that I never loved him half so dear as now. Try to think as if I died when I was little, and was buried somewhere. Tell him that I never loved him half so dear. Love some good girl, that will be true to you, and worthy of you. If he don't bring me back a lady, and I don't pray for my own self, I'll pray for all. My last tears, and my last thanks, for uncle!"

He stood, long after I had ceased to read, still looking at me.

Ham spoke to him. Mr. Peggotty was so far sensible of *his* affliction, that he wrung his hand.

Slowly, at last he moved his eyes from my face. Then he said, in a low voice:

"Who's the man? I want to know his name."

Ham glanced at me, and suddenly I felt a shock that struck me back.

"Mas'r Davy!" implored Ham. "Go out a bit, and let me tell him what I must. You don't ought to hear it, sir."

I felt the shock again. I sank down in a chair.

"For some time," Ham faltered, "there's been a servant about here. There's been a gen'lm'n too. Both of 'em belonged to one another."

Mr. Peggotty stood fixed as before, but now looking at him.

"The servant," pursued Ham, "was seen along with—our poor girl —last night. He was thought to have gone, but he was hiding. Doen't stay, Mas'r Davy, doen't!"

I felt Peggotty's arm round my neck, but I could not have moved if the house had been about to fall upon me.

"A strange chay and hosses was outside town, this morning," Ham went on. "The servant went to it, Em'ly was nigh him. The t'other was inside. He's the man."

"For the Lord's love," said Mr. Peggotty. "Doen't tell me his name's Steerforth!"

"Mas'r Davy," exclaimed Ham, in a broken voice, "it ain't no fault of yourn—his name is Steerforth, and he's a damned villain!"

Mr. Peggotty pulled down his rough coat from its peg in a corner.

"Bear a hand with this! I'm struck of a heap, and can't do it," he said, impatiently.

Ham asked him whither he was going.

"I'm a going to seek my niece. I'm a going to seek my Em'ly. I'm a going, to stave in that theer boat, and sink it where I would have drownded *him*, if I had had one thought of what was in him! I'm a going to find my poor niece in her shame, and bring her back. No one stop me! I tell you I'm a going to seek my niece!"

CHAPTER 29

The Beginning of a Long Journey

The news of what had happened soon spread through the town; insomuch that as I passed along the streets next morning, I overheard the people speaking of it at their doors. Many were hard upon her, some few were hard upon him, but towards her second father and her lover there was but one sentiment. Among all kinds of people a respect for them in their distress prevailed, which was full of gentleness and delicacy.

It was on the beach, close down by the sea, that I found them. They looked worn; and I thought Mr. Peggotty's head was bowed in one night more than in all the years I had known him.

"My dooty here, sir," said Mr. Peggotty, "is done. I'm a going to seek her. That's my dooty evermore."

I told him I had not gone to-day, fearing to lose the chance of being of any service to him; but that I was ready to go when he would.

"I'll go along with you, sir," he rejoined, "to-morrow."

In the morning I was joined by Mr. Peggotty and by my old nurse, and we went at an early hour to the coach office.

Our first pursuit was to look for a lodging for Peggotty, where her brother could have a bed. We were so fortunate as to find one, over a chandler's shop, only two streets removed from me.

Mr. Peggotty told me that he meant "to set out on his travels," that night.

After dinner we sat for an hour or so near the window, without talking much; and then Mr. Peggotty got up, and brought his oilskin bag and his stout stick, and laid them on the table.

He promised to communicate with me, when anything befell him; and bade us both, "Good-bye!"

CHAPTER 30

Blissful

PEGGOTTY's business, being settled, I took her down to the office one morning to pay her bill. Mr. Spenlow had stepped out, but as I knew he would be back directly, I told Peggotty to wait.

But neither Peggotty nor I had eyes for him, when we saw, in company with him, Mr. Murdstone.

"Ah, Copperfield!" said Mr. Spenlow. "You know this gentleman, I believe?"

I made my gentleman a distant bow. Peggotty barely recognised him.

"I hope," he said, "that you are doing well?"

"It can hardly be interesting to you," said I.

We looked at each other, and he addressed himself to Peggotty.

"I am sorry to observe that you have lost your husband."

"It's not the first loss I have had in my life," replied Peggotty. "I have not worn any body's life away. I have not frightened any sweet creetur to an early grave!"

He eyed her gloomily—remorsefully I thought—for an instant; and said: "We are not likely to encounter soon again; a source of satisfaction to us both, no doubt." With that, he paid the money for his licence; and, receiving it neatly folded from Mr. Spenlow, went out of the office.

Mr. Spenlow seemed to think, that my aunt was the leader of the state party in our family, and that there was a rebel party commanded by somebody else—so I gathered while we were waiting for Mr. Tiffey to make out Peggotty's bill of costs.

Old Tiffey handed it to Mr. Spenlow. Mr. Spenlow, went over the items with a deprecatory air—and handed it back to Tiffey with a bland sigh.

"Yes," he said. "That's right."

I paid Tiffey in bank notes. Peggotty then retired to her lodging, and Mr. Spenlow and I went into Court, where we had a divorce-suit coming on.

Mr. Spenlow told me this day week was Dora's birthday, and he would be glad if I would come down and join a little picnic on the occasion.

I saw Dora in the garden sitting on a seat under a lilac tree, in a white chip bonnet and a dress of celestial blue.

There was a young lady with her—Miss Mills, and Dora called her Julia.

Jip was there, and Jip *would* bark at me again. When I presented my bouquet, he gnashed his teeth with jealousy.

"Oh, thank you, Mr. Copperfield! What dear flowers!" said Dora.

"You'll be so glad to hear, Mr. Copperfield," said Dora, "that that cross Miss Murdstone is not here. She has gone to her brother's marriage, and will be away at least three weeks. Isn't that delightful?"

"She is the most disagreeable thing I ever saw," she added. "You can't believe how ill-tempered and shocking she is, Julia."

"Yes, I can, my dear!" said Julia.

"*You* can, perhaps, love," returned Dora, with her hand on Julia's.

I shall never have such a ride again. I have never had such another. There were only those three, their hamper, and the guitar-case, in the phaeton; and, of course, the phaeton was open; and I rode behind it, and Dora sat with her back to the horses, looking towards me.

It was a green spot, on a hill, carpeted with soft turf. There were shady trees, and heather, and, as far as the eye could see, a rich landscape.

It was a trying thing to find people here, waiting for us; and my jealousy, even of the ladies, knew no bounds.

We all unpacked our baskets, and employed ourselves in getting dinner ready.

I was very merry, and attached myself to a young creature in pink, with little eyes, and flirted with her desperately.

The young creature in pink had a mother in green; and I rather think the latter separated us from motives of policy. Howbeit, there was a general breaking up of the party, while the remnants of the dinner were being put away. I strolled off by myself among the trees, when Dora and Miss Mills met me.

"Mr. Copperfield and Dora," said Miss Mills, with an almost venerable air. "Enough of this. Do not allow a trivial misunderstanding to wither the blossoms of spring."

I took Dora's little hand and kissed it—and she let me! I kissed Miss Mills's hand; and we all seemed, to my thinking, to go straight up to the seventh heaven.

We stayed up there all the evening. We strayed to and fro among the trees: I with Dora's shy arm drawn through mine.

But we heard the others laughing and talking, and calling "Where's Dora?" They wanted Dora to sing.

I was happier than ever when the party broke up. Mr. Spenlow being a little drowsy after the champagne—and being fast asleep in a corner of the carriage, I rode by the side and talked to Dora.

122

"Mr. Copperfield," said Miss Mills, "come to this side of the carriage a moment. I want to speak to you. Dora is coming to stay with me, the day after to-morrow. If you would like to call, I am sure papa would be happy to see you."

When I awoke next morning, I was resolute to declare my passion to Dora, and know my fate. Happiness or misery was now the question.

At last, arrayed for the purpose at a vast expense, I went to Miss Mills's, fraught with a declaration.

I was shown into a room up-stairs, where Miss Mills and Dora were. Jip was there.

Miss Mills was conversational for a few minutes, and then left the room. I don't know how I did it. I had Dora in my arms. I was full of eloquence. I told her I should die without her. I told her that I idolised and worshipped her. Jip barked madly all the time.

When Dora hung her head and cried, and trembled, my eloquence increased so much the more.

Well, well! Dora and I were sitting on the sofa by-and-by, quiet enough, and Jip was lying in her lap, winking peacefully at me. I was in a state of perfect rapture. Dora and I were engaged.

I suppose we had some notion that this was to end in marriage. But, in our youthful ecstasy, I don't think that we really looked before us or behind us; we were to keep our secret from Mr. Spenlow; but the idea never entered my head, that there was anything dishonourable in that.

Miss Mills gave us her blessing, and the assurance of her lasting friendship.

CHAPTER 31

My Aunt Astonishes Me

I WROTE to Agnes as soon as Dora and I were engaged and tried to make her comprehend what a darling Dora was.

Of Steerforth, I said nothing. I only told her there had been sad grief at Yarmouth, on account of Emily's flight; and that on me it made a double wound, by reason of the circumstances attending it. I knew how quick she always was to divine the truth, and that she would never be the first to breathe his name.

While I had been away from home lately, Traddles had called twice or thrice.

"My dear Copperfield," cried Traddles, punctually appearing at my door, "how do you do?"

"My dear Traddles," said I, "I am delighted to see you at last. But I have been so much engaged—"

"Yes, I know," said Traddles. "Yours lives in London, I think."

"Oh yes. Near London."

"Mine, perhaps you recollect," said Traddles, with a serious look, "lives down in Devonshire—one of ten. Consequently, I am not so much engaged as you—in that sense."

I inquired how Mr. Micawber was?

"He is quite well, Copperfield, thank you," said Traddles. "I am not living with him at present."

"No?"

"No. You see the truth is," said Traddles, in a whisper, "he has changed his name to Mortimer, in consequence of his temporary embarrassments; and he don't come out till after dark—and then in spectacles. There was an execution put into our house, for rent."

I told him that he should make a solemn resolution to grant no more loans of his name, or anything else, to Mr. Micawber.

"My dear Copperfield," said Traddles, "I have already done so, because I begin to feel that I have not only been inconsiderate, but that I have been positively unjust to Sophy."

We turned back towards my chambers, and met Peggotty on the way. We were very surprised, coming higher up, to find my outer door standing open, and to hear voices inside.

What was my amazement to find my aunt there, and Mr. Dick! My aunt sitting on a quantity of luggage, with her two birds before her, and her cat on her knee, like a female Robinson Crusoe, drinking tea. Mr. Dick leaning thoughtfully on a great kite, such as we had often been out together to fly, with more luggage piled about him!

"My dear aunt!" cried I. "Why, what an unexpected pleasure!"

"Holloa!" said my aunt to Peggotty, who quailed before her awful presence. "How are you?"

"You remember my aunt, Peggotty?" said I.

"We have only met each other once before, you know," said my aunt. "A nice business we made of it then! Trot, my dear, another cup."

I handed it dutifully to my aunt, who was in her usual inflexible state of figure.

I knew my aunt sufficiently well to know that she had something of importance on her mind, and that there was far more matter in this arrival than a stranger might have supposed.

"Trot," said my aunt at last, when she had finished her tea, "have you got to be firm, and self-reliant?"

"I think so, aunt."

"Then why, my love," said my aunt, looking earnestly at me, "why do you think I prefer to sit upon this property of mine to-night?"

I shook my head, unable to guess.

"Because," said my aunt, "I'm ruined, my dear!"

I could hardly have received a greater shock.

"All I have in the world is in this room, except the cottage; and that I have left Janet to let. To save expense, perhaps you can make up something here for myself. Anything will do. It's only for to-night. We'll talk about this, more, to-morrow."

I was roused from my amazement, and concern for her—by her falling on my neck, and crying that she only grieved for me.

"We must meet reverses boldly. We must live misfortune down, Trot!"

CHAPTER 32

Depression

As soon as I could recover my presence of mind, I proposed to Mr. Dick to come round to the chandler's shop, and take possession of the bed which Mr. Peggotty had lately vacated.

In the morning I arrived at the office and sat down in my shady corner, looking up at the sunlight on the opposite chimney-pots, and thinking about Dora; until Mr. Spenlow came in, crisp and curly.

"How are you, Copperfield?" said he. "Fine morning!"

"Beautiful morning, sir," said I. "Could I say a word to you before you go into Court?"

"By all means," said he. "Come into my room."

I followed him into his room.

"I have some rather disheartening intelligence from my aunt."

"No!" said he. "Dear me!"

"She has met with some large losses."

"You as-tound me, Copperfield!" cried Mr. Spenlow.

I shook my head. "Indeed, sir," said I, "her affairs are so changed, that I wished to ask you whether it would be possible—to cancel my articles?"

What it cost me to make this proposal, nobody knows.

"To cancel your articles, Copperfield? Cancel?"

I explained with tolerable firmness, that I really did not know where my means of subsistence were to come from, unless I could earn them for myself.

"I am extremely sorry to hear this, Copperfield," said Mr. Spenlow. "It is not usual to cancel articles for any such reason. It is not a convenient precedent at all. Far from it. At the same time—"

"You are very good, sir," I murmured.

"Don't mention it," said Mr. Spenlow. "I was going to say, if it had been my lot to have my hands unfettered—"

My hopes were dashed in a moment. In a state of despondency I left the office.

A hackney chariot coming after me, and stopping at my very feet, occasioned me to look up. A fair hand was stretched forth to me from the window; and the face I had never seen without a feeling of serenity and happiness was smiling down on me.

"Agnes!" I joyfully exclaimed. "What a pleasure to see you!"

"Is it, indeed?" she said, in her cordial voice.

"I want to talk to you so much!" said I. "Where are you going?"

She was going to my rooms to see my aunt. I dismissed the coachman, and she took my arm, and we walked on together.

My aunt had written her one of the old, abrupt notes. She had stated therein that she had fallen into adversity, and was leaving Dover for good. Agnes had come to London to see my aunt, between whom and herself there had been a mutual liking these many years. She was not alone, she said. Her papa was with her—and Uriah Heep.

"And now they are partners," said I. "Confound him!"

"Yes," said Agnes. "They have some business here; and I took advantage of their coming, to come too. I do not like to let papa go away alone, with him."

"Does he exercise the same influence over Mr. Wickfield?"

Agnes shook her head. "You would scarcely know the dear old house. They live with us now."

"They?" said I.

"Mr. Heep and his mother. He sleeps in your old room," said Agnes.

My aunt, being greatly pleased to see Agnes—received us with unimpaired good humour. When Agnes laid her bonnet on the table, I could not but think, how natural it seemed to have her there: how trustfully, although she was so young and inexperienced, my aunt confided in her.

We began to talk about my aunt's losses, and I told them what I had tried to do that morning.

"Which was injudicious, Trot," said my aunt, "but well meant."

I observed Agnes turn pale, as she looked attentively at my aunt. My aunt, patting her cat, looked very attentively at Agnes.

"Betsey Trotwood," said my aunt, who had always kept her money matters to herself: "—had a certain property. It don't matter how much; enough to live. She took her pigs," said my aunt, "to a foreign market; and a very bad market it turned out to be. I don't know what the Bank shares were worth but the Bank was at the other end of the world; it fell to pieces, and never will and never can pay sixpence; and Betsey's sixpences were all there. Now, Agnes, you have a wise head. So have you, Trot. What's to be done? Here's the cottage; it will produce, say seventy pounds a year. Well!—That's all we've got," said my aunt.

Agnes inquired if my rooms were held for any long term?

"You come to the point, my dear," said my aunt. "They are not to be got rid of, for six months at least, unless they could be underlet, and that I don't believe. I have a little ready money; and I agree with you, the best thing we can do, is, to live the term out here, and get Dick a bedroom hard by."

"I have been thinking, Trotwood," said Agnes, diffidently, "that if you had time—"

"I have a good deal of time, Agnes."

"I know you would not mind," said Agnes, "the duties of a secretary. Because," continued Agnes, "Doctor Strong has acted on his intention of retiring, and has come to live in London; and he asked papa, I know, if he could recommend him one."

"Dear Agnes!" said I. "What should I do without you!"

A knock came at the door.

"I think," said Agnes, turning pale, "it's papa. He promised me that he would come."

I opened the door, and admitted, not only Mr. Wickfield, but Uriah Heep.

"Well, Wickfield!" said my aunt; and he looked up at her for the first time. "I have been telling your daughter how well I have been disposing of my money for myself, because I couldn't trust it to you. We have been taking counsel together, and getting on very well, all things considered. Agnes is worth the whole firm, in my opinion."

"If I may umbly make the remark," said Uriah Heep, with a writhe, "I should be only too appy if Miss Agnes was a partner."

"You're a partner yourself, you know," returned my aunt, "and that's about enough for you, I expect. How do you find yourself, sir?"

Mr. Heep replied that he was pretty well, and hoped she was the same.

"I only called to say that if there was anything we could do, we should be really glad. I may go so far?" said Uriah, with a sickly smile at his partner.

"Uriah Heep," said Mr. Wickfield, in a monotonous forced way, "is active in the business, Trotwood. What he says, I quite concur in."

"You are not going, papa?" said Agnes, anxiously. "Will you not walk back with Trotwood and me?"

"I am bespoke myself," said Uriah. "But I leave my partner to represent the firm. Miss Agnes, ever yours! I wish you good-day, Master Copperfield, and leave my umble respects for Miss Betsey Trotwood."

With these words, he retired, leering at us like a mask.

We sat there, talking about our pleasant old Canterbury days. Mr. Wickfield, left to Agnes, soon became more like his former self; though there was a settled depression upon him, which he never shook off.

CHAPTER 33

Enthusiasm

MY first care, was to find the Doctor's house. It was not in that part of Highgate where Mrs. Steerforth lived, but quite on the opposite side of the little town.

When I reached the Doctor's cottage—I saw him walking in the garden, as if he had never left off walking since the days of my pupilage.

Knowing the utter hopelessness of attracting his attention from that distance, I made bold to open the gate, and walk after him, so as to meet him when he should turn round. When he did, and came towards me, he looked at me thoughtfully for a few moments, evidently without thinking about me at all; and then his benevolent face expressed extraordinary pleasure, and he took me by both hands.

"Why, my dear Copperfield," said the doctor; "you are a man! How do you do? I am delighted to see you. My dear Copperfield, how very much you have improved! You are quite—yes—dear me!"

I hoped he was well, and Mrs. Strong too.

"Oh dear, yes!" said the Doctor; "Annie's quite well, and she'll be delighted to see you. Mr. Jack Maldon is home. He couldn't bear the climate. Mrs. Markleham," said the Doctor, "was quite vexed about him, poor thing; so we have got him at home again."

"Now, my dear Copperfield, in reference to this proposal of yours. It's very gratifying and agreeable to me, I am sure; but don't you think you could do better?"

I became very glowing again, reminding the Doctor that I had already a profession.

"Certainly, your having a profession, makes a difference. But, my good young friend, what's seventy pounds a year?"

"If you will take such time as I have, and that is my mornings and evenings, you will do me such a service as I cannot express."

"Then be it so," said the Doctor, clapping me on the shoulder.

"And I shall be twenty times happier, sir," said I, "if my employment is to be on your Dictionary."

The Doctor stopped and smilingly clapped me on the shoulder again, "My dear young friend, you have hit it. It is the Dictionary!"

Our plans thus being arranged to our mutual satisfaction, the Doctor took me into the house to present me to Mrs. Strong.

They had postponed their breakfast on my account, and we sat down to table together.

We had not been seated long, when a gentleman on horseback came to the gate, and leading his horse into the little court, with the bridle over his arm, as if he were quite at home, tied him to a ring in the empty coach-house wall, and came into the breakfast parlour, whip in hand. It was Mr. Jack Maldon.

"Mr. Jack!" said the Doctor. "Copperfield!"

Mr. Jack Maldon shook hands with me; but not very warmly.

"I came out to inquire whether Annie would like to go the opera to-night," said Mr. Maldon, turning to her.

The Doctor, turned to her and said:

"You must go, Annie. You must go."

"I would rather not," she said to the Doctor. "I prefer to remain at home."

Without looking at her cousin, she asked me about Agnes, and whether she should see her; and was so much disturbed, that I wondered how even the Doctor could be blind to what was so obvious.

I was pretty busy now; up at five in the morning, and home at nine or ten at night. I had not revealed myself in my altered character to Dora yet, because she was coming to see Miss Mills in a few days, and I deferred all I had to tell her until then; merely informing her in my letters (all our communications were secretly forwarded through Miss Mills), that I had much to tell her.

Not satisfied with all these proceedings, but burning with impatience to do something more, I went to see Traddles. Mr. Dick, I took with me.

I took Mr. Dick, because acutely sensitive to my aunt's reverses, he had begun to worry himself out of spirits and appetite, as having nothing useful to do. Seriously apprehending that his malady would increase, unless we could put him in the way of being really useful, I made up my mind to try if Traddles could help us. Before we went, I wrote Traddles a full statement of all that had happened, and Traddles wrote me back a capital answer, expressive of his sympathy and friendship.

We found him hard at work. He received us cordially, and made friends with Mr. Dick, in a moment. Mr. Dick professed an absolute certainty of having seen him before, and we both said, "Very likely."

The first subject on which I had to consult Traddles was this.—I had heard that many men distinguished in various pursuits had begun life by reporting the debates in Parliament. I wished to know how I could qualify myself for this pursuit. Traddles now informed me that the mere mechanical acquisition necessary, thorough excellence in short-hand writing and reading, was about equal in difficulty to the mastery of six languages.

"I am very much obliged to you," said I. "I'll begin to-morrow."

Traddles looked astonished, as he well might; but he had no notion as yet of my rapturous condition.

I brought Mr. Dick on the carpet.

"You see," said Mr. Dick, wistfully, "if I could exert myself, Mr. Traddles—if I could beat a drum—or blow anything!"

Traddles, who would not have smiled for the world, replied:

"But you are a very good penman, sir. You told me so, Copperfield!"

"Excellent!" said I, and indeed he wrote with extraordinary neatness.

"Don't you think," said Traddles, "you could copy writings, sir, if I got them for you?"

Traddles and I concocted a scheme in virtue of which we got him to work next day, with triumphant success.

On a table by the window in Buckingham Street, we set out the work Traddles procured for him—which was to make, I forget how many copies of a legal document about some right of way. In a word, although we took great care that he should have no more to do than was good for him, and although he did not begin with the beginning of a week, he earned by the following Saturday night ten shillings and nine pence; and never, while

I live, shall I forget his going about to all the shops in the neighbourhood to change this treasure into sixpences, or his bringing them to my aunt arranged in the form of a heart upon a waiter, with tears of joy and pride in his eyes.

"No starving now, Trotwood," said Mr. Dick, shaking hands with me in a corner. "I'll provide for her, sir!" and he flourished his ten fingers in the air, as if they were ten banks.

A letter (Mr. Micawber never missed any possible opportunity of writing a letter) was addressed to me. "By the kindness of T. Traddles, Esquire, of the Inner Temple." It ran thus:

"My dear Copperfield,

"You may possibly not be unprepared to receive the intimation that something has turned up. I may have mentioned to you on a former occasion that I was in expectation of such an event.

"I am about to establish myself in one of the provincial towns of our favoured island in immediate connexion with one of the learned professions. Mrs. Micawber and our offspring will accompany me.

"If, on the eve of such a departure, you will accompany our mutual friend, Mr. Thomas Traddles, to our present abode, and there reciprocate the wishes natural to the occasion, you will confer a Boon.

Wilkins Micawber."

Learning from Traddles that the invitation referred to the evening then wearing away we went off together to the lodging which Mr. Micawber occupied.

"My dear Copperfield," said Mr. Micawber, "yourself and Mr. Traddles find us on the brink of migration."

Glancing round as I made a suitable reply, I observed that the family effects were already packed, and that the amount of luggage was by no means overwhelming. I congratulated Mrs. Micawber on the approaching change.

"It may be a sacrifice," said Mrs. Micawber, "to immure one's self in a Cathedral town; but surely, Mr. Copperfield, it is much more a sacrifice in a man of Mr. Micawber's abilities."

"Oh! You are going to a Cathedral town?" said I.

"To Canterbury. I have entered into arrangements, by virtue of which I stand pledged and contracted to our friend Heep, to assist and serve him in the capacity of—and to be—his confidential clerk."

I stared at Mr. Micawber, who greatly enjoyed my surprise.

"Of my friend Heep," said Mr. Micawber, "who is a man of remarkable shrewdness, I desire to speak with all possible respect."

Mr. Micawber drank two glasses of punch in grave succession. He then said with much solemnity:

"My friend Mr. Thomas Traddles has, on two several occasions, 'put his name,' if I may use a common expression, to bills of exchange for my accommodation. These sums, united, make a total, if my calculation is correct, amounting to forty-one, ten, eleven and a half. I beg to hand to my friend Mr. Thomas Traddles my I.O.U. for forty-one, ten, eleven and a half, and I am happy to recover my moral dignity."

With this introduction, Mr. Micawber placed his I. O. U. in the hands of Traddles, and said he wished him well in every relation of life. I am persuaded, not only that this was quite the same to Mr. Micawber as paying the money, but that Traddles himself hardly knew the difference until he had had time to think about it.

CHAPTER 34

A Little Cold Water

LITTLE Dora was quite unconscious of my desperate firmness, otherwise than as my letters darkly shadowed it forth. But, another Saturday came, and on that Saturday evening she was to be at Miss Mill's; and I was to go there to tea.

By this time, we were quite settled down in Buckingham Street, where Mr. Dick continued his copying in a state of absolute felicity.

Although Peggotty still retained something of her old sentiment of awe in reference to my aunt, she had received so many marks of encouragement and confidence, that they were the best friends possible. But the time had now come when it was necessary for her to return home, and enter on the discharge of the duties she had undertaken on behalf of Ham.

I took Peggotty to the coach-office and saw her off. She cried at parting, and confided her brother to my friendship as Ham had done.

I fatigued myself as much as I possibly could in the Commons all day, by a variety of devices, and at the appointed time in the evening repaired to Mr. Mill's street.

Dora came to the drawing-room door to meet me; and Jip came scrambling out, tumbling over his own growls, under the impression that I was a Bandit; and we all three went in, as happy and loving as could be. I soon carried desolation into the bosom of our joys—by asking Dora, if she could love a beggar?

"How can you ask me anything so foolish?" pouted Dora.

"Dora, my own dearest!" said I. "*I* am a beggar!"

"How can you be such a silly thing," replied Dora, slapping my hand, "as to sit there, telling such stories? I'll make Jip bite you!"

Her childish way was the most delicious way in the world to me, but it was necessary to be explicit, and I solemnly repeated:

"Dora, my own life, I am your ruined David!"

I looked so serious, that Dora began to cry. That was dreadful! I fell upon my knees imploring her not to rend my heart.

At last, I got her to look at me, with a horrified expression of face. Then I told her, how I loved her, how I felt it right to offer to release her from her engagement, because now I was poor; how I had no fears of poverty, if she had none, how I was already working with a courage such as none but lovers knew.

"Is your heart mine still, dear Dora?" said I, rapturously. "My own! May I mention something?"

"Oh, please don't be practical!" said Dora coaxingly. "Because it frightens me so!"

"Indeed I am not going to be, my darling!" I assured her. "But, Dora, my love, if you will sometimes think—just to encourage yourself—that you are engaged to a poor man—"

"Don't, don't! Pray don't!" cried Dora. "It's so very dreadful!"

"My soul, not at all!" said I cheerfully. "If you will sometimes think of that, and look about now and then at your papa's housekeeping, and endeavour to acquire a little habit—of accounts, for instance—"

Poor little Dora received this suggestion with something that was half a sob and half a scream.

"And if you would promise me to read a little—a little Cookery Book that I would send you, it would be so excellent for both of us. For our path in life, my Dora," said I, warming with the subject, "is stony and rugged now."

I had said enough. I had done it again. Oh, she was so frightened! Oh, take her to Julia Mills, and go away, please!

Miss Mills must have been born to be a blessing to us. She ascertained from me in a few words what it was all about, comforted Dora, and gradually convinced her that I was not a labourer, and so brought us together in peace. When we were quite composed, and Dora had gone upstairs to put some rose-water to her eyes, Miss Mills rang for tea.

We had only one check to our pleasure, and that happened a little while before I took my leave, when, Miss Mills chancing to make some allusion to to-morrow morning, I unluckily let out that, being obliged to exert myself now, I got up at five o'clock.

"Now don't get up at five o'clock, you naughty boy."

"My love," said I, "I have work to do."

"But don't do it!" returned Dora. "Why should you?"

"How shall we live without, Dora?" said I.

"How? Any how!" said Dora.

She seemed to think she had quite settled the question, and gave me such a triumphant little kiss, direct from her innocent heart, that I would hardly have put her out of conceit with her answer, for a fortune.

CHAPTER 35

A Dissolution of Partnership

ONE day, when I went to the Commons as usual, I found Mr. Spenlow in the doorway looking extremely grave, and talking to himself.

Instead of returning my "Good morning" with his usual affability, he looked at me in a distant, ceremonious manner, and coldly requested me to accompany him to a certain coffee-house. I complied, in a very uncomfortable state. I observed that he carried his head with a loftly air that was particularly unpromising; and my mind misgave me that he had found out about my darling Dora.

I followed him into an up-stairs room, and found Miss Murdstone there.

Miss Murdstone gave me her chilly finger-nails, and sat severely rigid. Mr. Spenlow shut the door, motioned me to a chair, and stood on the hearth-rug in front of the fireplace.

"Have the goodness to show Mr. Copperfield," said Mr. Spenlow, "what you have in your reticule, Miss Murdstone."

Miss Murdstone opened it and produced my last letter to Dora, teeming with expressions of devoted affection.

"I believe that is your writing, Mr. Copperfield?" said Mr. Spenlow.

I said, "It is, sir!"

"If I am not mistaken," said Mr. Spenlow, as Miss Murdstone brought a parcel of letters out of her reticule, tied round with the dearest bit of blue ribbon, "those are also from your pen, Mr. Copperfield?"

I took them from her.

"No, thank you!" said Mr. Spenlow, coldly, as I mechanically offered them back to him. "I will not deprive you of them. Miss Murdstone, be so good as to proceed!"

"I must confess to having entertained my suspicions of Miss Spenlow, in reference to David Copperfield, for some time. I observed Miss Spenlow and David Copperfield, when they first met. The depravity of the human heart is such—"

"You will oblige me, ma'am," interrupted Mr. Spenlow, "by confining yourself to facts."

"I have frequently endeavoured to find decisive corroboration of those suspicions, but without effect. On the return of Miss Spenlow from her visit to her friend Miss Mills, I imagined that the manner of Miss Spenlow gave me greater occasion for suspicion than before. Therefore I watched Miss Spenlow closely. Still," resumed Miss Murdstone, "I found no proof until last night. It appeared to me that Miss Spenlow received too many letters from her friend Miss Mills."

"Last evening after tea, I observed the little dog worrying something. I said to Miss Spenlow, 'Dora, what is that the dog has in his mouth? It's paper.' Miss Spenlow immediately put her hand to her frock, gave a sudden cry, and ran to the dog. I interposed, and said 'Dora, my love, you must permit me.'"

The little dog retreated under the sofa on my approaching him, and was with great difficulty dislodged by the fire-irons. At length I obtained possession of it. After perusing it, I taxed Miss Spenlow with having many such letters in her possession; and ultimately obtained from her, the packet which is now in David Copperfield's hand.

Mr. Spenlow, turning to me. "I beg to ask, Mr. Copperfield, if you have anything to say in reply?"

"There is nothing I can say, sir," I returned, "except that all the blame is mine."

"You are very much to blame, sir," said Mr. Spenlow. "When I take a gentleman to my house, no matter whether he is nineteen, twenty-nine, or ninety, I take him there in a spirit of confidence. If he abuses my confidence, he commits a dishonourable action, Mr. Copperfield."

"I feel it, sir, I assure you," I returned. "But I never thought so, before. I love Miss Spenlow to that extent—"

"Pooh! nonsense!" said Mr. Spenlow, reddening. "Pray don't tell me to my face that you love my daughter, Mr. Copperfield!"

"Could I defend my conduct if I did not, sir?" I returned, with all humility.

"Have you considered your years, and my daughter's years, Mr. Copperfield? Have you considered my daughter's station in life, the projects I may contemplate for her advancement, the testamentary intentions I may have with reference to her? Have you considered anything, Mr. Copperfield?"

"Very little, sir, I am afraid;" I answered, speaking to him as respectfully and sorrowfully as I felt; "but pray believe me, I have considered my own worldly position. When I explained it to you, we were already engaged—"

"I beg," said Mr. Spenlow, "that you will not talk to me of engagements, Mr. Copperfield!"

The otherwise immoveable Miss Murdstone laughed contemptuously in one short syllable.

"Will you grant me time—any length of time? We are both so young, sir—"

"You are right," interrupted Mr. Spenlow, nodding his head a great many times, and frowning very much, "you are both very young. It's all nonsense. Let there be an end of the nonsense. Take away those letters, and throw them in the fire. Give me Miss Spenlow's letters to throw in the fire; and although our future intercourse must, you are aware, be restricted to the Commons here, we will agree to make no further mention of the past."

No. I couldn't think of agreeing to it.

"Very well, Mr. Copperfield," said Mr. Spenlow, "I must try my influence with my daughter. Do you decline to take those letters, Mr. Copperfield?" For I had laid them down on the table.

Yes. I told him I hoped he would not think it wrong, but what could I do? I could not deny Dora, and my own heart.

"Confer with Miss Trotwood, or with any person with any knowledge of life," said Mr. Spenlow, adjusting his cravat with both hands. "Take a week, Mr. Copperfield."

I submitted; and, with a countenance as expressive as I was able to make it of dejected and despairing constancy, came out of the room.

When I got to the office, I fell into a state of torment about Dora. The idea of their frightening her, and making her cry, and of my not being there to comfort her, was so excruciating, that it impelled me to write a wild letter to Mr. Spenlow, beseeching him not to visit upon her the consequences of my awful destiny. I saw him, through the half-opened door of his room, take it up and read it.

He said nothing about it all the morning; but before he went away in the afternoon he called me in, and told me that I need not make myself at all uneasy about his daughter's happiness. He believed he was an indulgent father, and I might spare myself any solicitude on her account.

"You may make it necessary, if you are foolish or obstinate, Mr. Copperfield," he observed, "for me to send my daughter abroad again. I hope you will be wiser than that, in a few days. All I desire, Mr. Copperfield, is, that it should be forgotten."

I confided all to my aunt when I got home; and in spite of all she could say to me, went to bed despairing. I got up despairing, and went out despairing. It was Saturday morning, and I went straight to the Commons.

I was surprised, when I came within sight of our office-door, to see the ticket-porters standing outside talking together. I quickened my pace, and went hurriedly in.

Old Tiffey, for the first time in his life, was sitting on somebody else's stool, and had not hung up his hat.

"This is a dreadful calamity, Mr. Copperfield," said he, as I entered.

"What is?" I exclaimed. "What's the matter?"

"Don't you know?" cried Tiffey, and all the rest of them, coming round me.

"No!" said I, looking from face to face.

"Mr. Spenlow," said Tiffey. "Dead!"

They sat me down in a chair, untied my neckcloth, and brought me some water.

"He dined in town yesterday, and drove down in the phaeton by himself," said Tiffey, "having sent his own groom home by the coach—"

"Well?"

"The phaeton went home without him. The horses stopped at the stable gate. The man went out with a lantern. Nobody in the carriage."

"Had they run away?"

"They were not hot," said Tiffey, putting on his glasses; "no hotter, I understand, than they would have been, going down at the usual pace.

They found him a mile off, lying partly on the roadside, and partly on the path, upon his face. Whether he fell out in a fit, or got out, feeling ill before the fit came on—no one appears to know."

I cannot describe the state of mind into which I was thrown by this intelligence.

Tiffey told me, little thinking how interested I was in the story, that, paying all the just debts of the deceased, and deducting his share of outstanding bad and doubtful debts due to the firm, he wouldn't give a thousand pounds for all the assets remaining.

I suffered tortures all the time. Miss Mills reported to me, that my broken-hearted little Dora would say nothing, when I was mentioned, but "Oh, poor papa! Oh, dear papa!" Also, that she had no other relations than two aunts, maiden sisters of Mr. Spenlow, who lived at Putney, and who had not held any other than chance communication with their brother for many years.

These two ladies now emerged from their retirement, and proposed to take Dora to live at Putney.

Dora, clinging to them both, and weeping, exclaimed, "Oh yes, aunts! Please take Julia Mills and me and Jip to Putney!" So they went, very soon after the funeral.

CHAPTER 36

Wickfield and Heep

MY aunt, beginning, I imagine, to be made seriously uncomfortable by my prolonged dejection, made a pretence of being anxious that I should go to Dover to see that all was working well at the cottage, which was let.

Although it required an effort to leave Miss Mills, I fell rather willingly into my aunt's pretence, as a means of enabling me to pass a few tranquil hours with Agnes.

Arrived at Mr. Wickfield's house, I found, in the little lower room on the ground floor, where Uriah Heep had been of old accustomed to sit, Mr. Micawber plying his pen with great assiduity.

Mr. Micawber was extremely glad to see me.

He told me that he had become the tenant of Uriah Heep's old house; and that Mrs. Micawber would be delighted to receive me, once more, under her own roof.

I looked into the room still belonging to Agnes, and saw her sitting by the fire, at a pretty old-fashioned desk she had, writing.

My darkening the light made her look up. What a pleasure to be the cause of that bright change in her attentive face, and the object of that sweet regard and welcome!

"Ah, Agnes!" said I, "I have missed you so much, lately!"

"Indeed?" she replied. "Again! And so soon?"

In her placid sisterly manner; with her beaming eyes; with her tender voice; and with that sweet composure, which had long ago made the house that held her quite a sacred place to me; she soon won me from this weakness, and led me on to tell all that had happened since our last meeting.

"What ought I to do then, Agnes?" I inquired, after looking at the fire a little while. "What would it be right to do?"

"I think," said Agnes, "that the honourable course to take, would be to write to those two ladies and relate, as plainly and as openly as possible, all that has taken place; and I would ask their permission to visit sometimes, at their house. Considering that you are young, and striving for a place in life, I think it would be well to say that you would readily abide by any conditions they might impose upon you. I would entreat them not to dismiss your request, without a reference to Dora; and to discuss it with her when they should think the time suitable."

"But if they were to frighten Dora again, Agnes, by speaking to her," said I. "And if Dora were to cry, and say nothing about me!"

"I don't think, Trotwood," returned Agnes, "I would consider that. Perhaps it would be better only to consider whether it is right to do this; and, if it is, to do it."

I had no longer any doubt on the subject. But first I went down-stairs to see Mr. Wickfield and Uriah Heep.

I found Uriah in possession of a new, plaster-smelling office, built out in the garden; looking extraordinarily mean, in the midst of a quantity of books and papers. He accompanied me into Mr. Wickfield's room, which was the shadow of its former self—having been divested of a variety of conveniences, for the accommodation of the new partner—and stood before the fire, warming his back, and shaving his chin with his bony hand, while Mr. Wickfield and I exchanged greetings.

"You stay with us, Trotwood, while you remain in Canterbury?" said Mr. Wickfield, not without a glance at Uriah for his approval.

"Is there room for me?" said I.

"I am sure, Master Copperfield—I," said Uriah,—"I would turn out of your old room with pleasure, if it would be agreeable."

"No, no," said Mr. Wickfield. "Why should *you* be inconvenienced? There's another room. There's another room."

"Oh, but you know," returned Uriah, with a grin, "I should really be delighted!"

I had hoped to have no other companion than Agnes. But Mrs. Heep had asked permission to bring herself and her knitting near the fire, in that room.

She never left off, or left us for a moment. I had arrived early in the day, and we had still three or four hours before dinner; but she sat there, plying her knitting-needles as monotonously as an hour-glass might have poured out its sands.

At dinner she maintained her watch, with the same unwinking eyes.

After dinner, her son took his turn; and when Mr. Wickfield, himself, and I were left alone together, leered at me, and writhed until I could hardly bear it.

This lasted until bedtime. Next day the knitting and watching began again, and lasted all day.

I had not an opportunity of speaking to Agnes, for ten minutes. I could barely show her my letter. I proposed to her to walk out with me; but Mrs. Heep repeatedly complaining that she was unwell, Agnes charitably remained within, to bear her company. Towards the twilight I went out by myself.

I had not walked out far enough to be quite clear of the town, upon the Ramsgate road, where there was a good path, when I was hailed, through the dust, by somebody behind me. The shambling figure, and the scanty great-coat, were not to be mistaken. I stopped, and Uriah Heep came up.

"Where are you going?" said I.

"I am coming with you, Master Copperfield, if you'll allow me the pleasure of a walk with an old acquaintance."

"Uriah!" said I, as civilly as I could, after a silence.

"Master Copperfield!" said Uriah.

"To tell you the truth, I came out to walk alone, because I have had so much company."

He looked at me sideways.—"You mean mother."

"Why yes, I do," said I.

"Ah! But you know we're so very umble," he returned. "We must really take care that we're not pushed to the wall by them as isn't umble. All stratagems are fair in love, sir. You see," he said, still hugging himself in that unpleasant way, and shaking his head at me, "you're quite a dangerous rival, Master Copperfield. You always was, you know."

"Do you suppose," said I, constraining myself to be very temperate and quiet with him, on account of Agnes, "that I regard Miss Wickfield otherwise than as a very dear sister?"

"Well, Master Copperfield," he replied, "you perceive I am not bound to answer that question. You may not, you know. But then, you see, you may!"

"I am engaged to another young lady. I hope that contents you."

"Upon your soul?" said Uriah.

He caught hold of my hand, and gave it a squeeze.

"Before we leave the subject, you ought to understand," said I, breaking a pretty long silence, "that I believe Agnes Wickfield to be as far above you, and as far removed from all your aspirations, as that moon herself!"

"Peaceful! Ain't she!" said Uriah. "Very! Now confess, Master Copperfield, that you haven't liked me quite as I have liked you."

When we three males were left alone after dinner, he got into a more adventurous state. He had taken little or no wine; and I presume it was the mere insolence of triumph that was upon him, flushed perhaps by the temptation my presence furnished to its exhibition.

I had observed yesterday, that he tried to entice Mr. Wickfield to drink; and interpreting the look which Agnes had given me as she went out, had limited myself to one glass, and then proposed that we should follow her. I would have done so again to-day; but Uriah was too quick for me.

"Come, fellow-partner," said Uriah, "if I may take the liberty—now, suppose you give us something or another appropriate to Copperfield!"

I pass over Mr. Wickfield's proposing my aunt, his proposing Mr. Dick, his proposing Doctors' Commons, his proposing Uriah, his drinking everything twice; his consciousness of his own weakness, the ineffectual effort that he made against it; the struggle between his shame in Uriah's deportment, and his desire to conciliate him; the manifest exultation with which Uriah twisted and turned, and held him up before me.

"Come, fellow-partner!" said Uriah, at last, "I'll give you another one, and I umbly ask for bumpers, seeing I intend to make it the divinest of her sex."

Her father had his empty glass in his hand. I saw him set it down, look at the picture she was so like, put his hand to his forehead, and shrink back in his elbow-chair.

"Agnes," said Uriah, either not regarding him, or not knowing what the nature of his action was, "Agnes Wickfield is, I am safe to say, the divinest of her sex. May I speak out, among friends? To be her father is a proud distinction, but to be her usband—"

Spare me from ever again hearing such a cry, as that with which her father rose up from the table!

"What's the matter?" said Uriah, turning of a deadly colour. "You are not gone mad, after all, Mr. Wickfield, I hope? If I say I've an ambition to make your Agnes my Agnes, I have as good a right to it as another man. I have a better right to it than any other man!"

I had my arms round Mr. Wickfield, imploring him by everything that I could think of, oftenest of all by his love for Agnes, to calm himself a little. He was mad for the moment; tearing out his hair, beating his head, trying to force me from him, and to force himself from me, not answering a word, not looking at or seeing any one; blindly striving for he knew not what, his face all staring and distorted—a frightful spectacle.

He pointed to Uriah, pale and glowering in a corner, evidently very much out in his calculations, and taken by surprise.

"Look at my torturer," he replied. "Before him I have step by step abandoned name and reputation, peace and quiet, house and home."

"Don't be foolish, Mr. Wickfield. If I have gone a little beyond what you were prepared for, I can go back, I suppose? There's no harm done. You had better stop him, Copperfield, if you can," cried Uriah, with his long fore-finger pointing towards me. "He'll say something presently—mind you!—he'll be sorry to have said afterwards, and you'll be sorry to have heard!"

"I'll say anything!" cried Mr. Wickfield, with a desperate air. "Why should I not be in all the world's power if I am in yours?"

"Mind! I tell you!" said Uriah, continuing to warn me. "If you don't stop his mouth, you're not his friend!"

"Oh, Trotwood, Trotwood!" exclaimed Mr. Wickfield, wringing his hands. "What I have come down to be, since I first saw you in this house!"

He dropped into a chair, and weakly sobbed. The excitement into which he had been roused was leaving him. Uriah came out of his corner.

"I don't know all I have done, in my fatuity," said Mr. Wickfield, putting out his hands, as if to deprecate my condemnation. "*He* knows best," meaning Uriah Heep, "for he has always been at my elbow, whispering to me. You see the mill-stone that he is about my neck."

"You haven't need to say so much, nor half so much, nor anything at all," observed Uriah, half defiant, and half fawning. "You'll think better of it to-morrow, sir."

The door opened, and Agnes, gliding in, without a vestige of colour in her face, put her arm round his neck, and steadily said, "Papa, you are not well. Come with me!" He laid his head upon her shoulder, as if he were oppressed with heavy shame, and went out with her. Her eyes met mine for but an instant, yet I saw how much she knew of what had passed.

I went up-stairs into the quiet room where Agnes had so often sat beside me at my books. I heard the clock strike twelve, and was still reading, without knowing what I read, when Agnes touched me.

"You will be going early in the morning, Trotwood! Let us say good-bye, now!"

She had been weeping, but her face then was so calm and beautiful!

"Dearest Agnes!" I returned, "I see you ask me not to speak of to-night—but is there nothing to be done?"

"There is God to trust in!" she replied.

"Dear Agnes," I said, "you will never sacrifice yourself to a mistaken sense of duty, Agnes?"

More agitated for a moment than I had ever seen her, she took her hand from me, and moved a step back.

Oh! long, long afterwards, I saw that look subside, as it did now, into the lovely smile, with which she told me she had no fear for herself—I need have none for her—and parted from me by the name of Brother, and was gone!

CHAPTER 37

The Wanderer

WE had a very serious conversation in Buckingham Street that night, about the domestic occurrences I have detailed in the last chapter. My aunt was deeply interested in them, and walked up and down the room with her arms folded, for more than two hours afterwards.

When my aunt and I were left to ourselves by Mr. Dick's going to bed, I sat down to write my letter to the two old ladies.

I posted it, and had nothing to do then, but wait, as patiently as I could, for the reply. I was still in this state of expectation, and had been, for nearly a week; when I left the Doctor's one snowy night, to walk home.

My shortest way home—was through Saint Martin's Lane. As I passed the steps of the portico, I encountered, at the corner, a woman's face. I knew it. I had seen it somewhere. But I could not remember where.

On the steps of the church, there was the stooping figure of a man, who had put down some burden on the smooth snow, to adjust it; my seeing the face, and my seeing him, were simultaneous. I don't think I had stopped in my surprise; but in any case, as I went on, he rose, turned, and came down towards me. I stood face to face with Mr. Peggotty!

Then I remembered the woman. It was Martha, to whom Emily had given the money that night in the kitchen. Martha Endell—side by side with whom, he would not have seen his dear niece, Ham had told me, for all the treasures wrecked in the sea.

We shook hands heartily. At first, neither of us could speak a word.

"Mas'r Davy!" he said, gripping me tight, "it do my 'art good to see you, sir. Well met, well met!"

"Where were you going now?" I asked.

"Well!" he replied, shaking the snow out of his long hair, "I was a-going to turn in somewheers."

Two or three publicrooms opened out of the stable-yard; and looking into one of them, and finding it empty, and a good fire burning, I took him in there.

"I'll tell you, Mas'r Davy," he said,—"wheer all I've been, and what-all we've heerd. I've been fur, and we've heerd little; but I'll tell you!"

"When she was—lost," said Mr. Peggotty, "I know'd in my mind, as he would take her to them countries. When we see his mother, I know'd quite well as I was right. I went across-channel to France, and landed theer, as if I'd fell down from the sky."

I saw the door move, and the snow drift in. I saw it move a little more, and a hand softly interpose to keep it open.

"I found out an English gen'leman as was in authority," said Mr. Peggotty, "and told him I was a going to seek my niece. He got me them papers as I wanted fur to carry me through—I told him, best as I was able, what my gratitoode was, and went away through France."

"Alone, and on foot?" said I.

"Mostly a-foot," he rejoined.

"When I come to any town," he pursued, "I found the inn, and waited about the yard till some one turned up as know'd English. Then I told how that I was on my way to seek my niece, and they told me what manner of gentlefolks was in the house, and I waited to see any as seemed like her, going in or out. When it warn't Em'ly, I went on agen."

141

It was Martha at the door. I saw her haggard, listening face directly. My dread was lest he should turn his head, and see her too.

Overpowered by sudden grief, he sobbed aloud.

From some pocket in his breast he took out, with a very careful hand, a small paper bundle containing two or three letters or little packets, which he laid upon the table.

"This fust one come," he said, selecting it from the rest, "afore I had been gone a week. A fifty pound Bank note, in a sheet of paper, directed to me, and put underneath the door in the night. She tried to hide her writing, but she couldn't hide it from me!"

He folded up the note again, with great patience and care, in exactly the same form, and laid it on one side.

"This come to Missis Gummidge," he said, opening another, "two or three months ago." After looking at it for some moments, he gave it to me, and added in a low voice, "Be so good as read it, sir."

I read as follows:

"Dear, if your heart is hard towards me—ask him I have wronged the most—him whose wife I was to have been—before you quite decide against my poor poor prayer! If he should be so compassionate as to say that you might write something for me to read—I think he would, oh, I think he would, if you would only ask him, for he always was so brave and so forgiving—tell him then (but not else), that when I hear the wind blowing at night, I feel as if it was passing angrily from seeing him and uncle, and was going up to God against me. Tell him that if I was to die to-morrow (and oh, if I was fit, I would be so glad to die!) I would bless him and uncle with my last words, and pray for his happy home with my last breath!"

Some money was enclosed in this letter also. Five pounds. It was untouched like the previous sum, and he refolded it in the same way.

"What answer was sent?" I inquired of Mr. Peggotty.

"Missis Gummidge," he returned, "not being a good scholar, sir, Ham kindly drawed it out, and she made a copy on it. They told her I was gone to seek her, and what my parting words was."

"Is that another letter in your hand?" said I.

"It's money, sir," said Mr. Peggotty, unfolding it a little way. "Ten pound, you see. And wrote inside, 'From a true friend,' like the fust. But the fust was put underneath the door, and this come by the post, day afore yesterday. I'm a going to seek her at the postmark."

He showed it to me. It was a town on the Upper Rhine.

He gathered up the letters thoughtfully, smoothing them with his hand; put them into their little bundle; and placed it tenderly in his breast again. The face was gone from the door. I still saw the snow drifting in; but nothing else was there.

He rose, and I rose too; we grasped each other by the hand again, before going out.

"I'd go ten thousand mile," he said, "I'd go till I dropped dead, to lay that money down afore him. If I do that, and find my Em'ly, I'm content."

As he went out into the rigorous night, I saw the lonely figure flit away before us. I turned him hastily on some pretence, and held him in conversation until it was gone.

I returned to the inn yard, and, impressed by my remembrance of the face, looked awfully round for it. It was not there.

CHAPTER 38

Dora's Aunts

At last, an answer came from the two old ladies. They presented their compliments to Mr. Copperfield, and begged to forbear expressing, "through the medium of correspondence," an opinion on the subject of Mr. Copperfield's communication; but that if Mr. Copperfield would do them the favour to call, upon a certain day (accompanied, if he thought proper, by a confidential friend), they would be happy to hold some conversation on the subject.

To this favour, Mr. Copperfield immediately replied, with his respectful compliments, that he would have the honour of waiting on the Misses Spenlow, at the time appointed; accompanied, in accordance with their kind permission, by his friend Mr. Thomas Traddles of the Inner Temple. Having dispatched which missive, Mr. Copperfield fell into a condition of strong nervous agitation; and so remained until the day arrived.

I was in several minds how to dress myself on the important day. I endeavoured to hit a happy medium between the two extremes; my aunt approved the result; and Mr. Dick threw one of his shoes after Traddles and me, for luck, as we went down-stairs.

On our approaching the house where the Misses Spenlow lived, I was at such a discount in respect of my personal looks and presence of mind, that Traddles proposed a gentle stimulant in the form of a glass of ale.

This having been administered at a neighbouring public-house, he conducted me with tottering steps, to the Misses Spenlow's door.

I had a vague sensation of being, as it were, on view, when the maid opened it; and of wavering, somehow, across a hall with a weather-glass in it, into a quiet little drawing-room on the ground-floor, commanding a neat garden. Ultimately I found myself backing Traddles into the fireplace, and bowing in great confusion to two dry little elderly ladies, dressed in black, and each wonderfully like a preparation in chip or tan of the late Mr. Spenlow.

"Pray," said one of the two little ladies, "be seated."

They were both upright in their carriage, formal, precise, composed, and quiet.

"Mr. Copperfield, I believe," said one sister to Traddles.

This was a frightful beginning. Traddles had to indicate that I was Mr. Copperfield.

"Mr. Copperfield!" said the sister.

I did something—bowed, I supposed—and was all attention when the other sister struck in.

"My sister Lavinia," said she, "being conversant with matters of this nature, will state what we consider most calculated to promote the happiness of both parties."

I discovered afterwards that Miss Lavinia was an authority in affairs of the heart, by reason of there having anciently existed a certain Mr. Pidger, who played short whist, and was supposed to have been enamoured of her.

"We will not," said Miss Lavinia, "enter on the past history of this matter. Our poor brother Francis's death has cancelled that."

"We had not," said Miss Clarissa, "been in the habit of frequent association with our brother Francis; but there was no decided division or disunion between us."

Each of the sisters leaned a little forward to speak, shook her head after speaking, and became upright again when silent.

"Our niece's position, is much changed by our brother Francis's death," said Miss Lavinia; "and therefore we consider our brother's opinions as regarding her position as being changed too. We have no reason to doubt, Mr. Copperfield, that you are a young gentleman possessed of good qualities and honourable character; or that you have an affection for our niece."

I replied, that nobody had ever loved anybody else as I loved Dora. Traddles came to my assistance with a confirmatory murmur.

Miss Lavinia resumed:

"You ask permission of my sister Clarissa and myself, Mr. Copperfield, to visit here, as the accepted suitor of our niece. My sister Clarissa and I have been very careful indeed in considering this letter; and we have not considered it without finally showing it to our niece, and discussing it with our niece. We have no doubt that you think you like her very much."

"Think, ma'am," I rapturously began, "oh!——"

"It is owing to the difficulty of knowing whether your feelings are likely to endure or have any real foundation, that my sister Clarissa and myself have been very undecided how to act, Mr. Copperfield, and Mr.——"

"Traddles," said my friend, finding himself looked at.

"I beg pardon. Of the Inner Temple, I believe?" said Miss Clarissa, again glancing at my letter.

Traddles said, "Exactly so; I speak, if I may presume to say so, as one who has some little experience of such things, being myself engaged to a young lady—one of ten, down in Devonshire—and seeing no probability, at present, of our engagement coming to a termination."

"You may be able to confirm what I have said, Mr. Traddles," observed Miss Lavinia, evidently taking a new interest in him, "of the affection that

144

is modest and retiring; that waits and waits?"

"Entirely, ma'am," said Traddles.

Miss Lavinia turned my letter, and referred through her eye-glass to some orderly looking notes she had made on that part of it.

"It seems to us," said she, "prudent, Mr. Traddles, to bring these feelings to the test of our own observation. At present we know nothing of them, and are not in a situation to judge how much reality there may be in them. Therefore we are inclined so far to accede to Mr. Copperfield's proposal, as to admit his visits here."

"I shall never, dear ladies," I exclaimed, relieved of an immense load of apprehension, "forget your kindness!"

"We shall be happy," said Miss Clarissa, "to see Mr. Copperfield to dinner, every Sunday, if it should suit his convenience. Our hour is three."

I bowed.

"In the course of the week," said Miss Clarissa, "we shall be happy to see Mr. Copperfield to tea. Our hour is half-past six."

I bowed again.

"Twice in the week," said Miss Clarissa, "but, as a rule, not oftener."

I bowed again.

"Miss Trotwood," said Miss Clarissa, "mentioned in Mr. Copperfield's letter, will perhaps call upon us."

I intimated that my aunt would be proud and delighted to make their acquaintance; though I must say I was not quite sure of their getting on very satisfactorily together.

Miss Lavinia then arose, and begging Mr. Traddles to excuse us for a minute, requested me to follow her. I obeyed, all in a tremble, and was conducted into another room. There, I found my blessed darling stopping her ears behind the door, with her dear little face against the wall; and Jip in the plate-warmer with his head tied up in a towel.

Oh! How beautiful she was in her black frock, and how she sobbed and cried at first, and wouldn't come out from behind the door! How fond we were of one another, when she did come out at last; and what a state of bliss I was in, when we took Jip out of the plate-warmer, and restored him to the light, sneezing very much, and were all three reunited!

"My dearest Dora! Now, indeed, my own for ever!"

"Oh yes," said Dora, "but I am so frightened!"

"Frightened, my own?"

"Oh yes! I don't like him," said Dora. "Your friend," said Dora. "It isn't any business of his. What a stupid he must be!"

"My love! He is the best creature!"

"Oh, but we don't want any best creatures!" pouted Dora.

"My dear," I argued, "you will soon know him well, and like him of all things. And my aunt is coming here soon: and you'll like her of all things too, when you know her."

"No, please don't bring her!" said Dora, giving me a horrified little kiss, and folding her hands. "Don't. I know she's a naughty, mischief-making old thing! Don't let her come here, Doady!" which was a corruption of David.

I was charmed by her presently asking me, of her own accord, to give her that cookery-book I had once spoken of, and to show her how to keep accounts, as I had once promised I would.

But the cookery-book made Dora's head ache, and the figures made her cry. They wouldn't add up, she said.

Then I playfully tried verbal instruction in domestic matters. Sometimes, when we passed a butcher's shop, I would say:

"Now suppose, my pet, that we were married, and you were going to buy a shoulder of mutton for dinner, would you know how?"

My pretty little Dora's face would fall, and she would think a little, and then reply, perhaps, with great triumph:

"Why, the butcher would know how to sell it, and what need *I* know?"

So, when I once asked Dora, with an eye to the cookery-book, what she would do, if we were married, and I were to say I should like a nice Irish stew, she replied that she would tell the servant to make it.

I occasionally wished I could venture to hint to Miss Lavinia, that she treated the darling of my heart too much like a plaything; and I sometimes awoke wondering to find that I had fallen into the general fault, and treated her like a plaything too.

CHAPTER 39

Mischief

SHE came on a visit of a fortnight to the Doctor's. Mr. Wickfield was the Doctor's old friend, and the Doctor wished to talk with him, and do him good. It had been a matter of conversation with Agnes when she was last in town, and this visit was the result. She and her father came together. I was not much surprised to hear from her that she had engaged to find a lodging in the neighbourhood for Mrs. Heep, whose rheumatic complaint required change of air, and who would be charmed to have it in such company. Neither was I surprised when, on the very next day, Uriah, like a dutiful son, brought his worthy mother to take possession.

"You see, Master Copperfield," said he, as he forced himself upon my company for a turn in the Doctor's garden, "where a person loves, a person is a little jealous—leastways anxious to keep an eye on the beloved one."

"Of whom are you jealous, now?" said I.

He gave me a sidelong glance out of his sinister red eyes, and laughed.

"Really, Master Copperfield," he said, "—Well, I don't mind telling you," putting his fish-like hand on mine, "I'm not a lady's man in general, sir, and I never was, with Mrs. Strong."

"What do you mean?" said I.

"When I was but a numble clerk, she always looked down upon me. She was for ever having my Agnes backwards and forwards at her ouse, and she was for ever being a friend to you, Master Copperfield; but I was too far beneath her, myself, to be noticed."

"Well?" said I; "suppose you were!"

"—And beneath him too," pursued Uriah, very distinctly, and in a meditative tone of voice, as he continued to scrape his chin.

"Don't you know the Doctor better," said I, "than to suppose him conscious of your existence, when you were not before him?"

He directed his eyes at me in that sidelong glance again, he made his face very lantern-jawed, for the greater convenience of scraping, as he answered:

"Oh dear, I am not referring to the Doctor! Oh no, poor man! I mean Mr. Maldon!"

My heart quite died within me. All my old doubts, and apprehensions on that subject, all the Doctor's happiness and peace, all the mingled possibilities of innocence and compromise, that I could not unravel, I saw, in a moment, at the mercy of this fellow's twisting.

"He never could come into the office, without ordering and shoving me about," said Uriah. "I was very meek and umble—and I am. But I didn't like that sort of thing—and I don't!"

He left off scraping his chin, and sucked in his cheeks until they seemed to meet inside.

"I mustn't be put upon, as a numble person, too much. I can't allow people in my way. Really they must come out of the cart, Master Copperfield!"

"I don't understand you," said I.

"Don't you, though?" he returned, with one of his jerks. "I'm astonished at that, Master Copperfield, you being usually so quick! I'll try to be plainer, another time.—Is that Mr. Maldon a-norseback, ringing at the gate, sir?"

"It looks like him," I replied, as carelessly as I could.

Uriah stopped short, put his hands between his great knobs of knees, and doubled himself up with laughter.

On the next evening but one, which was a Saturday, I took Agnes to see Dora.

I was in a flutter of pride and anxiety; pride in my dear little betrothed, and anxiety that Agnes should like her.

Dora was afraid of Agnes. She had told me that she knew Agnes was "too clever."

But when she saw her looking at once so cheerful and so good, she gave a little cry of surprise, put her arms round Agnes' neck, and laid her innocent cheek against her face.

I never was so happy.

"I am so glad," said Dora, after tea, "that you like me. I didn't think you would."

Agnes said she was afraid I must have given her an unpromising character; but Dora corrected that directly.

"Oh no!" she said, shaking her curls at me; "it was all praise. He thinks so much of your opinion, that I was quite afraid of it."

We made merry about Dora's wanting to be liked, and Dora said I was a goose, and she didn't like me at any rate, and the short evening flew away on gossamer wings.

The time was at hand when the coach was to call for us. There was a hurried but affectionate parting between Agnes and herself; and Dora was to write to Agnes (who was not to mind her letters being foolish, she said), and Agnes was to write to Dora; and they had a second parting at the coach-door.

The stage-coach was to put us down near Covent Garden, where we were to take another stage-coach for Highgate.

When we had again alighted, and were walking in the starlight along the quiet road that led to the Doctor's house. I glanced at the serence face looking upward, and thought it was the stars that made it seem so noble.

"There has been no change at home," said Agnes, after a few moments.

"No fresh reference," said I, "to what we spoke of, when we parted last?"

"You must think less about it. Remember that I confide in simple love and truth at last. Have no apprehensions for me, Trotwood," she added, after a moment; "the step you dread my taking, I shall never take."

Although I think I had never really feared it, it was an unspeakable relief to me to have this assurance from her own truthful lips.

We were now within the little court-yard of the Doctor's cottage. It was growing late. There was a light in the window of Mrs. Strong's chamber, and Agnes, pointing to it, bade me good-night.

I saw a light in the Doctor's study. With the view of bidding him good-night, if he were yet sitting among his books, I looked in.

The first person whom I saw, to my surprise, was Uriah. The Doctor sat in his study chair, covering his face with his hands. Mr. Wickfield, sorely troubled and distressed, was leaning forward, irresolutely touching the Doctor's arm.

For an instant, I supposed that the Doctor was ill. I hastily advanced a step under that impression, when I met Uriah's eye, and saw what was the matter.

"At any rate," observed Uriah, with a writhe of his ungainly person, "we may keep the door shut. We needn't make it known to ALL the town."

Saying which, he went on his toes to the door, which I had left open, and carefully closed it.

"I have felt it incumbent upon me, Master Copperfield," said Uriah, "to point out to Doctor Strong what you and me have already talked about. You didn't exactly understand me, though."

"As you didn't understand me, Master Copperfield," resumed Uriah, "I may take the liberty of umbly mentioning, that I have called Doctor Strong's attention to the goings-on of Mrs. Strong."

148

I wonder now, that I did not try to shake the breath out of his body.

"I have mentioned to Doctor Strong that any one may see that Mr. Maldon, and the lovely and agreeable lady as is Doctor Strong's wife, are too sweet on one another. Really the time is come, when Doctor Strong must be told that Mr. Maldon is here for nothing else."

"You have had doubts, Wickfield," said the Doctor, without lifting his head. "You have had doubts."

"I had, at one time, certainly. I thought," said Mr. Wickfield, "that you wished to send Maldon abroad to effect a desirable separation."

"No, no, no!" returned the Doctor. "To give Annie pleasure, by making some provision for the companion of her childhood."

"I am sure," said Uriah, writhing himself into the silence like a Conger-eel, "that this is a subject full of unpleasantness to everybody. But since we have got so far, I ought to take the liberty of mentioning that Copperfield has noticed it too."

I turned upon him, and asked him how he dared refer to me!

"Oh! it's very kind of you, Copperfield," returned Uriah, undulating all over, "and we all know what an amiable character yours is; but you know that the moment I spoke to you the other night, you knew what I meant."

I saw the mild eye of the good old Doctor turned upon me for a moment, and I felt that the confession of my old misgivings and remembrances was too plainly written in my face to be overlooked.

We were silent again, and remained so, until the Doctor rose and walked twice or thrice across the room.

"I have been much to blame. I believe I have been very much to blame. I married that lady," said the Doctor, "when she was extremely young. I took her to myself when her character was scarcely formed. I knew her father well. I knew her well. I had taught her what I could, for the love of all her beautiful and virtuous qualities. I did her wrong; in taking advantage of her gratitude and her affection."

He walked across the room, and came back to the same place; holding the chair with a grasp that trembled, like his subdued voice, in its earnestness. "My life with this lady has been very happy. Until to-night, I have had uninterrupted occasion to bless the day on which I did her great injustice. I see how natural it is that she should have some regretful feeling towards her old companion and her equal. That she does regard him with some innocent regret, with some blameless thoughts of what might have been, but for me, is, I fear, too true. But, beyond this, gentlemen, the dear lady's name never must be coupled with a word, a breath, of doubt."

For a little while, his eye kindled and his voice was firm; for a little while he was again silent. Presently, he proceeded as before:

"It only remains for me, to bear the knowledge of the unhappiness I have occasioned, as submissively as I can. It is she who should reproach; not I."

"Gentlemen, I have shown you my heart. I am sure you will respect it. What we have said to-night is never to be said more. Wickfield, give me an old friend's arm to help me up-stairs!"

They went slowly out of the room together, Uriah looking after them.

"Well, Master Copperfield!" said Uriah, meekly turning to me. "The thing hasn't took quite the turn that might have been expected."

I needed but the sound of his voice to be so madly enraged as I never was before, and never have been since.

"You villain," said I, "what do you mean by entrapping me into your schemes? How dare you appeal to me just now, you false rascal, as if we had been in discussion together?"

As we stood, front to front, I saw so plainly, in the stealthy exultation of his face, what I already so plainly knew (I mean that he had forced his confidence upon me, expressly to make me miserable, and had set a deliberate trap for me in this very matter) that I couldn't bear it. The whole of his lank cheek was invitingly before me, and I struck it with my open hand with such force that my fingers tingled as if I had burnt them.

"Copperfield," he said at length, in a breathless voice, "have you taken leave of your senses?"

"I have taken leave of you," said I, wresting my hand away. "You dog, I'll know no more of you."

"Copperfield," he said, "there must be two parties to a quarrel. I won't be one."

"You may go to the devil!" said I.

The Doctor gave out that he was not quite well; and remained alone, for a considerable part of every day, during the remainder of the visit. It was not a subject I could discuss with Agnes, and Agnes certainly had not the least suspicion of what had passed.

Neither, I felt convinced, had Mrs. Strong then. Several weeks elapsed before I saw the least change in her. It came on slowly, like a cloud when there is no wind. Gradually, an unhappy shadow fell upon her beauty, and deepened every day.

When the visit at the Doctor's was still in progress, I observed that the postman brought two or three letters every morning for Uriah Heep, directed in a business-like manner by Mr. Micawber, who now assumed a round legal hand, and I was consequently much surprised to receive the following letter from his amiable wife:—

"CANTERBURY, *Monday Evening.*

"You will picture to yourself, my dear Mr. Copperfield, what the poignancy of my feelings must be, when I inform you that Mr. Micawber is entirely changed. He is reserved. He is secret. His life is a mystery to the partner of his joys and sorrows.

"But this is not all. Mr. Micawber is morose. He is severe. He is estranged from our eldest son and daughter, he has no pride in his twins, he looks with an eye of coldness even on the unoffending stranger who last became a member of our circle. The pecuniary means of meeting our expenses, kept down to the utmost farthing, are obtained from him with great difficulty.

"This is hard to bear. This is heart-breaking. If you will advise me, you will add another friendly obligation to the many you have already rendered me. With love from the children, and a smile from the happily-unconscious stranger, I remain, dear Mr. Copperfield,

"Your afflicted,
"Emma Micawber."

I did not feel justified in giving a wife of Mrs. Micawber's experience any other recommendation, than that she should try to reclaim Mr. Micawber by patience and kindness (as I knew she would in any case); but the letter set me thinking about him very much.

CHAPTER 40

Another Retrospect

Weeks, months, seasons, pass along. They seem little more than a summer day and a winter evening.

I have come legally to man's estate. I have attained the dignity of twenty-one. But this is a sort of dignity that may be thrust upon one. Let me think what I have achieved.

I have tamed that savage stenographic mystery. I make a respectable income by it. I am in high repute for my accomplishment in all pertaining to the art, and am joined with eleven others in reporting the debates in Parliament for a Morning Newspaper.

I have come out in another way. I have taken with fear and trembling to authorship. I wrote a little something, in secret, and sent it to a magazine, and it was published. Since then, I have taken heart to write a good many trifling pieces. Now, I am regularly paid for them. Altogether, I am well off; when I tell my income on the fingers of my left hand, I pass the third finger and take in the fourth to the middle joint.

We have removed from Buckingham Street, to a pleasant little cottage very near the one I looked at, when my enthusiasm first came on. My aunt, however (who has sold the house at Dover, to good advantage), is not going to remain here, but intends removing herself to a still more tiny cottage close at hand. What does this portend? My marriage? Yes!

It was a strange condition of things, the honeymoon being over, and the bridesmaids gone home, when I found myself sitting down in my own small house with Dora; quite thrown out of employment, as I may say, in respect of the delicious old occupation of making love.

It seemed such an extraordinary thing to have Dora always there. Sometimes of an evening, when I looked up from my writing, and saw her seated opposite, I would lean back in my chair, and think how queer it was that there we were, alone together as a matter of course.

It was such a wonderful thing, at first, to have her coming softly down to talk to me as I ate my supper. It was such a stupendous thing to know for certain that she put her hair in papers. It was altogether such an astonishing event to see her do it! I doubt whether two young birds have known less about keeping house than I and my pretty Dora did.

CHAPTER 41

Mr. Dick Fulfils My Aunt's Predictions

IT was some time now, since I had left the Doctor. Living in his neighbourhood, I saw him frequently; and we all went to his house on two or three occasions to dinner or tea. The Old Soldier was in permanent quarters under the Doctor's roof. She was exactly the same as ever, and the same immortal butterflies hovered over her cap.

"My dear soul," she said to him one day when I was present, "you know there is no doubt it would be a little pokey for Annie to be always shut up here."

The Doctor nodded his benevolent head.

"Therefore, my dear Doctor," said the Soldier, giving him several affectionate taps, "you may command me, at all times and seasons. Now, do understand that I am entirely at your service. I am ready to go with Annie to operas, concerts, exhibitions, all kinds of places; and you shall never find that I am tired. Duty, my dear Doctor, before every consideration in the universe!"

It was in vain for Annie to protest that she was weary of such things. Her mother's remonstrance always was, "Now, my dear Annie, I am sure you know better; and I must tell you, my love, that you are not making a proper return for the kindness of Doctor Strong."

This was usually said in the Doctor's presence, and appeared to me to constitute Annie's principal inducement for withdrawing her objections when she made any. But in general she resigned herself to her mother, and went where the Old Soldier would.

My aunt rubbed her nose sometimes when she happened to be alone with me, and said she couldn't make it out; she wished they were happier; she didn't think our military friend (so she always called the Old Soldier) mended the matter at all.

But one night, when I had been married some months, Mr. Dick put his head into the parlour, where I was writing alone.

"Trotwood," said Mr. Dick, laying his finger on the side of his nose, after he had shaken hands with me. "Before I sit down, I wish to make an observation. You know your aunt?"

"A little," I replied.

"She is the most wonderful woman in the world, sir!"

152

After the delivery of this communication, which he shot out of himself as if he were loaded with it, Mr. Dick sat down with greater gravity than usual, and looked at me.

"In short, boy," said Mr. Dick, dropping his voice to a whisper, "I am simple."

I would have qualified that conclusion, but he stopped me.

"Yes I am! She pretends I am not. She won't hear of it; but I am. I know I am. If she hadn't stood my friend, sir, I should have been shut up, to lead a dismal life these many years. But I'll provide for her! I never spend the copying money. I put it in a box. I have made a will. I'll leave it all to her. She shall be rich—noble!"

Mr. Dick took out his pocket-handkerchief and wiped his eyes.

"Now you are a scholar, Trotwood," said Mr. Dick. "You are a fine scholar. You know what a learned man, what a great man, the Doctor is. Not proud in his wisdom, condescending even to poor Dick, who is simple and knows nothing."

I delighted him by saying, most heartily, that the Doctor was deserving of our best respect and highest esteem.

"And his beautiful wife is a star," said Mr. Dick. "A shining star. But," bringing his chair nearer, and laying one hand upon my knee—"clouds, sir—clouds."

He looked so wistfully into my face, and was so anxious to understand, that I took great pains to answer him slowly and distinctly, as I might have entered on an explanation to a child.

"There is some unfortunate division between them," I replied. "Some unhappy cause of separation. A secret. It may be inseparable from the discrepancy in their years. It may have grown up out of almost nothing."

"Doctor not angry with her, Trotwood?" he said, after some time.

"No. Devoted to her."

"Then, I have got it, boy!" said Mr. Dick.

The sudden exultation with which he slapped me on the knee, and leaned back in his chair, with his eyebrows lifted up as high as he could possibly lift them, made me think him farther out of his wits than ever.

"A poor fellow with a craze, sir," said Mr. Dick, "a simpleton, a weak-minded person—present company, you know!" striking himself again, "may do what wonderful people may not do. I'll bring them together, boy. I'll try. They'll not blame *me*. They'll not object to *me*. They'll not mind what *I* do, if it's wrong. I'm only Mr. Dick. And who minds Dick? Dick's nobody! Whoo!" He blew a slight, contemptuous breath, as if he blew himself away.

One fair evening, when Dora was not inclined to go out, my aunt and I strolled up to the Doctor's cottage.

It was twilight. Mrs. Strong was just coming out of the garden, where Mr. Dick yet lingered, busy with his knife, helping the gardener to point some stakes. The Doctor was engaged with some one in his study. Mrs. Strong begged us to remain and see him. We went into the drawing-room with her, and sat down by the darkening window.

We had not sat here many minutes, when Mrs. Markleham, who usually contrived to be in a fuss about something, came bustling in, with her newspaper in her hand, and said, out of breath and sinking on the sofa, "I never had such a turn in all my life! I came upon the amiable creature—if you'll imagine my feelings, Miss Trotwood and David—in the act of making his will."

Her daughter looked round from the window quickly.

"In the act, my dear Annie," repeated Mrs. Markleham, "of making his last Will and Testament. I must tell you how it was. I took me to the Study, where I saw a light. I opened the door. In company with the dear Doctor were two professional people, evidently connected with the law, and they were all three standing at the table: the darling Doctor pen in hand. 'This simply expresses then,' said the Doctor—'the confidence I have in Mrs. Strong, and gives her all unconditionally.' Upon that, with the natural feelings of a mother, I said, 'Good God, I beg your pardon!' fell over the door-step, and came away through the little back passage where the pantry is."

Mrs. Strong opened the window, and went out into the verandah, where she stood leaning against a pillar.

I was conscious of Mr. Dick's standing in the shadow of the room, shutting up his knife, but who got first into the Study, I have forgotten. But this I know—that we saw the Doctor before he saw us, sitting at his table. That, as the Doctor moved his head, his wife dropped down on one knee at his feet, and, with her hands imploringly lifted, fixed upon his face the memorable look I had never forgotten.

"Doctor!" said Mr. Dick. "What is it that's amiss? Look here!"

"Annie!" cried the Doctor. "Not at my feet, my dear!"

"Yes!" she said. "I beg and pray that no one will leave the room! Oh, my husband and father, break this long silence. Let us both know what it is that has come between us!"

Mrs. Markleham here exclaimed, "Annie, get up immediately and don't disgrace everybody belonging to you by humbling yourself like that!"

"Mama!" said Annie. "Waste no words on me, for my appeal is to my husband, and even you are nothing here."

"Nothing!" exclaimed Mrs. Markleham. "Me, nothing! The child has taken leave of her senses. Please to get me a glass of water!"

I was too attentive to the Doctor and his wife, to give any heed to this request; and it made no impression on anybody else; so Mrs. Markleham panted, stared, and fanned herself.

"Annie!" said the Doctor, tenderly taking her hands in his. "My dear! If any unavoidable change has come, in the sequence of time, upon our married life, you are not to blame. The fault is mine, and only mine. There is no change in my affection, admiration, and respect. I wish to make you happy. I truly love and honour you. Rise, Annie, pray!"

But she did not rise. After looking at him for a little while, she sank down closer to him, laid her arm across his knee, and dropping her head upon it, said:

"If I have any friend here, who can speak one word for me, or for my husband in this matter; if I have any friend here, who can give a voice to any suspicion that my heart has sometimes whispered to me; if I have any friend here, who honours my husband, or has ever cared for me, and has anything within his knowledge, no matter what it is, that may help to mediate between us—I implore that friend to speak!"

There was a profound silence. After a few moments of painful hesitation, I broke the silence.

"Mrs. Strong," I said, "there is something within my knowledge, which I have been earnestly entreated by Doctor Strong to conceal, and have concealed until to-night."

She turned her face towards me for a moment, and I knew that I was right.

"Our future peace," she said, "may be in your hands."

Thus earnestly besought, I related plainly what had passed in that same room that night.

When I had finished, Annie remained, for some few moments, silent, with her head bent down as I have described. Then, she took the Doctor's hand and kissed it. Mr. Dick softly raised her; and she stood, when she began to speak, leaning on him, and looking down upon her husband—from whom she never turned her eyes.

"All that has ever been in my mind, since I was married," she said in a low, submissive, tender voice, "I will lay bare before you."

"Nay, Annie," said the Doctor, mildly, "I have never doubted you, my child."

"There is great need," she answered, in the same way, "that I should open my whole heart before the soul of generosity and truth, whom year by year, and day by day, I have loved and venerated more and more, as Heaven knows!"

"When I was very young," said Annie, "my first associations with knowledge of any kind were inseparable from a patient friend and teacher—the friend of my dead father—who was always dear to me. They never could have been, I think, as good if I had taken them from any other hands."

"Makes her mother nothing!" exclaimed Mrs. Markleham.

"Not so, mama," said Annie. "You know how young and inexperienced I was, when you presented him before me, of a sudden, as a lover. When so great a change came in the character in which I had so long looked up to him, I think I was sorry. But nothing could have made him what he used to be again: and I was proud that he should think me so worthy, and we were married."

"I never thought of any worldly gain that any husband would bring to me."

"Mama, forgive me when I say that it was *you* who first presented to my mind the thought that any one could wrong me, and wrong him, by

155

such a cruel and wicked suspicion."

"Me!" cried Mrs. Markleham.

"It was the first unhappiness of my new life," said Annie. "It was the first occasion of every unhappy moment I have known. Those moments have been more, of late, than I can count; but not—my generous husband!—not for the reason you suppose."

She raised her eyes, and clasped her hands, and looked as beautiful and true, I thought, as any Spirit. The Doctor looked on her, henceforth, as steadfastly as she on him.

"Mama is blameless," she went on, "of having ever urged you for herself, and she is blameless in intention everyway, I am sure,—but when I saw how many importunate claims were pressed upon you in my name; how generous you were, and how Mr. Wickfield, who had your welfare very much at heart, resented it; the first sense of my exposure to the mean suspicion that my tenderness was bought—and sold to you, of all men, on earth —fell upon me, like unmerited disgrace, in which I forced you to participate."

"It was at that time that mama was most solicitous about my Cousin Maldon. I had liked him:" she spoke softly, but without any hesitation: "very much. We had been little lovers once. If circumstances had not happened otherwise, I might have come to persuade myself that I really loved him, and might have married him, and been most wretched. There can be no disparity in marriage like unsuitability of mind and purpose."

I pondered on those words, as if they had some particular interest, or some strange application that I could not divine.

"There is nothing," said Annie, "that we have in common. If I were thankful to my husband for no more, instead of for so much, I should be thankful to him for having saved me from the first mistaken impulse of my undisciplined heart."

She stood quite still, before the Doctor, and spoke with an earnestness that thrilled me. Yet her voice was just as quiet as before.

"When he was waiting to be the object of your munificence, so freely bestowed for my sake, I thought it would have become him better to have worked his own way on. But I thought no worse of him, until the night of his departure for India. That night I knew he had a false and thankless heart."

"I have never, but in your presence, interchanged a word with him from that time; then, only when it has been necessary for the avoidance of this explanation. Years have passed since he knew from me, what his situation here was."

She sunk down gently at the Doctor's feet, though he did his utmost to prevent her; and said, looking up, tearfully, into his face:

"You never can know what it was to be devoted to you, with those old associations; to find that any one could be so hard as to suppose that the truth of my heart was bartered away. I was very young, and had no adviser. Between mama and me, in all relating to you, there was a wide division. If I shrunk into myself, hiding the disrespect I had undergone, it was because I honoured you so much, and so much wished that you should honour me!"

"Annie, my pure heart!" said the Doctor, "my dear girl!"

"I used to fear that I was unsuited to your learning and wisdom. If all this made me shrink within myself, it was still because I honoured you so much, and hoped that you might one day honour me."

"That day has shone this long time, Annie," said the Doctor.

She had her arms around the Doctor's neck, and he leant his head down over her, mingling his grey hair with her dark brown tresses.

"Oh, hold me to your heart, my husband! Never cast me out!"

In the silence that ensued, my aunt walked gravely up to Mr. Dick, without at all hurrying herself, and gave him a hug and a sounding kiss.

"You are a very remarkable man, Dick!" said my aunt, with an air of unqualified approbation; "and never pretend to be anything else, for I know better!"

CHAPTER 42

Intelligence

I MUST have been married, about a year or so, when one evening, as I was returning from a solitary walk, thinking of the book I was then writing—I came past Mrs. Steerforth's house.

I had never done more than glance at the house, as I went by with a quickened step. I do not remember that I ever saw a light in all the house. If I had been a casual passer-by, I should have probably supposed that some childless person lay dead in it.

As it was, I thought as little of it as I might. But my mind could not go by it and leave it, as my body did; and it usually awakened a long train of meditations. I walked on, and a voice at my side made me start.

"If you please, sir, would you have the goodness to walk in, and speak to Miss Dartle?"

I turned back, and inquired of my conductor, as we went along, how Mrs. Steerforth was. She said her lady was but poorly, and kept her own room a good deal.

When we arrived at the house, I was directed to Miss Dartle in the garden, and left to make my presence known to her myself.

She saw me as I advanced, and rose for a moment to receive me.

Our meeting was not cordial. We had parted angrily on the last occasion; and there was an air of disdain about her, which she took no pains to conceal.

"I am told you wish to speak to me, Miss Dartle;" said I.

"Pray has this girl been found?"

"No."

"And yet she has run away!"

I saw her thin lips working while she looked at me.

"Run away?" I repeated.

"Yes! From him," she said, with a laugh. "If she is not found, perhaps she never will be found. She may be dead!"

The vaunting cruelty with which she met my glance, I never saw expressed in any other face that ever I have seen.

"To wish her dead," said I, "may be the kindest wish that one of her own sex could bestow upon her, Miss Dartle."

She condescended to make no reply, but, turning on me with another scornful laugh, said:

"Do you wish to know what is known of her?"

"Yes," said I.

She rose with an ill-favoured smile.

"You will restrain any demonstrative championship or vengeance in this place, of course, Mr. Copperfield?"

I inclined my head, without knowing what she meant; and she said, "Come here!" Whereupon the respectable Mr. Littimer, made me a bow, and took up his position behind her.

"Now," said she, imperiously, without glancing at him, "tell Mr. Copperfield about the flight."

"Mr. James and myself have been abroad with the young woman, ever since she left Yarmouth under Mr. James's protection."

"Mr. James took quite uncommonly to the young woman; and was more settled, for a length of time, than I have known him to be since I have been in his service. The young woman was very improvable, and spoke the languages; and wouldn't have been known for the same country-person. I noticed that she was much admired wherever we went. What with her dress; what with the air and sun; what with being made so much of; what with this, that, and the other; her merits really attracted general notice."

Taking his hands from the seat, and placing one of them within the other, as he settled himself on one leg, Mr. Littimer proceeded, with his eyes cast down, and his respectable head a little advanced, and a little on one side:

"The young woman went on in this manner for some time, being occasionally low in her spirits, until I think she began to weary Mr. James by giving way to her low spirits and tempers of that kind; and things were not so comfortable. Mr. James he began to be restless again. The more restless he got, the worse she got; and I must say, for myself, that I had a very difficult time of it indeed between the two. Still matters were patched up here, and made good there, over and over again; and altogether lasted, I am sure, for a longer time than anybody could have expected."

"At last, Mr. James set off one morning, and left it in charge with me to break it out, that, he was gone. But Mr. James proposed that the young woman should marry a very respectable person, who was fully prepared to overlook the past, and who was, at least, as good as anybody the young woman could have aspired to in a regular way: her connexions being very common."

I was convinced that the scoundrel spoke of himself.

"I undertook the commission. The young woman's violence when she came to, after I broke the fact of his departure, was beyond all expectations. She was quite mad, and had to be held by force; or, if she couldn't have got to a knife, or got to the sea, she'd have beaten her head against the marble floor."

Miss Dartle, leaning back upon the seat, with a light of exultation in her face, seemed almost to caress the sounds this fellow had uttered.

"But when I came to the second part of what had been entrusted to me," said Mr. Littimer, "which anybody might have supposed would have been, at all events, appreciated as a kind intention, then the young woman came out in her true colours. Her conduct was surprisingly bad. If I hadn't been upon my guard, I am convinced she would have had my blood."

"I think the better of her for it," said I, indignantly.

"She got out in the night; forced the lattice of a window, that I had nailed up myself; dropped on a vine that was trailed below; and never has been seen or heard of, to my knowledge, since."

With that, he made a polite bow; and went away through the arch in the wall of holly by which he had come. Miss Dartle and I regarded each other for a little while in silence.

"This devil whom you make an angel of," said she, "I mean this low girl whom he picked out of the tide-mud," with her black eyes full upon me, and her passionate finger up, "may be alive,—for I believe some common things are hard to die. If she is, you will desire to have a pearl of such price found and taken care of. We desire that, too; that he may not by any chance be made her prey again. So far, we are united in one interest; and that is why I, who would do her any mischief that so coarse a wretch is capable of feeling, have sent for you to hear what you have heard."

I saw, by the change in her face, that some one was advancing behind me. It was Mrs. Steerforth, who gave me her hand more coldly than of yore.

"I have had some slight correspondence with your former friend, sir, but it has not restored his sense of duty or natural obligation. If, by the course which may relieve the mind of the decent man you brought here (for whom I am sorry—I can say no more), my son may be saved from again falling into the snares of a designing enemy, well!"

"Madam," I said respectfully, "I must say, even to you, having known this injured family from childhood, that if you suppose the girl, so deeply wronged, has not been cruelly deluded, and would not rather die a hundred deaths than take a cup of water from your son's hand now, you cherish a terrible mistake."

"It is no matter. Let it be. You are married, sir, I am told?"

I answered that I had been some time married.

"I understand you are beginning to be famous."

"I have been very fortunate," I said.

"You have no mother?"—in a softened voice.

"No."

"She would have been proud of you. Good night!"

As I moved away from them along the terrace, I could not help observing how steadily they both sat gazing on the prospect, and how it thickened and closed around them.

Reflecting on what had been thus told me, I felt it right that it should be communicated to Mr. Peggotty. Often now, had I seen him in the dead of night passing along the streets, searching, among the few who loitered out of doors at those untimely hours, for what he dreaded to find.

He kept a lodging over the little chandler's shop in Hungerford Market. Hither I directed my walk.

He was sitting reading by a window.

"Mas'r Davy! Sit ye down. You're kindly welcome, sir!"

"Mr. Peggotty," said I, "I have heard some news."

"Of Em'ly!"

He put his hand, in a nervous manner, to his mouth.

"It gives no clue to where she is; but she is not with him."

He sat down, looking intently at me, and listened in profound silence to all I had to tell. "Mas'r Davy, I have felt so sure as she was living—I have been so led on by it, and held up by it—that I doen't believe I can have been deceived. No! Em'ly's alive!"

"If she should come here," said I, "I believe there is one person, here, more likely to discover her than any other. Do you remember—Martha?"

"I have seen her in the streets," he answered with a shiver.

"But you don't know," said I, "that Emily was charitable to her, with Ham's help, long before she fled from home. Nor, that, when we met one night, and spoke together in the room yonder, over the way, she listened at the door. You say you have seen her. Do you think that you could find her? I could only hope to do so by chance."

"I think, Mas'r Davy, I know wheer to look."

"It is dark. Being together, shall we go out now, and try to find her to-night?"

We were not far from Blackfriars Bridge, when he turned his head and pointed to a solitary female figure flitting along the opposite side of the street. I knew it, readily, to be the figure that we sought.

I advised my companion, that we should not address her yet, but follow her.

He acquiescing, we followed at a distance: never losing sight of her, but never caring to come very near, as she frequently looked about.

She went on a long way. It was evident, from the manner in which she held her course, that she was going to some fixed destination. At length she turned into a dull, dark street, where the noise and crowd were lost; and I said, "We may speak to her now;" and, mending our pace, we went after her.

CHAPTER 43

Martha

WE were in the narrow water-side street by Millbank before we came up with her. At that moment she crossed the road, as if to avoid the footsteps that she heard so close behind; and without looking back, passed on even more rapidly.

A glimpse of the river through a dull gateway, seemed to arrest my feet. I touched my companion without speaking, and we both followed on that opposite side of the way; keeping as quietly as we could in the shadow of the houses, but keeping very near her.

There was, at the end of that low-lying street, a dilapidated little wooden building, probably an obsolete old ferryhouse. As soon as she came here, and saw the water, she stopped and presently went slowly along by the brink of the river, looking intently at it. I then signed to Mr. Peggotty to remain where he was, and emerged from the shade to speak to her.

At the same moment I said, "Martha!"

She uttered a terrified scream, and struggled with me with such strength that I doubt if I could have held her alone. But a stronger hand than mine was laid upon her; and when she raised her frightened eyes and saw whose it was, she made but one more effort and dropped down between us. We carried her away from the water to where there were some dry stones, and there laid her down, crying and moaning.

"Oh, the river!" she cried passionately. "Oh, the river! I know that I belong to it. It comes from country places—and it creeps through dismal streets, defiled and miserable—and it goes away, like my life, to a great sea, that is always troubled—and I feel that I must go with it!"

I have never known what despair was, except in the tone of those words.

Sinking on the stones, she took some in each hand, and clenched them up, as if she would have ground them.

"What shall I ever do!" she said, fighting thus with her despair. "How can I go on as I am, a solitary curse to myself, a living disgrace to every one I come near!" Suddenly she turned to my companion. "Stamp upon me, kill me! When she was your pride, you would have thought I had done her harm if I had brushed against her in the street. You can't believe—why should you?—a syllable that comes out of my lips. It would be a burning shame upon you, even now, if she and I exchanged a word."

"Martha," said Mr. Peggotty, "God forbid as I should judge you. Well!" he paused a moment, then went on. "You doen't understand how 'tis that this here gentleman and me has wished to speak to you. You doen't understand what 'tis we has afore us. Listen now! If you heerd," said Mr. Peggotty, "owt of what passed between Mas'r Davy and me, th' night when it snowed so hard, you know as I have been—wheer not—fur to seek my dear niece."

She put her hands before her face; but otherwise remained quiet.

"I have heerd her tell," said Mr. Peggotty, "as you was early left father-less and motherless, with no friend fur to take, in a rough sea-faring-way, their place. Maybe you can guess that if you'd had such a friend, you'd have got into a way of being fond of him in course of time, and that my niece was kinder daughter-like to me."

"According to our reckoning," he proceeded, "she is like, to make her own poor solitary course to London. We believe—that you are as innocent of everything that has befell her, as the unborn child! You've spoke of her being pleasant, kind, and gentle to you. You're thankful to her, and you love her. Help us all you can to find her, and may Heaven reward you!"

She looked at him hastily, and for the first time, as if she were doubt-ful of what he had said.

"Will you trust me?" she asked, in a low voice of astonishment.

"Full and free!" said Mr. Peggotty.

"To speak to her, if I should ever find her; shelter her, if I have any shelter to divide with her; and then, without her knowledge, come to you, and bring you to her?" she asked hurriedly.

We both replied together, "Yes!"

She lifted up her eyes, and solemnly declared that she would devote herself to this task, fervently and faithfully.

We judged it expedient, now, to tell her all we knew; which I recounted at length. She listened with great attention. It seemed as if her spirit were quite altered, and she could not be too quiet.

She asked when all was told, where we were to be communicated with, if occasion should arise. Under a dull lamp in the road, I wrote our two addresses on a leaf of my pocket-book. I asked her where she lived herself. She said, it were better not to know.

I took out my purse; but I could not prevail upon her to accept any money, nor could I exact any promise from her that she would do so at another time.

Again she repressed the tears that had begun to flow; and, putting out her trembling hand, and touching Mr. Peggotty, as if there was some healing virtue in him, went away along the desolate road.

We followed her at a short distance, our way lying in the same direc-tion, until we came back into the lighted and populous streets. We suffered her to take her own road, and took ours.

I had reached my own gate, when I was rather surprised to see that the door of my aunt's cottage was open.

I saw a man standing in her little garden.

He had a glass and bottle in his hand, and was in the act of drinking. I recognised the man whom I had once supposed to be a delusion of Mr. Dick's, and had once encountered with my aunt in the streets of the city.

He was eating as well as drinking, and seemed to eat with a hungry appetite.

The light in the passage was obscured for a moment, and my aunt came out. She was agitated, and put some money into his hand.

"What's the use of this?" he demanded.

"I can spare no more," returned my aunt.

"Is this all you mean to give me, then?"

"It is all I *can* give you," said my aunt. "You stripped me of the greater part of all I ever had," said my aunt. "You closed my heart against the whole world, for years and years. You treated me falsely, ungratefully, and cruelly. Don't add new injuries to the long, long list of injuries you have done me!"

"It's all very fine!—Well! I must do the best I can."

Taking two or three quick steps, as if I had just come up, I met him at the gate, and went in as he came out. We eyed one another narrowly in passing, and with no favour.

"Aunt," said I, hurriedly. "This man is alarming you again! Let me speak to him. Who is he?"

"Child," returned my aunt, taking my arm, "come in, and don't speak to me for ten minutes."

We sat down in her little parlour.

"Trot," said my aunt, calmly, "it's my husband."

"Your husband, aunt? I thought he was dead!"

"Dead to me," returned my aunt, "but living."

I sat in silent amazement.

"Betsey Trotwood," said my aunt, composedly, "believed in that man most entirely. She loved him, Trot, right well. He repaid her by breaking her fortune, and nearly breaking her heart. So she put all that sort of sentiment in a grave, and filled it up."

"My dear good aunt!"

"I left him," my aunt proceeded, "generously. He had been so cruel to me, that I might have effected a separation on easy terms for myself; but I did not. He sank lower and lower, married another woman, became a gambler, and a cheat. What he is now, you see."

She gave my hand a squeeze, and shook her head.

"He is nothing to me now, Trot. But, sooner than have him punished for his offences I give him more money than I can afford, at intervals when he reappears, to go away. I was a fool when I married him; and I am so far an incurable fool on that subject."

My aunt dismissed the matter with a heavy sigh.

CHAPTER 44

I Am Involved in Mystery

I received one morning by the post, the following letter, postmarked Canterbury, and addressed to me at Doctors' Commons:

"My dear Sir,

"Circumstances beyond my individual control have effected a severance of that intimacy which, has ever afforded me, gratifying emotions of no common description.

This fact, combined with the distinguished elevation to which your talents have raised you, deters me from presuming to aspire to the liberty of addressing the companion of my youth, by the familiar appellation of Copperfield! That name will ever be treasured among the muniments of our house with sentiments of personal esteem amounting to affection.

"You will naturally inquire by what object am I influenced, then, in inditing the present missive?

"I may be permitted to observe, in passing, that my brightest visions are for ever dispelled—that my peace is shattered and my power of enjoyment destroyed—that my heart is no longer in the right place—and that I no more walk erect before my fellow man.

"Placed in a mental position of peculiar painfulness, it is my intention to fly from myself for a short period, and devote a respite of eight-and-forty hours to revisiting some metropolitan scenes of past enjoyment. My feet will naturally tend towards the King's Bench Prison. In stating that I shall be (D. V.) on the outside of the south wall of that place of incarceration on civil process, the day after to-morrow, at seven in the evening, precisely, my object in this epistolary communication is accomplished.

"I confine myself to throwing out the observation, that, at the hour and place I have indicated, may be found such ruined vestiges as yet remain.

"Wilkins Micawber.

"P.S. Mrs. Micawber is *not* in confidential possession of my intentions."

I read the letter over several times. I believed that something important lay hidden at the bottom of this roundabout communication. I was still pursuing it, when Traddles found me in the height of my perplexity.

"My dear fellow," said I, "I have received a very singular letter, Traddles, from Mr. Micawber."

"I have received one from Mrs. Micawber," cried Traddles.

With that, Traddles produced his letter and made an exchange with me. I then entered on the perusal of Mrs. Micawber's epistle.

"My best regards to Mr. Thomas Traddles, I assure Mr. T. T. that I would not intrude upon his kindness, were I in any other position than on the confines of distraction.

"Mr. T. can form no adequate idea of the change in Mr. Micawber's conduct, of his wildness, of his violence. I have become accustomed to hear Mr. Micawber assert that he has sold himself to the D. Mystery and secrecy have long been his principal characteristics. Last night, on being childishly solicited for two pence, to buy 'lemon-stunners'—a local sweetmeat—he presented an oyster-knife at the twins!

"May I now venture to confide to Mr. T. the purport of my letter?

"Mr. Micawber is going to London. Though he studiously concealed his hand, in writing the direction-card which he attached to the little brown valise, the eagle-glance of matrimonial anxiety detected d,o,n, distinctly traced. The West-End destination of the coach, is the Golden Cross. Dare I ask Mr. T. to endeavour to step in between Mr. Micawber and his agonised family? Oh no, for that would be too much!

"If Mr. Copperfield should yet remember one unknown to fame, will Mr. T. take charge of my unalterable regards and similar entreaties? In any case, he will *consider this communication strictly private, and on no account whatever to be alluded to, in the presence of Mr. Micawber*. If Mr. T. should ever reply to it, a letter addressed to M. E., Post Office, Canterbury, will be fraught with less painful consequences than any addressed immediately to one, who subscribes herself in extreme distress.

"Mr. Thomas Traddle's respectful friend and suppliant,

"EMMA MICAWBER."

"What do you think of that letter?" said Traddles.

"What do you think of the other?" said I.

"I think that the two together, Copperfield," replied Traddles, "mean more than Mr. and Mrs. Micawber usually mean in their correspondence— Poor thing! It will be a charity to write to her, and tell her that we will not fail to see Mr. Micawber."

I had often thought of the Micawbers, and to recall how shy Mr. Micawber was of me when he became clerk to Uriah Heep.

However, I now wrote a comforting letter to Mrs. Micawber, in our joint names, and we both signed it. As we walked into town to post it, Traddles and I decided that we would be very punctual in keeping Mr. Micawber's appointment.

Although we appeared at the stipulated place a quarter of an hour before the time, we found Mr. Micawber already there.

He had relinquished his legal suit of black for the purposes of this excursion, and wore the old surtout and tights, but not quite with the old air; his very eyeglass seemed to hang less easily, and his shirt collar, though still of the old formidable dimensions, rather drooped.

"Gentlemen!" said Mr. Micawber, after the first salutations, "you are friends in need, and friends indeed."

We acknowledged his politeness, and made suitable replies. He then directed our attention to the wall.

"I was about to observe that I again behold the serene spot where some of the happiest hours of my existence fleeted by."

"Made so, I am sure, by Mrs. Micawber," said I. "I hope she is well?"

"Thank you," returned Mr. Micawber, whose face clouded at this reference, "she is but so-so. And this," said Mr. Micawber, nodding his head sorrowfully, "is the Bench!"

"When I was an inmate of that retreat I could look my fellow-man in the face, and punch his head if he ever offended me. My fellow-man and myself are no longer on those glorious terms!"

Turning from the building in a downcast manner, Mr. Micawber accepted my proffered arm on one side, and the proffered arm of Traddles on the other, and walked away between us.

"Oh, you are in low spirits, Mr. Micawber," said Traddles.

"I am, sir," interposed Mr. Micawber.

"How is our friend Heep, Mr. Micawber?" said I, after a silence.

"My dear Copperfield," returned Mr. Micawber, bursting into a state of much excitement, and turning pale. "In whatever capacity you ask after my employer, I beg, without offence to you, to limit my reply to this— that whatever his state of health may be, his appearance is foxy; not to say diabolical. You will allow me, to decline pursuing a subject which has lashed me to the utmost verge of desperation in my professional capacity."

I expressed my regret for having innocently touched upon a theme that roused him so much.

I then mentioned that it would give me great pleasure to introduce him to my aunt, if he would ride out to Highgate, where a bed was at his service.

We walked on, arm-in-arm, again; found the coach in the act of starting; and arrived at Highgate without encountering any difficulties by the way.

We went to my aunt's house rather than to mine, because of Dora's not being well. My aunt presented herself on being sent for, and welcomed Mr. Micawber with gracious cordiality.

Mr. Dick was at home. He was by nature so exceedingly compassionate of anyone who seemed to be ill at ease, that he shook hands with Mr. Micawber, at least half-a-dozen times in five minutes.

"The friendliness of this gentleman," said Mr. Micawber to my aunt, "to a man who is struggling with a complicated burden of perplexity and disquiet, is trying, I assure you."

"My friend Mr. Dick," replied my aunt, proudly, "is not a common man."

"That I am convinced of," said Mr. Micawber.

"You are a very old friend of my nephew's, Mr. Micawber," said my aunt. "I wish I had had the pleasure of seeing you before."

"Madam," returned Mr. Micawber, "I wish I had had the honour of knowing you at an earlier period. I was not always the wreck you at present behold."

"I hope Mrs. Micawber and your family are well, sir," said my aunt.

"The subsistence of my family, ma'am," returned Mr. Micawber, "trembles in the balance. My employer——"

Here Mr. Micawber provokingly left off; and began to peel the lemons that had been under my directions set before him, together with all the other appliances he used in making punch.

"Your employer," said Mr. Dick, jogging his arm as a gentle reminder.

"My employer, ma'am—Mr. Heep—once did me the favour to observe to

166

me, that if I were not in the receipt of the stipendiary emoluments appertaining to my engagement with him, I should probably be a mountebank about the country, swallowing a sword-blade, and eating the devouring element."

Mr. Micawber then resumed his peeling with a desperate air.

My aunt eyed him attentively.

I should have taken him up at this point, but for the strange proceedings in which I saw him engaged; whereof his putting the lemon-peel into the kettle, the sugar into the snuffer-tray, the spirit into the empty jug, and confidently attempting to pour boiling water out of a candle-stick, were among the most remarkable. He clattered all his means and implements together, rose from his chair, pulled out his pocket-handkerchief, and burst into tears.

"Mr. Micawber," said I, "what is the matter? Pray speak out."

"What is *not* the matter? Villainy is the matter; baseness is the matter; deception, fraud, conspiracy, are the matter; and the name of the whole atrocious mass is—HEEP!"

My aunt clapped her hands, and we all started up as if we were possessed.

"The struggle is over!" said Mr. Micawber, violently gesticulating with his pocket-handkerchief, "I'll put my hand in no man's hand," said Mr. Micawber, gasping, puffing, and sobbing, to that degree that he was like a man fighting with cold water, "until I have—blown to fragments—the—a —detestable—serpent—HEEP! I'll partake of no one's hospitality, until I have—a—moved Mount Vesuvius—to eruption—on—a—the abandoned rascal—HEEP! Refreshment—a—underneath this roof—particularly punch —would—a—choke me—unless—I had—previously—choked the eyes—out of the head—a—of—interminable cheat, and liar—HEEP! I—a—I'll know nobody—and—a—say nothing—and—a—live nowhere—until I have crushed—to—a—undiscoverable atoms—the—transcendent and immortal hypocrite and perjurer—HEEP!"

I really had some fear of Mr. Micawber's dying on the spot. But now, when he sank into a chair, steaming, and looked at us, with every possible colour in his face that had no business there, and an endless procession of lumps following one another in hot haste up his throat, I would have gone to his assistance, but he waved me off, and wouldn't hear a word.

"No, Copperfield!—No communication—a—until—Miss Wickfield—a —redress from wrongs inflicted by consummate scoundrel—HEEP!" (I am quite convinced he could not have uttered three words, but for the amazing energy with which this word inspired him when he felt it coming.) "Inviolable secret—a—from the whole world—a—no exceptions—this day week —a—at breakfast time—a—everybody present—including aunt—a—and extremely friendly gentleman—to be at the hotel at Canterbury—a—where —Mrs. Micawber and myself—Auld Lang Syne in chorus—and—a—will expose intolerable ruffian—HEEP! No more to say—a—or listen to persuasion—go immediately—not capable—a—bear society—upon the track of devoted and doomed traitor—HEEP!"

With this last repetition of the magic word, Mr. Micawber rushed out of the house; leaving us in a state of excitement, hope, and wonder, that reduced us to a condition little better than his own.

CHAPTER 45

Mr. Peggotty's Dream Comes True

By this time, some months had passed, since our interview on the bank of the river with Martha. I had never seen her since, but she had communicated with Mr. Peggotty on several occasions. Nothing had come of her zealous intervention; nor could I infer, from what he told me, that any clue had ever been obtained, for a moment, to Emily's fate.

I was walking alone in the garden, one evening, about a fortnight afterwards, when I saw a figure beyond, dressed in a plain cloak. It was bending eagerly towards me, and beckoning.

"Martha!" said I, going to it.

"Can you come with me?" she inquired, in an agitated whisper. "I have been to him, and he is not at home. I wrote down where he was to come, and left it on his table with my own hand. They said he would not be out long. I have tidings for him. Can you come directly?"

My answer was to pass out of the gate immediately.

I stopped an empty coach that was coming by, and we got into it. When I asked her where the coachman was to drive, she answered "Anywhere near Golden Square! And quick!"—then shrunk into a corner, with one trembling hand before her face, and the other making the former gesture, as if she could not bear a voice.

We alighted at one of the entrances to the Square she had mentioned, where I directed the coach to wait, not knowing but that we might have some occasion for it. She laid her hand on my arm, and hurried me on to one of the sombre streets, of which there are several in that part, where the houses were once fair dwellings in the occupation of single families, but have, and had, long degenerated into poor lodgings let off in rooms. Entering at the open door of one of these, and releasing my arm, she beckoned me to follow her up the common staircase, which was like a tributary channel to the street.

We proceeded to the top storey of the house. Two or three times, by the way, I thought I observed in the indistinct light the skirts of a female figure going up before us. As we turned to ascend the last flight of stairs between us and the roof, we caught a full view of this figure pausing for a moment, at a door. Then it turned the handle, and went in.

"What's this!" said Martha, in a whisper. "She has gone into my room.

What is she doing? I don't know her!"

I knew her. I had recognised her with amazement, for Miss Dartle.

Martha softly led me up the stairs; and then, by a little back door which seemed to have no lock, and which she pushed open with a touch, into a small empty garret with a low sloping roof: little better than a cupboard. Between this, and the room she had called hers, there was a small door of communication, standing partly open. Here we stopped, breathless with our ascent, and she placed her hand lightly on my lips.

A dead silence prevailed for some moments. Martha kept one hand on my lips, and raised the other in a listening attitude.

"It matters little to me her not being at home," said Rosa Dartle, haughtily, "I know nothing of her. It is you I come to see."

"Me?" replied a soft voice.

At the sound of it, a thrill went through my frame. For it was Emily's!

"Yes," returned Miss Dartle, "I have come to look at you. What? You are not ashamed of the face that has done so much?"

The resolute and unrelenting hatred of her tone, its cold stern sharpness, and its mastered rage, presented her before me, as if I had seen her standing in the light.

"I have come to see," she said, "James Steerforth's fancy; the girl who ran away with him, and is the town-talk of the commonest people of her native place; the bold, flaunting, practised companion of persons like James Steerforth. I want to know what such a thing is like."

There was a rustle, as if the unhappy girl, on whom she heaped these taunts, ran towards the door, and the speaker swiftly interposed herself before it. It was succeeded by a moment's pause.

When Miss Dartle spoke again, it was through her set teeth, and with a stamp upon the ground.

"Stay there!" she said, "or I'll proclaim you to the house, and the whole street! If you try to evade *me,* I'll stop you, if it's by the hair, and raise the very stones against you!"

A frightened murmur was the only reply that reached my ears. A silence succeeded. I did not know what to do. Much as I desired to put an end to the interview, I felt that I had no right to present myself; that it was for Mr. Peggotty alone to see her and recover her. Would he never come? I thought, impatiently.

Miss Dartle placed herself in a chair, within view of the door and looked downward, as if Emily were crouching on the floor before her. Being now between me and the light, I could see her curled lip, and her cruel eyes intently fixed on one place, with a greedy triumph.

"Listen to what I say!" she said; "and reserve your false arts for your dupes. Do you hope to move *me* by your tears? No more than you could charm me by your smiles, you purchased slave."

"Oh, have some mercy on me!" cried Emily. "Show me some compassion, or I shall die mad!"

"It would be no great penance," said Rosa Dartle, "for your crimes. Do you know what you have done? Do you ever think of the home you have laid waste?"

"Oh, is there ever night or day, when I don't think of it!" cried Emily. "Oh, home, home! Oh dear, dear uncle, if you ever could have known the agony your love would cause me when I fell away from good, you never would have shown it to me so constant, much as you felt it; but would have been angry to me, at least once in my life, that I might have had some comfort!"

Rosa Dartle sat looking down upon her, as inflexible as a figure of brass.

"*Your* home! Do you imagine that I bestow a thought on it, or suppose you could do any harm to that low place, which money would not pay for, and handsomely? *Your* home! You were a part of the trade of your home, and were bought and sold like any other vendible thing your people dealt in."

"Oh, not that!" cried Emily. "Have some respect for them, as you are a lady, if you have no mercy for me."

"I speak of *his* home—where I live. Here, is a worthy cause of division between lady-mother and gentleman-son; of grief in a house where she wouldn't have been admitted as a kitchen girl; of anger, and repining, and reproach. This piece of pollution, picked up from the water-side, to be made much of for an hour, and then tossed back to her original place!"

"No! no!" cried Emily, clasping her hands together. "I had been brought up as virtuous as you or any lady, and was going to be the wife of as good a man as you or any lady in the world can ever marry. If you live in his home and know him, you know, perhaps, what his power with a weak, vain girl might be. I don't defend myself, but I know well, and he knows well, or he will know when he comes to die, and his mind is troubled with it, that he used all his power to deceive me, and that I believed him, trusted him, and loved him!"

Rosa Dartle sprang up from her seat; recoiled; and in recoiling struck at her, with a face of such malignity, so darkened and disfigured by passion, that I had almost thrown myself between them. The blow, which had no aim, fell upon the air.

"*You* love him? *You*?" she cried, with her clenched hand, quivering as if it only wanted a weapon to stab the object of her wrath.

She slowly, very slowly, broke into a laugh, and pointed at Emily with her hand, as if she were a sight of shame for gods and men.

"*She* love!" she said. "That carrion! And he ever cared for her, she'd tell me. Ha, ha! The liars that these traders are!"

"I came here, you pure fountain of love," she said, "to see—what such a thing as you was like. I was curious. I am satisfied. Also to tell you, that you had best seek that home of yours, with all speed, and hide your head among those excellent people who are expecting you, and whom your money will console."

Her rage got the better of her again, for a moment; but it passed over her face like a spasm, and left her smiling.

"Hide yourself," she pursued, "if not at home, somewhere. Let it be somewhere beyond reach; in some obscure life—or, better still, in some obscure death."

"Oh me, oh me!" exclaimed the wretched Emily, in a tone that might have touched the hardest heart, I should have thought; but there was no relenting in Rosa Dartle's smile. "What, what, shall I do?"

"Do?" returned the other. "Live happy in your own reflections! Consecrate your existence to the recollection of James Steerforth's tenderness —he would have made you his serving-man's wife, would he not?—Marry that good man, and be happy in his condescension. If this will not do, die! There are doorways and dust-heaps for such deaths, and such despair— find one, and take your flight to Heaven!"

I heard a distant foot upon the stairs. It was his, thank God!

She moved slowly from before the door when she said this, and passed out of my sight.

"But mark!" she added, slowly and sternly, opening the other door to go away, "I am resolved, for reasons that I have and hatreds that I entertain, to cast you out."

The foot upon the stairs came nearer—nearer—passed her as she went down—rushed into the room!

"Uncle!"

A fearful cry followed the word. I paused a moment, and, looking in, saw him supporting her insensible figure in his arms. He gazed for a few seconds at the face; then stooped to kiss it—oh, how tenderly!—and drew a handkerchief before it.

"Mas'r Davy," he said, in a low tremulous voice, when it was covered, "I thank my Heav'nly Father as my dream's come true! I thank Him hearty for having guided of me, in His own ways, to my darling!"

With those words he took her up in his arms; and, with the veiled face lying on his bosom, and addressed towards his own, carried her, motionless and unconscious, down the stairs.

CHAPTER 46

The Beginning of a Longer Journey

IT was yet early in the morning of the following day, when, as I was walking in my garden with my aunt (who took little other exercise now, being so much in attendance on my dear Dora), I was told that Mr. Peggotty desired to speak with me. He came into the garden to meet me half-way, on my going towards the gate; and bared his head, as it was always his custom to do when he saw my aunt, for whom he had a high respect.

She drew her arm through Mr. Peggotty's, and walked with him to a leafy little summer-house there was at the bottom of the garden, where she sat down on a bench, and I beside her. There was a seat for Mr. Peggotty, too, but he preferred to stand, leaning his hand on the small rustic table.

"I took my dear child away last night," Mr. Peggotty began, as he raised his eyes to ours, "to my lodging, wheer I have a long time been expecting of her and preparing fur her. It was hours afore she knowed me right; and when she did, she kneeled down at my feet, and kinder said to me, as if it was her prayers, how it all come to be."

"She come," said Mr. Peggotty, dropping his voice to an awestricken whisper, "to London. She—as had never seen it in her life—alone—without a penny—young—so pretty—come to London. A'most the moment as she lighted heer, all so desolate, she found (as she believed) a friend; a decent woman as spoke to her about the needlework as she had been brought up to do, about finding plenty of it fur her, about a lodging for the night, and making secret inquiration concerning of me and all at home. When my child," he said aloud, and with an energy of gratitude that shook him from head to foot, "stood upon the brink of more than I can say or think on—Martha, trew to her promise, saved her!"

I could not repress a cry of joy.

"She had know'd of her bitter knowledge wheer to watch and what to do. She come, white and hurried, upon Em'ly in her sleep. She says to her, 'Rise up from worse than death, and come with me!' Them belonging to the house would have stopped her, but they might as soon have stopped the sea. 'Stand away from me,' she says, 'I am a ghost that calls her from beside her open grave!' She told Em'ly she had seen me, and know'd I loved her, and forgive her."

"She attended on Em'ly," said Mr. Peggotty, who had released my hand, and put his own hand on his heaving chest; "then she went in search of me; then in search of you, Mas'r Davy. My niece is found."

He ceased to speak, and his hand upon the table rested there in perfect repose, with a resolution in it that might have conquered lions.

"You have quite made up your mind," said I to Mr. Peggotty, "as to the future, good friend? I need scarcely ask you."

"Quite, Mas'r Davy," he returned; "Our future life lays over the sea. No one can't reproach my darling in Australia. We will begin a new life over theer!"

I asked him if he yet proposed to himself any time for going away.

"I was down at the Docks early this morning, sir," he returned, "to get information concerning of them ships. In about six weeks or two months from now, there'll be one sailing—I see her this morning—went aboard—and we shall take our passage in her."

"Em'ly," he continued, "will keep along with me—poor child, she's sore in need of peace and rest!—until such time as we goes upon our voyage. She'll work at them clothes, as must be made; and I hope her troubles will begin to seem longer ago than they was, when she finds herself once more by her rough but loving uncle."

My aunt nodded confirmation of this hope, and imparted great satisfaction to Mr. Peggotty.

"Theer's one thing furder, Mas'r Davy," said he, putting his hand in his breast-pocket, and gravely taking out the little paper bundle I had seen before, which he unrolled on the table. "Theer's these heer banknotes—fifty pound, and ten. This money, I shall put up jest afore I go, in a cover d'rected to him; and put that up in another, d'rected to his mother. I shall tell her, in no more wureds than I speak to you, what it's the price on; and that I'm gone, and past receiving of it back."

I told him that I thought it would be right to do so—that I was thoroughly convinced it would be, since he felt it to be right.

"I said that theer was on'y one thing furder," he proceeded with a grave smile, when he had made up his little bundle again, and put it in his pocket; "but theer was two. I warn't sure in my mind, when I come out this morning, as I could go and break to Ham, of my own self, what had so thankfully happened."

"And do you wish me to go with you?" said I.

"If you could do me that kind favour, Mas'r Davy," he replied, "I know the sight on you would cheer 'em up a bit."

My little Dora being in good spirits, and very desirous that I should go —as I found on talking it over with her—I readily pledged myself to accompany him in accordance with his wish. Next morning, consequently, we were on the Yarmouth coach, and again travelling over the old ground.

As we passed along the familiar street at night—Mr. Peggotty, in despite of all my remonstrances, carrying my bag—I felt reluctant to be present when Mr. Peggotty first met his sister and Ham.

After a stroll about the town, I went to Ham's house. Peggotty had now removed here for good; and had let her own house to the successor of Mr. Barkis in the carrying business, who paid her very well for the goodwill, cart, and horse. I believe the very same slow horse that Mr. Barkis drove, was still at work.

I found them in the neat kitchen, accompanied by Mrs. Gummidge, who had been fetched from the old boat by Mr. Peggotty himself. I doubt if she could have been induced to desert her post, by any one else. He had evidently told them all. Both Peggotty and Mrs. Gummidge had their aprons to their eyes, and Ham had just stepped out "to take a turn on the beach." He presently came home, very glad to see me; and I hope they were all the better for my being there. We spoke, with some approach to cheerfulness, of Mr. Peggotty's growing rich in a new country, and of the wonders he would describe in his letters. We said nothing of Emily by name, but distantly referred to her more than once. Ham was the serenest of the party.

I thought I had read in his face that he would like to speak to me alone. I therefore resolved to put myself in his way next evening, as he came home from his work.

It was easy to come in his way, as I knew where he worked. I met him at a retired part of the sands, which I knew he would cross, and turned back with him, that he might have leisure to speak to me if he really wished.

"Mas'r Davy, shall you see her, d'ye think?"

"It would be too painful to her, perhaps," said I.

"I have thowt of that," he replied. "So 'twould, sir, so 'twould."

"But Ham," said I, gently, "if there is anything that I could write to her, for you, in case I could not tell it; if there is anything you would wish to make known to her through me; I should consider it a sacred trust."

We walked a little farther in silence, and then he spoke.

"'Tan't that I forgive her. 'Than't that so much. 'Tis more as I beg of her to forgive me, for having pressed my affections upon her. Odd times, I think that if I hadn't had her promise fur to marry me, sir, she was that trustful of me, in a friendly way, that she'd have told me what was struggling in her mind, and would have counselled with me, and I might have saved her."

With a slight wave of his hand, as though to explain to me that he could not enter the old place, he turned away. As I looked after his figure, crossing the waste in the moonlight, I saw him turn his face towards a strip of silvery light upon the sea, and pass on, looking at it, until he was a shadow in the distance.

The door of the boat-house stood open when I approached; and, on entering, I found it emptied of all its furniture, saving one of the old lockers, on which Mrs. Gummidge, with a basket on her knee, was seated, looking at Mr. Peggotty. He leaned his elbow on the rough chimney-piece, and gazed upon a few expiring embers in the grate; but he raised his head, hopefully, on my coming in, and spoke in a cheery manner.

"Come, according to promise, to bid farewell to't, eh, Mas'r Davy?" he said, taking up the candle. "Bare enough, now, an't it?"

"Indeed you have made good use of the time," said I.

"Why, we have not been idle, sir. Missis Gummidge has worked like a— I doen't know what Missis Gummidge an't worked like," said Mr. Peggotty, looking at her, at a loss for a sufficiently approving simile.

Mrs. Gummidge, leaning on her basket, made no observation.

We looked into the other little room, and came back to Mrs. Gummidge, sitting on the locker.

"Dan'l," said Mrs. Gummidge, suddenly deserting her basket, and clinging to his arm, "my dear Dan'l, the parting words I speak in this house is, I mustn't be left behind. Doen't ye think of leaving me behind, Dan'l! Oh, doen't ye ever do it!"

Mr. Peggotty, taken aback, looked from Mrs. Gummidge to me, and from me to Mrs. Gummidge, as if he had been awakened from a sleep.

"My good soul," said Mr. Peggotty, shaking his head, "you doen't know what a long voyage, and what a hard life 'tis!"

"Yes I do, Dan'l! I can guess!" cried Mrs. Gummidge. "But my parting words under this roof is, I shall go into the house and die, if I am not took. I can dig, Dan'l. I can work. I can live hard. I can be loving and patient

174

now—more than you think, Dan'l, if you'll on'y try me. I'll go with you and Em'ly, if you'll on'y let me, to the world's end! I know how 'tis; I know you think that I am lone and lorn; but, deary love, 'tan't so no more! I ain't sat here, so long, a watching, and a thinking of your trials, without some good being done me. Mas'r Davy, speak to him for me! I knows his ways, and Em'ly's, and I knows their sorrows, and can be a comfort to 'em, some odd times, and labour for 'em allus! Dan'l, deary Dan'l, let me go 'long with you!"

And Mrs. Gummidge took his hand, and kissed it with a homely pathos and affection, in a homely rapture of devotion and gratitude, that he well deserved.

We brought the locker out, extinguished the candle, fastened the door on the outside, and left the old boat shut up, a dark speck in the cloudy night. Next day, when we were returning to London outside the coach, Mrs. Gummidge and her basket were on the seat behind, and Mrs. Gummidge was happy.

CHAPTER 47

I Assist At an Explosion

WHEN the time Mr. Micawber had appointed so mysteriously, was within four-and-twenty hours of being come, my aunt and I consulted how we should proceed; for my aunt was very unwilling to leave Dora. Ah! how easily I carried Dora up and down stairs, now!

We were disposed to arrange that she should stay at home, and be represented by Mr. Dick and me, when Dora again unsettled us by declaring that she never would forgive herself, and never would forgive her bad boy, if my aunt remained behind, on any pretence.

"But, aunt," said Dora, coaxingly. "You must go. I shall lead my naughty boy *such* a life, if he don't make you go. Besides," said Dora, putting back her hair, and looking wonderingly at my aunt and me, "why shouldn't you both go? I am not very ill indeed. Am I?"

"Why, what a question!" cried my aunt.

"What a fancy!" said I.

"Yes! I know I am a silly little thing!" said Dora, slowly looking from one of us to the other, and then putting up her pretty lips to kiss us as she lay upon her couch. "Well, then, you must both go, or I shall not believe you; and then I shall cry!"

I saw, in my aunt's face, that she began to give way now, and Dora brightened again, as she saw it too.

"There! Now you'll go, won't you? You'll only be gone one night, and Jip will take care of me while you are gone. Doady will carry me up-stairs before you go, and I won't come down again till you come back."

We agreed, without any more consultation, that we would both go, and that Dora was a little Impostor, who feigned to be rather unwell, because she liked to be petted. She was greatly pleased, and very merry; and we four, that is to say, my aunt, Mr. Dick, Traddles, and I, went down to Canterbury by the Dover mail that night.

We all became very anxious and impatient, when we sat down to breakfast. As it approached nearer and nearer to half-past nine o'clock, our restless expectation of Mr. Micawber increased. And I looked out of the window to give early notice of Mr. Micawber's coming.

Nor had I long to watch, for, at the first chime of the half-hour, he appeared in the street.

"Here he is," said I, "and not in his legal attire!"

"Gentlemen, and madam," said Mr. Micawber, "good morning! My dear sir," to Mr. Dick, who shook hands with him violently, "you are extremely good."

"Have you breakfasted?" said Mr. Dick. "Have a chop!"

"Not for the world, my good sir!" cried Mr. Micawber, stopping him on his way to the bell; "appetite and myself, Mr. Dixon, have long been strangers."

"Now, sir," said my aunt to Mr. Micawber, as she put on her gloves, "we are ready for Mount Vesuvius, or anything else, as soon as *you* please."

"Madam," returned Mr. Micawber, "I trust you will shortly witness an eruption. Mr. Traddles, I have your permission, I believe, to mention here that we have been in communication together?"

"It is undoubtedly the fact, Copperfield," said Traddles, to whom I looked in surprise. "Mr. Micawber has consulted me, in reference to what he has in contemplation; and I have advised him to the best of my judgement."

"Unless I deceive myself, Mr. Traddles," pursued Mr. Micawber, "what I contemplate is a disclosure of an important nature."

"Highly so," said Traddles.

"Perhaps, under such circumstances, madam and gentlemen, I would beg to be allowed a start of five minutes by the clock; and then to receive the present company, inquiring for Miss Wickfield, at the office of Wickfield and Heep, whose Stipendiary I am."

My aunt and I looked at Traddles, who nodded his approval.

"I have no more," observed Mr. Micawber, "to say at present."

When the time was expired, Traddles gave her his arm; and we all went out together to the old house, without saying one word on the way.

We found Mr. Micawber at his desk, in the turret office on the ground floor, either writing, or pretending to write, hard.

As it appeared to me that I was expected to speak, I said aloud:

"How do you do, Mr. Micawber?"

"Mr. Copperfield," said Mr. Micawber, gravely, "I hope I see you well?"

"Is Miss Wickfield at home?" said I.

"Miss Wickfield, I have no doubt, will be happy to see old friends."

He preceded us to the dining-room—and flinging open the door of Mr. Wickfield's former office, said, in a sonorous voice:

"Miss Trotwood, Mr. David Copperfield, Mr. Thomas Traddles, and Mr. Dixon!"

I had not seen Uriah Heep since the time of the blow. Our visit astonished him, evidently. He frowned to that degree that he almost closed his small eyes, while the hurried raising of his gristly hand to his chin betrayed some trepidation or surprise. A moment afterwards, he was as humble as ever.

"Well, I am sure," he said. "This is indeed an unexpected pleasure! Mr. Copperfield, I hope I see you well. Mrs. Copperfield, sir, I hope she's getting on. We have been made quite uneasy by the poor accounts we have had of her state, lately."

I felt ashamed to let him take my hand, but I did not know yet what else to do.

"Micawber, tell 'em to let Miss Agnes know—and mother. Mother will be quite in a state, when she sees the present company!" said Uriah, setting chairs.

"You are not busy, Mr. Heep?" said Traddles.

"No, Mr. Traddles," replied Uriah, resuming his official seat, and squeezing his bony hands. "Not so much so as I could wish. Not but what myself and Micawber have our hands pretty full in general, on account of Mr. Wickfield's being hardly fit for any occupation, sir. You've not been intimate with Mr. Wickfield, I think, Mr. Traddles?"

"No, I have not been intimate with Mr. Wickfield," returned Traddles; "or I might perhaps have waited on you long ago, Mr. Heep."

There was something in the tone of this reply, which made Uriah look at the speaker again, with a very sinister and suspicious expression. But, seeing only Traddles, with his good-natured face, he dismissed it as he replied, with a jerk of his whole body:

"I am sorry for that, Mr. Traddles. You would have admired him as much as we all do."

Agnes, now ushered in by Mr. Micawber, was not quite so self-possessed as usual, I thought; and had evidently undergone anxiety and fatigue. But her earnest cordiality, and her quiet beauty, shone through with a gentle lustre.

I saw Uriah watch her while she greeted us; and he reminded me of an ugly and rebellious genie watching a good spirit. In the meanwhile, some slight sign passed between Mr. Micawber and Traddles; and Traddles, unobserved except by me, went out.

"Don't wait, Micawber," said Uriah.

Mr. Micawber stood erect before the door, most unmistakably contemplating one of his fellow-men, and that man his employer.

"What are you waiting for?" said Uriah. "Micawber! did you hear me tell you not to wait?"

"Yes!" replied the immovable Mr. Micawber.

"Then why *do* you wait?" said Uriah.

"Because I—in short choose," replied Mr. Micawber, with a burst.

Uriah's cheeks lost colour, and an unwholesome paleness, still faintly tinged by his pervading red, overspread them. He looked at Mr. Micawber attentively, with his whole face breathing short and quick in every feature.

"You are a dissipated fellow, as all the world knows," he said, with an effort at a smile, "and I am afraid you'll oblige me to get rid of you. Go along! I'll talk to you presently."

"If there is a scoundrel on this earth," said Mr. Micawber, suddenly breaking out again with the utmost vehemence, "with whom I have already talked too much, that scoundrel's name is—HEEP!"

Uriah fell back. Looking slowly round upon us with the darkest and wickedest expression, he said, in a lower voice:

"This is a conspiracy! You have met here, by appointment! You are playing Booty with my clerk, are you, Copperfield? None of your plots against me; I'll counterplot you! Micawber, you be off."

"Mr. Micawber," said I, "deal with him as he deserves!"

"You are a precious set of people, ain't you?" said Uriah, in the same low voice, and breaking out into a clammy heat, "to buy over my clerk, who is the very scum of society—Miss Trotwood, I'll stop your husband shorter than will be pleasant to you. Miss Wickfield, you had better not join that gang. Think twice, you, Micawber, if you don't want to be crushed. Where's mother?" he said, suddenly appearing to notice, with alarm, the absence of Traddles.

"Mrs. Heep is here, sir," said Traddles, returning with that worthy mother of a worthy son. "I have taken the liberty of making myself known to her."

"Who are you to make yourself known?" retorted Uriah.

"I am the agent and friend of Mr. Wickfield, sir," said Traddles, in a composed business-like way. "And I have a power of attorney from him in my pocket, to act for him in all matters."

"The old ass has drunk himself into a state of dotage," said Uriah, turning uglier, "and it has been got from him by fraud!"

"Something has been got from him by fraud, I know," returned Traddles quietly; "and so do you, Mr. Heep."

"Ury—!" Mrs. Heep began, with an anxious gesture.

"Will you hold your tongue, mother, and leave it to me?"

Though I had long known that his servility was false, and all his pretences knavish and hollow, I had had no adequate conception of the extent of his hypocrisy, until I now saw him with his mask off. The malice, insolence, and hatred he revealed; the leer with which he exulted in the evil he had done, at first took even me by surprise, who had known him so long, and disliked him so heartily.

After some rubbing of the lower part of his face, he made one more address to me, half whining, and half abusive.

"You think it justifiable, do you, Copperfield, you who pride yourself so much on your honour and all the rest of it, to sneak about my place, eaves-dropping with my clerk? Mr. What's-your-name, you were going to refer some question to Micawber. There's your referee. Why don't you make him speak?"

Mr. Micawber produced from his pocket a foolscap document, folded in the form of a large letter. Opening this packet, he began to read as follows:

" 'Dear Miss Trotwood and gentlemen——' "

" 'I appear before you to denounce probably the most consummate Villain that has ever existed,' " Mr. Micawber, without looking off the letter, pointed the ruler, like a ghostly truncheon, at Uriah Heep.

"In an accumulation of Despair, and Madness, I entered the Firm, nominally conducted under the appellation of Wickfield and—HEEP, but in reality, wielded by—HEEP alone. HEEP, and only HEEP, is the Forger and the Cheat.' "

Uriah, more blue than white at these words, made a dart at the letter, as if to tear it in pieces.

"The Devil take you!" said Uriah, "I'll be even with you."

"Approach me again, you—you—you HEEP of infamy," gasped Mr. Micawber, "and if your head is human, I'll break it."

Mr. Micawber, when he was sufficiently cool, proceeded with his letter.

" 'The stipendiary emoluments were not defined, beyond the pittance, of twenty-two shillings and six per week. The rest was left contingent on the value of my professional exertions; in other and more expressive words, on the baseness of my nature, the cupidity of my motives, the poverty of my family. Need I say, that it soon became necessary for me to solicit from —HEEP—pecuniary advances towards the support of Mrs. Micawber, and rising family? Need I say that this necessity had been foreseen by—HEEP? That those advances were secured by I.O.U.'s and other similar acknowledgments, known to the legal institutions of this country? And that I thus became enmeshed in the web he had spun for my reception?' "

" 'Then it was that I found that my services were constantly called into requisition for the falsification of business, and the mystification of an individual whom I will designate as Mr. W. That Mr. W. was imposed upon, kept in ignorance, and deluded, in every possible way.' "

" 'When Mr. W. was least fit to enter on business—HEEP was always at hand to force him to enter on it. He obtained Mr. W.'s signature under such circumstances to documents of importance, representing them to be other documents of no importance. He induced Mr. W. to empower him to draw out, thus, one particular sum of trust-money, amounting to twelve six fourteen, two, and nine, and employed it to meet pretended business charges and deficiencies which were either already provided for, or had never really existed. He gave this proceeding, throughout, the appearance of having originated in Mr. W's own dishonest intention, and of having been accomplished by Mr. W.'s own dishonest act; and he has used it ever since, in order to torture and constrain him.'"

"You shall prove this, you Copperfield!" said Uriah, with a threatening shake of the head. "All in good time!"

"Ask—HEEP—if he ever kept a pocket-book," said Mr. Micawber; "will you?"

I saw Uriah's lank hand stop, involuntarily, in the scraping of his chin.

"Or ask him," said Mr. Micawber, "if he ever burnt one. If he says yes, and asks you where the ashes are, refer him to Wilkins Micawber, and he will hear of something not at all to his advantage!"

The triumphant flourish with which Mr. Micawber delivered himself of these words, had a powerful effect in alarming the mother; who cried out in much agitation:

"Ury, Ury! Be umble, and make terms, my dear!"

"Mother!" he retorted, "will you keep quiet?"

Mr. Micawber, proceeded with his composition.

"'Second. HEEP has, on several occasions, systematically forged, to various entries, books, and documents, the signature of Mr. W.'"

Mr. Micawber read on, almost smacking his lips:

"'To wit, Mr. W. being infirm, and it being within the bounds of probability that his decease might lead to some discoveries, and to the downfall of—HEEP's—power over the W. family, unless the filial affection of his daughter could be secretly influenced from allowing any investigation of the partnership affairs to be ever made, the said—HEEP—deemed it expedient to have a bond ready by him, as from Mr. W., for the beforementioned sum of twelve six fourteen, two and nine, with interest, stated therein to have been advanced by—HEEP—to Mr. W. to save Mr. W. from dishonour; though really the sum was never advanced by him, and has long been replaced. The signatures to this instrument, purporting to be executed by M. W. and attested by Wilkins Micawber, are forgeries by—HEEP. And I have the document itself, in my possession.'"

Uriah Heep, with a start, took out of his pocket a bunch of keys, and opened a certain drawer; then, suddenly bethought himself of what he was about, and turned again towards us, without looking in it.

"And I have since relinquished it to Mr. Traddles," said Mr. Micawber.

"It is quite true," assented Traddles.

"Ury, Ury!" cried the mother, "be umble and make terms. I told the gentleman at first, when he told me up-stairs it was come to light, that I would answer for your being umble, and making amends."

"Why, there's Copperfield, mother," he angrily retorted, "he would have given you a hundred pounds to say less than you've blurted out!"

"I can't help it, Ury," cried his mother. "I can't see you running into danger, through carrying your head so high. Better be umble."

Mr. Micawber promptly resumed his letter.

"'Third. And last. I am now in a condition to show that Mr. W. has been for years deluded and plundered, in every conceivable manner, to the pecuniary aggrandisement of the avaricious, false, and grasping—HEEP.

That his last act, completed but a few months since, was to induce Mr. W. to execute a relinquishment of his share in the partnership, and even a bill of sale on the very furniture of his house, in consideration of a certain annuity, to be well and truly paid by—Heep—on the four common quarter-days in each and every year. That these meshes; beginning with alarming and falsified accounts of the estate of which Mr. W. is the receiver, at a period when Mr. W. had launched into imprudent and ill-judged speculations, and may not have had the money, for which he was morally and legally responsible, in hand; going on with pretended borrowings of money at enormous interest, really coming from—Heep— and by—Heep—fraudulently obtained or withheld from Mr. W. himself. Bankrupt, as he believed, his sole reliance was upon the monster in the garb of man, who, by making himself necessary to him, had achieved his destruction.' "

There was an iron safe in the room. The key was in it. A hasty suspicion seemed to strike Uriah; and, with a glance at Mr. Micawber, he went to it, and threw the doors clanking open. It was empty.

"Where are the books?" he cried, with a frightful face. "Some thief has stolen the books!"

Mr. Micawber tapped himself with the ruler. "*I* did, when I got the key from you as usual—but a little earlier—and opened it this morning."

"Don't be uneasy," said Traddles. "They have come into my possession. I will take care of them, under the authority I mentioned."

What was my astonishment when I beheld my aunt make a dart at Uriah Heep, and seize him by the collar with both hands!

"*I* want," said my aunt, "my property! Agnes, my dear, as long as I believed it had been really made away with by your father, I wouldn't breathe a syllable of its having been placed here for investment. But, now I know this fellow's answerable for it, and I'll have it! Trot, come and take it away from him!"

I hastened to put myself between them, and to assure her that we would all take care that he should make the utmost restitution of everything he had wrongly got.

"I will tell you what must be done," said Traddles.

"Has that Copperfield no tongue?" muttered Uriah. "I would do a good deal for you if you could tell me that somebody had cut it out."

"My Uriah means to be umble!" cried his mother. "Don't mind what he says, good gentlemen!"

"What must be done," said Traddles, "is this. First, the deed of relinquishment, that we have heard of, must be given over to me now—here."

"Suppose I haven't got it," he interrupted.

"But you have," said Traddles; "therefore you know, we won't suppose so. Then," said Traddles, "you must prepare to disgorge all that your rapacity has become possessed of, and to make restoration to the last farthing. All the partnership books and papers must remain in our possession; all your books and papers; all money accounts and securities, of both kinds. In short, everything here."

"We shall maintain possession of these things; and beg you—in short, compel you—to keep your own room, and hold no communication with any one."

"I won't do it!" said Uriah, with an oath.

"Maidstone Jail is a safer place of detention," observed Traddles; "Copperfield, will you go round to the Guildhall, and bring a couple of officers?"

Here, Mrs. Heep broke out again, crying on her knees to Agnes to interfere in their behalf, exclaiming that he was very humble, and it was all true, and if he didn't do what we wanted, she would, and much more to the same purpose; being half frantic with fears for her darling.

He wiped his hot face with his hand. "Mother, hold your noise. Let 'em have that deed. Go and fetch it!"

"Do you help her, Mr. Dick," said Traddles, "if you please."

Mr. Dick accompanied her as a shepherd's dog might accompany a sheep. But, Mrs. Heep gave him little trouble; for she not only returned with the deed, but with the box in which it was, where we found a banker's book and some other papers that were afterwards serviceable.

"Good!" said Traddles, when this was brought. "Now, Mr. Heep, you can retire to think: there is only one thing to be done; and that it must be done without delay."

Uriah, pausing at the door, said:

"Copperfield, I have always hated you. You've always been an upstart, and you've always been against me. Micawber, you old bully, I'll pay *you*!"

Mr. Micawber remained supremely defiant of him, until he had slunk out at the door.

"The veil that has long been interposed between Mrs. Micawber and myself, is now withdrawn," said Mr. Micawber.

Mr. Dick, my aunt, and I, went home with Mr. Micawber.

His house was not far off; and as the street-door opened into the sitting-room, he bolted in with a precipitation quite his own, and exclaiming: "Emma! my life!" rushed into Mrs. Micawber's arms.

"Emma!" said Mr. Micawber. "The cloud is passed from my mind. Mutual confidence, so long preserved between us once, is restored, to know no further shedding of tears. Welcome misery, welcome houselessness, welcome hunger, rags, tempest, and beggary! Mutual confidence will sustain us to the end!"

"Mr. Micawber, I wonder you have never turned your thoughts to emigration," said my aunt.

"Madam," returned Mr. Micawber, "it was the dream of my youth."

"Aye?" said my aunt, with a glance at me. "Why, what a thing it would be for yourselves and your family, Mr. and Mrs. Micawber, if you were to emigrate now."

"Capital, madam, capital," urged Mr. Micawber, gloomily.

"Capital?" cried my aunt. "But you are doing us a great service—have done us a great service, I may say, for surely much will come out of the fire—and what could we do for you, that would be half so good as to find the capital? Here are some people David knows, going out to Australia shortly. If you decide to go, why shouldn't you go in the same ship? You may help each other. Think of this now, Mr. and Mrs. Micawber. Take your time, and weigh it well."

"There is but one question, my dear ma'am, I could wish to ask," said Mrs. Micawber. "The climate, I believe, is healthy?"

"Finest in the world!" said my aunt.

"Just so," returned Mrs. Micawber. "Now, *are* the circumstances of the country such, that a man of Mr. Micawber's abilities would have a fair chance of rising in the social scale?"

"No better opening anywhere," said my aunt, "for a man who conducts himself well, and is industrious."

"I entertain the conviction, my dear madam," said Mr. Micawber, "that it is, under existing circumstances, the land, the only land, for myself and family; and that something of an extraordinary nature will turn up on that shore. It is no distance—comparatively speaking; and though consideration is due to the kindness of your proposal, I assure you that is a mere matter of form."

CHAPTER 48

Another Retrospect

I AM again with Dora, in our cottage. I do not know how long she has been ill. It is not really long, in weeks or months; but, in my usage and experience, it is a weary, weary while.

I have begun to fear, remotely, that the day may never shine, when I shall see my child-wife running in the sunlight with her old friend Jip.

He is, as it were suddenly, grown very old. It may be, that he misses in his mistress, something that enlivened him and made him younger; but he mopes, and his sight is weak, and his limbs are feeble.

Dora lies smiling on us, and is beautiful, and utters no hasty or complaining word. She says that we are very good to her; that her dear old careful boy is tiring himself out, that my aunt has no sleep, yet is always wakeful, active, and kind. Sometimes, the little bird-like ladies come to see her; and then we talk about our wedding-day, and all that happy time.

It is evening; and I sit by the bed, her face turned towards me. We have been silent, and there is a smile upon her face. I have ceased to carry my light burden up and down-stairs now. She lies here all the day.

"Doady!"

"My dear Dora!"

"I want to see Agnes. Very much I want to see her."

"I will write to her, my dear."

"Will you?"

"Directly."

"You are very lonely when you go down-stairs, now?" Dora whispers, with her arm about my neck.

"How can I be otherwise, my own love, when I see your empty chair?"

"My empty chair!" She clings to me for a little while, in silence. "And you really miss me. Even poor, giddy, stupid me?"

"My heart, who is there upon earth that I could miss so much?"

"Oh, husband! I am so glad, yet so sorry!" creeping closer to me, and folding me in both her arms. She laughs and sobs.

"Only give Agnes my dear love," she says, "and tell her that I want very, very much to see her."

It is night; and I am with her still. Agnes has arrived; has been among us, for a whole day and an evening. She, my aunt, and I, have sat with Dora since the morning, all together. We have not talked much, but Dora has been perfectly contented and cheerful. We are now alone.

Do I know, now, that my child-wife will soon leave me? They have told me so. I hold her hand in mine, I hold her heart in mine, I see her love for me, alive in all its strength. I cannot shut out a pale lingering shadow of belief that she will be spared.

"I am going to say something, Doady, I have often thought of saying, lately. You won't mind?" with a gentle look.

"Mind, my darling?"

"Doady, dear, I am afraid I was too young."

I lay my face upon the pillow by her, and she looks into my eyes, and speaks very softly.

"I was such a silly little creature! I am afraid it would have been better, if we had only loved each other as a boy and girl, and forgotten it."

"We have been very happy, my sweet Dora."

"I was very happy, very. But, as years went on, my dear boy would have wearied of his child-wife."

"Oh, Dora, dearest, dearest, do not speak to me so."

"I loved you far too well, to say a reproachful word to you, in earnest— it was all the merit I had, except being pretty—or you thought me so."

"Oh, how my poor boy cries! Hush! Now, make me one promise. I want to speak to Agnes. Send her up to me; and while I speak to her, let no one come—not even aunt. I want to speak to Agnes, quite alone."

I promise that, immediately; but I cannot leave her, for my grief.

"I said that it was better as it is!" she whispers.

"Oh, Doady, after more years, you never could have loved your child-wife better than you do at this moment; I know I was once too young and foolish. It is so much better as it is!"

Agnes is down-stairs, when I go into the parlour; and give her the message. She disappears, leaving me alone with Jip.

How the time wears, I know not: until I am recalled by my child wife's old companion. More restless than he was, Jip crawls out of his house, and looks at me, and wanders to the door, and whines to go up-stairs.

"Not to-night, Jip! Not to-night!"

He comes very slowly back to me, licks my hand, and lifts his dim eyes to my face.

"Oh, Jip! It may be, never again!"

He lies down at my feet, stretches himself out as if to sleep, and with a plaintive cry, is dead.

CHAPTER 49

Mr. Micawber's Transactions

I was to go abroad. That seemed to have been determined among us from the first. The ground now covering all that could perish of my departed wife, I waited only for what Mr. Micawber called the 'final pulverisation of Heep,' and for the departure of the emigrants.

At the request of Traddles, most affectionate and devoted of friends in my trouble, we returned to Canterbury: I mean my aunt, Agnes, and I. We proceeded by appointment straight to Mr. Micawber's house; where, and at Mr. Wickfield's, my friend had been labouring ever since our explosive meeting.

"Well, Mr. and Mrs. Micawber," was my aunt's first salutation after we were seated. "Pray, have you thought about that emigration proposal of mine?"

"My dear madam," returned Mr. Micawber. "Our Boat is on the shore, and our Bark is on the sea."

"That's right," said my aunt. "I augur all sorts of good from your sensible decision. Arrange it in any way you please, sir," said my aunt.

"Madam," he replied, "Mrs. Micawber and myself are deeply sensible of the very considerate kindness of our friends and patrons. What I wish is, to be perfectly business-like, and perfectly punctual."

"I propose," said Mr. Micawber, "Bills—a convenience to the mercantile world. But if a Bond, or any other description of security, would be preferred, I should be happy to execute any such instrument. As between man and man."

My aunt observed, that in a case where both parties were willing to agree to anything, she took it for granted there would be no difficulty in settling this point. Mr. Micawber was of her opinion.

The matter being thus amicably settled, Mr. Micawber gave Mrs. Micawber his arm, and glancing at the heap of books and papers lying before Traddles on the table, said they would leave us to ourselves; which they ceremoniously did.

"My dear Copperfield," said Traddles, leaning back in his chair, "I must do Mr. Micawber the justice to say," Traddles began, "that although he would appear not to have worked to any good account for himself, he is a most untiring man when he works for other people. I never saw such a fellow. If he always goes on in the same way, he must be, virtually, about two hundred years old, at present. The heat into which he has been continually putting himself; and the distracted and impetuous manner in which he has been diving, day and night, among papers and books is quite extraordinary."

"There's Mr. Dick, too," said Traddles, "has been doing wonders! As soon as he was released from overlooking Uriah Heep, whom he kept in such charge as I never saw exceeded, he began to devote himself to Mr. Wickfield."

"Dick is a very remarkable man," exclaimed my aunt; "and I always said he was. Trot, you know it."

"I am happy to say, Miss Wickfield," pursued Traddles, at once with great delicacy and with great earnestness, "that in your absence Mr. Wickfield has considerably improved. Relieved of the incubus that had fastened upon him for so long a time, and of the dreadful apprehensions under which he had lived, he is hardly the same person."

"Now, let me see," said Traddles, looking among the papers on the table. "Having counted our funds, and reduced to order a great mass of unintentional confusion in the first place, and of wilful confusion and falsification in the second, we take it to be clear that Mr. Wickfield might now wind up his business, and his agency-trust, and exhibit no deficiency or defalcation whatever."

"I am happy to hear you say so," answered Agnes, steadily. "Dear Mr. Traddles and dear Trotwood, papa free with honour, what could I wish for! I have always aspired, if I could have released him from the toils in which he was held, to render back some little portion of the love and care I owe him, and to devote my life to him. Our wants are not many. If I rent the dear old house, and keep a school, I shall be useful and happy."

"Next, Miss Trotwood," said Traddles, "that property of yours."

"Well, sir," sighed my aunt. "If it's gone, I can bear it; and if it's not gone, I shall be glad to get it back."

"It was originally, I think, eight thousand pounds, Consols?" said Traddles.

"Right!" replied my aunt.

"I can't account for more than five," said Traddles, with an air of perplexity.

"—thousand, do you mean?" inquired my aunt, with uncommon composure, "or pounds?"

"Five thousand pounds," said Traddles.

"It was all there was," returned my aunt. "I sold three, myself. One, I paid for your articles, Trot, my dear; and the other two I have by me. When I lost the rest, I thought it wise to say nothing about that sum, but to keep it secretly for a rainy day. I wanted to see how you would come out of the trial, Trot; and you came out nobly—persevering, self-reliant, self-denying! So did Dick."

"Then I am delighted to say," cried Traddles, beaming with joy, "that we have recovered the whole money!"

"Don't congratulate me, anybody!" exclaimed my aunt. "How so, sir?"

"You believed it had been misappropriated by Mr. Wickfield?" said Traddles. "And indeed it was sold, by virtue of the power of management he held from you; but I needn't say by whom sold, or on whose actual signature. It was afterwards pretended to Mr. Wickfield, by that rascal, that he had possessed himself of the money to keep other deficiencies and difficulties from the light."

We all remained quiet; Agnes covering her face.

"Well, my dear friend," said my aunt, after a pause, "and you have really extorted the money back from him?"

"Why, the fact is," returned Traddles, "Mr. Micawber had so completely hemmed him in, and was always ready with so many new points if an old one failed, that he could not escape from us. I really don't think he grasped this sum so much for the gratification of his avarice, as for the hatred he felt for Copperfield."

"And what's become of him?"

"I don't know. He left here," said Traddles, "with his mother, who had been clamouring, and beseeching, and disclosing, the whole time."

"Do you suppose he has any money, Traddles?" I asked.

"Oh dear, yes, I should think so," he replied, shaking his head, seriously. "I should say he must have pocketed a good deal, in one way or other. But, I think you would find, Copperfield, if you had an opportunity of observing his course, that money would never keep that man out of mischief."

"And now, touching Mr. Micawber," said my aunt.

"Well, really," said Traddles, cheerfully, "I must, once more, give Mr. Micawber high praise. But for his having been so patient and persevering for so long a time, we never could have hoped to do anything worth speaking of."

"Now, what would you give him?" inquired my aunt.

"Oh! Before you come to that," said Traddles, a little disconcerted, "those I. O. U.'s, and so forth, which Mr. Micawber gave him for the advances he had—"

"Well! They must be paid," said my aunt. "What's the amount altogether?"

"Why, Mr. Micawber has entered the transactions—he calls them transactions—with great form, in a book," rejoined Traddles, smiling; "and he makes the amount a hundred and three pounds, five."

"Now, what shall we give him, that sum included?" said my aunt. "Agnes, my dear, you and I can talk about division of it afterwards. What should it be? Five hundred pounds?"

Upon this, Traddles and I both struck in at once. We both recommended a small sum in money, and the payment, without stipulation to Mr. Micaw-ber, of the Uriah claims as they came in. We proposed that the family should have their passage and their outfit, and a hundred pounds; and that Mr. Micawber's arrangements for the repayment of the advances should be gravely entered into, as it might be wholesome for him to suppose him-self under that responsibility.

We went back next day to my aunt's house—not to mine; and when she and I sat alone, as of old, before going to bed, she said:

"Trot, do you really wish to know what I have had upon my mind lately?"

"Indeed I do, aunt."

"Would you ride with me a little way to-morrow morning?" asked my aunt. "At nine," said she. "I'll tell you then, my dear."

At nine, accordingly, we went out in a little chariot, and drove to Lon-don. We drove a long way through the streets until we came to one of the large hospitals. Standing hard by the building was a plain hearse. The driver recognised my aunt, and in obedience to a motion of her hand at the window, drove slowly off; we following.

"You understand it now, Trot," said my aunt. "He is gone!"

"Did he die in the hospital?"

"Yes."

We drove away, out of town, to the churchyard at Hornsey. "Better here than in the streets," said my aunt. "He was born here."

We alighted; and followed the plain coffin to a corner I remember well, where the service was read consigning it to the dust.

"Six-and-thirty years ago, this day, my dear," said my aunt, as we walked back to the chariot, "I was married. God forgive us all!"

We took our seats in silence; and so she sat beside me for a long time, holding my hand. At length she suddenly burst into tears, and said:

"He was a fine-looking man when I married him, Trot—and he was sadly changed!"

It did not last long. After the relief of tears, she soon became composed, and even cheerful. Her nerves were a little shaken, she said, or she would not have given way to it. God forgive us all!

CHAPTER 50

Tempest

ONE evening when the time was close at hand, I was alone with Peggotty and her brother. Our conversation turned on Ham. She described to us how tenderly he had taken leave of her, and how manfully and quietly he had borne himself.

"I am thinking," said I, "that I'll go down again to Yarmouth. There's time, and to spare, for me to go and come back before the ship sails. My mind is constantly running on him, in his solitude; I am restless, and shall be better in motion. I'll go down to-night."

In the evening I started, by that conveyance, down the road I had traversed under so many vicissitudes.

"Don't you think that," I asked the coachman, in the first stage out of London, "a very remarkable sky? I don't remember to have seen one like it."

"Nor I—not equal to it," he replied. "That's wind, sir. There'll be mischief done at sea, I expect, before long."

There had been a wind all day; and it was rising then, with an extraordinary great sound. In another hour it had much increased, and the sky was more overcast, and blew hard.

And we were often in serious apprehension that the coach would be blown over. Sweeping gusts of rain came up before this storm, like showers of steel; and, at those times, when there was any shelter of trees or lee walls to be got, we were fain to stop, in a sheer impossibility of continuing the struggle.

When the day broke, it blew harder and harder. I had been in Yarmouth when the seamen said it blew great guns, but I had never known the like of this, or anything approaching to it. We came to Ipswich—very late, having had to fight every inch of ground since we were ten miles out of London.

As we struggled on, nearer and nearer to the sea, from which this mighty wind was blowing dead on shore, its force became more and more terrific. Long before we saw the sea, its spray was on our lips. When at last we got into the town, the people came out to their doors, all aslant, and with streaming hair, making a wonder of the mail that had come through such a night.

I put up at the old inn, and went down to look at the sea. Coming near the beach, I saw, not only the boatmen, but half the people of the town, lurking behind buildings.

Joining these groups, I found bewailing women whose husbands were away in herring or oyster boats. Grizzled old sailors were among the people, shaking their heads, as they looked from water to sky, even stout mariners, disturbed and anxious, levelling their glasses at the sea from behind places of shelter, as if they were surveying an enemy.

The tremendous sea itself, when I could find sufficient pause to look at it, in the agitation of the blinding wind, the flying stones and sand, and the awful noise, confounded me. As the high watery walls came rolling in, and, at their highest, tumbled into surf, they looked as if the least would engulf the town.

Not finding Ham among the people whom this memorable wind had brought together, I made my way to his house. It was shut; and as no one answered to my knocking, I went, by back ways and bye-lanes, to the yard where he worked. I learned there, that he had gone to Lowestoft, to meet some sudden exigency of ship-repairing in which his skill was required; but that he would be back to-morrow morning, in good time.

I was very much depressed in spirits; very solitary; and felt an uneasiness in Ham's not being there, disproportionate to the occasion. I was persuaded that I had an apprehension of his returning from Lowestoft by sea, and being lost. This grew so strong with me, that I resolved to go back to the yard before I took my dinner, and ask the boat-builder if he thought his attempting to return by sea at all likely?

The boat-builder, with a lantern in his hand, was locking the yard-gate. He quite laughed, when I asked him the question, and said there was no fear; no man in his senses, or out of them, would put off in such a gale of wind, least of all Ham Peggotty, who had been born to seafaring.

I went to bed, exceedingly weary and heavy; but, on my lying down, all such sensations vanished, as if by magic, and I was broad awake, with every sense refined.

For hours I lay there, listening to the wind and water; imagining that I heard shrieks out at sea; but I was tired now, and, getting into bed again, fell—off a tower and down a precipice—into the depths of sleep.

The thunder of the cannon was so loud and incessant, that I could not hear something I much desired to hear, until I made a great exertion and awoke. It was broad day—eight or nine o'clock; the storm raging, in lieu of the batteries; and some one knocking and calling at my door.

"What is the matter?" I cried.

"A wreck! Close by!"

I sprung out of bed, and asked, what wreck?

"A schooner, from Spain or Portugal, laden with fruit and wine. Make haste, sir, if you want to see her! It's thought, down on the beach, she'll go to pieces any moment."

The excited voice went clamouring along the staircase; and I wrapped myself in my clothes as quickly as I could, and ran into the street.

I looked out to sea for the wreck, and saw nothing but the foaming heads of the great waves. A half-dressed boatman, standing next to me, pointed with his bare arm. Then, oh great Heaven, I saw it, close in upon us!

One mast was broken short off, six or eight feet from the deck, and lay over the side, entangled in a maze of sail and rigging. Some efforts were even then being made, to cut this portion of the wreck away; for, I plainly descried her people at work with axes, especially one active figure with long curling hair, conspicuous among the rest. But the sea, sweeping over the rolling wreck, made a clean breach, and carried men, spars, casks, planks, bulwarks, heaps of such toys, into the boiling surge.

The ship was parting amidships, and I could readily suppose so, for the rolling and beating. Four men arose with the wreck out of the deep, clinging to the rigging of the remaining mast; uppermost, the active figure with the curling hair.

Again we lost her, and again she rose. Two men were gone. The agony on shore increased more. I found myself one of these, frantically imploring a knot of sailors whom I knew, not to let those two lost creatures perish before our eyes.

They were making out to me, in an agitated way—that the life-boat had been bravely manned an hour ago, and could do nothing; and that as no man would be so desperate as to attempt to wade off with a rope, and establish a communication with the shore, there was nothing left to try; when I noticed that some new sensation moved the people on the beach, and saw them part, and Ham come breaking through them to the front.

I ran to him—I held him back with both arms; and implored the men with whom I had been speaking, not to listen to him, not to do murder, not to let him stir from off that sand!

A cry arose on shore; and looking to the wreck, we saw the cruel sail, with blow on blow, beat off the lower of the two men, and fly up in triumph round the active figure left alone upon the mast.

Against such a sight, and against such determination as that of the calmly desperate man who was already accustomed to lead half the people present, I might as hopefully have entreated the wind. "Mas'r Davy," he said, cheerily grasping me by both hands, "if my time is come, 'tis come. If 't an't, I'll bide it. Lord above bless you, and bless all! Mates, make me ready! I'm a going off!"

I was swept away, but not unkindly, to some distance, where the people around me made me stay. Then, I saw him standing alone, in a seaman's frock and trousers: a rope in his hand, or slung to his wrist: another round his body: and several of the best men holding, at a little distance, to the latter, which he laid out himself, slack upon the shore, at his feet.

The wreck, was breaking up and the life of the solitary man upon the mast hung by a thread. He had a singular red cap on—not like a sailor's cap, but of a finer colour; and he was seen by all of us to wave it. I saw him do it now, and thought I was going distracted, when his action brought an old remembrance to my mind of a once dear friend.

Ham watched the sea, standing alone, until there was a great retiring wave, when, with a backward glance at those who held the rope which was made fast round his body, he dashed in after it, and in a moment was buffeting with the water.

He was hurt. I saw blood on his face, from where I stood; but he took no thought of that.

And now he made for the wreck, lost beneath the rugged foam, borne in towards the shore, borne on towards the ship, striving hard and valiantly. The distance was nothing, but the power of the sea and wind made the strife deadly. At length he neared the wreck—when, a high, green, vast hill-side of water, seemed to leap up and the ship was gone!

Some eddying fragments I saw in the sea, as if a mere cask had been broken. Consternation was in every face. They drew him to my very feet—insensible—dead. He was carried to the nearest house, I remained near him, busy, while every means of restoration were tried; but he had been beaten to death by the great wave, and his generous heart was stilled for ever.

As I sat beside the bed, a fisherman, who had known me when Emily and I were children, and ever since, whispered my name at the door.

"Sir, will you come over yonder?"

The old remembrance that had been recalled to me, was in his look. I asked him, terror-stricken, leaning on the arm he held out to support me:

"Has a body come ashore?"

He said, "Yes."

"Do I know it?" I asked then.

He answered nothing.

But, he led me to the shore. And on that part of it where she and I had looked for shells, two children—on that part of it where some lighter fragments of the old boat, blown down last night, had been scattered by the wind—among the ruins of the home he had wronged—I saw him lying with his head upon his arm, as I had often seen him lie at school.

CHAPTER 51

A New Wound, and the Old

No need, Steerforth, to have said: "Think of me at my best!" I had done that ever; and could I change now, looking on this sight!

They brought a hand-bier, and laid him on it, and covered him with a flag, and took him up and bore him on towards the houses. All the men who carried him had known him, and gone sailing with him, and seen him merry and bold. They carried him through the wild roar, a hush in the midst of all the tumult; and took him to the cottage where Death was already.

But, when they set the bier down on the threshold, they looked at one another, and at me, and whispered. I knew why. They felt as if it were not right to lay him down in the same quiet room.

We went into the town, and took our burden to the inn. I knew that the care of it, and the hard duty of preparing his mother to receive it, could only rest with me; and I was anxious to discharge that duty as faithfully as I could.

I chose the night for the journey, that there might be less curiosity when I left the town.

Upon a mellow autumn day, I arrived at Highgate. I walked the last mile, thinking as I went along of what I had to do; and left the carriage that had followed me all through the night, awaiting orders to advance.

I had not, at first, the courage to ring at the gate; and when I did ring, my errand seemed to me to be expressed in the very sound of the bell. The little parlour-maid came out:

"Is anything the matter, sir?—Mr. James?———"

"Hush!" said I. "Yes, something has happened, that I have to break to Mrs. Steerforth. She is at home?"

The girl anxiously replied that her mistress saw no company, but would see me. Her mistress was up, she said, and Miss Dartle was with her. What message should she take up-stairs?

Giving her a strict charge to be careful of her manner, and only to carry in my card and say I waited, I sat down in the drawing-room.

The house was so still that I heard the girl's light step up-stairs. On her return, she brought a message, to the effect that Mrs. Steerforth was an invalid and could not come down; but, that if I would excuse her being in her chamber, she would be glad to see me. In a few moments I stood before her.

At her chair, as usual, was Rosa Dartle. From the first moment of her dark eyes resting on me, I saw she knew I was the bearer of evil tidings.

"I am sorry to observe you are in mourning, sir," said Mrs. Steerforth.

"I am unhappily a widower," said I.

"You are very young to know so great a loss," she returned. "I hope Time will be good to you."

"I hope Time," said I, looking at her, "will be good to all of us. Dear Mrs. Steerforth, we must all trust to that, in our heaviest misfortunes."

The earnestness of my manner, and the tears in my eyes, alarmed her. The whole course of her thoughts appeared to stop, and change.

"When I was last here," I faltered, "Miss Dartle told me he was sailing here and there. The night before last was a dreadful one at sea. If he were at sea that night, and near a dangerous coast, as it is said he was; and if the vessel that was seen should really be the ship which———"

"Rosa!" said Mrs. Steerforth, "come to me!"

She came, but with no sympathy or gentleness. Her eyes gleamed like fire as she confronted his mother, and broke into a frightful laugh.

"Now," she said, "is your pride appeased, you madwoman? *Now* has he made atonement to you———with his life! Do you hear?—His life!"

Mrs. Steerforth, fallen back stiffly in her chair, and making no sound but a moan, cast her eyes upon her with a wide stare.

"Aye!" cried Rosa, smiting herself passionately on the breast, "look at me! Moan, and groan, and look at me! Look here!" striking the scar, "at your dead child's handiwork!"

The moan the mother uttered, from time to time, went to my heart.

"Do you remember when he did this?" she proceeded. "Do you remember when, in his inheritance of your nature, and in your pampering of his pride and passion, he did this, and disfigured me for life? Look at me, marked until I die with his high displeasure; and moan and groan for what you made him!"

"Miss Dartle," I entreated her. "For Heaven's sake———"

"I *will* speak!" she said, turning on me with her lightning eyes. "Be silent, you! Look at me, I say, proud mother of a proud false son! Moan for your nurture of him, moan for your corruption of him, moan for your loss of him, moan for mine!"

"Oh Miss Dartle, shame! Oh cruel!"

"I tell you," she returned, "I *will* speak to her. No power on earth should stop me, while I was standing here! Have I been silent all these years, and shall I not speak now? I loved him better than you ever loved him!" turning on her fiercely.

"Look here!" she said, stroking the scar again, with a relentless hand. "When he grew into the better understanding of what he had done, he saw it, and repented of it! I could sing to him, and talk to him, and attain with labour to such knowledge as most interested him; and I attracted him. When he was freshest and truest, he loved *me*."

"When he grew weary, I grew weary. As his fancy died out, I no more tried to strengthen any power I had. We fell away from one another without a word. Moan? Moan for what you made him; not for your love. I tell you that the time was, when I loved him better than you ever did!"

She stood with her bright angry eyes confronting the wide stare, and the set face; and softened no more, when the moaning was repeated, than if the face had been a picture.

"Miss Dartle," said I, "if you can be so obdurate as not to feel for this afflicted mother—if his faults cannot," I went on, "be banished from your remembrance, in such an hour; look at that figure, even as one you have never seen before, and render it some help!"

All this time, the figure was motionless, rigid, staring; moaning in the same dumb way from time to time, with the same helpless motion of the head; but giving no other sign of life. Miss Dartle suddenly kneeled down before it, and began to loosen the dress.

"A curse upon you!" she said, looking round at me, with a mingled expression of rage and grief. "It was in an evil hour that you ever came here! A curse upon you! Go!"

Later in the day, I returned, and we laid him in his mother's room. Miss Dartle never left her; doctors were in attendance, many things had been tried; but she lay like a statue, except for the low sound now and then.

CHAPTER 52

The Emigrants

ONE thing more, I had to do, before yielding myself to the shock of these emotions. It was, to conceal what had occurred, from those who were going away; and to dismiss them on their voyage in happy ignorance. In this, no time was to be lost.

I took Mr. Micawber aside that same night, and confided to him the task of standing between Mr. Peggotty and intelligence of the late catastrophe.

He zealously undertook to do so, and to intercept any newspaper through which it might, without such precautions, reach him.

"If it penetrates to him, sir," said Mr. Micawber, striking himself on the breast, "it shall first pass through this body!"

The Micawber family were lodged in a little, dirty, tumble-down public-house, whose protruding wooden rooms overhung the river. My aunt and Agnes were there, busily making some little extra comforts, in the way of dress, for the children. Peggotty was quietly assisting, with the old insensible work-box, yard measure, and bit of wax-candle before her, that had now outlived so much.

"And when does the ship sail, Mr. Micawber?" asked my aunt.

"Madam," he replied, "I am informed that we must positively be on board before seven to-morrow morning."

"Heyday!" said my aunt, "that's soon. Is it a sea-going fact, Mr. Peg-gotty?"

" 'Tis so, ma'am. She'll drop down the river with that theer tide. If Mas'r Davy and my sister comes aboard at Gravesen', arternoon o' next day, they'll see the last on us."

"And that we shall do," said I, "be sure!"

"My love," said Mr. Micawber, clearing his throat in his magnificent way, "my friend Mr. Thomas Traddles is so obliging as to solicit, in my ear, that he should have the privilege of ordering the ingredients necessary to the composition of a moderate portion of that Beverage which is peculiarly associated, in our minds, with the Roast Beef of Old England. I allude to—in short, Punch. Under ordinary circumstances, I should scruple to entreat the indulgence of Miss Trotwood and Miss Wickfield, but——"

"I can only say for myself," said my aunt, "that I will drink all happiness and success to you, Mr. Micawber, with the utmost pleasure."

"And I too!" said Agnes, with a smile.

Mr. Micawber immediately descended to the bar, where he appeared to be quite at home; and in due time returned with a steaming jug. I could not but observe that he had been peeling the lemons with his own clasp-knife.

"That's well," said my aunt, nodding towards Mr. Peggotty, "and I drink my love to you all, and every blessing and success attend you!"

Mr. Peggotty put down the two children he had been nursing, one on each knee, to join Mr. and Mrs. Micawber in drinking to all of us in return; and when he and the Micawbers cordially shook hands as comrades, and his brown face brightened with a smile, I felt that he would make his way, establish a good name, and be beloved, go where he would.

Even the children were instructed, each to dip a wooden spoon into Mr. Micawber's pot, and pledge us in its contents. When this was done, my aunt and Agnes rose, and parted from the emigrants. It was a sorrowful farewell. They were all crying; the children hung about Agnes to the last; and we left poor Mrs. Micawber in a very distressed condition, sobbing and weeping by a dim candle, that must have made the room look, from the river, like a miserable lighthouse.

In the afternoon of the next day, my old nurse and I went down to Gravesend. We found the ship in the river, surrounded by a crowd of boats; a favourable wind blowing; the signal for sailing at her mast head. I hired a boat directly, and we put off to her; and getting through the little vortex of confusion of which she was the centre, went on board.

Mr. Peggotty was waiting for us on deck.

As my eye glanced round this place, I thought I saw sitting, by an open port, with one of the Micawber children near her, a figure like Emily's; it first attracted my attention, by another figure parting from it with a kiss; and as it glided calmly away through the disorder, reminding me of—Agnes! But in the rapid motion and confusion, and in the unsettlement of my own thoughts, I lost it again; and only knew that the time was come when all visitors were being warned to leave the ship.

"Is there any last wured, Mas'r Davy?" said he. "Is there any one forgotten thing afore we parts?"

"One thing!" said I. "Martha!"

He touched the younger woman I have mentioned on the shoulder, and Martha stood before me.

"Heaven bless you, you good man!" cried I. "You take her with you!"

She answered for him, with a burst of tears. I could speak no more, at that time, but I wrung his hand; and if ever I have loved and honoured any man, I loved and honoured that man in my soul.

The time was come. I embraced him, took my weeping nurse upon my arm, and hurried away.

As the sails rose to the wind, and the ship began to move, there broke from all the boats three resounding cheers, which those on board took up, and echoed back, and which were echoed and re-echoed. My heart burst out when I heard the sound, and beheld the waving of the hats and handkerchiefs.

Then I saw her, at her uncle's side, and trembling on his shoulder. He pointed to us with an eager hand; and she saw us, and waved her last good-bye to me. Aye, Emily, beautiful and drooping, cling to him with the utmost trust of thy bruised heart; for he has clung to thee, with all the might of his great love!

CHAPTER 53

Absence

It was a long and gloomy night that gathered on me, haunted by the ghosts of many hopes, of many dear remembrances, many errors, many unavailing sorrows and regrets.

I went away from England; not knowing, even then, how great the shock was, that I had to bear. I left all who were dear to me, and went away; and believed that I had borne it, and it was past. As a man upon a field of battle will receive a mortal hurt, and scarcely know that he is struck, so I, when I was left alone with my undisciplined heart, had no conception of the wound with which it had to strive.

If my grief were selfish, I did not know it to be so. I mourned for my child-wife, taken from her blooming world, so young. I mourned for him who might have won the love and admiration of thousands, as he had won mine long ago. I mourned for the broken heart that had found rest in the stormy sea; and for the wandering remnants of the simple home, where I had heard the night-wind blowing, when I was a child.

When this despondency was at its worst, I believed that I should die. Sometimes, I thought that I would like to die at home; and actually turned back on my road, that I might get there soon. At other times, I passed on farther away, from city to city, seeking I know not what, and trying to leave I know not what behind.

For many months I travelled with this ever-darkening cloud upon my mind. Some blind reasons that I had for not returning home—reasons then struggling within me, vainly, for more distinct expression—kept me on my pilgrimage.

In three months more, a year would have passed since the beginning of my sorrow. I determined to make no resolutions until the expiration of those three months.

The three months gone, I resolved to remain away from home for some time longer; so settled myself for the present in Switzerland, to resume my pen; to work.

I worked patiently and hard. I wrote a Story, out of my experience, and sent it to Traddles, and he arranged for its publication very advantageously for me; and the tidings of my growing reputation began to reach me from travellers whom I encountered by chance. After some rest and change, I fell to work, in my old ardent way, on a new fancy, which took strong possession of me.

Agnes! I cannot say at what stage of my grief it first became associated with the reflection, that in my wayward boyhood, I had thrown away the treasure of her love. I could not forget that the feeling with which she now regarded me had grown up in my own free choice and course. That if she had ever loved me with another love—and I sometimes thought the time was when she might have done so—I had cast it away. I had bestowed my passionate tenderness upon another object; and what I might have done, I had not done; and what Agnes was to me, I and her own noble heart had made her.

I had always felt my weakness, in comparison with her constancy and fortitude; and now I felt it more and more. Whatever I might have been to her, or she to me, if I had been more worthy of her long ago, I was not now. The time was past. I had let it go by, and had deservedly lost her.

I made no effort to conceal from myself now, that I loved her, that I was devoted to her; but I brought the assurance home to myself, that it was now too late, and that our long-subsisting relation must be undisturbed.

Three years had elapsed since the sailing of the emigrant ship. Three years. Long in the aggregate, though short as they went by. And home was very dear to me, and Agnes too—but she was not mine—she was never to be mine. She might have been, but that was past!

CHAPTER 54

Return

I LANDED in London on a wintry autumn evening. It was dark and raining, and I saw more fog and mud in a minute than I had seen in a year. I walked from the Custom House to the Monument before I found a coach; and although the very house-fronts, looking on the swollen gutters, were like old friends to me, I could not but admit that they were very dingy friends.

For some changes in the fortunes of my friends, I was prepared. My aunt had long been re-established at Dover, and Traddles had begun to get into some little practice at the Bar, in the very first term after my departure. He had chambers in Gray's Inn, now.

They expected me home before Christmas; but had no idea of my returning so soon.

The well-known shops, however, with their cheerful lights, did something for me; and when I alighted at the door of the Gray's Inn Coffee-house, I had recovered my spirits.

"Do you know where Mr. Traddles lives in the Inn?" I asked the waiter, as I warmed myself by the coffee-room fire.

"Holborn Court, sir. Number two."

Being very anxious to see the dear old fellow, nevertheless, I despatched my dinner, in a manner not at all calculated to raise me in the opinion of the chief waiter, and hurried out by the back way. Number two in the Court was soon reached; and an inscription on the door-post informing me that Mr. Traddles occupied a set of chambers on the top storey, I ascended the staircase.

In the course of my stumbling up-stairs, I fancied I heard a pleasant sound of laughter.

Groping my way more carefully, I found the outer door. I knocked.

A small sharp-looking lad, half-footboy and half-clerk, presented himself.

"Is Mr. Traddles within?" I said.

"Yes, sir, but he's engaged."

"I want to see him."

After a moment's survey of me, the sharp-looking lad decided to let me in.

"Good God!" cried Traddles, looking up. "It's Copperfield!" and rushed into my arms, where I held him tight.

"All well, my dear Traddles?"

"All well, my dear, dear Copperfield, and nothing but good news!"

We cried with pleasure, both of us.

"My dear fellow!" said Traddles. "And grown so famous! My glorious Copperfield! Good gracious me, *when* did you come, *where* have you come from, *what* have you been doing? Why, my dear Copperfield," said Traddles, sticking his hair upright with both hands, and then putting his hands on my knees, "I am married!"

"Married!" I cried joyfully.

"Lord bless me, yes!" said Traddles—"by the Rev. Horace—to Sophy —down in Devonshire. Why, my dear boy, she's behind the window curtain! Look here!"

To my amazement, the dearest girl in the world came at that same instant, laughing and blushing, from her place of concealment. And a more cheerful, amiable, honest, happy, bright-looking bride, I believe (as I could not help saying on the spot) the world never saw. I kissed her as an old acquaintance should, and wished them joy with all my might of heart.

"Dear me," said Traddles, "what a delightful re-union this is! You are so extremely brown, my dear Copperfield! God bless my soul, how happy I am!"

"And so am I," said I.

"And I am sure I am!" said the blushing and laughing Sophy.

We sat round the fire; while the sharp boy produced the tea-things. After that, he retired for the night, shutting the outer-door upon us with a bang. Mrs. Traddles, with perfect pleasure and composure beaming from her household eyes, having made the tea, quietly made the toast as she sat in a corner by the fire.

She had seen Agnes, she told me, while she was toasting. "Tom" had taken her down into Kent for a wedding trip, and there she had seen my aunt, too; and both my aunt and Agnes were well, and they had all talked of nothing but me. "Tom" had never had me out of his thoughts, she really believed, all the time I had been away. "Tom" was the authority for everything. "Tom" was evidently the idol of her life; never to be shaken on his pesdestal by any commotion; always to be believed in, and done homage to with the whole faith of her heart, come what might.

I had not seen a coal fire since I had left England three years ago; though many a wood fire had I watched, as it crumbled into hoary ashes, and mingled with the feathery heap upon the hearth, which not inaptly figured to me, in my despondency, my own dead hopes.

I could think of the past now, gravely, but not bitterly; and could contemplate the future in a brave spirit. Home, in its best sense, was for me no more. She in whom I might have inspired a dearer love, I had taught to be my sister. She would marry, and would have new claimants on her tenderness: and in doing it, would never know the love for her that had grown up in my heart. It was right that I should pay the forfeit of my headlong passion. What I reaped, I had sown.

Thoroughly tired, I went to bed too, at midnight; passed the next day on the Dover coach; burst safe and sound into my aunt's old parlour while she was at tea (she wore spectacles now); and was received by her, and Mr. Dick, and dear old Peggotty, who acted as housekeeper, with open arms and tears of joy.

CHAPTER 55

Agnes

My aunt and I, when we were left alone, talked far into the night. How the emigrants never wrote home, otherwise than cheerfully and hopefully; how Mr. Micawber had actually remitted divers small sums of money, on account of those "pecuniary liabilities." Mr. Dick, as usual, was not forgotten. My aunt informed me how he incessantly occupied himself in copying everything he could lay his hands on, how it was one of the main joys and rewards of her life that he was free and happy.

"And when, Trot," said my aunt, patting the back of my hand, as we sat in our old way before the fire, "when are you going over to Canterbury?"

"I shall get a horse, and ride over to-morrow morning, aunt, unless you will go with me?"

"No!" said my aunt, in her short abrupt way. "I mean to stay where I am."

"Oh, Trot," I seemed to hear my aunt say once more; and I understood her better now—"Blind, blind, blind!"

We both kept silence for some minutes. When I raised my eyes, I found that she was steadily observant of me.

"You will find her father a white-haired old man," said my aunt, "though a better man in all other respects—a reclaimed man. You will find her," pursued my aunt, "as good, as beautiful, as earnest, as disinterested, as she has always been. If I knew higher praise, Trot, I would bestow it on her."

"Has Agnes any—" I was thinking aloud, rather than speaking.

"Well? Hey? Any what?" said my aunt, sharply.

"Any lover," said I.

"A score," cried my aunt, with a kind of indignant pride. "She might have married twenty times, my dear, since you have been gone!"

"No doubt," said I. "No doubt. But has she any lover who is truly worthy of her? Agnes could care for no other."

Slowly raising her eyes to mine, she said:

"I suspect she has an attachment, Trot."

"A prosperous one?" said I.

"Trot," returned my aunt gravely, "I can't say. I have no right to tell you even so much. She has never confided it to me, but I suspect it."

"If it should be so," I began, "and I hope it is—"

"I don't know that it is," said my aunt curtly.

"If it should be so," I repeated, "Agnes will tell me at her own good time. A sister to whom I have confided so much, aunt, will not be reluctant to confide in me."

I rode away, early in the morning, for the scene of my old school days. I cannot say that I was yet quite happy, in the hope that I was gaining a victory over myself; even in the prospect of so soon looking on her face again.

The well-remembered ground was soon traversed, and I came into the quiet streets, where every stone was a boy's book to me. I went on foot to the old house and looking, as I passed, through the low window of the turret-room where first Uriah Heep, and afterwards Mr. Micawber, had been wont to sit, saw that it was a little parlour now, and that there was no office. Otherwise the staid old house was, as to its cleanliness and order, still just as it had been when I first saw it. I requested the new maid who admitted me, to tell Miss Wickfield that a gentleman who waited on her from a friend abroad, was there; and I was shown up the grave old stair-case (cautioned of the steps I knew so well), into the unchanged drawing-room. The books that Agnes and I had read together, were on their shelves; and the desk where I had laboured at my lessons, many a night, stood yet at the same old corner of the table. All the little changes that had crept in when the Heeps were there, were changed again. Everything was as it used to be, in the happy time.

The opening of the little door in the panelled wall made me start and turn. Her beautiful serene eyes met mine as she came towards me. She stopped and laid her hand upon her bosom, and I caught her in my arms.

"Agnes! my dear girl! I have come too suddenly upon you."

"No, no! I am so rejoiced to see you, Trotwood!"

"Dear Agnes, the happiness it is to me, to see you once again!"

I folded her to my heart, and for a little while, we were both silent.

With her own sweet tranquillity, she calmed my agitation; led me back to the time of our parting; spoke to me of Emily, whom she had visited, in secret, many times; spoke to me tenderly of Dora's grave.

"And you, Agnes," I said, by and by. "Tell me of yourself. You have hardly ever told me of your own life, in all this lapse of time!"

"What should I tell?" she answered, with her radiant smile. "Papa is well. You see us here, quiet in our own home; our anxieties set at rest, our home restored to us: and knowing that, dear Trotwood, you know all."

"All, Agnes?" said I.

She looked at me, with some fluttering wonder in her face.

"Is there nothing else, Sister?" I said.

Her colour, which had just now faded, returned, and faded again. She smiled; with a quiet sadness, I thought; and shook her head.

"You will wait and see papa," said Agnes, cheerfully, "and pass the day with us? Perhaps you will sleep in your own room? We always call it yours."

I could not do that, having promised to ride back to my aunt's, at night; but I would pass the day there, joyfully.

"I must be a prisoner for a little while," said Agnes, "but here are the old books, Trotwood, and the old music."

"Even the old flowers are here," said I, looking round.

"I have found a pleasure," returned Agnes, smiling, "while you have been absent, in keeping everything as it used to be when we were children. For we were very happy then, I think."

"Heaven knows we were!" said I.

She smiled again, and went out at the door by which she had come.

It was for me to guard this sisterly affection with religious care. It was all that I had left myself, and it was a treasure. If I once shook the foundations of the sacred confidence and usage, in virtue of which it was given to me, it was lost, and could never be recovered. I set this steadily before myself. The better I loved her, the more it behoved me never to forget it.

When I returned, Mr. Wickfield had come home, from a garden he had, a couple of miles or so out of town, where he now employed himself almost every day.

After tea we three sat together, talking of the by-gone days.

"My part in them," said Mr. Wickfield, shaking his white head, "has much matter for regret, Trotwood, you well know. But I would not cancel it, if it were in my power."

I could readily believe that, looking at the face beside him.

"I should cancel with it," he pursued, "such patience and devotion, such fidelity, such a child's love, as I must not forget, no! even to forget myself."

"I understand you, sir," I softly said.

"But no one knows, not even you," he returned, "how much she has done, how much she has undergone, how hard she has striven."

She had put her hand entreatingly on his arm, to stop him; and was very, very pale.

"Well, well!" he said with a sigh, dismissing, as I then saw, some trial she had borne, or was yet to bear, in connexion with what my aunt had told me. "Well! I have never told you, Trotwood, of her mother. Has any one?"

"Never, sir."

"It's not much—though it was much to suffer. She married me in opposition to her father's wish, and he renounced her. She prayed him to forgive her, before my Agnes came into this world. He was a very hard man, and her mother had long been dead. He repulsed her. He broke her heart."

Agnes leaned upon his shoulder, and stole her arm about his neck.

"She had an affectionate and gentle heart," he said; "and it was broken. I knew its tender nature very well. No one could, if I did not. She loved me dearly, but was never happy. She was always labouring, in secret, under this distress; and being delicate and downcast at the time of his last repulse —for it was not the first, by many—pined away and died. She left me Agnes, two weeks old; and the grey hair that you recollect me with, when you first came."

He kissed Agnes on her cheek.

"My love for my dear child was a diseased love, but my mind was all unhealthy then. I say no more of that. I am not speaking of myself, Trotwood, but of her mother, and of her. If I give you any clue to what I am, or to what I have been, you will unravel it, I know."

Agnes rose up from her father's side, before long; and going softly to her piano, played some of the old airs to which we had often listened in that place.

"Have you any intention of going away again?" Agnes asked me, as I was standing by. "I think you ought not, Trotwood," she said, mildly. "Your growing reputation and success enlarge your power of doing good."

"What I am, you have made me, Agnes. You should know best."

"*I* made you, Trotwood?"

"Yes! Agnes, my dear girl!" I said, bending over her. "I tried to tell you, when we met to-day, something that has been in my thoughts since Dora died. You remember, when you came down to me in our little room —pointing upward, Agnes?"

"Oh, Trotwood!" she returned, her eyes filled with tears. "So loving, so confiding, and so young! Can I ever forget?"

"As you were then, my sister, I have often thought since, you have ever been to me. Ever pointing upward, Agnes; ever leading me to something better; ever directing me to higher things!"

She only shook her head; through her tears I saw the same sad quiet smile.

"I want you to know, that all my life long I shall look up to you, and be guided by you, as I have been through the darkness that is past. Whatever betides, whatever new ties you may form, whatever changes may come between us, I shall always look to you, and love you, as I do now, and have always done. You will always be my solace and resource."

She softly played on, looking at me still.

"I really believe, that you could be faithfully affectionate against all discouragement, and never cease to be so, until you ceased to live.—Will you laugh at such a dream?" I said.

"Oh, no! Oh, no!"

For an instant, a distressful shadow crossed her dear face; but, even in the start it gave me, it was gone; and she was playing on, and looking at me once more with her own calm smile.

As I rode back in the lonely night, the wind going by me like a restless memory, I thought of this, and feared she was not happy. *I* was not happy; but, thus far, I had faithfully set the seal upon the Past.

CHAPTER 56

A Light Shines On My Way

THE year came round to Christmas-time, and I had been at home above two months. I had seen Agnes frequently. However loud the general voice might be in giving me encouragement, and however fervent the emotions and endeavours to which it roused me, I heard her lightest word of praise as I heard nothing else.

Between my aunt and me there had been something, in this connexion, since the night of my return, which I cannot call a restraint, or an avoidance of the subject, so much as an implied understanding that we thought of it together, but did not shape our thoughts into words. When, according to our old custom, we sat before the fire at night, we often fell into this train; as naturally, and as consciously to each other, as if we had unreservedly said so. But we preserved an unbroken silence. I believed that she had read, or partly read, my thoughts that night; and that she fully comprehended why I gave mine no more distinct expression.

This Christmas-time being come, and Agnes having reposed no new confidence in me, a doubt that had several times arisen in my mind—whether she could have that perception of the true state of my breast, which restrained her with the apprehension of giving me pain—began to oppress me heavily.

It was—what lasting reason have I to remember it!—a cold, harsh, winter day. There had been snow some hours before; and it lay, not deep, but hard-frozen on the ground.

"Riding to-day, Trot?" said my aunt, putting her head in at the door.

"Yes," said I, "I am going over to Canterbury. It's a good day for a ride."

"I hope your horse may think so, too," said my aunt; "but at present he is holding down his head and his ears, standing before the door there, as if he thought his stable preferable."

My aunt, I may observe, allowed my horse on the forbidden ground, but had not at all relented toward the donkeys.

"He will be fresh enough, presently!" said I.

"The ride will do his master good, at all events," observed my aunt, glancing at the papers on my table. "Ah, child, you pass a good many hours here! I never thought, when I used to read books, what work it was to write them."

"It's work enough to read them, sometimes," I returned. "As to the writing, it possesses its own charms, aunt."

"Ah! I see!" said my aunt. "Ambition, love of approbation, sympathy, and much more, I suppose? Well: go along with you!"

"Do you know anything more," said I, standing composedly before her chair—she had patted me on the shoulder, and sat down in my chair, "of that attachment of Agnes?"

She looked up in my face a little while, before replying:

"I think I do, Trot."

"Are you confirmed in your impression?" I inquired.

"I think I am, Trot."

She looked so steadfastly at me: with a kind of doubt, or pity, or suspense in her affection: that I summoned the stronger determination to show her a perfectly cheerful face.

"And what is more, Trot—" said my aunt.

"Yes!"

"I think Agnes is going to be married."

"God bless her!" said I, cheerfully.

"God bless her!" said my aunt, "and her husband too!"

I echoed it, parted from my aunt, went lightly down-stairs, mounted, and rode away.

I found Agnes alone. She put down her book on seeing me come in; and having welcomed me as usual, took her work-basket and sat in one of the old-fashioned windows.

I sat beside her on the window-seat, and we talked of what I was doing, and when it would be done, and of the progress I had made since my last visit. Agnes was very cheerful; and laughingly predicted that I should soon become too famous to be talked to, on such subjects.

"So I make the most of the present time, you see," said Agnes, "and talk to you while I may."

As I looked at her beautiful face, observant of her work, she raised her mild clear eyes, and saw that I was looking at her.

"You are thoughtful to-day, Trotwood!"

"Agnes, shall I tell you what about? I came to tell you."

She put aside her work, as she was used to do when we were seriously discussing anything; and gave me her whole attention.

"My dear Agnes, do you doubt my being true to you?"

"No!" she answered, with a look of astonishment.

"Do you doubt my being what I always have been to you?"

"No!" she answered, as before.

"Do you remember that I tried to tell you, when I came home, what a debt of gratitude I owed you, dearest Agnes, and how fervently I felt towards you?"

"I remember it," she said, gently, "very well."

"You have a secret," said I. "Let me share it, Agnes."

She cast down her eyes, and trembled.

"I could hardly fail to know, even if I had not heard—but from other lips than yours, Agnes, which seems strange—that there is some one upon whom you have bestowed the treasure of your love. Do not shut me out of what concerns your happiness so nearly! If you can trust me as you say you can, and as I know you may, let me be your friend, your brother, in this matter, of all others!"

With an appealing, almost a reproachful glance, she rose from the window; and hurrying across the room as if without knowing where, put her hands before her face, and burst into such tears as smote me to the heart.

And yet they awakened something in me, bringing promise to my heart. Without my knowing why, these tears allied themselves with the quietly sad smile which was so fixed in my remembrance, and shook me more with hope than fear or sorrow.

"Agnes, I cannot bear to see you so, and think that I have been the cause. My dearest girl, dearer to me than anything in life, if you are unhappy, let me share your unhappiness. If you are in need of help or counsel, let me try to give it to you. If you have indeed a burden on your heart, let me try to lighten it. For whom do I live now, Agnes, if it is not for you?"

"Oh, spare me! I am not myself! Another time!" was all I could distinguish.

"I must say more. I cannot let you leave me so! For Heaven's sake, Agnes, let us not mistake each other after all these years, and all that has come and gone with them! I must speak plainly. Do not have any lingering thought that I could envy the happiness you will confer; that I could not resign you to a dear protector, of your own choosing."

She said in a low voice, broken here and there, but very clear:

"I owe it to your pure friendship for me, Trotwood—to tell you, you are mistaken. If I have sometimes, in the course of years, wanted help and counsel, they have come to me. If I have sometimes been unhappy, the feeling has passed away. If I have ever had a burden on my heart, it has been lightened for me. If I have any secret, it is—no new one; and is—not what you suppose."

"Agnes! Stay! A moment! Dearest Agnes! When I came here to-day, I thought that nothing could have wrested this confession from me. But, Agnes, if I have indeed any new-born hope that I may ever call you something more than Sister——"

Her tears fell fast; but they were not like those she had lately shed, and I saw my hope brighten in them.

"Agnes! Ever my guide, and best support! If you had been more mindful of yourself, and less of me, when we grew up here together, I think my heedless fancy never would have wandered from you. When I loved Dora, even then, my love would have been incomplete, without your sympathy. I had it, and it was perfected. And when I lost her, Agnes, what should I have been without you, still!"

Closer in my arms, nearer to my heart, her trembling hand upon my shoulder, her sweet eyes shining through her tears, on mine!

"I went away, dear Agnes, loving you. I stayed away, loving you. I returned home, loving you!"

"I am so blest, Trotwood—my heart is so overcharged—but there is one thing I must say."

"Dearest, what?"

She laid her gentle hands upon my shoulders, and looked calmly in my face.

"Do you know, yet, what it is?"

"I am afraid to speculate on what it is. Tell me, my dear."

"I have loved you all my life!"

It was nearly dinner-time next day when we appeared before my aunt. She was up in my study, Peggotty said, which it was her pride to keep in readiness and order for me. We found her, in her spectacles, sitting by the fire.

"Goodness me!" said my aunt, peering through the dusk, "who's this you're bringing home?"

"Agnes," said I.

As we had arranged to say nothing at first, my aunt was not a little discomfited. She darted a hopeful glance at me, when I said "Agnes"; but seeing that I looked as usual, she took off her spectacles in despair, and rubbed her nose with them.

"By-the-by, aunt," said I, after dinner; "I have been speaking to Agnes about what you told me."

"Then, Trot," said my aunt, turning scarlet, "you did wrong, and broke your promise."

"You are not angry, aunt, I trust? I am sure you won't be, when you learn that Agnes is not unhappy in any attachment."

"Stuff and nonsense!" said my aunt.

As my aunt appeared to be annoyed, I thought the best way was to cut her annoyance short. I took Agnes on my arm to the back of her chair, and we both leaned over her. My aunt with one clap of her hands, and one look through her spectacles, immediately went into hysterics, for the first and only time in all my knowledge of her.

The hysterics called up Peggotty. The moment my aunt was restored, she flew at Peggotty, and calling her a silly old creature, hugged her with all her might. After that, she hugged Mr. Dick (who was highly honoured, but a good deal surprised); and after that, told them why. Then we were all happy together.

We were married within a fortnight. Traddles and Sophy, and Doctor and Mrs. Strong, were the only guests at our quiet wedding. We left them full of joy; and drove away together. Clasped in my embrace, I held the source of every worthy aspiration I had ever had; the centre of myself, the circle of my life, my own, my wife; my love of whom was founded on a rock!

"Dearest husband!" said Agnes. "Now that I may call you by that name,

I have one thing more I wish to tell you."

"Let me hear it, love."

"It grows out of the night when Dora died. She sent you for me."

"She did."

"She told me that she left me something. Can you think what it was?"

I believed I could. I drew the wife who had so long loved me, closer to my side.

"She told me that she made a last request to me, and left me a last charge."

"And it was——"

"That only I would occupy this vacant place."

And Agnes laid her head upon my breast, and wept; and I wept with her, though we were so happy.